"Welcome, my wyrmlings . . . my children," came the whispered, rasping voice emerging from the scarlet jaws. "It pleases me to see you kill—to learn the rapture of bloodletting, and of terribly lethal might."

A green head beside the mighty red lowered, eyes blinking lazily as it regarded an emerald-colored wyrmling, the newt Crematia had mangled in the pursuit of her prey.

"Weakness will not be tolerated." The words dripped like venom from the crimson jaws while the green dragon head licked forward, the tongue hissing a soft sound.

Immediately the crippled wyrmling uttered a yelp of pain, thrashing through a circle as its jaws snapped and claws swiped at an unseen enemy. Abruptly it froze, trembling, the tiny mouth gaping soundlessly, frothing with bubbles. The little dragon shrieked for a long moment until it vanished in an explosive shower of scales, flesh, and bones.

"Mercy is weakness—and weakness is death!" hissed the head of the Dark Queen.

From the Creators of the DRAGONLANCE® Saga

THE LOST HISTORIES

The Lost Histories
Volume VI

The Dragons

Douglas Niles

**To Margaret and Tracy,
for reasons that every
Krynnophile will understand**

DRAGONLANCE® Saga
The Lost Histories
Volume VI

THE DRAGONS
©1996 TSR, Inc.
All Rights Reserved.

First Printing: October 1996
Printed in the United States of America.
Library of Congress Catalog Card Number: 95-62252

9 8 7 6 5 4 3 2 1

8374XXX1501

ISBN: 0-7869-0513-1

TSR, Inc.
201 Sheridan Springs Rd.
Lake Geneva, WI 53147
U.S.A.

TSR Ltd.
120 Church End, Cherry Hinton
Cambridge CB1 3LB
United Kingdom

Prologue
Fiery Beginnings

circa 8500 PC

Crematia awakened to yearning, an awareness of a deep and fundamental need. She twitched, driven by knowledge that she lacked something . . . something essential to her comfort, even her life. Slowly, over a measureless span of time, that longing coalesced into a specific desire.

Fire.

Compelling but terribly distant, a blaze of heat called from somewhere beyond her tightly restricted universe. Seductive and alluring, powerfully radiant, the sensation tantalized her, until she knew without understanding that she had been summoned.

She reacted by pure instinct, driven by an urge ingrained into every fiber of her being. Lashing out in sudden anger, Crematia pushed and struck the resistant barrier of her world, initial frustration only increasing her desperation. She stiffened her neck, straining mightily toward the draw of magnificent warmth.

But still that radiance was masked by her enveloping barrier. With growing agitation, she pushed and prodded, squirming and flexing her supple body, then recoiling as the constraints of her universe pressed her back.

And in that frustration, Crematia learned the power of fury. A snarl rattled her tiny body as rage gave her strength. She struck blindly, snapping, clawing, frenzy infusing the cramped, squirming body with irresistible determination.

Pushing now, Crematia flexed, straightening her long neck, driving against the pernicious barrier. The front of her head was a sharpened beak, and when she pressed this hooked cutter against the leathery membrane, she felt the surface yield slightly. Compelled to new efforts by her fury, she swept against the barrier with her forelimbs, finding that, like her snout, her paws were equipped with sharp edges that tore and ripped at the stubborn impediment.

And then that glorious heat was there, radiating against her face, warming her eyes and caressing her nostrils. But that teasing suggestion of life only made the enclosing barrier that much more infuriating. Desperately, frantically, Crematia clawed, pulling the tough fabric out of the way, widening the gap. Finally her head pushed through, and wonderful warmth stroked her neck, kissed her shoulders with the promise of full and immediate immersion.

With a final push, driving with her rear limbs and clawing with her forelegs, the serpentine creature wriggled through the gap, leaving a hollow leathery sphere collapsing behind her. She blinked, straining to observe and study her surroundings, to clear away the film of murk that coated her eyes. At the same time, she stretched, feeling a glorious freedom, a lack of constraint that allowed her to extend her supple neck, to twist and lash her tail.

The environment was cloaked in shadow, but everywhere Crematia felt magnificent warmth against her scales. Twisting instinctively, curling about, she let the heat wash over her, bringing a trembling vibrancy to her slender reptilian body. Awkwardly she stretched as wings still gummy from the egg slowly, stickily unfurled. The sensation of space was exhilarating, though almost immediately she sensed a new discomfort, a gnawing ache in her belly.

As yet she could see nothing of shape or color, but she discerned a flaring brightness that she knew intuitively was the source of that wonderful heat. Deeply attracted, she hobbled toward the light. Her feet were unsteady beneath her, and she slipped, stumbling and jarring her chin painfully against a hard surface.

Jabbing with instantaneous fury, she snapped her jaws on the obstacle. The bite was painful, but the expression of rage deeply satisfying. Again she lunged toward the bright flickers, her vision clearing with every heartbeat. She saw tongues of orange heat rise, waver, disappear, to be replaced immediately by more of the dancing flares. The bright tendrils encircled her, rising in a protective curtain, shimmering and pulsing with relentless infernal energy.

A dark shape moved across the curtain of light, bringing another vigorous growl from Crematia's chest, causing her scarlet scales to shiver. Feeling anew the hollow pain in her gut, she froze, sniffing, staring. She saw a round form, smaller than herself, covered with smooth fur. A pair of bright spots glowed, widening as her sharp snout jabbed forward.

The furry creature shrieked when Crematia's beaklike jaw stabbed through its soft pelt. A wonderfully intoxicating aroma engulfed the huntress, and she sensed the elixir mingled her enemy's pain and its pathetic fear. As the dying form twitched a few times and then lay still, she knew with a thrill of anticipation that much of her life would be devoted to the re-creation in countless victims of these twin talismans of suffering.

Warm wetness flowed across Crematia's nostrils, and she discovered another tool of her body—a tongue, supple and forked, that could curl from her mouth to lick that wetness. The taste was sweet, so succulent that the serpentine body shivered in anticipation. Jabbing forward again, chewing and tearing, Crematia relished the tender meat and sweet blood of her first kill.

There was very little meat in the tiny corpse, but in her hunger, she greedily swallowed the small, warm heart and crunched the frail bones, sucking the marrow from each. Shaking drops of blood and fur from her jaws, she lifted her head, peering around with increasingly sensitive eyes, ready to kill again.

Crematia was vaguely aware of other shapes all around her, serpentine, scaly bodies emerging from a great nest of bones. With talon and fang they pulled ahead, climbing and clawing over each other, each striving instinctively to move beyond the others. In an atmosphere of seething intensity, hunger seemed to fill the air, driving the red dragon female with growing urgency. Uncertain why, she knew beyond doubt that as the wyrmlings explored outward, continued to move away from the nest, she would have to go first!

She saw another huddled furry shape scuttle past, and her hunger flared anew. Pouncing quickly, she slashed with lightning-fast claws and brought the little four-legged creature to a halt. Each squirming twist of the body, each keening cry brought another shiver of pleasure through her body. Again there was that intoxicating scent of blood, and she tasted the sweet liquid, relished the struggles of the creature in her talons. Crematia was vaguely saddened when those struggles grew still, when the little heart ceased to pulse forth its crimson nectar.

Once more she ate, this time focusing on the tastier morsels—flesh, heart, and brain. She left the bones and entrails behind, knowing that there would be more prey, more killing, just ahead. The food was good, warm and fulfilling in her belly, but she wanted—no, she *needed*—more.

In a frenzy, she dashed after another of the creatures as the little furball scurried away in panic. Abruptly a green and scaly shape, similar to Crematia but a trifle smaller, darted in front of her, reaching talons toward the prey. But the red wyrmling caught her emerald nestmate by the rear foot, twisting the leg, sinking her fangs into the twitching thigh. With a hissing, hateful shriek, the emerald serpent thrashed on the ground. Ignoring the weakling, the crimson killer leapt ahead of her nestmate to bear the bundle of flesh to the ground.

Again she was patient, investigating the wriggling creature, enjoying the sound of its plaintive, terrified bleats. Crematia quivered in pleasure as she took one of the stubby, kicking legs and twisted it off to a new crescendo of wailing. She snapped another leg and tore at the moist flesh with her jaws, holding the still breathing and trembling creature pinned with one of her forepaws.

Then, deliberately, she gouged out the bright little eyes, savoring each as the pathetic being wriggled frantically. Only after the struggles had faded almost to nothing did the red jaws dart outward and pull chunks of meat from the dying torso, swallowing until she had her fill. The green wyrmling still wailed plaintively, crawling on her three good legs, dragging the limb mangled by Crematia until she reached the gristly waste left from the red's feasting. The emerald serpent tore into the remains with greedy abandon.

The crimson female loped forward on increasingly sturdy legs, circling a great pile of wriggling bodies and leaking, colorful shells. Chromatic dragons slithered over each other, while more sticky wyrmlings emerged in the midst of the massive bones that framed the nest. A low hissing rose from that tangled thatch, and it pleased Crematia to know that she listened to the hunger of many frantic nestmates.

Dozens of little forms wriggled from the tangle of bones and webbing, dropping to the ground, trying to shake the muck of their birthing away. Serpents of black and green, white and blue—and a few more of red—crept forth, killing and devouring the furry creatures when they could, snapping at nestmates who dared venture too close.

Slow-witted prey moved with desperate, waddling steps away from the deadly wyrmlings, but the creatures were unable to escape the vicinity of the nest. With the initial frenzy of starvation past, many of the serpents had, like Crematia, discovered the pleasure of torture, of a slow and leisurely kill. The survivors tried to get away but were trapped by a void of space, a precipice on all sides of the nest. Shrieks and wails echoed, drowning out the dull hissing of emerging wyrmlings.

Crematia bulled forward, head high, chest outthrust, and everywhere her siblings gave way, forked tongues flickering along the ground before the red dragon's feet. The illumination she had earlier observed now flared anew, rising higher and faster and brighter than ever, and the red wyrmling—followed by the creeping pack of her fellow nestlings—prowled closer. Her hunger sated, she sought to satisfy her curiosity.

The tongues of fire resolved themselves into individual dancing pillars. Each was huge, rising from a chasm that Crematia perceived as a gulf completely encircling the lofty pillar supporting the nest. It was that same chasm that trapped the teeming pack of the hatchlings' prey, holding the creatures together with their lethal hunters atop the spire. The flames leapt from the bottomless gulf surrounding the nest, soaring high into the air and shedding blistering heat across the newborn dragons.

Crematia sensed a white sibling blinking, cowering away from the heat, and a sense of superiority curled her leathery lip into a sneer. The heat was a welcome embrace to her, and it was strange to contemplate that to this pale, colorless dragon, it seemed to be a discomfort.

But now her eyes began to focus on images even beyond those lofty flames. She saw a dark landscape, scarred by peak and chasm, stretching into the smoky distance beneath a lightless sky. In places, flares leapt upward from an abyssal crevasse, or streams of liquid fire flowed and spilled and gathered into bubbling, hellish lakes. This was a vast expanse, and immediately Crematia wanted to see it all, to fly over it, to claim the entire realm as her own!

A form took shape in the near distance, just beyond the

circle of fire, and the scarlet serpent felt an awakening of new emotions—awe and fear. A massive, serpentine image writhed there, looming ever higher into the air, growing more distinct and omnipresent as vaporous tendrils of flesh came together, solidifying. The writhing pillars separated, twisting into supple sections.

As the shape surged higher and closer, the wyrmling saw monstrous heads illuminated by the fire. Four . . . no, *five* great necks rose, each supporting a crocodilian head. The body below these heads was lost in the darkness of the chasm, but even so, the shadowy shape rivaled some of the distant mountains in size.

Already Crematia perceived that the central, the mightiest of these visages was as pure a red as her own crimson scales. This awareness puffed out her chest with another dose of pride, and she lifted her head arrogantly above the huddled mass of her fellow hatchlings.

"Welcome, my wyrmlings . . . my children," came the whispered, rasping voice emerging from the scarlet jaws. "It pleases me to see you kill—to learn the rapture of bloodletting, and of terribly lethal might."

A green head beside the mighty red lowered, eyes blinking lazily as it regarded an emerald-colored wyrmling, the newt Crematia had mangled in the pursuit of her prey.

"Weakness will not be tolerated." The words dripped like venom from the crimson jaws while the green dragon head licked forward, the tongue hissing a soft sound.

Immediately the crippled wyrmling uttered a yelp of pain, thrashing through a circle as its jaws snapped, claws swiped at an unseen enemy. Abruptly it froze, trembling, the tiny mouth gaping soundlessly, frothing with bubbles. The little dragon shrieked for a long moment until it vanished in an explosive shower of scales, flesh, and bones.

"Mercy is weakness—and weakness is death!" hissed the green head.

The wedge-shaped image of crimson drifted lower, leathery lids drooping lazily over the hot embers of twin eyes. Yet Crematia sensed that there was nothing sleepy, nothing but keen alertness, in the deceptively casual inspection. When the cruel jaws parted again, when more words rasped out, the red wyrmling tensed, as if the mighty being's speech was directed at her alone.

"You must never show mercy! Remember this, my wyrmlings: Mercy is weakness, and weakness is death!"

"Mercy is weakness, and weakness is death!" The echoes came in harsh whispers as a hundred vibrant wyrmlings, profoundly moved, repeated the words of their mistress.

Again came the rumbled lesson, and Crematia shivered to a thrill of learning. It was a teaching that she knew she would never forget.

"Remember, my children . . . be strong!" hissed the crimson jaws. "For in strength shall you gain mastery, and in mastery shall come your vengeance!"

Crematia's mind flared at the thought of vengeance. She knew intuitively that it was a goal worth one's whole being, one's very life.

"I am your mother and your queen," continued the soft but forceful voice. "My will is your command; my pleasure gives reason to your lives. And my whim is instant death."

Abruptly the blue head darted toward a pair of white wyrmlings who twitched restlessly at the fringe of the pack. Mighty jaws gaped, and in an explosion of brightness, a crackling bolt of energy shot from the dragon's mouth, sizzling into the distracted newborns, spattering them into a drifting haze of white scales.

"You must be ruthless—always!" The voice dropped to a soft, almost gentle whisper, but there was no wyrmling who did not grant the queen full attention.

"When you go forth into the world, your task will be to find your strongest enemy and kill him. When that foe is slain, you shall again find your strongest enemy and kill him. For every enemy that you slay, another will appear—and that one, in turn, must die."

The monstrous head inhaled, a measured drawing of breath that roared like a cyclone. After a long pause, the crimson jaws spoke again. "This shall be the course of your lives, my wyrmlings . . . knowing your foes, finding them, and bringing about their utter destruction."

"I will find my enemy and kill him," Crematia murmured, a sense of destiny growing within her, seething and boiling into instinctive hatred, a fury that would provide passion and purpose to her life.

All of the monstrous heads swung back and forth, five pairs of fiery eyes glittering with ambition and cruelty. Crematia shivered with joy at the power she beheld there. Once more the red dragon head rose above the others, fixing its penetrating gaze on the wyrmlings of the same color.

"Your father was Furyion, mightiest of my sons," rumbled the Queen of Darkness, and Crematia knew the words were meant for her and her crimson siblings. "He was tricked by the cunning of a gold dragon, lured to his death by the one known as Aurora. And though he claimed Aurora's life with his last act, there will come to be children of the metal dragons.

"Know this, my precious ones: These children, the metal wyrms of Paladine, are your enemies. Much time will pass before you journey to Krynn, but when you go there, you will do my bidding, seeking and slaying your enemies." Another blast of fire exploded from the gaping jaws, a beautiful inferno raging, crackling in the air, slowly melting away.

"Remember," growled the queen, "mercy is weakness!"

"And weakness," Crematia echoed, her voice mimicking the Dark Queen's menacing tone, "is death."

PART 1

Chapter 1
A Nest in the Grotto

circa 8000 PC

In a place unimaginably far from the Abyssal home of the Dark Queen's brood, a different world took shape, gradually emerging from the chaos of godly dreams. This was a realm of sunlight and water, of jagged mountain ranges, vast oceans, and verdant forests. Beneath one of the mightiest summits, within the bedrock of a stony massif, was hidden another, quite different nest. The eggs sheltered here gleamed in the colors of precious metals, remaining undisturbed for a timeless expanse.

Finally movement stirred, metallic shells rupturing to allow scaly wyrmlings to emerge. Every bit as hungry, as keenly intelligent as Crematia and her kin-dragons, these creatures were also as different from the chromatic dragons as were the icebound mountains from the placid sea.

From the beginning, there were thirteen in all, bright serpentine creatures of glistening metallic colors, pushing through the minor encumbrances of filmy metallic shells. Lazily stretching, uncoiling, curling gracefully, the wyrmlings clustered in the comfort and warmth and security of the nest. An aura of peace sheltered them, a soothing essence lingering from the great females, the five metallic matriarchs who had been dead for centuries.

Here brass jaws gaped in a long, unconscious yawn, revealing rows of needle-sharp teeth. There a copper body stretched with lean, instinctive grace, perching with precise balance on the edge of the nest even as it continued to slumber. A wyrmling of bright bronze scales, squat and muscular, slowly pulled itself through the mass of the others, rising to curl in the midst of the mound of metal-colored scales and shimmering, folded wings.

The thirteen included serpents both male and female, examples of copper and brass, silver, bronze, and gold. All were vigorous, active and strong, and with growing animation, each carved out a space for itself within the confines of the sheltering bowl that was their birthplace.

Still, there was never any question but that Darlantan and Aurican would vie for mastery within the nest. Silver Darlantan's lightning pounce killed the bat that was the hatchlings' first prey, but it was Aurican's audacious grasp that stole that morsel, allowing the golden serpent to enjoy the first feast. Then together the two quick, graceful serpents showed their nestmates how to snatch the elusive mammals from the air. It was a splendid game—a leap and grab as a great cloud of the fliers swept into or out of the grotto brought down a squirming, squeaking bundle of meat and blood. The hunting was easy and nearly always successful. Copper Blayze, with his lightning speed, soon became even more adept than Darlantan and Aurican, though poor, bronze Aysa never quite got the hang of it at all.

Later it was Aurican who discovered that the water trickling onto the shelves of the grotto walls was the purest and sweetest to drink. But it was Darlantan who learned that a sharp tug on the tail would bring the precariously perched drinker tumbling down in a hissing bundle of scales, fangs, and claws. Thus was the first game created.

Aurican was also the one who learned that they could pry gems loose from the nest. All the wyrmlings were fascinated by the bright, multicolored baubles that had been embedded into the finespun metal wire. Most of the nestmates played games, throwing the stones back and forth, but the golden male preferred simply to hold a single large gemstone, caressing and admiring it for a long period of reflection.

These awakenings, gradual discoveries of sustenance and fellowship and competition in the grotto, were gradual things, occurrences that would be measured over many lifetimes by human standards. But to Darlantan, the wyrmlings were just *here*, within this grotto surrounding the deep nest of gemstones and finespun wire. Eating when they needed to, sleeping often and for long intervals, the nestmates passed the time and slowly grew.

But as their size expanded, they also became more powerful, faster and keener of understanding. Curiosity grew as alert minds began to consider the possibilities of things other than bats, water, and the nest. The brass male, Smelt, was the first to voice these questions.

"What's there?" he wondered, straining to study the stalactites dangling from the ceiling. "Or down here?" when he scratched at the floor. Sometimes he scrutinized the shadowy tunnel leading away from the grotto. "And what about in there? Is it just the Darkness Beyond? Does somebody live in there? And where do the bats go when they fly out of here?"

Of course, since Smelt persisted in asking questions for which his nestmates had no answers, they tended to regard him as a rather chatty pest. Still, chirping incessantly at any of the wyrmlings who would listen, the brass was always ready for a conversation.

Together the thirteen nestmates explored over a timeless, sunless era, working their way through the wondrous springs, rivulets, rocks, and holes of the grotto. To the newtlings, the cave was a universe, a world of unparalleled adventure and timeless wonder. A soft glow permeated the air, arising in pale incandescence from the nest. The grotto was pleasantly warm, and the stony floor was lined in many places with beds of plush moss. No fewer than a dozen springs trilled splashing water down the walls, and this steady flowage filled numerous pools before the overflow drained away through niches and cracks in the floor.

A lone passageway connected the grotto to a place the wyrmlings knew only as the Darkness Beyond. The corridor was wide and lofty, but cloaked in sinister shadows. Compared to the moist, airy grotto, the place seemed forlorn and frightening, and for a long time, neither Auri nor Dar dared to venture there.

Naturally none of the other eleven had any inclination at all toward blazing such a new trail. For one thing, there was no water in this winding tunnel, and the entire brood delighted to play in and drink from the pools and trickles of clear liquid that sparkled throughout the grotto. But even more than this, the Darkness Beyond seemed a peculiarly uninviting place, and for the first span of their lives, the wyrmlings were content to remain in their cave.

Of course, this span would be measured in centuries by human standards, but the serpentine neophytes had no such form of reckoning. To them, life was the unchanging, eternal grotto, and it was good. There was plenty to eat, for the bats dwelt all along the roof of the cave, and the serpents quickly became adept at upward pounces and deliberate, crawling stalks. Lightning-fast Blayze, the copper male, could even flip onto his back and snatch two bats with his forepaws—and, with luck, one or two more with the rear!

Frequently Burll, an ever-hungry bronze male with more brawn than brains, waited for Blayze to perform his trick. Burll then jumped upon his copper nestmate, snatching as many bats as he could, fending off the enraged Blayze until the bronze wyrmling could gulp down his stolen morsels.

Often Darlantan and the others killed bats for the sheer joy of the hunt, for the thrill of the fatal, spine-cracking bite.

The silver male sometimes took more than he could eat, though hapless Aysa was generally ready to help finish off any surplus. Aurican, unlike his silver brother, was always more precise. He killed a bat and ate it, then killed and ate another, inevitably completing his repast without waste.

Frequently the bats departed, swirling through the tunnel into the Darkness Beyond, their keening cries fading only slowly into the distance. Sometimes when their prey was gone, one or more of the dragons would suffer from gnawing hunger, going to the cavern entrance and waiting anxiously for the return of the bats. Inevitably the flying pack returned sooner or later, in a great, shrieking cloud of wings and fur.

Upon these returns, the bats brought scents and tastes with them, clues that triggered in Darlantan's mind the notion that perhaps there were things beyond the grotto worth knowing. A moist and loamy must sometimes coated the muzzle of a bat that the silver wyrmling slew, and it was a spoor that particularly intrigued him. He determined that one day he would follow the bats and learn the nature and origin of this scent.

But that time remained some vague, unmeasurable interval in the future. For now, there were brothers and sisters to tug from the walls, games of stalk-and-tag around the looming, gem-studded bowl of the nest, and a growing measure of clicks, barks, woofs, and hoots, sounds that were becoming increasingly recognizable to one another.

All thirteen of the metallic wyrmlings were active, killing and feeding with increasing frequency as larger bodies required ever greater supplies of meat. Their competition was fierce and instinctive—often a metallic scale or two flaked to the floor, pulled loose by a jealous slash or protective swipe. Aurican perfected a clever trick, pointing his snout in one direction while he was actually watching somewhere else from the corner of his eye. Lulling his nestmate into a false sense of security, he was frequently able to snatch away a bat or interrupt the drink of an unsuspecting sibling.

The wyrmlings were finding that they had to eat many bats in order to keep from going hungry. For the first time,

Darlantan became aware of a strange sensation: It seemed that this perfect enclosure, their paradise, was becoming too confining. Frequently he wrestled with this sensation, feeling it rise to a new level of urgency on one occasion when he crouched impatiently, waiting for the return of the bats, who had swarmed forth on one of their regular forays.

"We'll get some food soon?" squawked Aurican in the chirping dialect in which the nestmates conversed. The golden wyrmling padded up to Darlantan's side. Auri's proud head was upraised as he peered irritably into the shadowy tunnel.

Darlantan looked, too, understanding exactly the sounds his brother had made. "Let's stay here and listen," he squawked in reply. "Bats will come."

Woofing, Aurican indicated his impatience, and Darlantan nodded, suddenly sharing a gnawing hunger that, before his brother's suggestion, had been nonexistent. Together the two wyrmlings crept toward the yawning shadow, the winding tunnel leading outward from the grotto. Darlantan wasn't really *that* hungry—and he knew the bats would be back soon, because they always came back—but for some reason, he suddenly pounced, landing with a rattling growl in the very mouth of the dark corridor.

Aurican would not be outdone. He raced along the far wall, head and body held low against the floor, shimmering wings tight across his spiny back. Tongue flickering, tasting the air, he scuttled forward, belly low against the smooth floor while the golden wyrmling's yellow eyes glittered brightly in the murky shadows.

Then the grotto was a fading presence behind them. As chilly darkness settled around them, Darlantan realized he could still see, but there was a cloudy vagueness to this place that was very different from the cavern of the nest. That strangeness was not so much frightening as it was exciting, enticing. Auri was still a bright snake of color, darting along the base of the wall, then freezing, sniffing and tasting with a tongue that was like a flash of golden foil.

The other side of the cavern was too far away from his brother, so Darlantan crept down the center of the passageway. Though the ceiling was high and the walls far apart, after the vaulted spaciousness of the grotto, this place seemed strangely confining. He crouched low, studying each gentle curve as they approached it, then charging forward in a clatter of claws on stone and finally halting, seeking sounds and scents.

The cavern was long, and the two dragons paced each other around numerous bends. Despite the chill, Dar's heart pounded with increasing exhilaration, his body trembling as they alternately lunged and froze, advancing in tandem with steadily increasing confidence.

Awareness of a change grew gradually, until the pair abruptly came to a simultaneous, awe-stricken halt. Darlantan stared upward at such a gulf of shadowy space that he scarcely dared to breathe. For a brief moment, he felt dizzy, forcibly resisting an urge to spring forward, to launch himself into that void. He trembled in place for many heartbeats until, once more, curiosity allowed him to move. Again Auri hurried to keep up.

Dar's nostril's itched suddenly, and he sneezed with a burst of sound that brought both of them to a halt.

It was a good thing, too, because the gulf of space he had observed above also extended downward. The cavern floor ended abruptly about a half-pounce ahead of where the two dragons now crouched, once more overcome by awe.

The space around them was as dark as the cavern they had just traversed, but it was also unspeakably, infinitely *huge*. Darlantan knew without a moment's questioning that they had discovered the Darkness Beyond. If there was a surface, any object out there, he couldn't see it.

Looking up, he discerned that the connecting cavern emerged from the side of a rock surface, and the cliff arched outward, an unclimbable overhang looming into the distant shadows. To the right, the face of sheer stone curled away, bending back out of sight in a short distance. To the left, it did the same, though in that direction the shelf upon which they stood curved along the face of rock, offering a path along a wide, smooth ledge.

Once again the silver nostrils twitched, teased by a tickling sensation, but this time Darlantan ducked his neck and shook his head, stifling any outburst. At the same time, he realized that the tickling sensation was caused by a smell, although it was an odor with a tangible presence unique among the many aromas in the nest.

"Look!" Auri hissed, inclining the wedge of his head in a subtle pointing gesture.

The odor was coming from around the cliff, in the direction of the continuing ledge. Darlantan was startled by an impression that he could actually *see* this scent—at least, he perceived a wisp of whitish vapor trailing through the air. When he blinked and stared again, it was gone. Still, he felt certain he had seen something.

"The smell is from there," he hissed in certainty, and Aurican nodded.

"Be quiet—and be careful," the gold replied.

Side by side, heads low and bodies taut, the two dragons started along the ledge leading away from the cave mouth. The shelf of rock was mostly flat, though it sloped dangerously near the edge and was barely wide enough for the two to move without touching wings. Darlantan, on the outside, felt a vague sense of menace in having the Darkness Beyond so close at his side. He took care to place each foot with precision, gripping tightly with his needle-sharp claws.

The wonders of this exciting excursion were not over. Darlantan squinted suddenly as the brightest light he had ever seen flared before him. Sparks trailed downward as the spot of brilliance remained poised in the air, then began to move very slowly.

"Fire!" Auri gasped, and Darlantan knew the word was right.

Instinct dropped filmy inner lids across the dragons' eyes, and they stared in wonder and awe, but even now, as newtlings, neither felt any glimmer of fear. Instead, Dar's heart pounded with anticipation. He felt an urge to leap forward, to gulp down that source of flame, but he resisted.

The fire, Dar could see now, was on the end of a long, thin object. As the flare of first brightness faded, he discerned that the stick was in turn connected to another thing—and that thing was a creature! It radiated an inner warmth that reminded Darlantan of a bat, though it was much, much bigger than any of the winged fliers.

The stick, with its flaming end trailing brightness through the air, moved up toward the being's face. There the fire came to rest over a hooked protuberance, a curling stem that ended in a blunt, upturned bowl. Fire surged brightly again, and Dar sensed that it was being drawn into the protuberance. Moldy leaves seemed to smolder there, and vapors rose from the bowl in that tangible smell that Darlantan again realized he could see!

Abruptly a huge cloud of that visible smell emerged from the being, and then the creature turned to regard the two serpents with eyes that were luminous in their own right—not like the fire, but possessing a certain soft brilliance that in a sense was even hotter. And in that gaze, Darlantan saw a kinship, an abiding intelligence that reached out to touch him deeply.

Below those eyes was a snout. This was not nearly as magnificent a muzzle as a dragon's, to be sure, but impressive enough. It hooked outward from the being's face, curving forward to terminate in two massive, flexing nostrils. Darlantan watched in fascination as those twin apertures gave vent to additional puffs of the gray odor.

Beneath the snout was a flexible hole where the curved, leaf-burning protuberance was attached—clearly a mouth, though the opening was pathetic and shriveled compared to a dragon's maw. The rest of the creature's front, so far as the silver wyrmling could see, was a cascade of wiry bristles, a shaggy mat similar to bat's fur, only longer and bushier. This thick coating draped far down the being's chest.

Abruptly the smoking horn detached from the creature's mouth, held in some sort of crude claw, a paw that lacked any talons, so far as Darlantan could see. That limb swept into a gesture, as if embracing the two dragons, drawing them forward with growing wonder.

"Hello, little newtlings," said the being. "I was wondering when you would get here. . . ."

Chapter 2
Patersmith

circa 7500 PC

"There should have been twenty of you," Patersmith explained, his shoulders slumping in a posture of uncharacteristic sadness.

The bewhiskered tutor stood at the rim of the jeweled nest, gazing at the seven tarnished orbs that remained within amid the litter of scraps and shells. For a moment, the sturdy, short-legged figure stood still, as if he had forgotten the attentive audience on the grotto floor.

Darlantan and his nestmates were gathered in a circle about their tutor, who often addressed them from the height of the nest. Yet now Patersmith's attention was turned inward, staring into the soft depression where the hatchlings had been protected for so long. The thirteen wyrmlings waiting to hear his next words might have been all but forgotten, so far as the silver male could tell. He remembered the spheres within that enchanted nest, knowing that there had been one each of gold, silver, and brass, and two of copper and of bronze. Long ago those eggs had resembled the brilliant metallic sheen of the wyrmlings' scales. For some time, however, they had shriveled and dried, until now they were merely wrinkled balls in different shades of brown.

"It is a sadness beyond measure that these wyrmlings never had the chance to live," declared Patersmith.

"But why didn't they come out with the rest of us?" Smelt asked.

"I cannot say for sure, but I suspect the cause is the fading of spell magic from Krynn. There was enough of your mothers' sorcery left to protect the thirteen of you, but not the rest."

"But what is this magic? How did it protect us?" probed Aurican alertly.

"You should have had your mothers here when you were born . . . but that was not to be. Instead, they wove this nest and cast their spells of sustenance and protection. It was all they could do."

"What is spell magic, and where did it go?" asked Aurican, perplexed as he tried to follow the lesson with his usual careful concentration.

"Much of it is a mystery, vanished with the great queen dragons. Their spell magic was a thing of wonder, a power that could transcend the laws of the mortal world—until it disappeared. Perhaps this is another legacy of the Dark One's lingering hatred."

"What is the Dark One?" queried Darlantan, shivering under an involuntary sense of menace.

"She who is hated by Paladine and all goodness."

"Teacher, what is hate?" asked Aurican.

"That is a good question, but not an easy one to answer. In truth, it requires another tale."

"Then tell us, please!" clamored Oro and Mydass, golden sisters who, like their brother Aurican, had an apparently endless appetite for stories, ballads, and legends.

"I have a tale!" chirped Smelt. "When I was hunting a bat, it—"

"Shhhh!" hissed Dar and Auri, anxious to stop the brass dragon before his story wandered into its inevitably complex and pointless course.

Sulking, Smelt hung his head while Patersmith sighed and drew deeply on his pipe.

"You dragons are the favored ones, the sons and daughters of Paladine himself. The Platinum Father watches over you. It was he who bade me come here to teach you."

"If we are the favored of the Platinum Father," inquired Aurican pointedly, "that would indicate that there are those who are *not* so favored. Who are these others?"

"Ah, always with the questions, my golden pupil. You will learn that Krynn is peopled with a multitude of lesser creatures, slow-witted, weak, and short-lived for the most part. Still, they strive to exist on the world, and when at last you come forth into daylight, you shall share the land with them."

"But who are these creatures?" Darlantan asked, trying to picture a being that was neither dragon nor bat nor Patersmith. At the same time, he tried to imagine what daylight was like. Patersmith had told the wyrmlings about the sun, and though Dar found the concept terribly intriguing, it was also almost impossible for him to imagine.

"Perhaps first you will meet the griffons who glide through mountain skies. Of course, you are mightier than they and could make them your prey or your slaves. But perhaps you will have the wisdom to treat them with dignity and honor and will find that their service, rendered willingly, can be far greater than anything compelled."

"So long as the griffon doesn't take my bats!" declared copper Blayze, with a hissing growl.

"Ah, my quick-tempered one. I suspect that, when at last you fly above Krynn, you shall find yourself amazed that you once ate bats."

"But surely we will still need food," growled Burll,

drawing his bronze brows into deep furrows along the foreridge of his thick-boned skull.

"Surely indeed, my hungry one," said Patersmith with a deep chuckle. "It's just that you have, as yet, no real awareness of the incredible banquet that awaits you. And this is the source of our lesson."

"More food?" Burll inquired hopefully.

"No . . . more variety. You will learn that the diversity of the world is its greatest strength, just as it is among yourselves."

"You mean like the color of our scales?" probed Aurican, who, as usual, was a thought or two ahead of his nestmates.

"That is an example, albeit a minor one. More to the point are the things that make you different, for these are the things that make you all, as a clan, strong."

"Like Aurican wondering about magic all the time?" Dar suggested. "He's the only one who does that."

"Aye—or Smelt, who talks more than all the rest of you put together. Or you yourself, Darlantan. Always you must be doing something, going somewhere, stretching your legs. I can only imagine what it will be like when you learn to fly. And Blayze, so fast. Ever do you leave your nestmates behind." The tutor's gentle eyes smiled at the copper male and chuckled. "And with your temper, speed can be a useful attribute, as least while you live among bigger, stronger dragons."

"Am I different, like everybody else?" inquired Burll plaintively.

"Look at your strapping shoulders, the muscles that pulse beneath your bronze scales. Is there another of your nestmates so strong?"

"No," concluded the bronze, with a pensive nod of his head. "I guess not."

"He's even got muscles inside his skull!" cackled Blayze, provoking Burll to spit a sharp spark of lightning.

Immediately the copper flew at his nestmate, spattering acid from his own jaws, until Aurican and Darlantan pulled the hissing, slashing serpents apart. Stiff-winged and growling, the two combatants settled back into their places while Patersmith cleared his throat sternly.

"What other creatures shall we meet, teacher?" asked Aurican, impatient with the diversion.

"Ogres are the oldest. They have erected mighty cities across the world. From these, they have gone forth to enslave humankind, perhaps the shortest-lived and most wretched of the two-legs."

"Are the humankinds like bats?" asked Burll, his earlier anger forgotten as his tongue flickered across ever-hungry jaws.

"Bigger than bats," Patersmith declared, "and more entertaining, though they are far lesser creatures than you dragons."

"But are there other beings who dwell long lives of proper meditation and reflection?" pressed Aurican, his brow furrowed by concern.

"Ah yes. There are the elves, of course. Indeed, they are shy folk and hide in the thickest of forests. But I do not doubt you will find some common understandings with them, should you persuade one to emerge from his grove long enough to talk to you!"

"I should like that. Or perhaps I shall go into their groves instead," Auri murmured, so quietly that only Darlantan could hear.

"But back to matters of Paladine and the dragons of metal. These eggs, here. I am afraid we shall never know what happened to the seven that remain unborn."

"Then tell us about our mothers!" pressed Oro. "What of them and their tale?"

"Yes, a tale!" Aurican's head rose from the scaly crowd of wyrmlings. "Will you share it with us?" The gold dragon held a large multifaceted ruby in his foreclaw. As his bright yellow eyes focused on the teacher, he unconsciously sat back and passed the bauble back and forth between his paws.

"Ah, my Auri . . . ever the balladeer. In the case of this tale, however, I fear it is too dark for you wee nestlings. Nay, that one shall wait until later."

Patersmith turned back to his pupils, eyes sparkling above the cascading shower of whiskers. Pacing along the rim of the nest on his bowed legs, the tutor regarded each of the wyrmlings with a look of deep sympathy and warm understanding.

It was a look they had come to know, and to cherish, very well. Since the coming of Patersmith, the lives of the nestmates had changed significantly.

For one thing, the first tentative explorations in language had become whole volumes of words that the nestlings shared with each other and with their tutor. They had already heard of many adventures, ballads, and legends of Aurora and Argyn and their other mothers, the five matriarchs of metal dragonkind who had dwelt in peace and wisdom.

Occasionally the tales had hinted of darker realities, of wyrms named Furyion or Korrill or Corrozus. But Patersmith would turn away their questions when the wyrmlings pressed about these mysterious hints.

"Is this tale of our mothers also a tale of the chromatic dragons and the Dark One?" asked Darlantan, recognizing the tutor's reticence.

"Yes. You see well, my son."

"And will they come for us next?" asked Aysa, with a fearful look around the grotto.

"I should say not, for the chromatic dragons are gone. . . driven from the world by the heroism of your mothers. With them went the power of spell magic, and many would say the tally is fair. No, the thing that harmed these eggs is not so much the coming of an enemy as the waning of a friend."

"And magic—that is the friend?" Auri pressed.

"Aye, and the chromatic dragons are the enemies. Though you will learn, my nestlings, that still there are many other threats, dangers and evils of which you will one day be aware."

"What tale can you share, then, Patersmith?" asked Burll, the sturdy bronze wyrmling who was not at all shy about speaking up. Indeed, it was a good thing he was willing to question their tutor, since he often had to have things explained to him two or three times before he understood.

"Perhaps . . . perhaps a tale of magic."

At his words, the brood of dragons sat as if on cue, stilling any jostling and restless shifting. For of all the tales told by Patersmith, those about magic were without fail the most entertaining.

"Aurora was your mother," began the teacher in the ritual singsong of a proper lesson. Smith nodded to Aurican, and to his golden sisters, Mydass and Oro. "She of the golden scales and mighty power . . . but, too, she who had captured the wisdom and poetry of the ages within her being and her mind.

"Her magic was a wonder of the world. With a whispered word she could change her shape from dragon to eagle, soaring the skies of Krynn like a keen-eyed bird of prey."

Darlantan had neither seen nor heard about eagles, yet the word conjured an image of a sleek, feather-winged shape gliding through air that was not black, not cloaked in shadow. It was an image that inflamed his heart and caused his fledgling wings to twitch uncontrollably.

"Ah, Dar . . . one day you will fly among the eagles," murmured Smith, noticing the young dragon's agitation. "But just as Aurican must wait for his tales of nightmare and horror, so must you spend time on the ground before you strain for the skies."

"Aye, teacher," Darlantan pledged, bowing respectfully. Yet his wings still stretched as he settled himself more firmly among his siblings, determined to listen. He could scarcely stand to wait—he wanted to fly right *now*.

One of those restless silver wings brushed against Blayze, who was still glowering at Burll through the pack of attentive wyrmlings. The copper spat, drops of acid searing into Darlantan's wing, and the silver dragon whirled in a blur of scales and teeth. His own breath exploded, frosty ice gusting through the grotto as he hurled himself at the hot-tempered Blayze.

For several seconds, they tumbled and rolled, tails lashing, scales of copper and silver flaking into the air. Blayze was quick, but Darlantan was big and strong, and he easily pressed the copper to the ground. Silver jaws clamped over the metallic brown neck, and it was then that Patersmith stopped them with a word spoken in a hushed and soothing tone.

"Mercy," he said, stepping down from the nest to balance on his bowed legs. He touched each of the battling dragons with his hand, and Darlantan felt the rage go out of him like an exhalation of breath.

"Mercy," repeated the tutor. "Always show mercy to each other, and even to your enemies."

"But does that not make me vulnerable?" asked Blayze, scowling darkly, hissing at Darlantan.

"On the contrary, mercy makes you strong, for it creates loyalty and friendship. And you will learn that he who has loyal friends has great strength.

"But I was speaking of Aurora's magic . . . of her spells of fire that could raise a conflagration from a sodden forest, or hiss a small lake of water into steam."

Again the tutor used words that the dragons had never heard, but once more their tiny minds fashioned images to the sounds and began to picture a world that was beyond the enclosure even of the Darkness Beyond.

"Aurora and her sisters used their spell magic to fashion this nest, breathing upon the most precious stones in the world, forming them into a suitable crib for their precious offspring. It was this enchantment that insured your bed was always warm, and that should have seen all of you to a birth undisturbed by dangers.

"In those days of magic, all of your mothers knew great spells. But ever was Aurora the greatest." At the continuing words, the golden wyrmlings puffed with visible pride.

"It is said that she even caused a mountain to disappear once, bringing to death one of her mortal enemies when that dragon of white flew directly into an immovable cliff."

"Was that a dragon of our enemies?" asked Aysa.

"Yes, my daughter. You should know that those were days of violence, for the Queen of Darkness was ever jealous of your beautiful mothers, of their metal scales and keen wisdom and, perhaps most of all, of their eternal patience."

"And that jealousy brought war?" stated Darlantan, who had deduced many facts about the past from things that Patersmith did *not* say.

"That was the birth of war as such. The sons of the queen were so treacherous that even your mothers' magic was barely enough to prevent their ultimate success."

"But spell magic let our mothers win!" Oro asserted, glaring about with a golden glint, challenging any of her nestmates to dispute her claim.

"In the end, it did, though that struggle cost Aurora her life. Still, her spells were mighty. With them she could fly without wings, could at one time battle enemies in two different places."

"Master, you told us that you speak of 'those days of magic.' " The questioner was Kenta, one of Darlantan's silver sisters. "By that do you mean those days are over?"

"Aye, my gleaming daughter. In that age of evil and dreams, when your mothers battled the five sons of the Dark Queen, sorcery was a power held by all dragons. It was inherent might that only served to prove your ancestors' status as masters of all the world."

"But what happened to the magic?" asked Aurican, frowning, thrashing his golden tail. He glared about the grotto, as if he would fix with his sharp stare the culprit who had worked that audacious theft. In his hands, the ruby bauble had begun to glow faintly, casting a soft, fiery light between the wyrmling's clutching golden claws.

"Spell magic passed from Krynn with the death of Aurora," declared Smith, with a sad shake of his whiskers and his head. "The only sorcery in the world now is that embodied by creatures such as yourselves—in the breath weapons that you spit at each other like petulant children, and in the might that will enable some of you to assume different shapes, to walk among the elves and men of the world as one of them."

"But there are no spells?" Aurican asked again.

"No. Except, perhaps, in the tiniest vestiges—such as you yourself have brought to that piece of rock."

Aurican looked down in surprise, blinking at the soft illumination that radiated from the stone.

"A nice trick, that—pretty to see, simple to work. But that is the extent of magic that remains in the world. There is no use in searching nor in seeking. The power of true, world-shaking sorcery has vanished, never to return. It faded with the passing of your mothers, leaving Krynn a colder, darker place."

"Perhaps I will bring it back," Auri mused, so softly that only Darlantan could hear, though Patersmith looked at the golden wyrm sharply as Aurican spoke more firmly.

"I *will*. I say this now, to my tutor and my nestmates: Spell magic will again belong to our world."

Chapter 3
First Wings

circa 7000 PC

Thirteen metallic shapes padded silently along the winding passageway, following the bow-legged figure of their mentor as he led them from the grotto at a surprisingly fast jog. Aurican was in the lead, of course. In fact, the sleek and golden dragon paced directly beside the tutor, his proud golden head upraised, nearly as high off the floor as Patersmith's own bewhiskered visage.

Darlantan was right behind. He strained to see past his brother's shoulder, succeeding because he was slightly larger than Auri. The other eleven nestlings trailed behind, loping gracefully to keep up on what their tutor had promised would be a memorable excursion.

Biting back a twitch of irritation, Dar saw Patersmith turn

and speak softly to Aurican. The silver dragon couldn't hear what was said, and he felt the familiar resentment. Auri was always getting special tidbits of learning from their tutor.

Usually it had something to do with magic. All the dragons had been impressed by the stories of the sorcerous powers of their matriarchs, but none had latched on to those tales with the obsessive intensity of Aurican. Many times had he boasted to Darlantan of his intention to discover the ancient magic that had been lost with the elder dragons, until at last the silver had grown short-tempered every time he heard about his brother's pointless wish.

Often Darlantan reminded himself of Patersmith's lesson: Aurican's obsession with magic made him different, and was therefore good. Even when it seemed bad, like Blayze's temper, or Smelt's endless chatter, these were the traits that would make them strong. At least, so the bearded tutor said.

But Dar's musings were interrupted as the procession approached the end of the tunnel. Before him, the Darkness Beyond expanded to overwhelm his senses. He advanced and stood poised lightly at the lip of the lofty precipice.

The gulf of shadowy space had become familiar to the young dragons, and especially to Darlantan, in the vast expanse of time since Patersmith had come to join him. Whereas Auri was entranced by the tutor's stories of magic, Dar found himself raptly listening to descriptions of the world beyond their vast but shadow-cloaked environment.

He imagined an expanse of bright skies and was desperately curious about the sun, of which he had heard much but never seen even a trace. Too, he was intrigued and fascinated by the whole idea of weather—water and ice tumbling from above, heavy clouds billowing thicker than the smoke from Patersmith's pipe across the sky. All of that sounded suspiciously like magic, and he wanted to see, to learn for himself, if these things that the tutor was suggesting were really true.

"Darlantan, my silver son," declared the tutor.

Now it was his turn to enjoy the smith's favor, and Dar wasted no time in nudging Auri aside.

"You shall be the first. All the world awaits beyond, and

now it is time for you to take wing." His eyes rose and took in the rest of the brood. "Time for *all* of you to fly."

Several of the dragons, Aysa in particular, gasped nervously at the prospect, but Darlantan's wings stood stiffly to the sides, beating rhythmically as he readied himself for that first leap. His heart pounded as he looked at the vast darkness with eagerness and anticipation.

"Remember, your body will know what to do, though your mind will not. Therefore, don't try to think. Let yourself sail through the air and fly, my children!"

Without hesitation or reflection, Darlantan hurled himself into the void and, for a heart-stuttering second, commanded his wings to beat, to carry him upward. Immediately he plunged nose downward, then flipped over onto his back, careening wildly as wind whipped past his face, lashing across his scales. He strove to bend the unwilling membranes of his wings. Only then did he remember the words of Patersmith to relax, allowing his body to direct itself without interference from his mind.

Instinct took over, and those leathery membranes, as shimmering bright as quicksilver, scooped into the air. Dar's nose came up, and he felt the pressure of wind as his stroking wings found their natural pace. Soon he was climbing, banking, turning, feeling the air soar past with a rush of speed. He wheeled through a graceful arc, back toward the grotto's ledge, and for the first time in his life, he regarded that sheltered cavern from a distant perspective.

The nook was burrowed into the side of a massive stone pillar, a formation that was very wide above, then tapered to a narrow shaft below, so that the column dangled like a gigantic fang from the ceiling. Only the black tunnel was visible, but he knew that within lay the sacred grotto.

Below was a giant lake, extending into the far distance of the Darkness Beyond. That darkness was much less threatening when one was a part of it, Darlantan reflected, rearing back as he approached the ledge. Flaring his wings, he landed in a skidding slide that knocked Oro and Aysa tumbling and hissing to the sides. Darlantan spun about and pranced to the edge of the cliff with the confident air of one who has just demonstrated his innate superiority.

He was giddy with a consuming sense of exhilaration. Only the cautionary raising of Patersmith's hand held him from lunging forth and once again taking flight. But the tutor was eminently fair, and his guidance was not to be questioned. Darlantan knew it was someone else's turn.

Gradually the silver dragon realized that his twelve nestmates regarded him with expressions ranging from awe to astonishment. Aurican's inner eyelids lowered as his golden head swung appraisingly from the gulf of darkness to the taut, stiff-winged form of his silver Kin-dragon.

"Splendid start," Patersmith declared, puffing on his pipe and beaming at Darlantan, whose wings fanned excitedly. "Now, who's to be next?"

Kenta and Turq were ready and bobbed their silver heads, but it was Aurican who stepped to the rim of the cliff and sprang into space with a prodigious leap. He swept smoothly into a dive, spiraling and circling downward until he was lost in the shadows. After many heartbeats, he reappeared, slowly working his way back upward.

By then Kenta had flown, like Darlantan in a momentary tumble of silvery scales before she found her natural rhythm. Turq followed her sister with similar success, and then one after another the young dragons threw themselves into space. With varying levels of struggle they took wing, gliding over the water and then swooping upward with steadily growing confidence.

Copper Blayze, nimble as ever, swept outward with confidence. His wings stroked with keen and instinctive skill as he pressed them downward, banked easily, then climbed steadily toward the ceiling of the lofty cavern.

Smelt, in a flash of brass scales, swept past Blayze and tugged at his wing, sending the hot-tempered copper spinning toward the lake in a spitting, twisting bundle of fangs and claws. It wasn't until very much later that Smelt even dared return to the ledge, and even then the fuming Blayze hurled himself at his nestmate, almost sending both of them tumbling toward the dark waters of the lake.

Aysa was the last to fly. Not surprisingly, she tumbled

straight down from the perch. The bronze female fell so rapidly that Darlantan dived after her, certain she would smash into the waters far below. Though the silver male strained to catch up, in the end, Aysa learned on her own, spreading her wings and leveling off just a short distance above the still, inky-dark expanse of the giant pool.

Soon the wyrms had gathered back at the ledge, where Patersmith regarded them with expressions of contentment. He puffed and smoked, smiling gently, though to Darlantan, the old teacher's eyes seemed to moisten with melancholy.

"Come with us!" urged the silver dragon. "We'll fly throughout the Darkness Beyond!"

"Alas." Patersmith held up his arms. "These are very poor wings. No, without magic, it is impossible for me to fly with you. But it is time that all of you soared into the world and witnessed the wonders of which you have only heard."

"But how do we find the world through the darkness?" asked Kenta.

"There is a cave, similar to the door cave of your own grotto." The tutor pointed into the distant darkness. "Find it and fly, my wyrmlings, and you will find yourself in the world of light and sky."

"We go!" cried Darlantan, his wings buzzing audibly as he tensed for a leap into space. Excitement brought him to a fever pitch. It was fantastic to fly, but even more wonderful to think he would at last get a look at the sun and the sky and the whole world.

"Yes, go! You will fly to the Valley of Paladine. Beyond the darkness, you shall see this sacred place, sheltered in the High Kharolis. There you may hunt and sleep and fly, safe from the intrusions of the world."

Darlantan led the way, though Aurican and the other two silvers flew just behind his tail. The others strung out through the darkness as the dragon followed his memory of Patersmith's pointing finger. A light breeze moved the air of this vast place—a place that was really something far more concrete than the vague entity he had known as the Darkness Beyond. Already Dar could see the looming wall of this great, subterranean chamber. A sheet of dark rock rose from the edge of the still water, rising high overhead as it domed outward to form the cavern's lofty, vaulted ceiling.

Abruptly Aurican veered to the side, wings straining in a visible effort to gain speed. Darlantan tried to think, to remember. . . . Was it possible he was mistaken in his memory of Patersmith's indicated direction?

Then he understood: It was the wind! Aurican had sensed that breeze and known that it must originate from the passageway to the outside world.

Before the others could react, their golden sibling swept into a shadowy passage looming in the vast wall. Now it was Darlantan behind his nestmate's tail, straining to overtake Aurican. Yet even in his frustration, he retained a measure of caution. He knew he couldn't try to fly past Auri in this narrow passage, or more likely than not they'd both go crashing into the walls or ground.

And then they were into a realm that was so broad, so breathtakingly open that the young dragon forgot all about his petty duel. The blue of the sky was deeper, more perfect than any color Darlantan had ever imagined. Clouds puffed, impossibly white and serene in the azure vault that swept overhead. Mountain peaks surrounded the file of gliding, awestruck dragons, and these summits were etched into such precise clarity that Dar felt as though he should be able to reach out and touch each one. He saw, however, that the valley was wide, and every one of the lofty peaks was a considerable distance away.

The heights fully encircled this place. Even as they flew, the dragons looked upward to the horizon in all directions. Glaciers sparkled in the sunlight, draping the highest peaks in regal cloaks of ice. Cornices, like diamond-studded crowns, crested these ridges, and where the daylight sparkled along the summits, the gleaming reflection was brighter than fire.

Best of all, brightening the scene everywhere, glowing from the heights of the sky, shone the ball of brilliant illumination . . . and Darlantan knew that he had at last discovered the sun.

Chapter 4
Abyssal Flames

circa 5000 PC

The crude rabble of Crematia's quarry huddled in a small alcove in the floor of the Abyss. These creatures, however, were not like the furry rodents that had sustained her upon her emergence from the egg. Now the mighty red dragon held sway throughout the realm of her queen, taking any of the inhabitants she desired for the pleasure of her feasting.

Tail lashing in leisurely arrogance, Crematia eyed the wretched creatures with cruel detachment. This was a family of them, wide-eyed creatures who walked upright and wore the skins of animals over their own hairless hide. Now a male strutted and growled, brandishing his pathetic club while the female huddled against the wall, three or four nit-like children clinging to her skirts, her hands, and her hair.

"Please, O mighty one!" wailed the mother. "Show us mercy!"

Crematia's crimson maw curled into a sneer.

"Mercy is weakness," she declared, then made a slow intake of breath. "And weakness is *death*."

Finally the red dragon's jaws opened, and the expulsion of fire blossomed into an oily, searing bundle of flames around the helpless victims. The roaring of the blaze drowned the pathetic wails of the dying creatures, a fact that invariably held true, except when Crematia incinerated a very large number of victims at once. In these cases, she had been amused to discover that the dying could raise a wail loud enough to carry above the infernal din.

But such opportunities for mass execution were very rare indeed. Crematia had become the scourge of the Dark Queen's hellish realm, but so effective was her killing that there were only occasional targets left upon which she could vent her wrath. She had learned her lessons well, remembering the queen's commands as if they had been seared into her mind with the fiery force of dragonbreath.

"Find your strongest enemy and kill him," Takhisis had ordered. "Then find your new strongest enemy—for there will be one—and kill him."

To that end, Crematia had slain all the other red dragons that had emerged from the nest of her birth. With cunning and cruelty, she had tracked them down, males and females alike, and killed by fang or talon or fire. Occasionally she prolonged the suffering of a victim for her own entertainment, but never did she do so out of mercy.

The other chromatic dragons, the blacks, whites, blues and greens, had been taken elsewhere by the queen, or else Crematia would certainly have killed them as well. Now she was left with pathetic beings like these warm-blooded creatures clad in furs. They died at her whim, but were scarcely deserving of the term "enemy."

"Crematia . . . my Scarlet Daughter."

"Yes, my queen." The red dragon bowed low when she heard the voice of her mistress. The obedience was ingrained—she had seen too many nestmates perish because they had been slow to respond to the Dark Queen's abiding need for fealty and worshipful fawning.

The great five-headed image of Takhisis reared from the chasm in the base of the Abyss. Naturally it was the crimson head that fixed its twin eyes upon Crematia, that spread the mighty jaws to speak in a low and rumbling voice.

"It is time for your journey to commence."

The words were exciting, bringing twin wisps of sooty flame snorting from the crimson nostrils. For eons, Crematia had known that her mistress had some destiny, some great task, for her, and it was thrilling to hope the time had finally come for her commencement.

"My journey of vengeance, Honored Matriarch?" Crematia's heart flared into a blaze of anticipation. For too long had she been sharpening her cruelty and her skills against such pathetic targets as these primitives.

"Indeed. Know that others of your nest will journey through the planes behind you, but you are the one I have chosen to lead my children in their return to Krynn. You shall pave the way, and the others I will send when you are ready."

"I am prepared to go now, mistress," the red dragon pledged with a low, wide-winged bow.

"You must be courageous, my daughter, but not foolhardy. You shall know killing, and wreak terrible destruction in my name. Seek the wyrms of Paladine; learn their habits and their lairs. But do not risk yourself. Leave the dangers to your sisters and brothers, my lesser wyrms."

"I obey, my queen."

"Then it is time for you to depart."

Fire surged as the queen's crimson jaws gaped, billowing a cloud of infernal flame that swelled and crackled in the air. For several heartbeats, the flames raged, and when they faded, a smudge of oily smoke lingered like a tangible sphere floating in the air.

The smoke gathered into a swirling vortex, a tiny funnel that twisted with a gusty roar on the red stone of the ground. With a tightly focused spiral, the whirlwind spun like a grinding drill against the rock until it dissipated with an audible *pop* of sound.

In the space where it had been, a bright red ruby gleamed. Multiple facets flared and sparkled, reflecting the myriad fires rising from the horizons of the queen's realm.

"Eat this Talonstone and my blessing shall infuse you."

Crematia's head darted forward, and the huge ruby disappeared, rippling its way down the snaky length of her scaly throat.

"With this gem of potent enchantment shall you carry magic to Krynn. You will bear a power greater than that of any good dragon, for sorcery has been lost to them for many ages. You, the first of my children, shall be a creature mightier than any in that world, and with that power you shall commence to claim all of Krynn for me!"

"Aye, mistress!" pledged Crematia, her belly seething and flaming at the prospects of destruction and killing.

"Follow the passage. Make way to a world of lesser mortals and let them know your wrath and your will!" commanded the Dark Queen, her crimson head rearing like a mountain above. Five pairs of jaws spread wide, acid and lightning, gas and frost and flame all erupting skyward in a quintuple fanfare.

"Mercy is weakness, and weakness is death!" Crematia repeated reverently.

Her crimson wings spread wide, and the red dragon took to the air. Before her, the gate flamed into existence, a great circle of fire poised in space, burning with raging fury. Through that gap she saw a smoldering but sun-brightened sky and a landscape scarred by deep gorges and heaving, fiery mountains. Tucking her wings, narrowing into a streamlined dive, the red dragon swept through the gate, departing forever the Abyss that was her mistress's realm.

She emerged from a shower of flames and immediately pulled upward, straining for height. The gate had passed her into the bottom of a deep shaft of rock, but the space was so broad that she was able to swing through lazy spirals, gradually climbing up and out. Riding the upsurge of scalding gases past sheer walls of flame-scorched stone, the crimson serpent rose steadily higher.

Finally Crematia emerged from the top of a great smoldering mountain, the greatest summit in a vast and tangled range of such peaks. She knew intuitively that this was Darklady Mountain, a massif that had risen from the tortured land in honor of her queen's awful might. Slopes of dark debris, streaked with rusty red and trailing spumes of tar, marked the conical summit in slashes of color, like a crown encircling a lofty brow.

Smoke and ash filled the sky, whipped by the wind, trailing like horsetails from many of the loftiest summits. Wings spread wide, Crematia soared, looking into a volcano that seethed and pulsed with the rage of internal fire, then flying above another with a caldera that lay still and snowbound below. Rivers of lava scored some of the valleys, while others were shrouded in great, apparently eternal blankets of ice, frost, and snow.

The sun was a fire in the heavens, but the warmth of that great orb was muted by the clouds of smoke roiling through the skies. Everywhere mountains spumed and exploded, and great billowing expulsions of ash and toxic vapors layered the sky. The stench of the air was thick and acrid, and comfortingly familiar to the Abyss-bred serpent. She soared with a sense of serene exhilaration over soot-stained glaciers and peered with aloof condescension into deep, eternally shaded gorges.

After flying for a long time, the red dragon swept between the steep shoulders of two massive mountains and found herself over a region of foothills. The ground was rough and rocky, but lacked the height and the flaming intensity of the volcanic reach she had just traversed.

It was in a valley between a pair of rolling crests that she saw the first signs of life, walking figures that shuffled outward from a deep, well-protected cave mouth. Immediately she cloaked herself with a spell of invisibility, soaring low for a closer look, knowing she was safe from observation. Several upright figures tromped along the ground, each hulking body borne by a pair of gnarled legs. Some of the brutes clutched large limbs of wood— apparently weapons, the red dragon deduced as she watched the creatures suddenly close in on a mountain sheep, bashing the animal between them until it was slain.

Intrigued, Crematia continued her explorations, discovering many of these creatures inhabiting the foothills around the High Khalkists. She observed that they dwelled in clans and took shelter in high, shallow caves. They had scored a series of crude tracks, linking many of the tribes over these torturous mountain pathways. Her observations suggested that the clans were led by the biggest of the brutes, who seemed to be rough, crude folk, readily prone to violence.

In one place, she discovered a deep valley sheltered between the sheer walls below two lofty summits. Along the floor of the gorge were no fewer than a half dozen great caves, and a large number of the two-legged brutes seemed to dwell there.

Still invisible, the red dragon flew back and forth, finally discovering one gathering that intrigued her. Several of the largest of the bull warriors gathered here, and from these bristled headdresses of bright feathers, while ornaments of gold dangled over their broad chests. Whispering a word of magic, she canceled her spell of invisibility, appearing suddenly when she was just overhead. The dragon settled to the ground before the adorned beings, the downward blasts of her wings driving dust and debris into their faces.

Crematia saw the gnarled legs, hulking bodies, and strapping arms of these humanoids. She studied the sloping brows, the wide, tusked mouths, and the massive hands clutching knobbed clubs or boulders. The creatures cowered back from her but did not run away, except for one female who, clutching a squalling infant, darted from the pack.

The red dragon lowered her head, jaws gaping, and spat a blast of searing flame around the lumbering, terrified creature. The victim's scream rose to a piercing ring as the female, now a living torch, tumbled and thrashed across the ground. In a heartbeat, her life and that of her babe were snuffed away, leaving as a remnant two inter-mingled, blackened shapes. Satisfied that the smoldering corpses were ample demonstration of her might, Crematia regally swung back to regard the abject creatures cower-ing before her.

"How are you called?" she asked the largest of the band, who scarcely dared to raise a fearful eye from the ground when he heard her question.

"We are ogres, O mighty one! And we are your miser-able servants."

"Do you expect my mercy?" demanded the red dragon.

"No, O mighty one. Mercy is weakness!"

"And weakness is death," she concluded with a grim nod. "Your answers please me. You will make me wel-come and show me honor. And you, my hulking one, you shall be my general and my slave. What is your name?"

"I am the battle chieftain known as Ironfist, and my ene-mies quail at the sound of my approach!"

"That is good. Now, Ironfist, send messengers. You must prepare your fellow tribes for the arrival of my kin. Your clans will gather to my call. Know that I shall lead you to a mastery of the world!"

Chapter 5
Lords of Peak and Glade

circa 5000 PC

The stag lunged through the thicket, crushing brittle branches with the force of its headlong flight. Nostrils flaring, hooves drumming the ground, the mighty deer lowered branching antlers and bulled ahead, breaking into the clear with a snorting toss of its proud head. Now the animal galloped across a marshy meadow, each leaping step kicking up great clods of moist dirt. Stretching, reaching in long strides, the stag accelerated with a frantic burst of speed. Darting and veering, the great creature lunged over the muddy terrain, its hoofprints a scar of darkness across the wet landscape.

And following that advancing scar was a fast-moving shadow in the form of a serpentine body, with a long tail and broad, tapering wings.

Darlantan saw immediately that the clearing would be the animal's undoing. The silver dragon tucked his wings and dropped precipitously to land on the stag's heaving back. Metal-hard talons flexed, argent tips gripping the flesh of shaggy haunches, while Darlantan's forefeet drove their claws into the stag's powerful shoulders. The mighty deer stumbled, collapsing from the dragon's weight, but by then Dar's jaws had closed around the muscular neck, biting down hard, breaking the hapless animal's spine.

Tumbling to the ground, the stag rolled through the mud and shuddered to a halt. Darlantan pitched forward, but the graceful dragon spread his wings and glided very low. Blades of marsh grass brushed his belly for a moment, but then he swept upward, finally rising high enough above the ground that he could once more flap his wings and safely gain elevation.

Circling back to the bleeding body of the antlered deer, he bugled his success into the clear, crisp air of the High Kharolis. The blue sky, an azure so deep that it never failed to move Darlantan, fully enclosed the vast valley, vaulting overhead like a magical dome of turquoise resting upon the ring of mighty peaks. How he loved to soar through that sky, to experience the utter, liberating freedom of flight.

Now Kenta and Aysa, silver and bronze shapes against the snowfields, glided into view, and Darlantan knew the others would be following soon. His chest puffed outward in unconscious pride, and again he bellowed word of his triumph with a cry that echoed back and forth between the lofty summits. He saw another speck of brown metal and recognized Burll. Darlantan chuckled, knowing his bronze kin-dragon would never be late for an offering of food.

Proudly the silver male settled beside the corpse of his kill. His chest thrust outward as he watched his nestmates gliding closer. Darlantan's tail curled around the motionless body as he lifted his head as high as the elk's antlers had been when the animal was alive. The mighty denizen of the forest weighed more than the winged hunter that had brought it down, and the silver dragon knew this was the largest single kill in the history of his nestmates' lives.

Kenta, the first to land, dipped her head in a nod of approval, flexing her wings and straightening her tail in a display that Darlantan found strangely intoxicating. She had done the same thing before, this silver female, and he had come to relish the fleeting, uncanny sensation. Uncertain of why he did so, Darlantan felt compelled to offer her the tenderest morsel, ripping the tongue from the elk's mouth and extending it to her in a silver claw.

"Do you remember when we used to eat bats?" asked Kenta, gulping the tongue in a smooth slurp, rippling the scales all the way down her sinuous neck.

Darlantan chuckled as he tore away a hindquarter of the massive elk. "It would take as many bats as Patersmith has stories to equal the meat in this single haunch."

He tore into the meat, relishing the taste of the fresh blood, the warm fullness of each bite as he gulped it down. More of the band came into view now—Oro and Mydass, the golden females, with brass Smelt gliding swiftly behind them—so the silver took a generous portion of the kill and withdrew, allowing his nestmates a chance to share the proof of his hunting skill.

"You killed this?" Smelt asked. Darlantan nodded serenely, and the brass dragon continued. "I like deer—especially the big ones. They have so much meat. Do you want the heart, or can I have it?"

The silver dragon's attention remained upon Kenta, so Smelt pulled the bloody muscle from the stag's chest and swallowed it in a rippling gulp. "Too bad Aurican can't see this," he said, wiping a forked tongue across his crimson jaws.

"Where is our golden kin-dragon?" Darlantan asked, amused by the serpentine metallic shapes clustered around the rapidly diminishing corpse. It pleased him to feed his nestmates, but he wanted Aurican to behold his trophy before it was merely a clean-picked skeleton.

"Oh, I saw him flying toward the sunset, maybe a dozen

sunrises ago," Smelt explained while gulping a mouthful of venison. "He was in the foothills, and I flew along with him for a while. But it seemed as if he didn't want to talk." With another convulsive gulp, he swallowed, then swiveled his long neck toward the west. "He should have heard your summons, but maybe he's too far away. Or perhaps he made a kill of his own."

"Yes . . . perhaps," declared Darlantan, disappointed. Still, he brightened at the sight of the stag's bristling antlers as Smelt lifted the skull and used his serpentine tongue to slurp out the tender brain. It was as though the ghost of the great deer danced before them. At least that rack would provide some proof of his accomplishment. He could take the trophy into the cavern to show Patersmith, who still took pride in the accomplishments of his growing charges.

Restlessness soon took the place of reflection. Darlantan stood stiff-legged, flexing his wings. He would remember this place and return for the antlers, but for now he was ready to fly. Without a farewell, he departed, leaving his nestmates to break the joints and suck the marrow from the remnants of the kill.

A short time later, as he flew beside a high mountain ridge, he heard a squawk of outrage from the other side of the rocks, followed by a dragonlike bellow of anger. Tipping his wing, Darlantan veered up and over the crest, coming to rest on the jagged but solid summit of the ridge.

Below he saw Blayze crouched on a shoulder of rock, jaws gaping as he faced a fluttering, feather-winged creature that the copper dragon had trapped against the mountainside. The birdlike beast shrieked again, hooked beak widespread. Blayze's jaws spread wider, and Dar saw his nestmate's belly swell, ready to hurl forward the deadly acid of his breath weapon.

Before that lethal spume emerged, Darlantan pounced, sweeping downward, reaching with his claws as he swept past the ledge. He snatched the griffon—he recognized the feathered flier by its tawny feline hindquarters—in his claws and pulled it away, allowing his momentum to carry both the fliers down the mountainside, away from Blayze. The copper's blast of acid seared the rocky wall, trickling downward, hissing and burning against Darlantan's tail as the silver dragon swept the struggling creature to safety. Landing on his haunches on a lower shoulder of the slope, Darlantan held the squirming griffon off the rocks to avoid crushing the creature with his own weight.

"That wyrm took my prey!" hissed the griffon, twisting with surprising strength. A sharp beak jabbed Darlantan's neck, and with a yelp, the silver dragon threw the hawk-faced flier to the side, struggling to hold his balance on the steep mountainside.

"That was my fight, Darlantan!" snarled Blayze, still crouched over the mountain sheep. "I don't need your help!"

"I'm not trying to help you," Darlantan replied. "I just wanted to talk to the griffon."

That feather-winged flier, meanwhile, had spiraled away and come to rest on a knob of rock. Now it straightened powerful wings, smoothing ruffled feathers with long strokes of its hooked beak. Darlantan crouched above, studying the creature curiously. Blayze, after glaring at his silver nestmate, decided to eat instead of pursue the quarrel.

"Don't think you can kill me just because you saved me from that snake!" spat the griffon, rearing back on its feline hindquarters and flailing the air with powerful, taloned foreclaws.

"Why would I save you to kill you?" Dar asked, puzzled by the statement.

"Who knows? Why would your kin-dragon take my sheep when he could easily kill one of his own?" huffed the creature, casting a nervous glance up the mountainside. Darlantan saw that Blayze was crouched there, and when the copper raised his head, he saw jaws dripping with fresh blood.

"I saw the ewe first," huffed the half-hawk, half-lion creature, fixing bright yellow eyes upon the silver dragon. The griffon blinked appraisingly, and Darlantan sensed it was more curious than angry.

"Blayze never was much for waiting his turn," the silver serpent explained. "Was that courage or foolishness that was leading you to fight him?"

The griffon blinked in surprise, then settled back on all fours. Apparently he had decided Darlantan wasn't an immediate threat, for he began grooming his chest and shoulders with one foreleg's talons as he spoke.

"Actually, I didn't think I could escape. And I wouldn't have, if you hadn't swept me away. Why did you do that?"

"I've never met a griffon. My name is Darlantan. Do you have a name?"

"Ravenclaw, at your service. And I will remember you, silver Darlantan. But now, since my kill was taken, I must fly to the hunt."

With that, the griffon took wing, eagle feathers streaming in the mountain air, the sleek form gliding toward the lower valleys, where presumably he could hunt without interference from bullying dragons.

Darlantan also flew, but his course took him upward, not down, until he soared over the ramparts of the lofty range. He left behind the High Kharolis, the vast mountain range that domed over the grotto and its surrounding cavern. Dar's flight took him away from that timeless home, into lower regions of forest that the dragon had flown above, but rarely inspected.

As he flew he reflected on an old lesson—"Mercy is strength," Patersmith had said, "for it breeds friendship." Indeed, he felt a kinship with the griffon, a warm pleasure that the creature was still alive. He was glad he had been merciful; Blayze would have killed the creature.

Through many sunrises, he soared above vast woodlands, awed by the extent of forest. In places, ponds, streams, or lakes sparkled blue amid swaths of greenery. Occasionally a knob of rocky bluff jutted upward, and when he grew tired, the silver dragon invariably came to rest upon one of these. He relished the pastoral swath of green, vaster by far than the Valley of Paladine. The lush forests seemed to blanket an entire portion of the world with their deceptively soft-looking foliage.

Game was plentiful here, and each night he was able to kill a deer or pig for his sustenance. For sunrises that stretched into seasons and even longer he remained in the forest. If it hadn't been for the continuing absence of Aurican, Darlantan's exploration would have been a marvelous adventure. Yet the fact that his golden brother had been gone so long he found increasingly disturbing—either because something bad had happened, or because the gold had perhaps discovered something extremely fascinating. Aurican was quite capable of becoming so distracted by a wondrous discovery that he would quite forget to inform his nestmates.

Dar's emotions wrestled constantly between concern and envy. He wasn't at all certain if he hoped Aurican had been distracted by some discovery, for there were times when it would have satisfied him to find his brother in some kind of real distress—nothing so serious that Darlantan couldn't have immediately come to his aid, however. The silver dragon flew on in growing agitation, his concerns slowly gaining prominence over suspicion and jealousy.

Finally his persistence was rewarded by a glimpse of shimmering golden scales, a serpentine shape coiled in a small, tree-shaded clearing. Braying a greeting, Darlantan tucked his wings and angled between lofty pines to land precisely in front of his brother. The draft of his wings drove a great cloud of dust and pine needles into Auri's face, an effect that Darlantan found not displeasing.

"Greetings, Cousin," declared Aurican, blinking his eyelids, then sneezing a cloud of dust back at Darlantan. The gold dragon's head reached high above the ground, while his sinuous body curled between several trees.

The silver chuckled, wrapping his tail around a tree trunk and squatting on the loam beside the sinuous golden form. "The ground here is soft, but surely there's more than that to bring you so far."

"Shhh." Auri's inner eyelids lowered lazily, his snout subtly gesturing toward the woods.

Darlantan mimicked his brother's air of indolence, allowing his gaze to shift far to the side in their childhood game of misdirection. He sniffed with casual curiosity, startled by a strange and intriguing smell wafting through the air. The odor was curiously sweet and complex, suggesting a variety of sources.

But nothing unusual was visible.

For a long time, the two serpents remained still. Finally Darlantan saw movement. Several figures skulked through the forest, advancing cautiously amid the shelter of the trees, drawing closer to the meadow, clearly interested in observing the dragons. The beings were quite pathetic-looking. They walked on two legs like Patersmith, but were skinny, if perhaps a little taller than the tutor. Though hair dangled from the scalps of these creatures, their faces were completely barren of whiskers. They wore skins of supple leather around their loins; their legs and arms were bare, with additional leather strapped to their feet. Darlantan could smell the skin of elk and deer.

Finally the strangers emerged into the open, and Aurican tipped his head regally toward the newcomers, then turned to regard his nestmate, an expression of gentle rebuke in the downward curl of his snout.

"You startled them rather badly, you know," Auri explained. "I've spent many seasons trying to tame them. Actually, I'm rather impressed they returned so readily."

Darlantan studied the approaching figures, realizing that, despite the uniform slenderness of their physiques, they were well muscled, wiry sinew rippling visibly beneath their pale skin. They carried curved wooden weapons in their hands, and several were girded with slender blades worn at the waist. Their eyes were bright and curious, reflecting a certain natural intelligence.

Then the silver dragon noticed the ornaments. Dar blinked in astonishment and envy as he saw a chain of golden links, the metal smooth and polished to the same sheen as Auri's scales. The gold dragon inclined his head low, and one of the two-footed beings placed the beautiful chain over his head. Rising again, Aurican looked about proudly, letting the glimmering metal jangle down to his broad chest.

Then the gold dragon turned over his forepaw, and Darlantan saw that Auri clutched one of the gemstones he was so fond of caressing. This stone seemed to be a large, smooth-surfaced opal, and it remained floating in the air after the golden talons withdrew. Slowly, reverently, one of the two-legged creatures advanced, reaching out to stroke the opal, then finally drawing the stone to his skinny chest. With a bow at the onlooking dragons, the little being stepped backward to show the gift to his companions.

"They are called elves," Auri explained as more and more of the pale figures emerged from the woods. "Remember? Patersmith told us about them. They are possessed of certain skills that even a dragon might find useful—and, Dar, I think they have a knowledge of magic!"

Awed and once more a little jealous, Darlantan raised his own sinuous neck, his head rising just a bit higher than Aurican's. He looked at the gathering of Aurican's pets—his elves—and he found himself admiring their courage. He saw that they whispered and muttered among themselves, pointing at the two dragons, clearly conversing in some sort of crude language.

"They even speak," Auri explained, as if reading his nestmate's mind. "In fact, they have a wealth of lore. I have met a chieftain who tells tales of my mother, Aurora!"

"That seems an unusual discovery," Dar agreed, "for beings so small, with neither scales nor hair, to have lore of the ancients. It is strange that Patersmith did not tell us more about them."

"Perhaps he did not know, for he believes magic to be vanished from Krynn, and yet these elves can work magic on metal."

Darlantan watched and listened attentively as Aurican said something to one of the elves in a strange tongue. The elf then opened a satchel at his side and held up a powder of bright flakes in his hand. Darlantan stared, intrigued, as the elf let the stuff trickle back into the leather sack, a shower of miniature sparkles, each as bright as Aurican's scales.

"They bring the gold from the rivers like this, but then they work a spell of magic, weaving the dust into these links that adorn me."

"That is a wonder," Darlantan agreed. "But are you certain it is magic?"

"Look." Auri nodded toward the woods, where another elf was emerging into view. This was a tall, proud male, whose hair was dark, in contrast to the strawlike yellow of his fellows. He strode boldly up to Darlantan and raised a shimmering object in his hands, a thing so beautiful that the mighty dragon all but gasped in astonishment.

It was a necklace of links, a gently chiming chain as perfectly brilliant as Aurican's, save that it was made out of pure, gleaming silver.

Darlantan lowered his head in imitation of Auri's gesture of acceptance, allowing the elf to place the chain over his head. He felt the weight against his scales as he rose and allowed the chain to jangle down the length of his long neck. Now he, too, felt the adornment of the elves, and his earlier envy was replaced by a twinge of shame.

"Can you tell them I am grateful?" he asked Aurican, looking with renewed interest into the elf's deep, emerald-colored eyes.

"I will tell them for now, but soon you will know their language as well." The gold made a declaration in that lilting, musical tongue—it wasn't primitive at all, Dar realized—and the elves bowed toward Darlantan. The dark-haired male who had bestowed the silver necklace made a soft, pleasant-sounding reply.

"Now they invite us to journey into the forest with them," Aurican explained. "They were just about to take me there when you arrived, but they have extended the invitation to us both."

Darlantan eyed the woodlands skeptically. "The trunks are close together, Cousin," he said. "How do you intend to pass? Magic?"

Aurican smiled slyly, rearing back on his haunches and

placing his foreclaws onto the golden chain. "You are closer to the truth than you might think. Of course, spell magic was lost with our mothers, but we have within us the means."

Abruptly Darlantan wasn't looking at Aurican, but at a tall, handsome elf who stood in the place where the gold dragon had been. The elf threw back his head and laughed, and only then did Dar recognize his nestmate.

"That *is* magic!" he gasped. It was strange, even incomprehensible, to try to understand that this little creature was actually the mighty Aurican!

"You must join us," the gold dragon in the body of the elf said, bowing low and sweeping a hand before Darlantan.

"But . . ."

Unwilling to appear ignorant before Aurican and his pets, Darlantan reared back in the posture his golden nestmate had assumed, but nothing happened.

"Perhaps it is a gift only of gold dragons," Dar suggested, trying to conceal his disappointment.

"No, I suspect that it will work for you—albeit not for our nestmates of the brown metals. You must form a picture of your new shape," Aurican encouraged. "Choose what you will. I became an elf, in honor of our hosts. But any form is available. Just be sure it's something that will fit between the trees," he added with a grin.

And then Darlantan knew. His claws closed around the chain, and he felt the world expanding. In a heartbeat, he stood among the elves, securely balanced on his clawless feet. His stature was broader than the elves, though he was their equal in height.

"Very appropriate," Aurican declared with a pleased nod.

Darlantan touched the whiskers that cascaded from his chin, strangely delighted by the arcane transformation and pleased that he could make his shape a tribute to Patersmith. A moment later the sturdy figure of the tutor, his gnarled hand still touching the silver chain, followed the file of elves into the forest shadows.

Chapter 6
Nestmates

3553 PC

Darlantan coiled along the crest of the High Kharolis, content to allow the sun to glisten from his silver scales. He felt the warm breeze of summer ruffling his wings and tugging at the mane that had begun to bristle around his jowls. Lord of all within his sight, the silver dragon was pleased to reflect on his own invincibility.

The Valley of Paladine was a sprawling landscape below, vast and peaceful, but somehow confining as well. Darlantan realized the great mountain-flanked vale was shrinking in the same way the grotto had seemed to diminish so many centuries ago.

He knew it would soon be time to move, to once more fly toward new corners of Krynn. Of course, he had often explored the regions beyond the valley. He and his nestmates were well known among the griffons, Ravenclaw's descendants, who dwelt in the High Kharolis, as well as to the elves of the vast woodlands. Touching the curling bell of a ram's horn that Darlantan wore on his silver chain, he thought with deep affection of one elf in particular.

As to his nestmates, in the last dozen centuries, the growing dragons had spread far from the grotto. Smelt had learned a multitude of languages and become a fixture among mankind. Dar knew that many a city or town considered the benevolent brass dragon to be its special benefactor. Whole realms had been freed from the threat of ogres or lizard men, and Smelt was welcomed far and wide, feted to feasting and drinking whenever he appeared, and always finding partners for the conversation that was as important as food to the sociable brass dragon.

Burll and Blayze had taken more solitary paths. The bronze male had at last grown tired of the competition with his more quick-witted brothers. Burll had disappeared once, more than a thousand winters ago, returning only after many centuries, smelling of brine and fish. Now he spent much of his time in some distant, secret lair, revealing to Darlantan only that he dwelt beside an unimaginably huge tract of water.

Blayze had become increasingly irritable, taunting and fighting his nestmates relentlessly. He had killed many of the griffons of the High Kharolis, so that even Darlantan, who had always gotten along with the hawk-faced predators, had ultimately lost track of Ravenclaw's clan. Finally, after an acid-spitting incident in the grotto itself, Aurican, Darlantan, and Smelt had together chased the hot-tempered copper away from the high ridges. Occasionally one of the others encountered him in the Kharolis foothills, but always the copper dragon had fled these meetings, using his superior quickness to escape.

Certainly Blayze, too, had established a secret lair and probably gathered treasures there. Darlantan and the others would have welcomed him back at any time—in fact, the silver dragon couldn't even recall the nature of the argument that had resulted in Blayze's hasty exile. But it had been a hundred or more winters since the other nestmates had so much as seen their copper kin-dragon.

The females of all the metals had remained close to the grotto, bringing Patersmith morsels of food and dwelling in the ancestral cavern of their kind. The last time Darlantan had visited was scores of winters ago, and then he had been surprised to discover his sisters, under the guidance of Kenta and Oro, gathering metals and gems with which they were expanding the size of the nest.

For their own parts, Darlantan and his golden brother had taken to spending much time in the woods. Assuming the bodies of the elf and the bearded sage, they had dwelt for long seasons among the sylvan folk. Aurican, in fact, spent most of his time in the guise of his elven body, speaking, meditating, and debating with the elders of the clans. Together Auri and the elves had composed ballads and epics that they delighted in re-creating, much to Darlantan's boredom. The silver dragon enjoyed the elves, but he could never remain on the ground for long periods of time. As always, the glory of flight, the spread of his silver wings in the uncontested skies, was the thing that truly brought him to life.

The elves who had most appealed to the silver dragon were the clans of the dark-haired Elderwild, the tribes that refused to gather in the towns favored by the golden elves. The silver dragon had befriended one of the wild elves, a stoic warrior named Kagonos, and now his thoughts stirred with the memory of that friendship, a suggestion that he should fly to the east and seek out the brave in his forest haunts. Again Darlantan touched the ram's horn, thinking of its mate, borne by Kagonos, knowing that with the horn, the wild elf could summon him if he needed the dragon's aid. It was a symbol, a mark of the deep bond between them.

A strange scent came to him on the breeze, a spoor subtle and alluring. His head came up, and immediately he detected a flash of silver along the lower slope of the mountain. It was Kenta, and the female dragon's scent carried a shockingly powerful allure. She looked at him

with a sidelong glance and then, tail twitching, darted away. Urgent emotion thrummed within Darlantan—not fear, nor even alarm, but instead a kind of tingling excitement he had never before experienced.

Instinctively he pounced toward that metallic gleam, racing down the mountainside in a series of gliding leaps, then springing upward, seizing a crest of rock with his forefeet, pulling himself through a tight turn. He raced over the ground with explosive, catlike leaps, reluctant to take to the air for fear he would be unable to turn quickly to pursue his evasive quarry in a new direction.

But Kenta was crouching there, waiting for him. Head down, wings buzzing excitedly at his sudden approach, she leapt upward and glided away, trilling laughter in the air behind her . . . and leaving a trace of that wondrous, intoxicating elixir that had aroused Darlantan from his rest atop the mountain.

The silver male flew in earnest, body arrowed, long, powerful wing strokes quickly narrowing the gap between himself and the silver female. In fact, he gained on her so fast that—despite the game she had apparently initiated—he had the clear impression she wasn't actively trying to get away. Kenta's flight took her over white-capped peaks, around the ridges of lofty divides, and finally above a serenely rolling glacier piled deep with fresh, powdery snow.

The alluring silver female veered around a looming shoulder of rock, making a surprisingly sharp turn that Darlantan was unable to follow. He brushed the mossy knoll, but scrambled for footing and once again hurled himself into the air. The force of his pounce sent him soaring after Kenta, overtaking her in a quick rush of flapping wings.

Just before he caught her, she rolled, gliding on her back and rising before the diving Darlantan. He reared but was unable to avoid her as her jaws gaped and she hissed a frosty cloud of musk into Darlantan's face. The scent drove him further into his frenzy, and he reached for her with all four legs, even spreading his wings to try to clutch her to him.

The two silver bodies clashed with violent force, but there was a subtle grace to their entangling. Kenta's tail wrapped around Darlantan's, pulling him close. Instinctively he reciprocated, coiling his neck about hers, clawing at her silver scales in an attempt to merge the two mighty forms. Wings thrashed and scales gleamed and shimmered, frothing through the snow. Together the two large serpents skidded into the sloping glacier, tumbling down the incline in an avalanche of loose snow and flailing silver coils. Dragonwings beat rhythmically, driving up great drifts of powdery whiteness, and the pair rolled over and over, sliding for an eternity down the vast, rippling incline.

They reached the bottom and lay together as waves of loose, light snow cascaded around them. Still entangled, Darlantan shook his head, clearing away enough snow that they could breathe. His glistening brow was draped with tufts of frost as he looked over the surroundings, secure for the moment that the skies and snowfields were free of danger. Content with the icy landscape, he lowered his head to lie beside Kenta in the depression they had worn in the snow.

When next he awakened, spring had warmed the glacier, melting the loose powder into slush. Kenta was stirring beneath him, and stiffly, awkwardly, Darlantan dug them out of the deep trough their bodies had impressed into the snow. He shook himself, sending a cascade of ice crystals flying, and blinked at the bright skyline. He knew where he was, but how he had gotten here remained a hazy memory.

The draft of Kenta's wings pulled his attention around, and he watched the silver female take wing with serene, aloof grace. She made no move to look backward as she flew toward the mountains on the northern horizon. Restlessly Darlantan took to the air himself, choosing to fly in a southeasterly direction, possessed of an urge to find Aurican again.

Many winters had come and gone since last he had spent time at his golden nestmate's side, but even so, it wasn't hard to know where to look. Flying steadily, Darlantan soon left the mountains behind. He enjoyed the sight of the woodland blanketing the landscape below. A layer of treetops, lush and green in the ripeness of early summer, stretched to all sides, fading into the distant flatlands. He knew from earlier reconnaissance that this forest extended from the Kharolis Mountains to the glaciers in the south, the jagged Khalkists to the east, and countless leagues to the north, until the forestlands gradually merged into the plains.

Now, as he crossed over a broad river of clear aquamarine waters, his eyes were attracted by something in the distance, a bright image that broke the serene perfection of the forest. Soon he discerned spires, like giant, leafless tree trunks jutting high from a vast clearing. These towers were made of metal and shiny crystal, and it was the reflection of sunlight from these surfaces that had first drawn his eye.

Closer still, Darlantan saw that many elves labored in this clearing, bustling like ants with blocks of stone, sluices of water, and panels of glimmering metal or clear crystal. Only as he saw other elves working at the forest's edge with axe and chisel did he perceive the whole truth: The elves had *created* this clearing on purpose and were actively removing a great swath of formerly pastoral woodland.

Indeed, much had already been changed. Darlantan flew low, ignoring the waves of welcome from elven watchmen, gliding over an expanse of carefully formed ponds and bright gardens scored by paths of crushed white marble. Figures walked along these paths or gathered in sheltered groves around ponds and fountains, and the silver dragon knew instinctively that he would find Aurican here.

Settling to the ground on one of the few patches of grass broad enough to accommodate his arching wings, Darlantan lifted his head above the surrounding greenery.

"Hello, my silver friend. The elves wish to thank you for sparing their flowers."

The figure of a tall, golden-haired elven patriarch emerged from a nearby bower, striding toward Darlantan with long, graceful steps. In his hands, the elf held a large emerald, passing the stone back and forth with smooth, well-practiced gestures. Though his eyebrows were the snowy white of an elder's, his face scored by the lines of many centuries of life, Dar knew this was not an aged elf—indeed, it was not an elf at all.

"Greetings, Aurican. It is not hard to find the tribe now that they have smashed such a spread of forest."

"It is already a wonder, is it not?" asked Auri, gesturing with both hands to the gardens, the vista of lakes and swans and fountains. "Perhaps you would find a smaller form more comfortable while you have a look around."

Darlantan agreed his real body would be a liability here, and so he smoothly shifted into his favored alternate guise, the bearded elder he had selected for his first shapeshifting.

Aurican led his kinsman through a bower of roses, where another elf, tall and elegantly clad in golden robes, rose to meet them.

"Welcome, Darlantan," declared the serene patriarch, with a dignified bow.

"I thank you, Silvanos."

"He is the architect of this great project," Aurican said. "The elf who has brought his people together under one clan . . . and now would create a city as a proper holding for that clan."

"You do me great honor, Auri," declared the handsome elf, startling the silver dragon with the familiar nickname. "As you do, Darlantan. It is a rare privilege to entertain you as our guest."

"Thank you," replied Dar, nodding with the bearded sage's head. "Your transformation is extensive and . . . remarkable." Patersmith had trained him well. He wouldn't allow himself to be rude. Still, he found himself wondering at the vast scope of the construction. Why did these elves find it necessary, and why did Aurican seem to like it so much?

The silver dragon in the guise of the sage allowed himself to be shown the network of gardens. He accepted an invitation to dinner and enjoyed the finest feast of his life in a grand outdoor pavilion. Succulent roasts of meat were accompanied by breads and cheese, fruits and wines and puddings, until even the hungriest of the guests, which arguably was Darlantan, had been fully sated.

"Have you been to see the grotto recently?" asked Aurican, leaning back easily as the guests relaxed after the meal.

"It has been many winters," admitted the silver dragon through the sage's whiskers.

"For me as well," Auri said dreamily. "But I will go to see Patersmith . . . soon."

"That is a good idea," declared Darlantan, touched by a surprising wave of melancholy. "He has the females to keep him company, but I suspect he misses us."

"Yes . . . and there are changes, things occurring in Krynn, that I must bring to his attention."

Darlantan was about to ask what his Kin-dragon meant when a trill of flute music wafted through the pavilion. Aurican's elven eyelids closed, and the music so clearly pleased him that Dar found it impossible to interrupt his nestmate's contentment. Later, elven dancers enacted a graceful epic beneath a canopy of stars, and finally, around midnight, the balladeers began their interminable labors. Strings were tuned, and flutes chirped their light and airy notes in a growing melody of joyous music.

Aurican had already risen, his eyes fixed upon a chorus of male elves. The emerald he had been holding floated in the air, trailing after him as the gold dragon stepped precisely toward the gathered musicians. "I . . . I must join them," he declared absently as Darlantan stood at his side.

"I understand," the silver serpent replied to his ancient nestmate. "But you will understand, too, that it is time for me to depart."

The lyrics of the song had barely passed into their second verse by the time the body of the elder sage had carried Darlantan to the edge of the grove. Stepping into the middle of a large, grassy swath, he suddenly shimmered as starlight reflected in dazzling array from his silver wings, his cold and gleaming scales. And then he was in the air, leaving the swath of the city behind, a wound that was at last masked by a bandage of distance.

For many seasons, he flew aimlessly, following the great woodlands toward the foothills of the Khalkists. Where the plains began, he saw the distant blot on the horizon of a great, sprawling city, a place far larger than Silvanos's gathering of his clans. He had heard Smelt speak of this place, calling it Xak Tsaroth, and he had no desire to fly closer to it. Let the brass dragon serve as ambassador to man.

He skirted to the east, flying above the snow-frosted foothills of the Khalkists. Finally he came to one of his favorite places, a high mountain far to the south of the smoking heartland of the range. Upon this peak, Darlantan came to rest. He crouched on the shoulder of the lofty summit, eyes staring across the realms to the south. Soon he saw that which he sought: the wild elf Kagonos, alone, away from his people, running on one of his pathfinding treks, which often lasted for many days.

The warrior was painted with swirls of dark ink. His black hair trailed in a long braid, and he was naked and unarmed. Yet there was a lethal capability in his gait, in the calm assurance with which he crossed precipitous heights and trotted down loose, slippery, shale that belied his apparent helplessness. At his side, he bore the ram's horn, twin to the instrument hanging on Darlantan's silver chain.

Atop a nearby lower summit, the brave halted. The wind whipped his hair to the side as he stared at the mighty dragon, locking eyes with Darlantan for many long heartbeats. And then the Elderwild elf was gone, trotting around the shoulder of the mountain, following his private path as he worked his way through these lofty reaches.

Farther down, at the foot of the massif, Darlantan could see the clans of the wild elves in their great Gathering. The tribe's encampment filled the sheltered swale of a small, well-watered valley. Just beyond were the pristine forests of the great wilderness.

Darlantan was already restless. He trotted around the slopes of the great mountain, easily picking his way over steep cliffs and loose rock piles. Soon he came into view of the northern Khalkists, a reach of looming peaks and deep, shadowy valleys. The horizon there seemed always masked by a haze of smoke, which originated from fires within some of the mountains themselves. It was a place that had always intrigued the mighty silver dragon, but he had never explored it.

Nor did he feel that inclination now. Still not sure where he would fly, he eased forward and jumped from the ridge. As his wings spread, scooping into the air, he noticed movement close beside the foot of this mountain.

Gliding downward, he discerned a file of monstrous warriors skulking through a shadowy defile. The dragon quickly came to rest behind a ridge, cautiously raising his head for a look. He saw the hulking physiques, the hunched posture of these warriors, and though he had never seen their like before, he knew they could be only one thing.

Ogres.

In the next instant, he studied the direction followed by the monstrous band and realized that if they continued to circle around the base of the mountain, the ogres would be able to fall upon the Gathering of the Elderwild from above.

Now the silver dragon took to the air and spread his shimmering wings, great leathery sails so broad that they cast the gorge occupied by the ogre raiding party into shadows. One of the brutes, a great, tusked bull at the head of the file, pointed upward and bellowed, waving a large feather-draped staff. Others threw stones that sailed past the gliding dragon or bounced harmlessly off his silver scales. Darlantan looped back, seeing that the ogres were all within the deep ravine. The walls might have kept them safe from observation, he reflected grimly, but now the confining barrier would prove to be the ogres' undoing.

Darlantan's breath exploded as a blast of deadly frost, an eruption of ice that billowed through the gorge, rebounding from the enclosing walls to fill the entire length of the ravine. Icicles formed instantly on the stone walls, and the roaring of dragonbreath was matched by a chorus of wails, shouts, and howls—the cries of the dying ogres ringing upward from the rock-lined channel.

He swept past again, once more spewing his deadly frost against the ogre column, this time concentrating the attack against the front of the band, where he had spotted several stragglers trying to crawl away. The explosive chill once more filled the trough of the ravine, penetrating into the cracks and crannies where desperate ogres had sought shelter.

Quickly the mountain winds blew the frost away, revealing a pathway littered with dead, frozen ogres. The entire column was slain, the brutish warriors cast about on the ground, some stiffened as they tried to climb to safety, others huddled in bundles of miserable terror. All of the corpses were draped by the heavy cake of frost, leaving a landscape of lifelike creatures that were all clearly dead.

This was different killing, Darlantan realized as he flew across the plains toward the Kharolis Mountains. The slaying of the ogres was very unlike the taking of an elk or a deer; it was even a distinct change from the violence he had directed against an occasional rogue griffon who didn't show proper respect for a dragon's prey. This was very serious business, he realized, as it dawned on him that he was battling creatures who were fully capable of killing him in return.

The sensation was not unpleasant. In fact, the silver dragon knew he had done the right thing. It gladdened his heart that his might could be used for such a cause. Mercy, after all, must be tempered by strength.

Gliding onward, he toyed with the idea of looking for more ogres, of perhaps striking dead another war party of these brutish creatures. Certainly he knew they were the enemies of the elves, and it pleased him to do things that were of service—at least, to the Elderwild.

Ultimately he decided against that course. His wings tilted, carrying him back to the wide plain. For a while, he drifted dreamily, riding updrafts like a lazy condor, working his wings only when the air grew still.

But a focus quickly took shape in his mind, and he realized it was time to go to see Patersmith.

Chapter 7
A Farewell

3532 PC

The High Kharolis was in the full vibrancy of late spring. Streams gushed through valleys and canyons, and swaths of green extended upward, encroaching on terrain revealed by melting snowfields. As always, the heights dazzled and inspired Darlantan as he winged his way toward the grotto.

A flash of metallic scales, gleaming brown, attracted the silver dragon's attention to a deep gorge. Tucking his wings, he dived and swiftly banked around a cliff to see a slender copper shape winging rapidly away. Blayze flew low, following the course of the canyon. The copper dragon cast a quick glance behind him, saw Darlantan, and swept into an immediate dive.

The silver came after him, driving his wings hard, anxious to talk to his nestmate. Many hundreds of winters had passed since last these two ancient beings had exchanged a word, and Darlantan felt a strong urge to bring that stretch to an end.

"Blayze—wait!" he called when another bend in the canyon brought his cousin into view.

With a slashing turn, far tighter than Darlantan could have made, the supple copper dragon banked around and came to rest on a ledge of the canyon wall. Spitting in frustration, Darlantan settled on a nearby knob, a perch much too small for his giant body. Wings flapping, foreclaws clutching at rocks as they crumbled under his grip, Darlantan confronted Blayze.

The copper stared back, wings spread wide, neck outstretched. He hissed loudly, but Dar was relieved that his nestmate at least held his corrosive acid breath in check.

"I mean you no harm. I want to talk to you . . . to ask if you're going to see Patersmith," the silver dragon grunted, still trying to hold his balance. With a mutter of frustration, he changed shape, sitting easily in the body of the ancient sage.

"I see your big body has grown too clumsy for you!" sneered Blayze, flexing his wings arrogantly. "Now I could knock you off there with one claw!"

"But why?" Darlantan countered. He was tempted to point out that this frail-looking body was every bit as strong as his dragon form. Instead, he held his tongue, knowing his purpose was not to argue.

"I would kill you to spare my treasures, to keep your plundering claws from my lair!"

"I care nothing for your treasure! And I don't know where your lair is!"

"For hundreds of winters, I have gathered wealth there—baubles and metals and trinkets I have taken from ogres, from the lizard people, even from rich humans, the fools who prey on their own kind. Now the treasures are mine!"

"And yours they shall remain," Darlantan said gently.

"But I'm going to see our old teacher, and Aurican is, too. All I wanted to do was talk, to invite you to come with us."

The stiff copper wings relaxed slightly. "It . . . it has been a very long time . . . since I have visited the grotto and our tutor."

"Then come with me!"

For a moment, Darlantan thought Blayze would fly away. The copper lifted his serpentine neck, looking into the distance. Then he sighed and lowered his head.

"Very well. It's true that I miss our teacher's company . . . and yours as well, my kin-dragon," he admitted.

For the first time in centuries, the nestmates flew side by side, steady wing strokes bearing them to the Valley of Paladine and into the shadowy cavern. As Darlantan led Blayze through the long tunnel leading into the cavern of the lake and the sacred grotto, he sensed another serpentine form in the darkness before him. A sniff confirmed the acrid scent of well-burned soot, and he knew he followed in the wake of Burll. By the time the three metal dragons winged their way over the lake, they caught Aurican, also in flight, and moments later they met Smelt, the brass having just landed at the ledge leading to the grotto's entryway.

Upon entering, they found the females already gathered, the aged tutor standing dotingly over the huge basket of the nest. Though several of these dragons hadn't been here for centuries, there was no great ceremony to mark their arrival.

"These are your eggs," Patersmith explained as Aurican, Darlantan, Smelt, and the other males gathered around the gem-studded nest in the grotto. The mighty wyrms of metal, long necks arched high, stared in awe at the glittering array of perfect baubles lining the sacred bowl.

Darlantan saw numerous orbs of silver, and only then did his eyes go to Kenta, who, along with the other females, coiled regally across the mossy cushion of the grotto's floor. She was uninterested in meeting his gaze, holding her attention instead upon the tutor and the nest that had somehow become full of eggs.

Now Patersmith lectured in his most sonorous tones, and out of old habit, Darlantan paid full attention to his mentor.

"You must guard them well. This is the sacred trust of every metal dragon. You are serpents of Paladine, and as such, these are your treasured artifacts. They represent your future and give proof to your past."

"There are so many of them," Auri declared in awe. "Our numbers shall grow."

"It is the Platinum Father's wish that your descendants should populate Krynn, should make this a world of halcyon peace, of celebrated beauty, goodness, and high learning beyond compare. No task is more important than that you guard them well and protect these eggs against any danger."

At Patersmith's words, Darlantan suddenly remembered his frosty blast when he slayed the multitude of ogres.

"Are they safe here?" he asked, raising his silver head to regard the tutor.

"Their mothers will remain here until the eggs have hatched," Patersmith explained. "They will be as well protected as anything on Krynn."

"And you . . . you will be here as well?" asked Aurican, his gilded brow furrowing with concern. "You will remain with our precious eggs?"

"Alas, that is not to be," declared the bewhiskered tutor. For the first time, Dar noticed that Patersmith had somehow grown very, very old. His whiskers were white as snow, his posture stooped and frail.

"You are going away?" asked Darlantan, while the other males lifted their heads in mute question.

"In a sense, yes . . . yes, I am. My journey will not be a physical one. To you, my sons and daughters, I will appear to sleep. And my sojourn shall indeed be restful, if good fortune will only follow me."

Darlantan was seized by a startlingly strong emotion, a

tug of melancholy that seemed quite out of place in his massive, powerful self. He knew he would miss the aged tutor, and though his visits to the grotto had been rare in recent centuries, he found it difficult to imagine a life without the sage's patient insight and wise counsel.

"But what of us?" asked Aurican, his deep voice rising in a plaintive question. "While our sisters guard the eggs, what would you have us do?"

"Ah, Auri," chuckled Patersmith. "Here is where your brother Darlantan's wisdom may even have exceeded your own, for he has always understood that you should not do the things that *I* would have you do, but that you would do for yourself."

The silver dragon tried to speak but found that his throat was thickened in an awkward fashion. He couldn't shape the words, couldn't even think of what to say.

Patersmith came to stand before Smelt, reaching up to stroke the brass scales of his neck. "You always understood me," the old tutor declared. "Of all your nestmates, you have best learned the value of mercy and of friendship. Go back to your humans, my chatty one, and lead them in the ways of wisdom and goodness."

Next he came to Blayze, whose copper head drooped sadly in the face of the smith's departure. "Mind that temper, my quick one. But do not vanquish it entirely, for it is a force that lies at the heart of your clan's might. All of you could learn something from Blayze, for there may come a time when you need to fight. Then you shall find that anger can be a useful force, a thing that can enhance your strength and even overawe your enemies."

Patersmith chuckled. "Our copper nestmate has only to learn to wait for that time," he concluded gently.

"And Burll, my mighty one. Know that your strength is as the bedrock of the world, an underlying force upon which the dragons of Paladine can always depend. Do not think too hard, for you are a doer of deeds, not a philosopher."

Next the bearded elder came to Darlantan. He placed a weathered hand on the shoulder of silver scales, blinking back at the moisture that began to form in the watery old eyes.

"And Darlantan, my silver pride . . . you are the one who best knows the world as it was meant to be. You will see what must be done and do it. With your strength, there is hope that goodness may stand for many ages. And never forget the pure joy of flight."

The tutor's words moved the silver dragon, but already Patersmith had moved on to Aurican, the last of his hatchlings to say farewell.

"We owe you much, our teacher," murmured the gold dragon. Aurican had picked up a diamond from the nest, clutching it in his foreclaw as he gently nuzzled the sage's beard. Darlantan hung his head low, but couldn't help listening to the exchange.

"Hold your gems, my golden one. Share them well, for those stones may become the proof of your life, even the hope of the world. And your songs, too, are ballads that will endure."

"I would like you to carry this on your journey," Aurican said softly. He extended a golden forepaw, in the clasp of which he held a bright diamond. When he pulled his claws away, the stone floated in the air. "It is all the magic I have been able to work."

Patersmith took the stone, blinking back the moisture of his emotion. "Hold your faith, my golden one. You may find the means of greater power yet. I only regret that I shall not be here to share in your triumph."

Finally Patersmith laid himself upon a bier of fine stones in the rear of the sacred cave. He settled back peacefully, clasping his hands over his chest while his eyelids drooped shut. With a deep, shuddering sigh, he went to sleep. Then, as the thirteen dragons watched with breath held in check, the frail and weathered body slowly faded from sight until it had completely disappeared.

Chapter 8
Rising Fury

3493 PC

The ogres gathered in a mighty throng around their mistress, shouting, roaring, and cheering in a monstrous din. The stomping of their feet shook the ground as greatly as did the rumbles of the nearby volcanoes. Accolades and battle cries rang through the night in a rising tide of martial thunder. Hulking Blacktusk, the battle chieftain who was descended directly from Ironfist himself, led the hailing of their mistress's name, of her power and her might.

Crematia coiled in their midst, her crimson neck and head rising high into the air. The dragon's serpentine tail snaked through the legs of a massive bull ogre, and a dozen more of the brutes, clad in armor of stiffened leather studded with bronze spikes, stood arrayed in a stance of honor around her. They were armed with swords and held these weapons high, allowing the red dragon to temper the keen edges with a great explosion of her flaming breath.

Beyond the elite bodyguards were thousands more of the burly tusked warriors. Great knobbed clubs waved through the air like a sea of grass flowing back and forth in the currents of the wind. Numerous chieftains were bedecked in feathers and ornaments of gold. Instead of crude clubs, many of these leaders brandished long swords or axes with blades of jagged-edged bronze. They all thronged forward, praising their leader, sharing in the glory of her presence while they displayed their bravery and devotion.

"You are brave, my ogres!" crowed the red dragon, and a roaring chorus of approbation rose from the gathered throng. "And soon you shall vent your courage against the legions of our Dark Lady's enemies!"

The shouts rose to a thunderous crescendo, resounding from the high stone walls of the barren valley. Crematia allowed her leathery eyelids to droop lazily as she swept her gaze over the frenzied, noisy mob. Ogre skin was slicked with sweat, and tiny eyes gleamed furiously from many a flat-skulled face. She saw the spittle dripping from tusks, heard the pure hatred in so many of those lusty shouts.

In the center of the throng, a huge fire blazed upward, spilling a wash of bright light through the deep canyon. The black, smoky skies of the Khalkists glowered overhead as a pile of whole pine trunks crackled and flared with greedy flames. Fiery tendrils roared eagerly upward, as if they would challenge the sun with their heat and brightness.

As encouraging to Crematia as the frenzy of her own tribe was the fact that similar gatherings were occurring in other valleys throughout the Khalkist Range. The dragon clans of blue, black, white, and green had each claimed realms in the mountains and foothills. Her cousins were more numerous, of course, a dozen or more of each color to her solitary crimson presence. Yet still she was acknowledged as their lord, for she alone had received the blessing of the Dark Lady herself.

So it was only appropriate that none of those other ogre

bands was quite so large, nor were any of their dragon masters her equal in size, sorcery, or savagery. It pleased her to know this legion was but the vanguard of a mighty force that in time would sweep across Ansalon and spread the yoke of the Dark Queen's rule to all corners of the world.

And at last that time had come.

"Blacktusk," she growled in a rumbling purr. Her word settled the roaring and pulled the attention of the massive bull ogre to the red serpent coiled on the high rock.

"I am your slave, mistress!" cried that brute, whose maw was distinguished by a single, upward-jutting fang, an ivory tusk dark and discolored enough to have given the mighty chieftain his name.

"Tell me what the scouts have reported," demanded Crematia.

"The elves of the woodlands have spread throughout the forestlands of Ansalon," growled the hulking brute. "While we have been busy slaughtering and enslaving the humans on the plains, their long-lived allies have been establishing strong footholds to the south."

"Are they dangerous?"

"My crimson lady, barely two moons ago an entire war party, commanded by my own brother, Fire-eye, was destroyed by ice magic as it circled the southern mountain. From this we have learned that the elves possess the power of sorcery, the power the humans have told us has been lost for ages."

"I know this tale," Crematia said slowly. Her hooded eyes narrowed still further as she considered the disturbing implications. "Yet the skill of your Painmasters is sufficient to insure that your human slaves are not lying, is it not?"

"Aye, mistress. My torturers possess exquisite abilities. I believe these humans spoke the truth as they knew it, up until the time their tongues were ripped from their mouths. They believe that magic is gone from Krynn."

"So if the elves possess magic, they have kept it secret from their allies?"

"Well . . . we know that the alliance between humans and elves is tenuous at best. Would it not be natural for such a mighty truth to remain concealed from the short-lived, irresponsible men?"

"That is one possibility," the red dragon agreed.

Privately, she placed more credence in another theory. After all, she and her chromatic kin-dragons had been granted magic in the Abyss by the Queen of Darkness herself. Crematia was fairly certain that the elves had not, in fact, discovered a way to bring magic back to Krynn on their own. She knew it was far more likely that the icy attack had a different origin, and it was one the nature of which her ogres did not as yet need to know.

"Do you have prisoners?"

Blacktusk nodded. "Bring out the elves!" he roared.

Immediately strapping ogres rolled away a rock that had been placed to block the mouth of a small cave. A hulking warrior seized a chain and pulled forth a trio of golden-haired figures—elven warriors, unarmed but still clad in their supple chain mail. The tallest of these stepped before the others, who were obviously younger and very frightened. But the leader crossed his arms over his chest and glared defiantly up at the dragon.

"Shall I show mercy?" Crematia brayed the question so it could be heard by her entire gathered horde.

"Mercy is weakness!" The cry came back as a resounding chant, echoing from the mountain walls, thundering through the valley. "And weakness is death!"

Crematia's blast of fire exploded outward, engulfing the elves as the roar of the conflagration drowned out the echoes of the chant. By the time the oily flames had dispersed, the place where the three elves had died was marked only by a few cinders. Even these tumbled and drifted away, carried away by a light wind.

"When you sweep upon the elves, you shall have the aid of my dragonfire—and, too, of the ice and acid, the lightning and toxins, of my cousins. Even the mightiest elven warrior will be unable to face us!"

Once again the cheers rang out, reflected along with the torchlight from the high walls of the gorge, until the entire deep chasm resounded with thunderous shouts and flaring, surging flames. The bonfire surged higher as ogres threw dried pine trunks onto the mound of coals, and these timbers were quickly engulfed by renewed flames.

"Soon we march!" bellowed Crematia. "But before then, we feast!"

Now the roars swelled into a cheer, raucous shouts whooping upward, echoing from the high walls. A file of naked humans, linked by heavy bronze chains, was led into the chasm. Wailing and crying, cringing from the brutes roaring and slavering on every side, the hapless prisoners were dragged into the very center of the throng.

"Let the feasting commence!" crowed the red dragon.

Immediately the ogres surged toward the captives, burying the humans in a throng of heaving, burly bodies. Screams rose to hysteria, then swiftly faded. There had been nearly a hundred of the human sacrifices, so Crematia knew the feasting would continue for some time.

She herself had little interest in the gory proceedings. Instead, she launched into the air, flying above the throng, winging her way upward until she circled out of the gorge and flew among the lofty peaks that cast the canyon into an eternal shadow.

On a high ledge of a mountain she came to rest, tucking her wings and passing into a shadowy alcove. She inspected the surface of the stone, seeing only her own footprints in the soot she had scattered there. That was as it should be, since no other creature would even know that the level surface was here. Crematia's magic had concealed the entrance, causing it to blend in with the surrounding cliff so perfectly that even a passing eagle wouldn't be aware the place offered the possibility of a perch.

Probing inward with her head, Crematia quickly found the wall of stone across the narrow passage. Like the soot, this barrier was undisturbed. A single word blinked the magical barrier out of existence, and now the red dragon crept into a cavernous space deeper within the mountain. The familiar odor of magma was a refreshing balm, and she recognized the reptilian hint in the scent that was suggestive of her own spoor.

Twin pools of lava flared and bubbled, one each at opposite edges of the vaguely oval chamber. A stream of liquid rock, glowing bright yellow at the top and cooling to muted crimson near the bottom, spilled from a chute on the far wall, gathering in a trough that divided the stream and carried it to each of the two pools. Lava and flame cast the entire chamber in a glare of muted orange, accented by brighter swaths of red near the flowing rock itself.

The light of the fires was reflected in a multitude of gold and silver surfaces, coins and platters and statues that were scattered across the cavern floor. Among these treasures winked many a gem, viridescent emerald vying with scarlet ruby, both fading in the shadow of sparkling diamonds. These were the precious baubles she had brought from all corners of the Khalkists—or, more accurately, that the ogres had brought her in response to her demands.

But the true beauty of the cave lay in the nest, the basket of bones Crematia had woven with such care. It lay upon a large knob of dark rock, fully encircled by the streams of flowing lava. The red dragon stepped over that obstacle and climbed to the nest, her head soon rising above the upper rim, which was formed entirely of the staring skulls of human captives taken by the ogres and offered to Crematia in sacrifice.

She counted them, all thirteen of the crimson orbs, sleek and perfect, unblemished by any sign of cracking or discoloration.

"Be patient, my wyrmlings," she whispered, her long tongue slipping forth to stroke lovingly over each scarlet surface. "You will grow stronger for many years, but you are safe here. Know that your mother shall bring you into a world where your clan is master of all."

Only then did she turn, restoring the wall of stone with a casting of her magic. Finally she wove a greater spell, insuring that the illusion continued to mask the outside of the lair. With her wings spread wide into the night sky, Crematia took to the air, ready to lead her armies southward, toward the lands of the elves.

Chapter 9
First War

3489 PC

"Join me in a flight to the southern forests . . . and together we shall see the new wonders raised by House Silvanos," urged Aurican.

"Ah, the elves," said Smelt quickly. "I haven't visited among them for a long time. I will come."

"I have a lair to tend," Burll growled, shaking his head while Blayze looked around suspiciously, as though he thought his treasures were in danger that very moment.

The five male dragons were coiled atop the crest of the High Kharolis, each claiming one of a series of closely gathered peaks. The windless weather, and the fact that an overcast of gray clouds lurked not very far overhead, allowed them to converse with ease. They had spent a period of reflection and contemplation following the departure of their mentor, until the females had begun to make it clear that it was time for their mates to depart the grotto.

Darlantan had heard his brother's words, but his own heart was lingering toward the eastern wilds—a place of no cities, nothing but wilderness and plentiful prey.

"Even you, Darlantan . . ." It was as if Auri were reading his silver kin's mind. "Though we have only been in the grotto for a short time, you'll be amazed to see what these elves can accomplish in the space of a dozen winters!"

"I can fully imagine," declared Darlantan sourly, picturing how much of the woodland might have been flattened by now. He had never found a proper answer to the question of why the elves cloistered themselves so readily in that silent, aloof city?

Still, after this long period among his nestmates, he was not quite ready to vanish by himself, so he consented to join the flight. Even Burll and Blayze seemed to have some lingering need for communion, and in the end, five metal dragons took to the air, riding the high currents, coursing through empty skies. They were lords of air and land, following a leisurely course that gave them much time for hunting and for resting in pleasant bowers and shaded valleys.

Yet as they drew southward, Darlantan sensed an increasing urgency in Aurican's manner. The gold dragon resisted a suggestion that the flying nestmates spend a day lolling beside a perfect mountain hot spring, and when the others grudgingly took wing, he led them on with unseemly haste.

"What's your hurry, my cousin?" asked the silver dragon, straining to keep up with the fast-flying gold.

"Don't you smell it?" asked Auri, speaking through taut jaws as he maintained his streamlined flight.

And then Darlantan *did* notice the taint of soot and char, a bleak hint of smell rising from an expanse that appeared to be lush forest. The odor was out of place here, strange and menacing, with evil portent, though the woodland below still appeared pristine and undisturbed.

But as they flew on, this notion was proved to be a cruel deception. They saw one clearing that was utterly black, smelling of ash, and they knew that a great fire had raged there. Soon they passed over more such swaths of destruction, and when they reached the broad river that intersected these woodlands, Aurican uttered a groan of pure, heartbreaking dismay.

Darlantan swept low over waters he remembered as crystalline and pure, which had once flowed over a bed of pristine gravel. Now the surface was a scum of mud and grime, with blackened timbers floating everywhere. More than once he saw a body, bloated by decay but still draped with the long golden hair of an elf.

Farther they flew, and now the destruction was more common than the undisturbed forests. A great landscape had burned, and the blackened trunks jutted from the charred ground in a mocking remembrance of the verdant carpet that once had blanketed the ground. Once-green trees were scarred and scorched, leaves withered away. In places, even mighty trunks had been smashed to the ground by unimaginable force.

Then Aurican uttered a strangled wail, and Darlantan saw what was left of the domes and towers that had distinguished Silvanos's once-splendid city. The spires of crystal had been smashed, their circular bases jutting from the ruins like broken bottles. Finally the anguished gold dragon banked, swooping low, coming to rest in the midst of a broad, dust-blown square of bare dirt. The other four serpents silently accompanied their mighty brother, each of them looking around grimly, formulating images and speculation about the cause of the destruction.

Aurican padded away, shifting shape almost absently into the body of the lean, elderly elven sage he had so frequently favored. Darlantan came behind, stalking like a prowling cat in the silvery serpent that was his natural form. Only as Auri knelt beside a charred object, brushing away the soot to reveal a portion of a white marble bust and its cracked supporting pillar, did Dar realize that they were in the elegant garden his brother had shown him before.

And even with that memory, the place was unrecognizable. Only when the silver dragon stepped into a murky pit of mud did he realize that one of the elegant fountains had been filled with ashes and dirt. Shaking his foot, flicking the sticky goo from his talons, Dar followed the shambling form of Aurican through the ruins.

In one place, the frail figure who was the gold dragon scratched at the ground, clearing away muck to reveal a slab of white stone. Without visible effort, the elf's body lifted the object back onto a pair of pedestals that stood nearby, restoring a once-elegant bench. Only when he saw the stubs of the rosebushes jutting upward from the soot, forming a perfect ring, did Darlantan realize that this had been the sheltered nook where he had been welcomed by Silvanos.

For the first time, he wondered about that elven leader, and it was a startling thought: Where were all the elves? There were some bodies here, true, but not nearly enough to account for the city's population. Had they escaped into what remained of the forests? Or had they been hauled into captivity, perhaps slavery, by the invaders?

And that led to the natural consideration of who, or what, had done this, and here Darlantan had some specific ideas. He was tired of mourning, of probing through the wrack and ruin, and he decided that it was time to talk to Aurican. He found his brother, still in elven form, slumped over a splintered frame of wood entangled with slender wires. Aurican was weeping, tears streaking down the skin of his elven face. He looked up as the mighty silver dragon loomed over him, but his eyes remained distant and unfocused.

"This was a harp, Dar . . . it could make music sweet enough to break your heart. And now it's smashed . . . like this whole place, this whole people, smashed!" Auri collapsed, burying his face in his hands as his shoulders shook with the convulsive force of his sobbing.

"Remember, my brother, you are a dragon!" Darlantan

insisted forcefully, embarrassed by the wrenching display of emotion. "A mighty gold—patriarch of your clan!"

"And where was I when *this* was happening!" cried Auri, turning his face to the sky. "Where?"

"Stop it!"

Darlantan reached forward with a great forepaw and swept his brother's elven form off the ground. He lifted Auri into the air and shook him forcefully. "Who knows, or cares, where you were? You're here now, and you've seen what happened! What are you going to do about it?"

"Put me down." Aurican's voice was deadly calm, his face blank of emotion.

Darlantan gingerly set the elven body back on the ground and immediately reared back as he was confronted by a bristling serpent of gold, wings stiff and flapping with menace, lip curled into a fanged sneer. Raising his silver neck in response, Dar met his brother's furious glare, saw the hatred in the gold dragon's eyes flare and then, slowly, focus.

Aurican raised his taloned forepaws, revealing that he held several of his baubles, the gemstones he delighted in caressing, infusing them with the minor enchantments that were the limits of his sorcerous power. Now he took these stones, a bright diamond, crimson ruby, scintillating emerald, and smooth jade, and hurled them into the murk of the destruction. When he turned back to Darlantan, his reptilian face was blank of emotion.

"Who has done this?" Auri asked intently, his voice a rumbling growl.

"I have a guess that it was ogres," Darlantan replied grimly. Burll and Smelt joined them, and he described the large war party that he had destroyed in the southern Khalkists.

"And you think the target of their strike was the Elderwild?" asked Smelt.

"They were on a march to approach the elven camp and fall upon them unawares." Darlantan remembered the weapons bristling from the belts and fists of the mighty brutes and was more certain than ever that they had been plotting violence against the elves. With that memory came another fear: Had the wild elves suffered the same violence as the house elves of Silvanos? He pictured the serene wilderness with a shudder, wondering how much of it remained.

"I suggest we fly north, toward the Smoking Mountains," Blayze said, using their old nickname for the volcanic Khalkists. "We will find ogres there, and I am thinking that they will give us answers first, and then perhaps a measure of vengeance."

"Aye," growled Smelt, with Burll and Darlantan nodding in grim agreement. All turned their eyes to Aurican, who looked once more across the swath of destruction, then lifted his eyes toward the northern horizon.

"Let us fly, then," he declared. With regal grace and grim purpose, he took to the air, rising in a powerful downdraft of wind. Golden wings shimmered, shifting with the force of his long strokes, as the mighty serpent pulled himself into the sky.

The others followed, and it was a grim and silent quintet that winged over the wasted forestland. Darlantan flew at Aurican's right wing, for it was the silver's memory that guided them toward the realms of the ogres. Smelt, Blayze, and Burll trailed slightly to the rear, a little lower than the leading pair.

Before nightfall, Burll spotted a deer and took the hapless creature in a sudden dive. The group shared the feast and then once more, without speaking, took wing into the darkness. They flew through the following dawn, and still they soared on. Everywhere the wrack of war, the litter of chaos and destruction, had spread through the woods. In some places, the devastation was limited to isolated outposts, but elsewhere it had reduced huge swaths of forestland or meadow into burned char.

Darlantan lost track of the dawns and sunsets, the quickly killed deer or buffalo that sustained them in their steadfast flight. Gradually the ground rippled below them, the forests still claiming the surface of the land, yet yielding to the distinctive texture of hills. And then a range of mountains took shape before them, at first indistinguishable from dark cloud on the horizon, soon growing in definition and relief.

The distant Khalkists were a mass of conical peaks, shrouded by their eternal wreath of smoky cloud. Closer, rising as a lone summit away from the great center of the range, stood a single peak. The pyramidal block of stone lofted above a realm of lakes and woods, and Darlantan remembered the Gathering of the Elderwild he had seen among those pristine waters.

"It was on the other side of this mountain," he told Aurican.

"Then let us be ready to do battle," the gold replied with a low growl.

The red dragon appeared with shocking suddenness, a scarlet form that was, in an eyeblink of an instant, just *there*, hanging in the air, directly in Darlantan's path. The silver started to twist as his flight took him past the crimson wyrm. He saw the jaws gape and tried to bellow a warning to Burll.

But the first sound was the roar of an infernal furnace. Dar's head came around in time to see the bronze dragon fly fully into the hellish blossom of the dragonfire. Burll cried out, his wail a piercing, cloud-shaking keen of impossible pain—and then the cruelly burned dragon twisted and shriveled before Darlantan's horrified eyes. The once-powerful neck tucked and curled, metallic scales burned away to reveal charred and blackened flesh. The two wings of rippling membrane hissed away in an instant, leaving the horribly burned body looking even more unnatural as it tumbled from the dissipating ball of fire.

Now Darlantan's roar of warning was propelled by pure rage, echoed by the cries of Smelt and Blayze. Aurican, grimly silent, had already curled upward to reverse his course at the vicious red.

And then there were blue dragons there, nearly a dozen of them appearing as shockingly as had the lone red. It's *magic*—they're using sorcery against us! A portion of Dar's mind shouted the frightening realization even as his body reacted with pure violence.

Jaws gaping, Darlantan blasted the nearest blue dragon, freezing the monster's wings with the icy onslaught. Shrieking in fury and pain, the azure serpent twisted frantically before tumbling out of the sky. The silver body arrowed forward, crashing into the blue, and Dar bit down hard, snapping the hateful neck.

By then a roaring wave of fire crackled through the air as Smelt blasted his incendiary breath at one of the blues, while his fellow attackers spit crackling spears of lightning. Fire and electricity roared together in convulsive explosions, pounding with sound, quickly dissipating into a lingering aura of smoke. The stench of killing and destruction spread even faster than the visible vapors of lingering dragonbreath.

One of the blues shrieked and fell away, one wing burned off while the other flapped desperately, fruitlessly as the creature plunged to its doom. Even as it dwindled below, the echoes of its dying scream rose from the dusty ground to linger in the air.

But at least three of the lethal lightning blasts had torn into the roaring brass dragon, stilling his valiant maneuvers. Metallic scales flaked into the air as Smelt jerked violently, fatally around. Killed immediately, burned to a blackened corpse, he fell out of the sky with shocking finality.

Aurican swept into the melee with a bellowing cry of fury. His golden jaws spread wide as he spewed a massive fireball, a searing cloud of swirling flames that encompassed two of the blues. Oily fire licked across blue scales, scalding and burning. Both of the monstrous serpents screamed and writhed away. Fatally wounded, they struggled and wailed all the way to the ground far below.

Darlantan drove forward, taking position on Aurican's flank as the gold plunged after the diving, frantically twisting red. That murderous serpent, a monstrous female, crowed in an exultation of triumph as she banked sharply, driving toward a gap in the looming foothills.

"Kill her!" rasped Aurican as Darlantan, wings scooping great beats out of the air, passed his golden brother, desperately straining for altitude and speed.

The silver pressed onward, pulling to draw within range of their foe's crimson tail. His belly seethed, ready with a blast of frost, and he intuitively knew that the frigid blast would be deadly to the fire-breathing red. Just a bit closer and she would be his, frozen from the skies by the lethal blast of his icy breath.

But then the hateful serpent was *gone*—she simply vanished in the air as quickly as she had first appeared. Dar could only hope that she was still there, screened by some sort of invisibility magic. He strained forward, blasting the air with his lethal frost. A moment later he flew through the frigid wake of his own attack to find only empty space. The red had escaped.

Or had she? A cry of alarm pulled the silver dragon around in time to see the savage crimson wyrm land full on the back of Blayze, who strained to keep up a short distance behind Aurican. Her lethal breath surrounded the copper dragon's head as cruel claws ripped into Blayze's shoulders and wings. He screamed, twisting desperately to pull free from the inferno, but his scales had been scalded away, his jaws barren of flesh in a blackened, fang-baring snarl.

The red cast the dying copper away with a contemptuous gesture as another blue slashed in. Again lightning flickered in the cloudless sky, tearing into Blayze's ribs, ripping flesh and scales away in a gory slash. Spiraling lazily, as if he were learning to fly all over again, Blayze whirled downward—but this time he never pulled out of the dive.

Aurican and Darlantan flew at the blue dragon that had delivered the lethal blast. Darlantan's fury nearly blinded him, but a small portion of his mind reminded him that they were outnumbered, that it was wise to be cautious. Both dragons of metal swept apart as if on an unspoken command, veering out of the blue's path as a second bolt of lightning hissed through the air between them.

Twisting back, Darlantan drew a deep breath, feeling

the surging power of deadly frost fill his chest. His neck darted forward, pointing his head straight at the azure serpent. Argent jaws gaped as the explosion of dragonbreath wracked Darlantan's body, spuming forward to engulf one side of the Dark Queen's mighty wyrm.

The combined blasts of gold dragonfire and silver dragon ice pinned the blue in a fatal vise, burning away one wing as the other froze, then snapped into a thousand shards when the shrieking serpent tried to flex the once-powerful limb. The cry took on a piteous keen as the wyrm tumbled away, writhing in pain through the long fall to the ground.

"Flee!" Aurican gasped.

Darlantan was about to whirl around, to seek the red dragon with the last ounce of his vengeful determination. He whipped his head back, seeking some sign of the threat that had brought forth Auri's desperate command. He saw many targets, great serpents of new colors, black and white and green, sweeping through the sky.

Snarling, Darlantan realized they had no choice. Sweeping into a shallow dive behind Aurican, he cast another glance backward and watched the chromatic shapes dwindle in the distance.

Yet even when they had disappeared from view, he looked around anxiously, wondering where these new and deadly enemies had gone—and when they would be back.

Chapter 10
hope and fear

3489 PC

The treetops of the eastern forest grazed his belly as Darlantan strained for speed, driving his wings with all the power in his mighty shoulders. Beside him, Aurican rushed through the air in a blur of pulsing wings and sparkling metallic scales. The chromatic dragons had been left far behind, though the lingering images and smells and hurts of battle—and the knowledge of their tragic, horrifying defeat—jangled resoundingly in a chorus of grief and shock within Darlantan's memory.

"We can't go to the grotto. We don't dare," Aurican said, his voice startlingly calm, in contrast to the cacophony of emotions storming through Darlantan's mind.

"Why?" demanded the silver, until another moment's

thought made clear the danger—to the females, and, more importantly, to their eggs. "Where, then?"

"Let's find a place to talk. Remember, I'm not one who can fly all night," replied Aurican.

"Our meeting bluff is nearby," Dar remembered, recalling a promontory where he and Auri had held several councils with the elves.

The pair of dragons glided silently toward the sunset, looking for the knoll. Everywhere tall pines covered the ground, and though it was a relief to see an area where the terrain had not been scorched, Darlantan was so tired he would have welcomed a swath of devastation just for the chance to land and rest his wings. His side ached where blue dragon lightning had seared the scales from his flesh and cruel claws had torn into his flank. The deep gouges burned with an agony that threatened to drag him down, to fold him into a ball of suffering that would plunge, unlamented, into the tangled foliage below.

Never had he been hurt like this before! Through all the hunting that had marked his life, he had never considered the possibility that, somehow, serious injury could be inflicted upon *him*, the mighty Darlantan! His memory of the battle was still wrapped in a numbing cloud of disbelief. Perhaps this detachment was a blessing—at least he was able to continue the fast, desperate flight.

But the numbness did not extend to thoughts of his brothers, his ancient nestmates. Darlantan moaned aloud as his mind turned to the speedy Smelt's last moments, or the horrible barrage of flame that had knocked powerful Burll from the sky. His jaws curled into a snarl, claws clenching unconsciously as he pictured the crimson dragon of the Dark Queen slaying Blayze from behind. With an unconscious growl, he imagined the killing he would work against them . . . someday.

"Magic . . . dragons of evil and magic," mused Aurican. His golden wings stroked easily and gracefully, showing no sign of fatigue as the flight extended through the long hours of the night. "How did these things come to Krynn?"

"Perhaps the dragons have always been here, but they were hiding," growled Darlantan. "Waiting for the chance to attack."

"I don't think so. We have flown this world for thousands of winters. I cannot believe they could have escaped our notice for so long. And remember, it was only their use of spell magic that gave them their first advantage. I think the magic and the chromatic dragons came to Krynn together."

"A plague on together!" spat Dar. "Unless you know a way that we could steal the magic and kill the wyrms!"

"No . . . not yet. We must think, plan."

"A plague on plans as well!" barked Darlantan. "I say we should turn around and attack, take them by surprise."

"I share your desire for vengeance, Cousin. But we cannot win this fight alone. It is time that we counseled with others."

"Who?" demanded the silver dragon, but as he spoke he knew: the elves, of course. "We fly to the council knoll, do we not?"

Aurican nodded, straining visibly to lift his head again. Dar's own wounds pained him, and he knew the long flight was taking its toll upon his kin-dragon.

"But how did they get the magic?"

"It could only have come from a god or gods," Aurican declared. "The Dark Queen herself must have blessed them with sorcery in some distant place, then released them to carry that power to Krynn!"

"And another plague on *how* they did it!" snarled Darlantan, his fury at last pulling Aurican's golden head around. The silver dragon's pain had faded into the background of his awareness, replaced by a grim fire, an emotion more chilling than any he had ever felt.

He was learning to hate, he knew.

"Beware!" The sound was like the keening cry of an eagle, but Darlantan recognized the word spoken in the language of the griffons. Immediately he banked, and Aurican followed in a lazy spiral over the forest.

"Up there," the gold dragon said, and his silver cousin

angled his head, observing the winged creature diving toward them.

"A scion of Ravenclaw," Darlantan said as the griffon slowed with a rearing gesture. The massive feathered wings bore the creature easily between the two mighty serpents. "Have a care, my friend. There are new dangers in the skies."

"This I know, and I have come in turn to warn you. There are two dragons, deep black in color, who have claimed the meeting knoll. They disturbed one of my young a short time ago, when they landed there."

The pillar of cliff-draped rock was already in view, thrusting upward from the surrounding forest.

"We will kill them!" Dar pledged, his belly tightening at the prospects of revenge.

"But first you must find them, and that is why I warn you. After they landed, they changed . . . disappeared so that they cannot be seen. But still my nestling could smell them. He knew they were there."

"Invisibility magic!" hissed the silver dragon, feeling another surge of outrage.

"We will deal with them," said Aurican. "Of that you may be sure. And thank you for the warning."

"Be careful!" urged the griffon, banking into a gentle dive. Soon he was a speck fading into the distance.

They approached the craggy knoll of granite, the barren summit perhaps twice as high as the loftiest of the pines. The dragons of Paladine scrutinized the place, seeking some sign of the invisible dragons.

"There, to the left," murmured Darlantan, indicating a clearing where several saplings had been flattened.

"Right—and there, on the rocks, is the second," Auri said.

"Where the bushes are crushed," Darlantan agreed, feeling the killing frost swell in his belly.

Side by side, the two metal dragons winged toward the bluff. Darlantan lowered himself into a gentle glide, as if looking for a good place to land. He marked both dragons, not because he could see them but because their massive bodies had inevitably disturbed the crowded terrain. Nearing the flattened patch of grove, Dar abruptly lashed his head downward, exploding with a blast of surging, churning frost.

The enemy dragon shrilled its pain and fury, and Dar veered away as a fountain of acid exploded from frost-coated jaws. The black dragon, clearly outlined in rime, twisted upward, but the vengeful silver was too fast. Darlantan settled onto the snakelike serpent, crushing with his silver claws, squeezing his powerful jaws over the squirming throat. With a shudder, the black dragon grew still.

Aurican, Darlantan saw, had dispatched his foe with similar quickness. The pair of metal dragons tossed the limp corpses into the forest below and finally settled to rest on the rocky crest, tucking their wings and squatting between rough outcrops. With a shrug, Aurican shifted into his more compact two-legged form, and Darlantan quickly followed.

He found it a relief to tend to some mundane affairs, gathering some brush for a fire while Auri cleared the stones from the area where they had chosen to sleep. Finally they settled before a small blaze, both of them reflecting on the many centuries of their brothers' lives . . . and their violent ends. They talked of Burll's strength, of Smelt's lightning quickness. Together they imagined the deadly menace that hot-tempered Blayze would have become, should he have survived the first ambush long enough to embark on a quest for vengeance.

"That revenge shall be our task now," Aurican murmured, still speaking with the serene detachment that, under the circumstances, Darlantan found profoundly disturbing.

"Sssst!" The body of the bearded sage hissed the warning as the silver dragon heard an almost silent footfall from the thicket near the precipitous edge of the knoll.

Darlantan rose to his feet, unafraid. In fact, he almost hoped to see an ogre, or even a dragon, of the Dark Queen burst into view and give him a vent for his fury. He felt a swelling in his human chest, but he resisted the impulse to expand to his full size.

Instead of ogres, a pair of lithe figures emerged from the shadows, moving toward the welcoming warmth of the fire. Only elves could have approached so quietly, and the dragons recognized both of the sylvan visitors. One had hair of harvest-straw gold and was dressed in silken leggings and tunic, while the other was dark-haired, nearly naked, his body covered in swirls of dark war paint. At his side, he bore the horn of a mighty ram. Silvanos and Kagonos advanced and squatted beside the small fire, soaking up the welcome radiance, saying nothing as their ancient friends settled back beside them.

"We grieve for your splendid city," Aurican said, solemnly addressing the proud Silvanos.

"One of a hundred, a thousand tragedies of a scope too grand to comprehend," declared the revered leader of the elves. "And in truth, the destruction of buildings and lands and constructs is as nothing compared to the losses of fathers and mothers, sons and sisters, that have ravaged our people since the coming of the dragons."

Silvanos looked squarely across the fire, meeting the eyes of Auri and Dar as he struggled to blink back tears. His voice, when he spoke, was strangled by a very unelven passion.

"The coming of the ogres was a thing we could fight, and we did—but *dragons!* By all the gods, when they swept from the sky, breathing lightning and ice, burning acid and deadly poisonous gas, we could only flee to the woods."

"We are all elves of the forest now," said Kagonos, furrowing his dark eyebrows. His face and body were painted in the whorls and lines of the inky dye favored by his tribe, and his gray eyes were serious as they regarded the flesh cloaking the two dragons. "We would have warned you of the danger had we received word of your return in time. As it was, by the time the news arrived from the south, you had already been lured into Crematia's ambush."

"Ah . . . a good name for that fiery killer," Aurican observed, still speaking in the same infuriating tone of detachment. "What about the spell magic that she used? Did this Crematia creature bring it from the Abyss?"

"Aye, my friend," Silvanos agreed, his golden eyes keen as they studied Aurican. "What does that mean to you?"

"Simply that spell magic resides in the realms of the gods . . . that if we want to fight the power of sorcery, we shall have to seek powers of our own—powers that come from the gods."

"But not from the Abyss . . ." The golden-haired elf spoke with certainty.

"No . . . no, of course not." Auri's manner was breezy.

Silvanos held up a hand. "There are others, perhaps, who can help. Do not be alarmed by their appearance, for they travel under our protection."

Three elves, a trio of lithe but apparently elderly males, advanced into the clearing. Except for the colors of their robes, which were red, black, and white, respectively, the three might have been mirror images of each other. Each had long hair of iron gray, and they regarded the quartet with dark eyes that flashed with curiosity and something else.

The black-robed elf hung back, his gaze glaring with almost physical brightness, while the two in white and red took hesitant steps forward, bowing, regarding the transformed dragons with inscrutable expressions.

"I present Fayal Padran and Parys Dayl," murmured Silvanos, indicating the elves in red and white, respectively. The dark-garbed figure in the back stared silently. "And Kayn Wytsnall as well."

"Welcome to our humble fire," Dar offered.

"These are elves who would be mages. They have studied the ways of the gods." Silvanos stood and gestured the trio forward to the fire.

"We have already lived longer than most of our kind," cautioned red-robed Fayal Padran, raising a hand that was tipped with unusually long, slender fingers.

"How have you done this?" asked Aurican in honest curiosity.

"More pointedly, why are you here?" Darlantan interjected, fearing that his cousin might be about to embark on a long and pointless conversation.

It was Kayn Wytsnall, the elf in black, who replied.

"We are here because we have devoted our lives to the quest for magic—to bring the power of sorcery and spellcasting back to Krynn. Now it would seem that there is magic to be gained, and we have an idea where to look."

"And where is that?" pressed Aurican excitedly. He felt a strong affinity for these elves who would be wizards, Dar could tell.

"We have assembled the wisest men and elves to help us answer that question." Parys Dayl took over the explanation. His manner was easy, and the white robe swirled like smoke from his arms as he gestured expansively. "For years, priests have meditated, sages researched. . . ."

"And you have learned the answer?" Auri probed gently.

"We have learned that we shall have to seek from the gods themselves. But here we are limited, for we cannot look to the Platinum Father, nor the Queen of Darkness. They are the mighty gods who have chosen to withhold magic from the world, and they would be hostile to our pleas."

"Where, then?" demanded Darlantan.

The white robe replied, directing his dark and intense gaze exclusively at Aurican. "We believe the gods who might be more sympathetic to our . . . request can be reached, but to do so will require a long flight—a journey into realms beyond our world. That is why Silvanos suggested we speak to you."

"Yes . . . perhaps I could carry you. This is a quest I have always longed to undertake."

"It was our hope that you would feel this way," Parys Dayl said.

When his cousin turned to regard him, Darlantan had the distinct feeling he was looking into the face of the massive golden serpent, though Auri was still in the form of the elven sage. He knew, too, that Aurican had made up his mind with certain finality.

"We may be gone for a long time. Until we return, the cause of our vengeance will fall to you. Are you prepared?"

For a long time, Darlantan was silent. He wondered, hoped, thought about the future and the past. The silver dragon was ready to carry the war against the serpents of the Dark Queen, and he knew that he could exact revenge.

He was less certain about Aurican's quest. For all of his life, the gold dragon had spoken of gaining magic, of returning the power of sorcery to the peoples of Krynn. Yet now, when he considered the task, it seemed like an impossible deed. Still, there was the presence of magic in the evil dragons, and suddenly Darlantan could only hope that Aurican and the three brother mages were right: With the help of gods, spell magic *could* be brought to Krynn.

"Aye, my cousin."

Darlantan felt a quickening of hope as Aurican once again shimmered and grew, uncoiling across the top of the little knoll. The golden neck lowered, and the three mages climbed aboard, resting securely in the hollow between the gold dragon's shoulders. With a powerful, graceful leap, Aurican took to the air, and Silvanos, the wild elf, and the silver dragon watched until the fliers had vanished into the gathering dusk.

Chapter 11
Silver Death

3488–3480 PC

The ogre's face was lined with sweat, and he wiped a burly paw across his forehead, casting a spray of salty drops into the dense bushes beside the winding pathway. Behind him, a file of similar brutes, panting and dust-covered warriors clearly weary from a long march, plodded listlessly along the trail. Frustration and fatigue pervaded the air, rising like a stench from the mute, shuffling ogres.

This was the spearhead of a vast army, but for many weeks, the weary brutes had been embarked on a fruitless campaign against an invisible woodland foe. They had found one elven camp, long abandoned, but had encountered none of the sylvan warriors who were their quarry. Now, bored and apathetic, the brutish troops plodded listlessly through the summer heat.

A braying cry rang through the woods, like the sudden call of some trumpet-billed bird. Then the sound was repeated, and again, with a force that made clear this was no winged creature of the forest. The ogre halted, growling suspiciously as his eyes peered into the shadows. Movement slashed across his vision, too quick for the brute to recognize, but then he looked down and grunted in surprise.

A short arrow jutted from his chest. Another of the shafts struck him in the belly, and two more in the neck. With a gurgling, choking cry, the lead ogre fell face first onto the path.

Other ogres charged past the corpse of their comrade, bronze swords upraised. Three of the monsters advanced abreast, growling and snapping at the dense foliage, until a hailstorm of arrows greeted them. Death showered silently from the woods, slaying the trio, more arrows striking the brutes that were farther back in the file.

Then the wild elves were everywhere, attacking in answer to the sound of the ram's horn. Axes chopped and spears jabbed as the painted braves swarmed from the woods on both sides of the trail, striking ogres in their sagging gullets or muscled backs, slashing necks and hamstrings with quick, deadly blows. Shouts and cries from ogre and elf mingled with the clatter of blows, the deadly din of battle.

In seconds, the veteran ogre company dissolved into chaos. Those brutes still alive and unwounded turned toward the rear, stampeding down the path in a bellowing mass of terror. The wild elves killed those who fled too slowly, but showed little eagerness to press the pursuit. Soon the ogres who led the rout—those who had been at the rear of the marching column—slowed their pace to a shambling trot. The immediate threat was past, they sensed.

Until they came around a bend and found a massive, silver serpent coiled in their path. The lumbering ogres came to an abrupt halt, but before they could reverse their course, a blast of frost swirled from the gaping jaws. Icy air wilted the trees and slew the monstrous troops in a gusty wave of frigid death.

When the last of the ogres had been slain, the silver form shifted as Darlantan assumed the white-bearded body of the sage. Wild elves emerged from the brush and gathered around, looking at the frozen corpses littering the forest floor.

"It was a good trap," Kagonos announced approvingly as the wild elves gathered around the dragon in the depths of the forest clearing. "My braves counted more than a hundred slain, versus none of our own warriors."

"That is indeed good news," Darlantan said, momentarily wearied by the weight of wartime memories.

For many winters since the departure of Aurican, the elves had remained in the deepest woods, harassing the ogres who dared to penetrate into those forest homes, hiding from the chromatic dragons beneath the overwhelming canopy of trees. A long period of wet seasons prevented the drying that would have allowed the ogres to burn entire forests away, and the elves continued to take their toll among the enemy invaders. Kagonos himself led many sudden strikes, his painted Elderwild warriors appeared from the woods like apparitions, slaying ogres, pillaging treasure and supplies, then vanishing into the forest pathways.

Sometimes Darlantan joined in these strikes in the guise of a lean elven warrior. He fought using his hands or elven weapons, killing ogres with the stab of a spear or the twist of his powerful fingers. Often he employed a great, jagged-edged longsword that he had claimed from a slain enemy. There was no counting the number of brutish ogres who had been fatally gashed by that implacable blade.

During these years, Darlantan camped with Kagonos and his braves, stalking under the trees, using his sensitive nostrils and hearing to aid the wild elves in their seeking of prey and enemies. Of course, the keen senses of the elves were nearly as fine as his own, and Darlantan had grown used to young Elderwild braves calling his attention to a nearby doe or alerting him to the surreptitious movement of an enemy column.

Still, the elves accepted this strange warrior, followed him as he killed on his relentless quest for vengeance. Darlantan devised intricate ambushes, attacks that inflicted great damage on the foe while protecting the braves of the tribe. Leading these assaults with reckless abandon, the silver dragon in elven guise would strike hard, kill many ogres, then vanish before the brutish warriors could organize a counterattack.

At other times, Darlantan assumed his natural form and took his war to the dragons of the Dark Queen. He prepared ambushes of his own, and since Aurican's departure he had killed serpents of blue and black, of green and white. He became a mighty dragonslayer, vengeful and swift, attacking with power, speed, and implacable determination to surprise and confound the enemy serpents. He remained always alert, ready to foil even a teleporting dragon from making a surprise attack, and word of his deadly presence spread rapidly through the ranks of the Dark Queen's wyrms.

Always he hoped to strike at red Crematia, but that wily and hateful serpent consistently avoided the silver dragon's traps. Instead, she left for Darlantan many signs of her destruction, cities and villages and towns of elvenkind laid to waste. She delighted in the slaughter of whole herds of livestock. After selecting a few morsels for her own feast, she inevitably incinerated the rest of the hapless beasts with an expulsion of her hellish breath.

Still, in return, Darlantan laid waste to many an ogre's lair, becoming a scourge of the clans, viewed with every bit as much abhorrence by his enemies as the elves regarded Crematia and her villainous kin-dragons. He blasted marching columns of the brutes with his frosty breath, collapsed the caves and dens of their lairs with his brute strength.

Too, he aided the army of Silvanos—now under the command of the fierce and vengeful Quithas Griffontamer and the diminutive but resolute Balif—when it took to the field against the ogres. Though the elves fought under divided command, their tactics were effective. Quithas led his flying archers, mounted on fleet griffons, through a series of fast raids, while Balif led the troops on the ground, appearing when they were least expected, fighting solidly when the ogres expected them to run, and vanishing when the ogre chieftain Blacktusk, scion of Ironfist, drew up his legions for an offensive.

After the successful ambush, the elves once again scattered to the deep forest, and Darlantan took flight over the Plain of Vingaard. On the third day after the battle, he came upon a skirmish raging around a small, isolated farmstead. Hundreds of ogres had the place surrounded, while a small band of defenders had raised wooden barricades and sealed themselves into a compound of stone-walled courtyards and wooden barns.

The silver dragon flew low, blasting the attacking ogres with repeated explosions of lethal frost. The warriors within the makeshift fortress counterattacked, driving the rest of the brutes away as the silver serpent settled onto the muddy, trampled field.

One of the defenders approached the silver dragon without visible fear. The warrior was not, as Dar had first suspected, an elf. Instead, this leader had a thick beard and was wearing a costume of crudely tanned furs. The silver dragon knew that this was a human.

"I am called Tarn Iceblade," said the warrior. "We thank you for killing the ogres." He bowed quickly, then regarded Darlantan with sparkling, ice-blue eyes.

The silver dragon nodded in return, noting that the man was missing several fingers from his left hand. "And I am Darlantan. The ogres are my enemies as well. It pleases me to kill them when I can. But how did they catch you here on the open plain?"

"These are my people. We sought to defend this place, but it seemed as though we were going to be overwhelmed."

"You fight well. But the ogres were many, and they fight well also."

"We try to kill the bastards when we can—that's all. But

thanks for your help. We owe you our lives."

"We share an enemy. But why are you here, on this plain?"

"We're going to try to grow a crop. Only thus can the next winter be more prosperous than the last. Many are the elders and wee ones we buried in the high valleys with the spring thaw."

"But out here . . . surely the dragons will find you, if the ogres don't."

"My people must eat," Tarn replied, with a shrug of resignation that Darlantan found strangely moving. "But as I said, we thank you for your help in our fight."

The silver dragon took to the air again, impressed by this human. The Darlantan was pleased to scatter an entire legion of ogres that was apparently marching to reinforce the doomed attackers, and he returned to the forests with a sincere hope that Tarn Iceblade's tribe would have a successful harvest.

Then, finally, came a time when Darlantan and Kagonos met again upon the council knoll, the place where Aurican had departed from on his journey to the gods. The pair of venerable warriors sat in pensive silence around a fading fire, the dragon in his bearded human form. They had talked of strategies and battle plans, for Blacktusk was embarking on a new and implacable drive against the south. Yet their thoughts and hopes were elsewhere.

A rustling in the greenery silenced the two warriors' discussion, and they stared in taut anticipation as Silvanos emerged into view. He was somber, but stepped forward to embrace his kinsman with a hug of desperate, almost frenzied affection.

"They will come . . . tonight," murmured the elven patriarch.

Darlantan had sensed this as well, and now his eyes turned with intuitive direction toward the sky, knowing that they didn't have long to wait. He saw the winged form almost immediately, outlined against the stars, and his heart surged with a pulse of hope.

Aurican landed, and his change of shape was such a

smooth transition that by the time the golden wings had brushed down to the ground, four figures stood before the trio and their small campfire.

"Greetings, kin-dragon," said Auri in the voice of his elven body. Darlantan looked for some sign of his news, but the serene face was impassive.

Fayal Padran, in his robe of red, stood at Aurican's left, while white-garbed Parys Dayl advanced to his left. A fourth figure remained behind them, cloaked by the shadows, but Darlantan knew that Kayn Wytsnal was there as well.

"I am glad to see you," said Darlantan, his emotions overwhelming any attempt to speak further.

"And I." Auri's elven face was suddenly creased by a tight smile, as if he had seen things that had inspired him to wonder, and perhaps awe. His posture was proud, and the light of triumph gleamed in his eyes as he looked at Darlantan.

The newcomers knelt upon the ground, and Parys Dayl opened a satchel that Aurican had carried, revealing five large, glowing gems. The colors of the stones were clear and matched the array of hues Darlantan had come to despise: red, blue, black, white, and green.

"Behold the dragongems," said Fayal, his voice hushed with wonder. "And the means to defeat the wyrms of the Dark Queen."

"And welcome the return of magic to Krynn," added Aurican, eyes rising toward the distant, stormy sky.

Chapter 12
A Trap

3472 PC

Darlantan came to rest in a sheltered valley, secure behind the rising ridges of the Khalkist foothills. Years of war had inculcated him with careful habits. No sooner had his talons touched the loam of the meadow than he changed shape. He had carried the carcass of a small deer in his claws, and now he hoisted the fresh meat easily, resting the animal over his shoulders as he looked around.

The white-bearded human figure moved easily through the trees, skirting the clearing, insuring that he was unobserved. Only then did Darlantan proceed along the narrow, winding trail through the deep ravine. Sheer walls rose far over his head, barely an arm's length to either side, but instead of constricting him, they represented security to the transformed silver serpent. He was masked from the skies above by the overhanging walls, and any dragon that tried to pursue him would be greatly hampered by the narrow confines.

Of course, an ogre or two could squeeze in here, but then Darlantan almost hoped he would encounter a few of the brutish warriors. On another occasion some winters before, several heavily armed ogres had come upon an apparently frail, elderly human, and it had been the last mistake those particular monsters ever made.

Once he reached the cave, Darlantan sniffed the air, probing for any sign of danger. The shelter was large, with a ceiling arching high overhead. Though it was not deep, it remained dry and sheltered from the weather and was large enough that the silver dragon could have assumed his normal form if he had desired to do so. Yet he was content to remain in his two-legged guise.

The shadows were thick, but his golden eyes penetrated the darkness with ease, determining that the place was empty. Retaining his body in the shape of the bearded human elder, Darlantan advanced into the cave, shuffling through the dark recesses, insuring that nothing unsuspected lurked in concealment. Crouching beside a pile of dried wood that had apparently remained undisturbed since his last visit, the ancient dragon used his dexterous fingers to find the shard of flint and the steel knife blade that Kagonos had left here. With a few quick strikes, Dar started a fire—not because he was cold, but because he knew that Kagonos, when he came, would appreciate the warmth.

Flames crackled from the tinder, rising with cheery warmth and brightness, spreading light throughout the stone-walled shelter. For some time, Darlantan amused himself by watching his own human-shaped shadow cavort and gesture on the smooth stone of the cave wall. Finally he heard the almost silent sound of a footfall along the trail that ran along the ravine floor, and Darlantan looked up to see the wild elf jog into view. Kagonos bore the long-hafted axe that was his favored weapon, the ram's horn on its thong of leather, and was garbed in a supple breechcloth of doeskin. Otherwise he was naked, unadorned except for the elaborate designs of ink streaked across his chest, cheeks, and forehead.

He entered the alcove with a nod, squatting before the fire and absorbing the warmth from the small bed of coals. Unlike humans or other short-lived creatures meeting again after a winter's separation, these two long-lived beings felt no need for conversation to distill the silence of the wilderness. Instead, they sat in worldless fellowship around the heartening blaze.

After a time, the two friends shared the fresh venison Darlantan had brought, drinking water from a pure spring at the back of the cave. A feeling of kinship grew between them, rising in the air like heat radiating from the coals. With the addition of a few dry sticks, the fire became their balladeer, crackling bold lyrics, then fading into a soft postlude.

"Word comes by runner from the east." Kagonos, with his eyes closed, leaned back and laid his head against the rock wall of the little cave. He spoke slowly, reluctant to dispel the serene aura. "The blue dragons attack toward the coast. They fight in support of a large army, so all indications are that they will remain there for some time."

"And Crematia?" Darlantan's calm broke with the mention of his enemy's name. His voice quivered and his jaw clenched at the thought of the red dragon, who had eluded his best efforts over so many winters.

Kagonos only shook his head. "Perhaps she has been swallowed by Aurican's magic gems—the same way those stones ate the souls of the white and green dragons."

"Do you know what happened to those gems?" Darlantan asked.

"Silvanos tells me the griffons carried them deep into the mountains," Kagonos replied. "There they were buried so they would never be found. And with them are buried two of the Dark Queen's clans."

"It is only to be wished that Crematia could have been trapped as well," Dar agreed. "But I was with my brother a dozen sunrises ago, and he has seen not so much as a single crimson scale."

Still, the wild elf's words reminded him of something else as well, something more hopeful than he would have believed ten winters earlier. Darlantan reflected on the success that Aurican and he had with the dragongems. The stones possessed a powerful allure, the fundamental essence of magic bestowed by the gods themselves. Aurican had never explained much about the harrowing quest that had brought them to the dragongems, only hinting that the cost might prove to be high.

Yet the stones of life-trapping had proven to be potent and effective, so long as the evil dragons could be lured close enough for the magic to take effect. To this end, Darlantan and Aurican had devised an effective tactic, one that had served them well in two distinct campaigns. Darlantan had located the wyrms and goaded them into a reckless pursuit. Aurican completed the other portion of the trap, waiting somewhere in ambush, concealed in his elven guise and waiting for his kin-dragon to lead the chromatic serpents to him.

As the enraged wyrms swept past, Aurican brandished the magical gem and worked the spell of life-trapping. Powerful sorcery exploded in a cyclone of magic, pulling the dragons into the stone. Twice the plan had worked to perfection, and the dragons of white and green had been imprisoned.

"Any word as to the black dragons?" asked the wild elf.

"There is some good news," Dar replied, heartened by the prospects for imminent battle. "They are gathered in the mountains above Blacktusk, and the ogres are already marching against Sylvanos. Aurican is ready with the black dragongem. It is my plan to fly there from here."

"Have a care, my friend," Kagonos urged, his gray eyes serious within the spirals of his war paint.

"I shall. I am grateful that these serpents of black seem to lack some of the mastery of magic of Crematia and the blues."

"I will join you later. Good luck," said the elf.

"And to you, as well, my friend."

In silence, the white-bearded sage tottered into the

darkness. By the time Kagonos had curled up for a few hours' sleep, silver wings parted the night air, and Darlantan soared toward the foothills and the gathered armies of the ogre Blacktusk and the elvenking Silvanos.

Before dawn, he passed the low, cratered mountain where Aurican was hidden. Darlantan marked the spot well, but did not fly too closely nor make any attempt to spot the gold dragon, who would undoubtedly be concealed in the body of the elven patriarch.

By then, the great mass of the ogre army had come into view. The monstrous horde swarmed over the plain like ants crossing a vast field, and even from his lofty vantage, Darlantan was impressed by the speed of their advance. Then he saw tiny forms soaring over the treetops far below and knew that the elven griffonriders were sweeping in to attack. More antlike figures emerged from the forest, and the army of Silvanos took up positions of defense.

But Darlantan's eyes were fixed upon higher targets. He couldn't hear the clash of weaponry, elven steel against ogre bronze, ringing from the melee below. The screams of the wounded and dying, the hoarse bellows of Blacktusk's subcommanders and the lyrical trumpets of Silvanos's signalmen—all were carried away by the wind long before they rose to Darlantan's lofty vantage.

In any event, Darlantan knew those sounds and their attending violence were only peripherally important. The success or failure of this day would not be measured by elven and ogre dead, but by the results of his and Aurican's efforts to entrap the dragons of black.

Then he saw his targets: seven black shapes winging out of the mountains, flying high, but not quite at the lofty altitude of their silver foe. The dragons of the Dark Queen veered along the descending slopes of the foothills, intent upon the battle developing at the edge of the plains. They flew a straight course, in a gentle descent that steadily increased the speed of their approach.

Darlantan stroked the air, flying his fastest as he curled around to approach the black dragons from the side. He flew in deadly silence, wondering if these arrogant wyrms would allow him the luxury of a surprise attack. Winging onward, he closed the distance, still apparently unobserved.

Abruptly one of the black dragons looked up and spotted the swiftly diving silver, braying a warning to its six companions. Fully alerted, the formation swerved toward Darlantan, individual black dragons diverging slightly, confronting him with an array of talons and fangs, holding their searing, acidic breath ready for a deadly crossfire.

It would be death to fly into that vortex of fury. Darlantan could well imagine the corrosive cloud of acid that would rot his scales and dissolve his wings. Instead, the silver dragon dived straight down, so fast that wind whistled through his mane and battered his body. He veered away from the blacks, daring but one look back to see that they had all swept into the pursuit.

The distance separating pursuers from pursued was great, and Darlantan allowed himself to relax a little, sweeping along from the force of his momentum alone. He watched the conical mountain where Aurican was waiting grow larger in his view, looming to dominate all the lesser peaks around it. Finally the level flight began to slow him, and his silver wings once again worked through the air, reaching, propelling the shimmering dragon through the skies.

A stream of acid burned into his left wing with vicious, searing intensity, and Darlantan veered away with a bellow of pain. He strained for more speed, but each wing stroke brought another bolt of agony shooting into his side. In disbelief, he turned to see one of the black dragons curving away with startling agility and speed, whipping through a tight, curling turn to make another pass at him. While its fellows remained well back, the leading wyrm had somehow far outdistanced the others.

Darlantan noticed the quick, almost fluttering motion of the dragon's wings as it swerved away, cautious of the now-alerted silver. When the black made a quick loop, darting in to resume the attack, he understood: The black serpent was hastened by magic. The wyrm's speed was so great, its maneuvers so quick and nimble, that it seemed more like a bat or a bee than a great dragon.

Spewing a swath of freezing breath into the air, Darlantan forced the black to veer aside, but was unable to damage his enemy. With renewed determination, the silver dragon turned toward his mountaintop goal, wings straining, trying to build up speed against the sorcerously quickened pursuit of his foe. He ignored the pain in his scarred wing, using the injured flap to pull himself forward.

Then the rim of the high crater was approaching. Climbing gently, Darlantan pulled himself over the top, briefly spotting a tall elf who faced the pursuing dragons with a large gem of black clutched in his hands. Aurican was ready, and Dar would bring him his victims.

The silver dragon felt the pulse of magic as the first of the blacks, the magically hastened serpent, was swallowed by the powerful essence of the stone. The monster simply vanished from the air, the sound of a whirling vortex roaring through the crater of the lofty mountain. The rest of the midnight-dark dragons swept onward, bellowing in rage at the disappearance of their fellow.

A blast of magic swirled through the caldera, much stronger this time as Aurican's spell captured the spiritual force of six black dragons. Spray rose from the wet snowfields as the wind focused, whirling, rising into a raging funnel cloud. Aurican stood, his feet firmly planted, holding up the gem as the wind curled and blustered.

Abruptly Darlantan saw a flash of crimson, like a slash of living flame in the sky, and he knew that Crematia had arrived. The red was poised above the circular crater, and the silver dragon saw her tuck her wings and arrow toward Aurican—who had his back to the scarlet horror, his full attention still riveted upon the black stone pulsing in his hands. She rushed downward, jaws gaping, foreclaws outstretched.

"Beware!" cried Darlantan, veering through a sharp turn. Aurican still took no notice; his concentration was focused upon the swirling storm and the enchanted gem.

Crematia swept lower, jaws gaping as she approached the figure of the elf, but suddenly she noticed the silver form racing toward her from the side. At the same moment, the whirlwind of sound rose to a thunder, echoing and roaring through the crater, casting a cloud of debris through the air. The red dragon banked away as the swelling crescendo of magic roared in Darlantan's ears.

And Crematia disappeared, vanished as abruptly as the seven black dragons. The power of the dragongem was a surging wave in the bowl of the valley, a resonant force echoing with sorcery, magic potent enough to swallow the black dragons . . . and apparently Crematia as well.

The vortex of the cloud swept up the steep slope of the crater, finally rising to whirl around Aurican. The buffeting of the storm was tremendous, but still the elven figure didn't budge.

And then the wind was gone, snuffed out like a small candle by the pure magic of the dragongem. Aurican held the black stone in his hands, smiling at the silver serpent who wheeled overhead. The skies were clear of chromatic dragons.

"Now," Aurican shouted, his tone swelling with exultation, "bring me the blues!"

Chapter 13
Blues in Battle

3357 PC

Campaigns raged across the face of Ansalon, scoring bloody scars over each summer season. During the colder times, the vast armies rested, recouped, and prepared for the upcoming offensives. The tide of battle flowed over the plains of Vingaard, lapped at the foothills of the mountain ranges flanking that great flatland, and washed deep into lands that had once been hallowed forests.

However, with three clans of evil dragonkind imprisoned in the stones of life-trapping and Crematia nowhere to be seen, the blue wyrms had become more cautious. They still sent their lightning against helpless mortals on the ground, but no longer did they join in the great campaigns of Blacktusk's—and later his heir, Talonian's—vast army. Thus the elves of Silvanos and the elven leader's human allies were able to gradually drive back the evil force's most aggressive spearheads.

Crematia, by all reports, had disappeared at the time of the ambush of the black dragons, and Aurican had quietly voiced the hope that she had somehow been entrapped with her inky cousins. Still, the gems had been specifically forged for a particular kind of dragon, and in darker moments, the gold dragon speculated that the red female had simply teleported away to spare herself from Darlantan's attack. Thus, she could be biding her time, waiting for her revenge.

Yet finally, after a campaign of more than a hundred winters, victory lay within the grasp of Aurican, Darlantan, and their elven and human allies. Only the blue serpents remained, and the silver and gold had patiently awaited a chance to trap them within the remaining dragongem, the enchanted stone of blue.

Until that stone was stolen.

For once, the ogres used cunning instead of brute force. Bribed by great treasures, some humans had betrayed the rest of their kind, enabling the ogres to penetrate the heart of the army camp where the bluestone was being held for safekeeping. The monsters had made off with the orb, carrying the precious treasure somewhere into the Khalkists.

Now the army of elves and humans was encamped across a vast plain, several days' march from the forest that had been their only protection in the days before the dragongems. Silvanos and his human allies had taken this position with audacity, in a blatant attempt to lure Talonian into a final battle—a contest that would almost certainly decide the outcome of the war.

Beside that position rose a single, steep-sided mountain, and it was atop this peak that two long, serpentine forms sprawled with regal ease. Starlight reflected from glittering scales of silver, rippled along sleek wings of gold, as the ancient nestmates overlooked the flatland and its burden of twin armies.

The blot of Talonian's horde lay to the north, a dark

stain on the dark land. Moving hastily, camping without fires, the ogre chieftain had brought his troops on a brutal forced march, so desperate was he to meet the elves while the enchanted gem was unavailable to them. Now that massive swarm was encamped along the northern horizon, and even in the darkness, the two dragons could smell the stench of many thousand ogres, a bitter and acrid blight on the night wind.

On the plain below, sprawling for as far as they could see, were the innumerable sparkling cookfires of the human and elven force. Pickets were placed and the formations were encamped in company order, ready to fall into line in the morning. From the mountaintop, the glittering specks marking Silvanos's massive army stretched almost to the far horizon.

"Or is it even Silvanos's army anymore?" mused Aurican pensively. "He tells me there are ten humans for every elf in his ranks."

"That is good for the elves, then," Darlantan noted dryly, "for the humans will likely do ten times as much dying."

"Indeed," Auri agreed sagely, missing the irony his nestmate had intended.

Even to Darlantan humans, were short-lived and reckless beings, lacking the dignity and wisdom inherent in elves. Yet increasingly the silver dragon had discovered that he not only found humans to be fascinating, but that he also actually enjoyed their company. Perhaps because of the memories and legends of the benefactor Smelt, the humans had welcomed the assistance of the silver serpent with enthusiasm and gratitude, and Darlantan had been eager to help when he could. He had walked among humans many times during more recent years, finding a peculiar and enervating excitement in the chaotic tangles of their messy, disorganized cities. Many men seemed to be industrious and unpredictable folk, and though he couldn't explain his reaction, the silver dragon had long ago realized that he was fascinated by them. He also wanted to protect them, insofar as it was possible, from the depredations of the Dark Queen's wyrms.

"Tell me," Aurican asked, interrupting his kin-dragon's musings, "has the wild elf heard any word about the blue-stone?"

"The news is hopeful. Kagonos has located it, and has a chance of returning it to Silvanos. Unless he can do so—until he does, in any event—it will be up to us to stand against the Dark Queen's blues."

"It is fitting enough, if only to get the war over with," Aurican said with a sigh. "There are ballads to compose, lyrics to record . . . too many things that have been put aside for this priority of violence."

"And nestlings," said Darlantan, with a regretful sigh of his own. Increasingly he had been thinking about those silver eggs in the grotto. Long ago he had resolved that as soon as the war was won, he would return to that sacred cavern. He even entertained hopes of being present to see the wyrmlings crawl forth from their eggs, but of course that would depend on many things that were beyond the ability of even an ancient dragon to control.

"Do you remember how Kenta and Oro chased us away?" mused Aurican.

"The grotto has become a place for females and eggs," Dar agreed with a nod. "As though they forgot that we, too, had dwelt there for thousands of winters!"

"Not forgotten, no." The gold dragon was pensive. "Rather, it was as though they understand that it was time for us to leave, to move into this world as its permanent inhabitants. In fact, there is a rightness to what our females did."

"Have you heard word from them . . . our mates?" asked the silver.

"Oro finds ways to send me news, often by griffon. I heard over the last winter that the eggs are safe."

Content for the moment, Darlantan sighed and closed his eyes. Throughout the cool night, the nestmates rested side by side, Dar's neck lying on Auri's wing, silver tail curled around to make a pillow for golden head. The ancient dragons didn't sleep, but nevertheless were alert and ready with the dawn. At first light, Darlantan's eyes played across the field as the combined elven and human camp stirred, great regiments and legions taking shape, commencing a crawling advance to the north. Now Talonian's horde hove into view, angling down the bank of a great river, turning to meet the advancing foe.

Daylight spread across the plains as the sun rose, bright rays breaking through the patchwork of clouds in many places, leaving a blotchy pattern of shadow and light across the sweeping plain. Abruptly a flash of crimson splashed across the scene like a huge stain of blood, but Darlantan recognized her instantly.

"Crematia!" he hissed, pointing with the angle of his flaring snout.

Aurican, who had been scanning the north in search of the blue dragons, whipped his head around and stared. "It is as I surmised," the gold declared. "She was not trapped in the black gem. She merely wished us to believe so."

"I will kill her now," declared the silver dragon, crouching, wings spread, ready to fly.

"Wait, my brother." Aurican's voice held Dar back. "My scales cannot be burned by her fire. Let me go after her. You watch here for the blues, or wait for word from Kagonos."

Darlantan growled, but he knew Auri was right. The gold dragon's gilded scales were proof against Crematia's fiery breath, a protection that Darlantan could not claim.

"Fly with the speed of sorcery and the Platinum Father," Dar urged.

"I shall."

In the echo of that word, Aurican was gone, a rush of air swirling in his wake. Darlantan squinted and saw the golden form diving toward the red dragon. Crematia darted away at impossible speed, and Auri, though unenchanted, pursued like a shooting star. Rapidly the two dragons dwindled to tiny specks of color far out over the dusty plain.

Returning his taut, uneasy inspections to the north, Dar squinted along the horizon. The scourge of the blue dragons had been well reported by elven scouts as the vicious serpents spread a swath of devastation along the eastern coast of the world. Moving northward, they had continued their way along the shoreline of the great ocean. Recent reports told of their intentions to rejoin Talonian.

So they would have to come from the north, Darlantan knew.

Soon his certainty was rewarded as tiny flecks of azure appeared in the distance against the rusty brown of the plains. The blue dragons swept toward the field with relentless determination, flying in a broad wing. There were five of the serpents in all, soaring below the level of the puffy clouds that scudded through the sky.

Darlantan took wing immediately, climbing through the clouds into the thin, frosty regions where he had rarely ventured. He took an evasive, wayward course, using the largest of the cumulus clouds as concealment from the onrushing serpents. Finally, far above them, he circled and waited.

Every once in a while he glimpsed a blue wing or the trailing flick of a tail through the obscuring vapor. Mostly the view below was blocked by the thickening overcast, and this concealment suited Darlantan. The wyrms were flying well below the clouds, doubtless to insure that they would have plenty of time to react to an attack from above.

That is, an ordinary attack. But Darlantan had a new plan in mind, a tactic that would require careful timing and a measure of luck. The leading blue dragon blinked into view again in the gap between two nearby clouds, and the silver dragon put his plan into action.

The body of metallic sheen shifted and grew smaller in the instant of his thought, and in an eyeblink, it was the body of a frail, white-bearded sage poised high in the air. Lacking wings, the body naturally began to fall straight down, and here Darlantan hoped for the intervention of luck.

He plunged through the clouds, blinking away the tears that formed in his eyes from the buffeting force of the wind.

Tucking his arms around his skinny legs, he made himself as small an object as possible, a tiny ball of humanity plunging from the lofty clouds, directly toward the back of the leading blue dragon. Doubtless the following serpents would have noticed something as huge and visible as a dragon of gleaming silver, but none of them took notice of this insignificant fleck of nothing tumbling downward.

But in another eyeblink Darlantan became a dragon again, poised directly above the back of the massive blue. He struck his target with crushing force as the silver head whipped around. Jaws gaping, he blasted an explosion of killing frost into the startled face of the next blue in line.

Beneath him, the wyrm snapped and writhed, trying to bring those lethal jaws—and that deadly lightning—to bear. Darlantan's claws closed around the blue's throat, crushing and tearing, until his own fangs ripped through its scales. Slowing the descent with his outspread wings, the silver dragon twisted once more to make sure his foe was dead.

Then he released the lifeless carcass and dived toward the ground, sweeping away from the two armies clenched in their distant, sprawling struggle. Bellows of rage still echoed, and the acrid scent of spent lightning stung his nostrils as he drew deep breaths and strove for altitude.

Three blue arrows plunged from the sky in vengeful pursuit as Darlantan headed for the scant concealment of a range of rugged foothills. He dodged into a chasm, flying around a massive bluff and swinging over the plains again, leaving the blues straining to keep him in sight. Upward and still upward he rose, the powerful strokes of his wings carrying him high above the land, higher than he had ever flown before. Passing through the tenuous layer of clouds, Darlantan found himself in a realm of twilight chill, though the sun burned from just past zenith overhead. The wetness on his scales turned to frost, and he sensed that the blues struggled with the uncomfortable chill as they labored in pursuit.

But they still had their magic, and in a heart-stopping moment, the three blue serpents materialized in the air before him—and Darlantan knew he was defeated. A trio of cruel maws gaped as the mighty silver tried to veer aside, knowing he was too late. The blue dragons were arrayed in lethal formation, poised to kill no matter which way he turned.

Then a great *rock* was there, a massive orb that was somehow suspended in the sky. The surface was silvery and bright, coated with frost, and the great sphere was moving very fast, tumbling crazily into the midst of the aerial melee. Darlantan veered, dodging as the massive globe swirled past the chromatic dragons.

Lightning blasted, and shards of white-silver stones flew past Darlantan. But the blue dragon's aim had been thrown off by the great sphere of stone. His shot missed the silver serpent, instead splintering into the great, floating mass of rock. Dar had no time to ponder the mystery of the flying stone. He curled around the gradually rounded surface, realizing that the body of rock was monstrously huge. Certainly it would be visible to those on the ground, though he had never seen nor heard of such a body in the skies above Krynn.

Sudden darkness loomed, as if something had abruptly doused the sun. But then he saw that it was another sphere of rock streaking after the first, this one midnight black in color. Indeed, the stone was so dark as to resemble a hole in the sky more than any solid surface of rock. Again lightning blasted, and this time shards of the black orb exploded upward as the blue's bolt missed its target and gouged into the mysterious globe.

Flying faster, Darlantan curled away from the black object, now seeing another great rock heave into view. This one was as red as blood, and it seemed to trail the other two through the sky. With three blue dragons in pursuit, the silver veered toward this third massive sphere, hoping beyond belief the good fortune that had blessed him until now would hold firm.

Sensing the blues close on his tail, the silver serpent curved sharply, driving his wings through long strokes, almost skimming the surface of bright, blood-red rock.

The monstrous orb hurled past, obviously trailing the other two on a trajectory that would carry it even higher into the sky—above the clouds, above the loftiest dragon-flight, seemingly beyond the very air itself.

Darlantan twisted instinctively, warned by familiarity with his foes. Once more lightning spurted past, driving into the surface of the cosmic rock, missing the silver dragon by a mere hairsbreadth. Then the crimson orb was streaking away, leaving a trail of shards from the lightning strike that, like the black and silver debris from earlier blasts, tumbled lazily through the air, falling with deceptive grace toward the ground below. The three great spheres, white and black and red, coursed quickly upward and away.

Without the moons for cover, Darlantan relied on his speed once more. He pushed himself through the air, blinking against the onrush of wind, tilting into a plummeting headlong dive. The snaky line of the Vingaard River expanded into clarity, and once again the dragon of metal outdistanced his azure foes.

But there was still that magic, and abruptly two of the blue serpents popped into view below him. Jaws agape, they waited in perfect attack position as Darlantan curved his neck and stretched his wings, striving desperately to pull away.

The lightning exploded with a violent flash, though curiously the silver dragon heard no sound. For a moment, everything was impossibly bright.

And then there was no light at all.

Chapter 14
Darlantan's Triumph

3357 PC

Aurican dived, the scarlet-winged form of Crematia growing broad in his vision. With a bellow, he lunged, arrowing his body into a deadly spear, driving toward that hateful crimson matriarch. The long pursuit was over, he sensed . . . now they would finish their feud.

But the red dragon suddenly whipped about, halting in space, suspended by magic. Aurican veered, slashing at a crimson wing, and the two dragons met in the midst of a raging fireball, the combined blast of their lethal breath weapons. Still, neither of these mighty serpents could be badly hurt by fire, and so they broke apart, diving to regain speed, then swerving upward to recommence the fight.

Once again they clashed, Crematia now abandoning magic for the fury of fang and talon. Rending and tearing, they dived and coiled and twisted through the air. Aurican's fangs tore into the crimson scales of his enemy's belly. She screamed, folding her wings and dropping like a falling rock to escape the golden claws. As she plummeted, Aurican heard her muttering strange words, knew that she was casting a spell.

Abruptly a whirling shape materialized in the air, an elemental summoned by Crematia from a distant plane. Like a whirlwind, it roared after the gold dragon, tearing at Aurican's wing, ripping the leathery membrane. Twisting, he snapped at the bizarre creature, but it dodged nimbly away—until he incinerated the elemental by belching a cloud of furiously churning flame.

Crematia again took flight, diving and then flying with desperate speed, but Aurican closed the distance with his quarry. For long hours, they raced and fought through deep canyons, over lofty ridges, and among the jagged peaks of the southern Khalkists. Slowly the gold dragon drew close, sensing that victory was imminent.

Then, in the blink of an instant, she was gone, leaving a hole in the sky. Aurican knew that she had teleported away, but he had no way of tracking her. Grimly furious, he banked to the side, squinting into the distance as he sought any sign of crimson scales . . . but there was nothing.

A squawk from below drew his attention to a griffon. As the creature flew closer, Aurican banked toward the hawk-faced flyer.

"What is the word from the east?" asked Auri as the griffon curled around to match his course and altitude.

"The battle was raging. Darlantan was in battle with the blues, flying high above the field, until at last we lost sight of him."

"And the elves?"

"They did not fare badly. It looked as though Talonian might at last meet his defeat."

"If the blues can be trapped . . . all our hopes depend on that," Aurican said. "Forgive me, my friend, but I must hasten back there. But I would ask a question of you first."

"As you wish," declared the griffon, with a polite dip of its hawklike head.

"Your kind and ours have had many conflicts, many rivalries. Why, in the midst of all this, have you been such a loyal friend to my brother?"

"He showed my ancestor mercy once," replied the descendant of Ravenclaw simply. "I am grateful."

"Patersmith would be proud," murmured Aurican, not surprised. Leaving the griffon wondering what he meant, the gold dragon turned back to the east. He flew for many hours until, near sunset, he found himself above the two armies.

The battlefield was a scar across the greensward below, a great wound in the world that glistened with flesh and blood, with the debris of broken weapons and punctured bodies. Fires blazed in many places, where war machines had been overtaken and put to the torch by victorious elves, or the ogres' supply wagons had been captured and subsequently destroyed.

Aurican dived lower, wishing he could celebrate the victory, could share the joy that must be rampant in the elven camps by now. But there were good reasons why the gold dragon felt a lingering sense of melancholy. For one thing, Crematia had eluded him. For another, he was deeply concerned about his silver nestmate.

The gold dragon settled into the midst of the elven encampment, maintaining his true form as Silvanos and his chief general, Balif, came forward to greet him.

"What of the blues?" inquired Aurican with precipitate haste. His concern for his ancient nestmate forced him to set aside proper patience for formalities.

In reply, Silvanos pulled forth a stone of deepest turquoise. The large sphere pulsed with vitality as the hateful spirits of dragons thrummed and struggled within.

"There were but three of them left," explained the elven patriarch. "My Elderwild cousin regained the stone barely in time. Quithas, astride his griffon, returned it to me here. When the three blue dragons swept downward to aid the battle on the ground, they approached me carelessly, and I was able to capture their spirits in the stone."

"Darlantan . . . ?" Auri felt a sense of bleak despair, knowing that his silver brother would have given his life to prevent the blues from getting through. "Did he know that you had the stone . . . or . . . ?"

"He fought throughout the morning, killing two of the blues before they could reach us. But, no, he did not know that Kagonos had regained the gem."

"Where is he?"

Silvanos pointed toward the riverbank beyond the camp. Night's shadows had stretched across the plain, but in the glow of firelight, Auri saw the grief in his old friend's eyes.

"I'm sorry. You had best go now if you hope to speak with him."

The elven patriarch's words were a murmur, barely whispered through the evening breeze, following the gold dragon who had already taken wing.

Aurican flew fast and low, and quickly he found the battered silver form stretched in the soft mud flats of the riverbank. Darlantan lay beside the broad flowage, the Vingaard, that drained this whole vast plain. Now the mighty head rose stiffly as the golden dragon swept through the night skies, gliding toward his nestmate.

Then Aurican was at Darlantan's side, the serpentine body of pure gold coiling protectively around the battered silver flesh. With a glimmer of change, almost invisible in the starlight, the gilded serpent became again the kindly elven sage. Darlantan sighed as the hand, soft and soothing with the wisdom of millennia, gently stroked the gouged and burned scales at the base of his neck.

"The mud is cooling balm, and it helps to soften the pain," the silver dragon admitted, allowing his head to settle once again to the ground. Still, Aurican knew that the soft dirt could do nothing to ease the various wounds gouged into the mighty serpentine body.

"Did . . . did the blues reach Silvanos?" Darlantan asked.

"No, my cousin. You killed two of them. And by the

time the other three turned their attentions to the ground, Kagonos and his wild elves had regained the Bluestone. It was returned to Silvanos in time for him to capture the rest of the Dark Queen's wyrms."

"Crematia . . . as well?"

"Alas, no. I chased her across the plain, and through realms of smoke and sky, but she managed to elude me. The best I can claim is that she has gone to ground again. We can only hope that, with the loss of all her kin, she will remain aloof from the affairs of Krynn."

"She does not know of the grotto, the eggs?" whispered Darlantan, suddenly stiffening.

"They are safe," said Aurican. "Already some of the eggs are showing signs of motion. I understand that the females have their eye on a silver. They expect it will be the first of the hatchlings to emerge."

Darlantan nodded, trying to absorb this suggestion of a future destiny.

"My son . . ." Darlantan's voice trailed away with the wind, but Aurican sensed his nestmate's joy at the thought of his own offspring coming forth into the world. The gold took some comfort from this knowledge, finding that it helped him to ignore the cruel wounds.

"Kenta is there, watching?" the silver serpent asked, his tongue flicking between his long fangs as he stirred weakly in the mud.

"Of course."

"My son . . . the first of the hatchlings," Darlantan declared dreamily. "He shall be named Callak. Here . . . please see that he has this when he comes of age."

The silver wing shifted, revealing the curling ram's horn and its chain of fine links. Aurican gently lifted the artifact, cradling it reverently in his two hands.

"It is done, my cousin," declared the gold dragon with the body of the ancient elf. Drops of warm wetness trickled onto Darlantan's brow and snout as Auri failed to restrain his weeping.

Darlantan's eyes turned upward, toward the dark vault of the skies. He saw two moons there, a circle of red and another of white. Behind them trailed an orb of blackness, visible only as it blotted out the light of the stars.

"Even the heavens mark the passing of war," he said softly, "for they have placed their lights in our sky."

"Those moons mark more than the passing of war," Aurican said. Even through the haze of his wounds, Dar realized that his brother spoke very seriously. "They are the tombs of nothing less than gods—Lunitari, Solinari, and Nuitari."

"What gods are these?" Darlantan, who knew of few deities other than their own Platinum Father and his antithesis, the Queen of Darkness, asked.

"These were the three gods that gave magic to the world—the trio I visited with the brother mages. It was they who gave us the dragongems, that we might battle the scourge of the Dark Queen's dragons," said Auri regretfully, shaking his head in despair. "They are being punished by the greater gods for their transgression, though that transgression gave us our means for winning this war."

"I will join them soon," Darlantan said, once again yielding to that dreamy sense of departure. Then apparently something fought to bring his attention back to the present, and he forced himself to raise his head, to focus the increasingly vague center of his mind.

"Here," he said weakly, lifting his wing to reveal the three shards of moon that had tumbled to the ground with him.

"But how did these . . . ?" The gold dragon looked in wonder, shaking his head as he struggled to accept the reality of the stony fragments.

"The final battle took me . . . far," Darlantan explained. "Even to what I now see are these godmoons. The lightning of the blues blasted the shards loose from the very bedrock of the spheres."

"And these pieces . . . ?"

"They tumbled back to Krynn with me . . . but now I give them to you. Or perhaps I give them to the future." The silver head was upraised, the voice stronger than before. Those deep yellow eyes glowed, compelling the gold dragon to hear and obey as Darlantan gestured to the three large stones. One was as black as the encroaching night, another silver-white, while the third was as slickly red as fresh blood.

Aurican stood upright then, and in a shimmering of golden scales, he returned to his serpentine body. "I understand," he said softly.

Crouching over the stones, Auri reached out with open jaws. His tongue snaked forward and scooped up the black shard, quickly drawing it into the gaping maw. Tossing his head high, the gold dragon gulped down the stone, an awkward bulge rippling the shimmering scales along the length of the sinuous neck. With swift stabs of his mighty head, Aurican took the white, and finally the red segments of stone, swallowing them after the black.

"Good," Darlantan said as the silver head once again settled to the mud. "It is nearly finished. But it is time for you to fly."

"Soon." The great golden form settled beside the ravaged body of his ancient nestmate, and in silence, the great serpents felt the kinship of touch, a sensation familiar to them over scores of centuries.

"Your elf is coming," Aurican said some time later. Darlantan couldn't see, couldn't raise his head, but the scent of Kagonos came to him on the evening breeze. In the distance, the camp of Silvanos rang with cheers and celebration.

"I will speak with him alone before I go," Dar whispered. "Now, fly back to our grotto, my brother, and have an eye for my wyrmlings as well as your own."

"You have my promise that I shall do that, and I shall compose a ballad that will live for the ages: the tale of brave Darlantan's last battle."

"I think I would like that, to have a ballad. And now it is time."

With a nod and a last gentle touch to the silver-scaled neck, Aurican reared tall and shimmered in the pale starlight. Golden wings arced outward, scooped down to compress the air, and then he was gone, vanishing into the sky before the painted figure of the wild elf emerged from the darkness.

Chapter 15
Legacy

3357 PC

Aurican's chest swelled with warm power, a fulfilling goodness unique in the gold dragon's experience. He felt an impulse to breathe out, to spew an explosion of gas that would unleash this invigorating, barely contained power of magic within him.

Instead, he clenched his jaws and felt the pressure rise, a glow of sublime might swelling him, bearing his golden body through midnight skies. His wings carried him higher and higher, parting the cool, dark air, gleaming with shining brightness under the night skies. At first, he passed through wispy clouds, an ethereal atmosphere that masked the vast plain of Vingaard below and obscured the soft starlight glowing above. But still the golden wings drove downward, and Aurican rose, splitting the mists, shimmering like a metallic ghost in the formless space. The cool, moist air felt good against his wings and his scales, and droplets of water glowed like gems against the metallic sheen of his body.

And then the clouds were a soft blanket below him, rolling crests and swells, shadowy kettles and swales that seemed deceptively solid under the muted light from above. Still the pressure expanded within him, and though the force was great, the feeling was not unpleasant.

Looking upward, Aurican beheld the three moons in close alignment, rising in the east, preceding the arrival of dawn by many hours. First came crimson Lunitari, then the dark shadow of Nuitari, and finally the brightness of Solinari. The loss of the three magical shards that now seethed within Aurican had left no visible scars, at least none that the gold dragon could see, yet he keenly sensed their influence within him as the magic surged.

Faster flew Aurican, soaring through the skies like an arrow launched from a monstrous bow. The distant ridge of the High Kharolis came into view as the plains passed away beneath him, as a flight that would normally take him three days was accomplished in the space of a single night. On wings of the gods he glided, serene and aloof, grieving but triumphant.

With a keen sense of destiny, he dived toward the secret entrance to the Valley of Paladine. He wasted no time coming to rest on the ground, instead flying with deliberate speed through the long entry tunnel, then racing over the still and silent waters of the subterranean lake. Like a golden arrow, he shot through the secret cavern, gliding toward the sacred grotto and its precious trove.

Only when he reached the rim of rock beyond that sheltered cavern did he come to rest, and even then he paused only long enough to fold his massive wings against his flanks. He crept into the winding passage, smelling the familiar warmth of the grotto. Drawing that presence through his nostrils and into his deep chest, he was overwhelmed with thoughts of Darlantan, and of Smelt, Burll, and Blayze. He knew that he carried the legacy of them all.

Approaching the nest, he lifted his head, conscious of the metallic females gathered along the cavern walls, watching him with bright, golden eyes. Gold and silver, brass, bronze, and copper dragons, all studied their patriarch as he rose above the precious clutch of eggs. Shifting restlessly, wings fluttering in barely contained agitation, the females rose and crept closer, surrounding Aurican and the nest in a ring of metallic scales and intensely staring eyes.

Kenta curled protectively around one side of the nest, and Oro framed her silver sister on the other side. Aurican nodded at each of them, then turned his attention to the precious orbs protected within the sheltered confines. Carefully curling his tail behind him, he sat with precise dignity. Only then did he arc his long neck and lift his head to stare at the clutch of metallic spheres, his heart swelling with a sense of profound wonder.

The pressure within him grew stronger, and Aurican clearly understood what would happen next, yet this understanding did nothing to cool his wonder. The golden jaws spread wide, and Aurican breathed softly, sharing the essence of magic, the power that was a part of every dragon's being but that, in Aurican, had been expanded and amplified by the effect of the shards of the three moons of magic.

A glowing mist floated forth, coalescing in the air, seething and roiling with colors that varied from black to silver to red. The gases swirled more rapidly, spiraling about the nest, slowly settling downward, touching the surfaces of the eggs, stroking the metal shells with ethereal fingers. The vapor sparkled with a glimmering wetness, slowly vanishing, as if absorbed by the pulsing, living treasures.

For a long time, the glow remained, shifting from one egg to another, sometimes bright and focused, other times diffused, but always possessing a vibrant and inherent brilliance that would have shamed any light born of flame or sun. The brightness danced and swayed, cavorting back and forth like a living thing, and when the brilliance faded, it left a lingering aura within the eggs that was perfectly clear to Aurican and the female dragons. The tiny serpents sheltered within those eggs had been blessed by the essence of magic. The enchantment contained in the bodies of the three gods was bestowed upon the young dragons in the breath of their golden patriarch. It settled on the eggs, infusing the shells and the wyrmlings, enchanting them with a power that had been absent for millennia.

Time, in seasons and then in years, passed while Aurican and the females waited with the serene patience of their kind. Watching and expectant, the great serpents held their attention upon the nest. Beyond the grotto, winters and springs and summers cycled through the High Kharolis in succession, a pattern mounting into the dozens, then the scores.

Still the eggs glowed, and gradually the brightness increased until the entire grotto was illuminated as under a noonday sun. Very slowly and gradually, several of the eggs began to pulse and shimmer. A silver surface throbbed, and a golden membrane shimmered under the internal pressure of a sharp beak.

Ultimately the two eggs ruptured, tiny metal newtlings crawling forth. Shaking away the muck of the eggs, clawing each other roughly aside, the dragons struggled toward the edge of the nest. Another egg, a brass, twitched and thrashed, and then several copper spheres began to show signs of movement.

And then they were coming from everywhere. Enchanted by the breath of Aurican, surrounded by the aura of magic, the next generation of metal dragons poked and pushed their way into the world.

PART II

Chapter 16
Crematia's Lair

circa 3000 PC

The cavern of fire lay deep in the heart of the mountain, beneath an active volcano, with plunging roots descending into a tangled network of seething lava, searing gases, and barren, scorched rock. A vast lake of fire bubbled and surged here, waves of liquid lava rumbling and tossing in the grip of an eternal gale, propelled by the regular convulsions of heaving bedrock. From many places across the expanse of molten rock, black pillars of stone rose to merge with a lofty ceiling. Sheer rock walls, melted smooth by eons of infernal heat, surrounded the expanse, broken only by an occasional ledge or outcrop.

A layer of soot darkened the vast ceiling. Many crevasses and gaps pocked that irregular face of cracked stone, giving vent to the buildup of heat and pressure. Far above, invisible from the huge subterranean chamber, geysers of gas, flame, and ash scarred the landscape in the rugged heart of the Khalkists.

Yet those external signs had no significance to the great crimson being who coiled, torpid, deep within the hellish cavern. Here Crematia had come to recoup, to heal and to hide in complete safety. She knew that not even Aurican could follow her into this searing environment, and any lesser flesh, such as cloaked man or elf or ogre, would blister away within moments of arrival.

The red dragon was a tangled, snaky coil gathered along a narrow ledge above the lake of lava. Crematia's back and wings rested against the cliff wall, and the double lids remained closed over her eyes. The long tail curled back over her feet to end just before her wide nostrils. Those twin apertures flared slightly in a gradual cadence, the only clear proof that the mighty creature still lived.

Soot and ash had settled over the serpentine shape over the course of a long hibernation. The stuff was a sticky goo that gummed Crematia's eyelids and encumbered her wings. Yet even that murk couldn't conceal the vibrant crimson of the dragon's scales or the blood-red flaps of her massive, folded wings.

She slept as she had slumbered for hundreds of years. Perhaps it was the lethal heat that drove her into this lethargy, but more likely her evil spirit needed time to restore itself following the wretched conclusion of her initial campaign. While she slumbered, her body healed the wounds inflicted by the mighty gold dragon, and even at her ancient age, she continued to grow.

She knew that the other chromatic dragons were gone from Krynn, their souls swallowed by the gems of life-trapping. Certainly Crematia had vivid dreams while she lay all-unknowing, and there is no doubt but that in those dreams she saw, and feared, a gleaming serpent of gold. Her enemy spewed breath as fiery as her own, attacking with power and skill—the deadliest foe she had ever known. She recalled her queen's command . . . find her strongest enemy and kill him.

And Crematia knew she had failed.

Frequently the red body quivered in a sense of betrayal, an outrage at the fact that she had found such potent magic in the hands of her enemies. Sorcery was to have been *her* domain; the queen herself had promised this. And though Crematia had seen the three moons and knew that the gods who had given magic to the dragons of metal had been punished, the knowledge did nothing to soothe her hatred—or her desire for vengeance.

But when finally the scarlet serpent stirred, it was not in response to any dream. Though no sound could penetrate to the depths of her fiery lair, there came a deep and inaudible message, a summons on a purely magical level. She lifted her head slowly, blinking a film of dust and soot from her eyes. When she could see, the hot illumination of the cavern reminded her instantly of where she was.

Her first thought was of Aurican, and with that memory came a renewed pumping of her heart, a taut eagerness stiffening her body and her wings. These recollections came with a full measure of hatred, and when she was fueled by hatred, Crematia came truly, completely alive.

The red dragon's tail uncurled with a whiplike crack, lashing back and forth as she rose to stand, stiff-legged, at the brink of the ledge. A reflexive pounce hurled her into the air, wings spread wide to catch the updrafts raging from the lava lake below. These rising currents lifted her as she glided effortlessly around the vast chamber, and without stroking her wings, she was soon carried near to the ceiling. She veered easily between down-jutting spikes of rock, relishing the vibrant energy of returning vitality.

She banked and dived, delighting in the dizzying speed, the onrush of molten rock as she plunged toward the crimson liquid. Bubbles expanded and burst in the thick surface, and the serpent relished the spattering of lava as droplets flew into the air. At the last moment, she pulled out of her dive, skimming low over the roiling lake, arching her back to rise toward the ceiling again.

Once more she rode the fast-rising updrafts, but this

time she helped herself as well, climbing with powerful strokes, angling toward a black slit in the ceiling of the cavern. She knew that, once within the chimney, she wouldn't have the space to turn around, so she drove herself with increasing urgency, making an arrow of her body—an arrow with large, very powerful wings.

Then the stone walls were close beside her, the rush of venting air roaring in her ears, bearing her higher and higher. Still she flew, straining for altitude, reaching for greater lift and pushing down with relentless strength. Her momentum slowed, the walls of the shaft visible now as more than a blurred backdrop, but she also saw a gap overhead, sensed that the darkness churning beyond was the ash-laden sky of the Khalkists.

Belatedly Crematia thought of magic—she could easily levitate out of this deep lair—but she cast aside the notion in the instant it arose. She would do this with her strength, and with her hatred. Again she thought of Aurican, imagining the gold dragon winging through the mountainous skies beyond, relishing the picture of his surprise when his crimson nemesis suddenly appeared. Her wings pulsed, driving through the air, and she exploded upward with renewed speed.

Abruptly the chimney walls gave way to a breathtaking expanse of air—she was *free* again, soaring into the skies over Krynn. Banking, sideslipping away from the venting gases, she plunged crazily along the steeply descending slope of the volcano that had sheltered her for so long. Darklady Mountain was a massive peak, and she couldn't help but see her queen's majesty reflected in the vast conical summit. She shrieked a cry of fierce exultation, skimming through a pass between the great mountain and a lesser neighbor, rocketing into the chilly air of an eternally shadowed gorge.

In the depths, she flew above a roiling river, watching the brown waters churn into whitecaps, thunder through rapids, steadily erode a deeper and deeper channel. Again she roared, the sound of her voice forceful enough to break rocks loose from the overhanging cliffs, bringing miniature landslides cascading into the torrent.

Upward she flew again, working hard now, relishing her own labors as she cut from realm of spray and shadow into the gusty heights. Veering back and forth like a wyrmling, she dodged through the smoke and ash that streamed from the smoldering summits in long plumes. A hundred great mountains were visible from this high vantage, but all the peaks except Darklady herself were far below. She banked regally, gliding with the serene arrogance of one who is mistress of everything in her sight.

A swift reconnaissance showed her a deep valley where several caves lined the walls. Tiny beings scuttled between these caves or worked their way up and down the steep trails leading to the stream at the foot of the plunging mountainsides. Crematia wheeled into the murk of the clouds, unseen from the ground, content for now to know that ogres still dwelt in these mountains. She would make herself known to them soon enough, but first she had an even more urgent task.

Flying above a treeless but well-watered swale, she observed several spots of whiteness on the green grass of the high tundra. She swept closer with silent, deliberate speed, and before the mountain sheep knew they were under attack, she had crushed a plump ewe to the soft ground. The blood was sweet on her tongue, the scent intoxicating in her nostrils, and she tore off the head of her prey, swallowing the morsel in one convulsive gulp. The rest of the mutton was fresh and warm in her claws, but she would not eat further at the moment.

Instead, she clutched the carcass and took to the air again, winging with renewed purpose, a crimson arrow flying straight toward a specific destination. Crematia curved from her path only when a looming crag rose high enough to block her flight, but after each digression, she returned to the course she marked from ancient memory, reacquainting herself with the highest reaches of the Khalkists. Flying toward another great volcano, one almost massive enough to vie with Darklady for mastery of the range, she set her sights upon the lofty summit. In fact, her target was an even more specific location, a specific spot on the high cliff. Closer now, she banked slightly, making a direct line toward the magically enchanted place on the mountainside.

She saw with satisfaction that her concealment spell remained in effect, masking the ledge as a patch of inaccessible cliff. Landing there, she found the sturdy barrier of her wall of stone spell similarly undisturbed. Though hundreds of winters had passed since her last visit, she was not surprised that her arcane protections remained unaltered. For the first time in centuries, she called up the magic to negate that spell, and the surface of stone melted smoothly away in the breath of her dispelling, revealing the mouth of her secret cave.

Within, Crematia crept through the vast treasure chamber to the precious skull basket that was her nest. Trembling with anxiety, knowing that the future of her kind depended upon what she found, she looked over the brink of the bony container . . . and expelled a flicker of tender flame in an outburst of relief.

The clutch of crimson eggs lay perfect and unspoiled within, except for an irregular pulsing she detected in one, the largest of the orbs. Before her eyes, a slit appeared in that shell, a tiny beak pressing outward, tearing down. Frantic claws emerged, tugging, trying to widen the gap— until the little wyrmling fell back, exhausted.

For several heartbeats, Crematia watched the egg. Finally she ripped into the carcass of the sheep, raising a piece of meat over the nest. With a deliberate squeeze, she let a trickle of fresh blood splash onto the egg, aiming carefully so that the stream of red liquid spilled into the tear in the shell of the first hatchling. Immediately that leathery orb throbbed and pulsed, and then those claws were there again, tearing and slashing at the narrow gap. The little beak thrust outward, and Crematia dribbled more sweet blood, driving the wyrmling into a frenzy. Another inch of eggshell tore, and now two forefeet pushed outward, pulling, making room for the sharp-beaked head on its long, skinny neck.

Finally, with a heaving thrust of awkward rear legs, the little creature pushed itself free of the restraining shell. It stood, wobbly, flexing two mucus-coated wings, though one of the membranes remained creased and gooey, still bound from centuries of gestation. The red tail stood stiffly upright, and an instinctive growl rumbled from the scaly chest.

Crematia gobbled the rest of the mutton then, but only long enough to chew it thoroughly and to let the juices of her belly begin the process of digestion. Then, with a heave that rippled along the length of her supple, scarlet-scaled neck, she regurgitated the gory remains into the nest.

Immediately the sole wyrmling threw himself at the messy food, rending and growling with instinctive fury. Several other eggs now showed signs of movement, pulses and jabs as the blood-red spheres throbbed slightly, rocking from the labors of hatchlings trapped within. Soon another slit appeared, then another. Crematia saw more snouts and claws come into view, but she paid scant attention to these flailing efforts. Her attentions remained fixed upon the firstborn of the wyrmlings, which still gnawed ravenously on the gruesome mess of the ram's carcass.

"Enjoy your feast, my son." Crematia bent low over the savagely growling little dragon, puffing a wisp of flame around the scarlet shape. "Hear me, my proud wyrmling. Your name is Deathfyre, and you shall lead my serpents back to their mastery of Krynn."

The dragon paused in its feasting long enough to regard his mother with bright, hungry eyes. By the time the monstrous crimson matriarch had turned to the cave mouth, the wyrmling had already gone back to its feast.

Once back on the mountainside, Crematia restored her spells of protection, leaving the wall of stone as a physical barrier and the other illusion as full concealment for the secret niche. Only then did she launch herself into a sky that had been cloaked by the shadows of nightfall.

The red dragon flew with a different destination now, one that had been born in her dreams and set with the long centuries of hatred within her fiery cavern. Her targets were strangers, creatures she had never attacked before, but she felt no fear, only a growing onslaught of fresh, hot hatred. Her dreams had shown her that her newest victims possessed no magic—indeed, they abhorred sorcery in all its forms—so it was with sublime confidence that she sought out their lair.

A black mountain, long and slender, with a ridge crest like the edge of a serrated knife, rose into the darkness before her. She swept through the clouds, her dark-sensitive eyes staring along the slopes of the massif. Soon she saw it: a small crack, narrow and lightless, plunging into the depths of the world. Masking herself with a spell of invisibility, the red dragon flew low over the aperture.

Despite her distance from the source, she could sense the magical emanations rising from the opening, and she knew of the rare and enchanted treasures that lay within. Her inspection showed her other creatures—small, busy figures laboring at the mountain's foot, the quarry that had been shown to her in her dreams.

They were called dwarves, she knew, and they had come to the Khalkists during the time of her hibernation. Now they delved the stone, seeking to create great underground lairs, an entire city sculpted from the living bedrock of the mountain range. But Crematia knew there was another reason for their digging as well, and this was the key to the red dragon's hopes.

She settled downward beyond the gathering of dwarves. Despite the darkness, many of the little creatures labored in terraced fields, using massive horses to pull plows and till crops. Others worked with a clattering of picks and hammers on the construction of a great tower. Nearby, massive granite blocks were being dragged over smooth pathways by teams of horses and dwarves. On a stone-paved plaza nearby, another group, apparently novice warriors, worked under the tutelage of a sharp-tongued trainer, learning the use of hammer and shield in battle tactics.

It was before this latter group that Crematia appeared, negating her invisibility as she dropped to the ground. Rearing before the startled dwarves, she spread her jaws and belched out a great cloud of fire. Flames spurted and crackled across the training field, instantly incinerating those dwarves caught in the full blast, then spreading outward like a slick of oily liquid, surrounding, dragging down the hapless victims on the periphery of the gathering who had turned, far too slowly, in an attempt to run away.

The smoke cleared away to reveal dozens of charred, blackened bodies smoldering and sizzling in the wake of the inferno. Near the edge of the swath of darkness, a pathetic figure crawled, reaching with blackened, clawlike hands, then shuddering to the stillness of death. Only the soot and char moved, drifting away on the wind. Crematia turned toward the great doors of the tower, sensing that hundreds of pairs of eyes regarded her with a mixture of terror and awe.

"Here me, dwarven delvers! I am the angel of magic, and four of my eggs lurk in the bowels of your realms!"

The words echoed through the valley, rebounding from the surrounding heights as the tiny bearded figures quaked and trembled in awe.

"These are spheres of blue and black, of white and green. They belong to me, and they are death to any other who would steal them."

She snorted another cloud of flame, watched the soot scar the great doors before she continued. "You must find these orbs of magic, these baubles that are my eggs, and bring them forth. If you do not remove them from your mountain, the taint of my sorcery will spread inward to infest you all! And the fires of my breath shall be nothing compared to the awful plague wrought by my eggs!"

She heard a groan, as if from the mountain itself, and knew that her words created real horror in the dwarves, for they hated magic above all else.

"I shall return in one hundred sunrises," she declared with a growl. "Present these stones to me then, or face my wrath!"

Again she took wing, a scarlet killer whispering into the night, knowing that the dwarves would work hard to do her bidding.

Chapter 17
Lessons

circa 3000 PC

"And what is the effect of the teleport spell?" Aurican, in the guise he favored as the elven sage, scowled archly at the twisting silver form on the floor before him.

"I—I don't know, Master."

Callak was miserable, and certainly his mentor understood this—but, with equal certainty, the young silver dragon knew that misery was no excuse in his golden tutor's eyes. Indeed, sometimes it seemed to Callak that Aurican *liked* his wyrmling pupils to be miserable.

All of them except Auricus, that is, though even as he had the jealous thought, Callak felt a glimmer of guilt. In truth, his golden nestmate was more than a kin-dragon bonded by the linkage of a shared nest. He was his greatest friend, his best companion. Indeed, in the matter of magical tutoring, Aurican showed favoritism to his first-born son only because Auricus had so clearly earned it.

Already the young gold dragon was able to make himself invisible. He could create minor illusions that would amuse, frighten, or—most likely—irritate his numerous siblings. Arrogantly he levitated his prey, ignited fires in the grotto, disguised nuisances, like chips of ice, that he used to trip up his fellow nestmates. And his sense of magic detection was so well attuned that he was able to penetrate to the truth of just about every trick the other wyrmlings tried to play upon him.

Still, as the largest and most aggressive of the nestlings, Callak had been able to avoid the worst of Auricus's pranks. Indeed, with his size and quickness, there was no one who could best the silver wyrmling in any contest of physical skill, though his nestmates, and particularly copper Flash, never hesitated to try.

"If my question is too complicated, perhaps you would like me to write it out? On your snout, perhaps?" growled Aurican, the penetrating stare of his yellow eyes quickly bringing the young dragon's attention into focus.

"Teleportation!" he said brightly. "I—I think I remember. . . . It is the transportation of the caster from one point to another in the instant of casting!"

"Very good—though it is one thing to know the effect of a spell, and another, quite more involved, to be able to cast that same enchantment. The Platinum Father alone knows when the latter studies might open themselves to you."

"Aye, lord." Callak hung his head, with a sidelong glance to insure that none of the other nestlings mocked his discomfiture. But the dozens of wyrmlings—bronze, copper, brass, silver, and gold—sitting rigidly behind the silver made no gesture that could remotely be construed as rude. After all, even at the young age of three hundred winters, Callak was much larger than any of his fellow nestmates, a physical supremacy that now served to intimidate the wyrmlings from making any mocking or insulting remarks.

Yet it was far more than his size that accounted for Callak's aloof mastery—in matters nonmagical, at least—of the grotto. His eyes drifted to the nest and saw the curled ram's horn suspended there on its fine silver chain. Kenta had placed it there, and none of the wyrmlings could look at it without recalling the esteemed heritage of the silver dragons.

All the young dragons had been schooled on the tales of brave Darlantan, whose final sacrifice had brought victory to the metal dragons and their allies during the Dragon War. For one thing, the silver matriarch, Kenta, had insured that her mate's valor was known to all the hatchlings. Aurican himself often spoke of the mighty serpent, invariably in tones both impassioned and affectionate. With great ceremony, he explained the legacy of the ram's horn, told them that someday the greatest of the silver serpents would bear that artifact as proof of their sire's legacy and wisdom.

It was a collection of tales that never failed to move Darlantan's offspring, Callak and his proud brother Arjen, and his sisters Daria, Starr, and Splendor. Even tiny Agon, crippled and malformed since emerging from his silver egg, allowed his chest to puff out when the name of their heroic sire was invoked.

All knew, too, of Smelt and Burll and Blayze. The silvers were not the only wyrmlings who had lost their sire before hatching. But it was Callak who felt the greatest burden of that history. Natural master of all the lesser wyrms, he engaged in constant rivalry with Auricus, while at the same time striving to learn the lore of magic as taught by the wise elder.

Now, however, as Aurican lectured sternly, the wyrms of the brown metals were content to let the silver absorb the browbeating. Bronze Bolt and brass Dazzall carefully averted their eyes as Callak mutely looked for support.

Copper-scaled Tharn, meanwhile, merely smirked and flexed his wings, no doubt still seething because of a recent trick the silver male had played. Indeed, Callak couldn't suppress a smile as he remembered his deception. The copper had eagerly pounced upon an object that looked like the plump carcass of a newly slain deer, only to discover that the silver dragon had used a minor illusion to create that appearance over a muckhole of brackish water and quicksand. The prank had resulted in a week of careful watching, as Callak had spent each waking moment since in wary anticipation of Tharn's revenge.

"The teleport spell works like this!" declared Auricus, suddenly appearing in the midst of the gathered wyrmlings. The golden dragon was poised in the air a good high jump off the ground, and before he could start flying, he plunged to the floor, sending several of the coppers tumbling and scrambling to get out of his way.

"And it's a good thing you can teleport!" Callak jabbed with a delighted sneer. "That way you won't have to learn how to use your wings!"

"I can fly!" Auricus insisted, sitting up and flexing the shimmering flaps of brilliant gold. "It's just that it's not as much fun as magic."

Callak knew his kin-dragon spoke the truth—at least, the truth as it appeared from Auric's perception—but just the same, the whole notion seemed crazy to the young silver. After all, he had learned that flying was simply the best thing there could possibly be, and no mastery of magic would ever make him feel any different.

"I think that's enough of our lessons for now," declared the tutor, with a stern glare between Auricus and Callak. "I suggest you fly to the valley, perhaps paying visits to your mothers."

In the moment of the suggestion, the wyrmlings were off, flashes of metal gleaming down the corridor and into the cavern of the great lake. The race evolved as always, with Callak in the lead, head and neck arrow-straight, wings all but buzzing from the strain of his flight. The others trailed behind, darts of metal hurtling through the air. Wind whistled over their scales, and the darkness passed in a blur.

The flash of gold went by him so quickly that the silver dragon wobbled in the air, almost losing control. In disbelief, he strained even harder, but could only watch as the golden tail pulled away. Within moments, Auricus had disappeared into the distance.

By the time Callak had led the rest of the brood into the sunlight warming the Valley of Paladine, Auricus had assumed a position of casual ease on the lordly rock that dominated the valley floor. Licking traces of rabbit fur from his jowls, the golden dragon regarded his approaching nestmates with an affected air of great boredom.

"Whatever in Krynn is the reason for your delay?" he asked, golden eyebrows rising in a mask of perplexity.

"You've learned another spell, I see," replied Callak sourly, having figured out by now that his nestmate had employed some kind of enchantment that greatly increased his speed. "What do you call this one?"

"It's the haste spell—quite a simple casting, really. Would you like me to teach you?" Auricus asked, innocently lowering his translucent inner eyelids.

"No, I would not!" huffed the silver wyrmling, lashing his tail in frustration. "I'm still trying to learn what each spell is called, while it seems that you're casting them one right after the other."

Auricus frowned. "Well, sometimes I *have* to. It's the only way I have to keep you from beating me all the time. After all, you're faster and stronger, and you can fly for days at a time, while I need to land for rest after each sunset."

It intrigued Callak to think that his golden nestmate actually felt he was getting the poor end of the competition. After all, the gold's sire was their collective tutor, and Auricus's intelligence often made the rest of his nestmates feel slighted and inferior. Still, if even Auricus could feel like this, Callak decided that life, perhaps, was not so unfair after all.

As to the other males, Bolt and Tharn had already shown tendencies toward the solitary life that had occupied the later years of their fathers. Each had discovered his patriarch's secret hoard and returned with tales of mystery and wonder, aggressively guarding against any hint that would lead to the location of their ancestral treasures. Dazzall, in the meantime, had made many friends among the humans who populated Krynn in ever-increasing numbers.

With a flexing of his silver wings, Callak took to the air, at first skimming the soft grass that layered the Valley of Paladine. He flew in long, lazy circles, and over a leisurely afternoon, he spiraled far above the valley floor. Finally he approached the ridges themselves, the precipitous heights that encircled the vale.

First he passed the reclining form of Oro, greeting Auricus's mother with a respectful nod. The mighty gold was stretched along a high crest so that, with just a turn of her head, she could see a hundred miles to the west or the east. She blinked lazily as the silver wyrmling flew onward.

Finally Callak saw another silver form, the sinuous shape coiled around the summit of a steep, conical peak. He came to rest beside Kenta, curling under her wing, nudging her flank with his snout. She was serenely placid, barely aware of him as he tried to recline with the regal grandeur of an adult dragon.

But soon Callak grew restless again. Then, inevitably, his narrow wings swept outward to carry the silver serpent over his steadily expanding world.

Chapter 18
Intransigents

circa 3000 PC

Crematia spread her wings wide, gliding through the cool night air, drawing close to the black pyramidal mountain she had visited a hundred days before. She broke from the overcast and screeched a warning of her presence, enjoying the panicked maneuvers of the dwarves as they scattered from their fields and roads, scrambling chaotically in a hundred different directions. Like ants revealed beneath an overturned log, they darted about in a vast and instantaneous reaction to her presence, a reaction that pleasantly reassured Crematia of her own might.

Yet by the time the red dragon's echo had returned from the opposite elevation, every one of the dwarves on the ground had disappeared. Crematia blinked, wondering if her aging eyes were suffering from the effects of minimal light. But no—she could see the roads and trails, even spot the picks and shovels dropped by the scattering work crews as they had funneled into an apparently infinite number of holes, niches, hatches, and caves. Her first impression had been right: The dwarves had all vanished.

She settled to the ground on the still-scorched paving stones of the plaza, the same place where she had earlier demonstrated her infernal might. Now she raised her head to the massive stone doors leading into the mountainside, allowing a deep growl to rumble from her belly. She sensed the reverberations of the sound vibrating the great gates, and she trusted that the import of her message was reaching the dwarves, who were no doubt cowering within. Still, it frustrated her that she was unable to attack, even to see, the wretched denizens huddling within their stone shelter.

Patiently Crematia waited, and while she did, she studied this valley of dwarves. The tower on the mountainside was a secure fortification. She saw that steel shutters had been drawn across the windows and doors, a barrier that might possibly prove resistant even against the killing heat of her breath. And the great gates of the dwarven city were set deep into an alcove in the wall of the mountainside, anchored by huge stone hinges and reinforced by straps of heavy steel. She could see slits and gaps above the entryway, and imagined that the resourceful creatures would no doubt find ways to attack her through these openings if she made an attempt to smash the sturdy gates.

Still, the dwarves were vulnerable otherwise. Their terraced hills were lush with crops approaching harvest, a harvest that Crematia could eliminate in a few hours. And she took it for certainty that the bearded creatures would not be content to dwell within their mountain for a long time without glimpse of the sun. After all, they obviously had labored with nearly inexhaustible energy on a variety of major projects throughout the valley of their realm.

So she was not surprised when a tiny aperture opened in the base of the great gate and a figure came out. The tiny fellow was dressed in a blue robe that trailed along the ground far behind him. His chest was as broad as a barrel, his arms strapping, terminating in powerful, callused hands. Though he wore no weapon at his waist, he bore a satchel of leather over his shoulder.

Naturally Crematia could have slain the dwarf with a slap of her forepaw or a minor sneeze of her breath. But she was impressed by the fellow's courage and curious about his intentions. She held her violent impulses in abeyance, at least long enough to hear what the dwarf had to say.

"Who are you?" she demanded, punctuating her question with a puff of black smoke.

"I am Bayrn Takwing, a chieftain of this delving," the dwarf replied, with a belligerent glare, as if he would have welcomed the dragon's precipitous attack—a notion that lingered temptingly in Crematia's mind.

"Have you obeyed me?" she demanded, once again sparing the insolent dwarf with a supreme effort of will.

"We have here one of your 'eggs,' Mighty Killer," declared the dwarf, glaring upward with an audacious display of ill temper.

"Then you have failed me, for I bade you bring four of them," growled Crematia, rearing back in unconscious surprise at the dwarf's manner. "Know that I am not one who is tolerant of failure."

Fire swelled in her belly, barely restrained from lethal release. Smoke puffed from her nostrils, but something in the dwarf's manner held her in check.

The fellow's beard bristled, and he slung the satchel forward, opening its mouth to allow a perfect sphere of white to tumble out. The stone sat still on the stony road, but seemed nevertheless to move with some sense of inner vitality. It pulsed and radiated, brightening the surrounding ground with a wash of icy light.

"And you have lied to us, for this is no more an egg than you are a horse. It is a gemstone, and you should be glad that it's magic. Because of that, we're content to be rid of it, and you are welcome to take it away from here. Otherwise, understand that you'd not be seeing its likeness again."

"Bold words for a dwarf whose city cowers behind

him." Crematia was amused more than angered. Indeed, she was almost grateful, as she felt her hopes flaring at the sight of the dragongem. "Know that my displeasure has wasted greater realms than yours."

"Bah! We're safe enough." The burly dwarf crossed his arms over his chest and made a great production of turning to the side and spitting casually into the dust.

Crematia reared back, seized by a deep rage. It had been many hundreds of years since anyone had dared to speak to her like this. "Do not expect mercy from me, foolish dwarf. Mercy is weakness, and weakness is death!"

"Oh, sure, you could kill me now, maybe even break down a few of our doors. But then you'd never see another one of these stones."

"So you admit the others are within your delvings? You dare to hold them from me?"

"They're down there somewhere. Our priests have felt the magic, and they don't like it much, neither. But there's no sayin' when we'll get down to the stones themselves."

"I shall return in another one hundred sunrises, and you will produce all of the stones. Otherwise your city will die."

"No. You'll take this white stone and be gone for now. You should come back in one hundred years. By then, we might have one of these stones for you."

"One hundred winters?" demanded Crematia, aghast. Her belly swelled, fire surging anew, pressure rising from the involuntary fuel of her rage.

"And if you damage our crops, or indeed even *try* to damage our city—not that you'd have any luck—then you can consider those stones gone forever."

Crematia clenched her jaws and snatched up the whitestone, forcibly resisting the temptation to sear this insolent dwarf into charcoal. He would have the other stones, she knew, and she could force herself to wait for a while before they became hers.

So instead of destroying this place, she took to the air, already resolved to wait the hundred winters—what was that time, really?—before she returned.

Chapter 19
Deathfyre

2698 PC

A red dragon male was the first to hatch, and he proved to be the largest and most powerful of Crematia's large brood. He grew with a quickness that astonished and delighted the venerable matriarch, displaying cruelty and malice, bullying his nestmates, and immediately asserting his superiority. Even as a wyrmling, he ate voraciously, once killing and devouring one of his weaker siblings when his mother had been slow to bring fresh food.

By the time he had entered his second century, Deathfyre was flying as swiftly as an eagle and bringing down prey that varied in size from young dwarves to the burly, spiral-horned rams that dared to graze in the heights of the Khalkists. He took a keen delight in killing and invariably tortured even the meanest of his prey with a deft cruelty that fascinated and impressed his savage matriarch.

By his two hundredth winter, Deathfyre had flown far beyond his mother's lofty vales. Sometimes he returned with meat—even humans and elves fell to his cruel claws—and other times with rare treasures, or news. He mastered a tribe of minotaurs and brought new bands of ogres into the fold of Crematia's gathering horde.

And in his third century, he returned with the bakali.

The craven lizard men swarmed in some stagnant fen in the lowlands. Deathfyre had demonstrated his power by slaying several of the tribe's elite warriors, finally blinding the chieftain as a reminder of his superiority. Then he had ordered the bakali to march into the mountains, to gather beneath the red dragon lair on Darklady Mountain. Bearing their maimed and eyeless ruler—a great, spike-spined lizard with strapping shoulders and brawny arms—on a feather-draped litter, a file of savage warriors encamped around the steaming springs of the Khalkist valleys.

Crematia herself remained close to the lair, for her other hatchlings were not so strong nor so capable as Deathfyre. She tutored and trained them, punished every weakness or tendency toward mercy, rewarding cruelty, always demonstrating the efficacy of merciless violence.

Every hundred winters, she journeyed to the dwarven home, and twice since her first successful visit had she come away with a dragongem. Now, corresponding to the arrival of Deathfyre's legion and the growing maturity of her other offspring, who numbered thirteen in all, the interval had passed again, and it was time to collect the last gem, the blackstone.

Her proud son accompanied her, the two dragons winging eastward through smoking, ash-laden skies. Deathfyre was already two-thirds of Crematia's own serpentine length, with the black mane of an adult bristled in a steadily thickening thatch around his cruel jowls. He was a strong, swift flyer, and the scarlet matriarch shivered with a thrill of pride. She admired his sleek frame, the sinewy muscle rippling beneath the crimson perfection of his scales.

Arriving over the dwarven vale, Crematia wasn't surprised to see that all the dwarves had once again taken shelter within their underground lair by the time she and Deathfyre settled toward the ground. She bade her son to remain watchfully back from the gates, then stalked forward with her crimson head held high. The great red dragon had already resolved upon at least one thing: After the dwarven king gave her this last stone, he would have no more hold over her, and thus she would slay him as just punishment for his past insolences.

Unfortunately the wretched delvers had apparently anticipated her intent, for this time, no berobed dwarf emerged to present her with the gem. Instead, a small hatch in the base of the gate swung open, and a sphere of perfect blackness rolled forth. Momentum carried the stone to Crematia's feet, and by the time she looked back at the gate, the hatch had slammed shut and she heard the sound of metal bolts being drawn.

She opened her mouth and belched a searing cloud of fire against the gates, taking minimal satisfaction from the slick surface of melted stone, the scorched blackness that now ringed the city's entryway. Changing shape with a twinkling of magic, Crematia stood in the flesh of a tall human woman, her body a shape of slender curves and flowing red hair clad in a gown of shimmering green. She reached down and picked up the blackstone, then turned back to Deathfyre.

A volley of arrows arced from small gaps in the mountainside, but the few that reached her merely bounced from the green silk and fell to the ground. She laughed, the sound a gaily trilling chime, as she strolled casually up to the red serpent, reaching upward to caress her scion's shoulder with a slender human hand.

"They seek to spite me," Crematia declared in amusement, turning to regard the concealed dwarves with a coy, even playful, smile. She gestured with her other hand, to the lush fields of grain and fruit, terraced fields covering the gently sloping mountainside in every direction.

"I told them to expect no mercy from me. But perhaps they did not believe me. Now, my bold son, show them that we know the meaning of spite as well as they."

For a long day, the young red dragon frolicked through the croplands, scorching with his breath, rending with talons, crushing with the wallowing weight of his great body. Crematia sat with the relaxed dignity of an amused lady, reclining in the shade of a great oak tree, occasionally tasting of some melon or grape brought to her by Deathfyre.

Once she rose and strolled tauntingly before the great gates. She laughed as arrows arced toward her, skipped nimbly out of the path of some of the missiles. Others she transformed into harmless flowers with a flick of her hand, or dissolved into sparks with a snap of her fingers. Always she taunted the dwarves, waving at them, summoning them to come out in a cooing, playful voice.

Only when the harvest had been thoroughly mauled, grain burned or crushed into mud, fruit squashed and broken, trees of ancient orchards snapped into kindling, did Crematia shift back to the body of her serpentine self. In the waning light of dusk, the two dragons took wing, coursing through the skies, vanishing into the shadowy gorges of the high Khalkists. Flying under moonlit skies, they soon left the ruined dwarven realm far behind. As she flew, the ancient female relished the memory of thousands of dwarven eyes, glaring with impotent hatred at the leisurely departure of their omnipotent enemies.

Returning to the valley of fire that half encircled Darklady Mountain, the two dragons found their legions of bakali and ogres eagerly waiting. For many seasons, the monstrous warriors had been gathering here, training and learning and worshiping their mighty crimson mistress. Now that the dragons had flown to retrieve the last dragongem, the troops knew that at last the period of waiting was almost done. Masses of troops thronged across the ground, shouting accolades and hoarse cheers, whooping in raw delight as the pair of serpents flew overhead, bellowing and snorting flames.

The mighty reds came to rest on a flat shelf of rock at the foot of the lofty peak, a natural stage where they could rise above their assembled horde. The promontory and its two illustrious occupants were visible from across the entire floor of the valley. Deathfyre bristled in stiff-winged pride while Crematia lifted her supple neck, raising her head far above the gathered horde.

This was an area naturally lighted by the fiery rivers of lava flowing down the Darklady's slopes and from gouts of flame and bubbling rock that frequently erupted from fissures on the valley floor. Yet now the ogres augmented the illumination, igniting great bonfires before the raised platform so that the two mighty red dragons were brightly lit in angry, surging flames, their crimson bodies slick and alight in the brightness cast by the massive pyres.

Crematia reared still higher, clutching the blackstone in her claws and raising it above the lustily cheering mass. Her twelve lesser offspring brayed and roared, adding their accolades to the wave of noise.

Finally four bakali shamans who had demonstrated remarkable talent—and great loyalty to Deathfyre—came forward. The lizard men priests, like the rest of their kind, were lean and supple creatures, marked by protruding muzzles and low, sloping brows. Forked tongues darted from fanged jaws, while heavy tails stretched behind, lending balance to the strangely dainty walk of the monstrous warriors.

Each of three bakali shamans carried a single dragongem of green, white, or blue. The fourth knelt before the still-upraised Crematia, tilting its snakelike head, leaning far backward to balance on its outflung tail.

The dragon abruptly dropped to her belly, crimson scales stopping a hairsbreadth short of smashing the shaman to the ground, a blow that would have certainly broken the wretched creature's spine. Yet the bakali remained faithfully rigid, singing the praises of the mighty red wyrm. Pleased, Crematia gave it the blackstone.

All four of the stone-bearing bakali marched between Crematia and Deathfyre, then started up the steep slope of the mountainside. Each clutched its stone in one taloned foreclaw, with the other hand pulling upward to aid in the long ascent. Crematia watched for a long time, relishing the awestruck silence of the legions gathered behind her as they, too, observed the four shamans gradually disappear into the darkness and haze of the heights.

"Fly with me, my children!" cried Crematia, taking to the air with a downblast of wind. She soared low over a sea of bakali and ogres and was lifted, borne aloft by the force of their relentless cheers. Behind the crimson matriarch, Deathfyre and the other red dragons took wing, following their mistress in an awe-inspiring flight over the massed army. Red wings filled the sky, like deadly awnings spreading above the rumbling horde.

Gradually the serpents climbed until they, like the lizard men shamans, had disappeared from the view of the legions on the ground. Even so, as she looked down, Crematia could still see the raging bonfires and the jagged streaks of the lava rivers crossing the valley floor. But now her eyes turned skyward as she strove steadily through the night. The air was warm, tainted with sulfurous gases from the bowels of Krynn. Often she tasted the metallic taint of copper or iron, solids rendered into vapor by the heat within Darklady Mountain.

Finally the lofty summit was there, emerging from the murk, the rim of the crater a sharp-edged circle in the sky. Crematia and her young came to rest along the crest, facing the plunging shaft, feeling the infernal heat baking against their faces and breasts. The giant matriarch loomed over them all, with mighty Deathfyre rising large to one side. The lesser serpents of her wyrmlings perched, still and patient, to either side along the rim of the Darklady's crater.

For a long time, Crematia made them wait, knowing the bakali would climb the mountain slowly. She watched carefully, and when Hodyo showed signs of slinking back from the inferno, she seared the end of his tail with a blast of breath, then sneered as he nearly toppled forward in a panicked effort to escape.

"Show strength, my dragons! Welcome the Darklady's heat! Fire is your spirit and your soul, and it shall not harm you—it sustains and renews. Remember, *never* show weakness!"

Finally she discerned a glowing brightness down the mountainside, soon recognizing the illumination of the whitestone. The green and blue were next to appear, and she had located all four of the bakali shamans before she found the sleek, inky perfection of the blackstone.

Though the lizard men had labored throughout the long night on an ascent that few, if any, landbound creatures had ever attempted before, they showed only eagerness as they reached the rim of the mighty crater, kneeling on the stony crest, two to each side of Crematia. The mountain rumbled, waves of heat blasting upward, billowing clouds of smoke and ash roiling in the bottomless depths.

"Splendid work, my shamans. . . . You have earned our queen's pleasure."

The bakali shivered, their faces pressed abjectly to the ground. Each clutched its dragongem tightly to its scaly chest as the grumbling in the mountain grew to a palpable tremor. Fire roared, and ash swirled through the air like stinging needles of hot sleet.

"See, my children . . . she rises to show her magnificence."

Now the bakali and the dragons looked toward the massive crater, where the billowing clouds of smoke had evolved into five distinct pillars. The central, and mightiest, was lit by an internal stream of flaming gas, glowing brightly with a crimson light. The columns of smoke on either side writhed and twisted like lesser snakes, alternately pale or dark, while the red central pillar rose even higher, spuming flame and ash into the sky.

"Now, shamans—*jump!*" Crematia barked her command, head rearing back to insure that each of the bakali obeyed.

Her precaution was unnecessary. At the command, each of the shamans leapt exultantly from the rim of the crater, clutching its dragongem worshipfully as it vanished into the gulf of fire and smoke. Immediately the mountain roared, waves of heat and light bursting into the sky.

"Now fly, my children! Take wing with me!" The mighty red took to the air, the thirteen younger serpents following. They circled the lofty summit, fighting their way through churning clouds of roiling air, watching as more and more convulsions rocked the Darklady.

"Deathfyre, fly to the valley. Lead the army away to the south," commanded Crematia as sections of rock slipped away from the summit, tumbling in landslides toward the lowlands masked by smoke and dust.

The red male swept away, and the matriarch turned her attention back to the mountain, secure in the knowledge that her scion would lead the army to safety. For a long time, the great summit rumbled and shook, firing clouds of debris into the air. Even as sunrise illuminated the sky, this remained a region of perpetual shadows. The red dragons circled through the murk, wyrmlings flying behind their mighty matriarch, glimpsing the shuddering, conical peak through gaps in the swirling smoke.

Abruptly the top of the mountain exploded, the force of the blast sending even mighty Crematia reeling through the skies. She plunged downward and away, pulling herself out of the dive and guiding her nestlings—except Deathfyre—back toward the shattered summit.

But now there was more than smoke and ash roiling through the air. Crematia's heart pounded at a glimpse of blue wing slicing through the edge of the cloud, at a green tail that flickered into sight, then vanished. Then scaly shapes passed to all sides, giant serpentine bodies borne by leathery wings.

At last the slopes of Darklady Mountain tumbled away, shattered by convulsive explosions, wracked by mighty destruction. Lava surged into the air, gouts of liquid rock sizzling through the clouds, splattering against the heaving ground below. Rocks as big as Crematia's wing floated past, tossed like marbles by the violent pressure of the dying mountain.

The pressure of noise shook the air with thunderous force, but the crimson matriarch exulted in the violence, knowing that the convulsions were nothing less than the power of the Dark Queen. More of the summit was blasted into dust, and she brayed loudly, a shrill cry of delight.

One whole shoulder of the massive peak sloughed away, thundering downward in an avalanche of dust, gravel, and flaming debris. More slopes fell, some collapsing inward, others falling out, sliding with glacial power into the smoldering, trembling valleys below. Colors flashed within that roiling murk, here a patch of white and blue, there a blur of green, a smudge of perfect black.

Then they were all around, filling the skies, crying deep challenges and exulting in freedom after long centuries of confinement. The chromatic dragons of the Dark Queen, released from their prisons in the dragongems, swept away from the mountain that had now collapsed into three lesser, but still mighty, summits. The wyrms of Takhisis bellowed their joy at their freedom and roared with rage at the thought of vengeance that had been too long denied.

"Fly, my kin-dragons!" cried Crematia. "Take wing with me to the south, where our armies march—and where we shall take our revenge against the elven lands!"

Chapter 20
Memories of Light and Darkness

2693 PC

Aurican drifted in a pleasant haze of memory and reflection. Sprawled across the great mountain ridge of the High Kharolis, he knew as he looked down that he was watching Callak and Auricus chase each other's tails through a maze of valleys and gorges. Specks of bright metal darted, looped, and raced in the full enthusiasm of youthful flight, their gold and silver wings a blur of shimmering reflection.

Yet a part of the mighty gold's mind could almost believe that it was himself and Darlantan down there, perfecting those maneuvers for the first time, chasing and wrestling, hunting together or tormenting their kindragons of the brown metals. When he drifted into these reflections, he felt like a young wyrmling again, ready to flex his wings and buzz like a hummingbird through the vast realm of the sky.

But when he shifted and stretched, he was vividly reminded that he was an ancient dragon now. His wings crackled, comfortable in repose but reluctant to respond to the commands of elderly muscles. His neck and back were sore, and he wanted nothing more than to absorb the warmth of the sun soaking through the shiny metallic scales. Was it his imagination, or did his spine actually creak as he raised his head to look off the other side of the mountain? He was slightly restless—worried, perhaps, about some unnamed threat to the nestlings, but not so agitated that he felt it necessary to move.

Though, in fact, these youngsters gave him many things to worry about. Callak and Aurican, of course, were strong and proud, and would someday be worthy heirs to the silver and gold clans. Auri learned magic with real talent, and his silver nestmate showed promise in the arcane arts as well. But they were impetuous and reckless in ways that disturbed the venerable gold, as if they didn't acknowledge the possibility of danger, the threat implicit in the Queen of Darkness and her currently dormant dragons. Naturally Aurican tended to forget that he and Darlantan had lived for thousands of years before becoming aware of that menace.

And the males of the brown metals were even more worrisome. Flash was every bit as selfish and hot-tempered as his sire, Blayze, had been. The younger copper showed little patience for the concerns of his nestmates and had been quick to bite—or even to spit a nasty stream of acid—when his young kin-dragons displeased him. From an early age, he had shown a tendency to wander off, to hunt and dwell by himself. Flash had located his sire's lair, Auri knew, but he feared that the vast treasures concealed therein had spoiled the young copper, making him even more suspicious and resentful of the others.

And Brunt, the offspring of strong, thick-skulled Burll,

had sadly shown little of his sire's placid nature. Like Flash, Brunt had found a separate lair, and he spent much of his time hoarding treasures and avoiding the company of the rest of Paladine's brood. Whether it was the same place Burll had used Aurican didn't know, but the young bronze always returned from his journeys with the scents of brine and fish that had distinguished the elder bronze.

At least Dazzall had carried on the sociable legacy of Smelt. He was already well known among humans and had proven to be a peacemaker among the nestmates. Although he was a passable student of magic, he lacked the concentration of Auricus or the native intelligence of Callak.

Aurican's attention drifted as his head swept through a serene, regal inspection. He saw the two lakes, where Oro and Kenta had gone to their final rest, side by side, their waters now emerald green following the spring melt, and sighed with loneliness. He was acutely aware that he was the last of his nestmates, the only one of Patersmith's pupils still alive.

It had been within the last fifty winters that the two elder females had finally weakened. Kenta had gone first, crawling from the lair into the mountains, laying herself on the ice so that she had been entombed by the thawing of spring. Then, the next year, golden Oro had followed her silver cousin into the realm beyond life.

Aurican thought about a thing he had learned from elves and humans, the strange concept of love. He had tried to understand this intangible bond. He knew that it connected mates to each other, and even stretched between siblings, parents and children, and close friends. Silvanos had once confessed that, despite their differences, he and Kagonos had shared a bond that could only be described as love. Yet when Auri looked at the place where Oro was buried or thought of the death of Darlantan, he wondered how the two-legs could bear it— to have such a bond torn apart in the short life span that was, at least in the case of humans, inevitable. While the ancient gold was saddened by the loss of his mate and his kin-dragon, their deaths had left him lonely, but not grief-stricken. Indeed, the very thought of an end to life made him more curious than anything else.

Aurican was not at all certain about whatever awaited one when mortal flesh at last yielded to death. To be sure, he had spent time—centuries, in fact—on the study of this particular question. Yet the mystery had eluded even the most penetrating of his meditations, researches, and self-posed queries. Even his dreams, normally a potent source of learning, had yielded little insight.

His musings, like so many of his reflections, made Aurican feel like a relic from an earlier era. Had he really ever been a wyrmling, sleek and supple like Auricus? Or were those memories merely dreams? For that matter, was there, in the present, a significant difference between a dream and a memory of the distant past?

This had been the question of philosophy that had occupied his thoughts for the last dozen or so winters, and he had yet to determine a truly satisfying answer. Naturally there were differences between dreams and memories, but were they *significant* when viewed from the portal of the present? With a pleasant drooping of his leathery lids, so that they half covered the still-clear orbs of his golden eyes, Aurican began to review the arguments in favor and opposed.

He thought in particular of Daria, the boldest of the female silver nestlings. She had always spoken of very vivid dreams, and several times Aurican had dreamed of Daria's destiny . . . a danger and a fate that would be revealed to her in a dream. He made a vow to speak to her of this, for he had the strong feeling that he himself would be dead before this destiny was made clear.

"Grandfather!"

A shout of forceful urgency brought his musings to an abrupt halt. Raising his head so quickly that a jolt of pain shot down to his shoulders, Aurican looked around for the source of the noise.

Little Agon was flying toward him, flapping his small wings with desperate urgency. "Grandfather Aurican!"

"Yes . . . what is it?" he asked as the silver wyrmling

came to rest on the mountainside slightly below the venerable gold. Agon was a likeable and enthusiastic wyrm, stunted in size since emerging from his egg, but popular among all of his kin-dragons. Much to Aurican's pleasure—and surprise—the runty silver had demonstrated almost as much magical aptitude as had golden Auricus.

"I heard something! It was loud, braying like a horn, and it seemed as if it were calling me. But I couldn't see anything! What was it?"

"Where did it come from?"

"Th-the east, I think. But I was flying with Dazzall, and he said he didn't hear anything."

Aurican's brow furrowed. He saw Dazzall as the brass dragon winged upward to join them. In moments he had landed, nodding his head in confirmation of Agon's words.

"A horn, you say? Like a trumpet?"

"Yes, Grandfather!" Agon said with a vigorous nod.

The gold dragon remembered the ram's horn, safely stored in the grotto, but he knew that another of the horns existed. That one was borne by the wild elves, and long ago Darlantan had told him its purpose: the Kagonesti could use the ram's horn to summon help from the silver dragons, in a call that was audible to the wyrms of argent alone.

"Here come Callak and Auricus," Agon noted, and the venerable gold saw that the pair were also flying upward, laboring hard toward the ancient's lofty vantage. Both were stiff-necked, straining their wings in obvious urgency.

Immediately Aurican hurled himself into the air, and his wings responded as needed, sweeping outward to channel and guide the wind, easily steering his flight. Callak and Auricus fell into formation as the elder dived past them, trailed by Agon and Dazzall.

"Did you hear something?" Aurican asked the young silver.

"Yes, Grandfather—a horn, with a strangely compelling sound."

"But you heard nothing?" the ancient demanded, turning to his golden scion. Auricus shook his head. "That seals it, then. What you heard was the ram's horn of the Kagonesti. Gather the others. We have important matters to discuss."

Before he could settle to the ground on the floor of the Valley of Paladine, Aurican was startled by a shimmer of magic below. A two-legged figure appeared instantly, and he realized that someone had teleported here. As he landed, the mighty gold saw that the newcomer was an elf. A river of blood trickled down the flank of the battered figure, and the dragon saw that his robes of regal silver had been rent and torn by cruel violence. The fellow looked up, took a weak step forward, and then fell to the ground.

Aurican scrutinized the stranger even as his gold dragon body shifted and shrank. Quickly the elder stood upright as he adjusted to his familiar elven body. He saw that the stranger had been gouged by a sword thrust to the side, and noticed by the irregular tears on the rich garment that the blade's edge had been cruelly serrated—in other words, a weapon that no elf would wield.

"Greetings, honored elf," Aurican said softly as Auricus and Callak came to rest behind him. They had not yet mastered the talent of the shapechange, and their metallic, reptilian heads rose over his shoulders as he regarded the battered newcomer. Dazzall and Agon held back slightly but also listened.

"Can you hear me? Do you come from Silvanost?" pressed the elder dragon. He had lived for a while in Silvanos's city, already a legendary place of crystal palaces and towers rising from an island in the midst of a mighty river. Now Aurican pictured that pastoral place, which had been peaceful for centuries, and the golden serpent felt a shiver of deep, chilling alarm.

At the name, the elf's eyelids flickered. His right eye was swollen shut, distorted by a purple bruise and cruel gouges on his cheek, but his left opened to regard Aurican with an expression of palpable terror.

"Again . . . she comes again," croaked the elf, a spatter of bloody drool trickling from his lip.

"Who?" asked Callak and Auricus at the same time, urgency hissing in the words.

"Crematia," declared Aurican, without any question in his voice. He looked again at the sword wound, then sniffed. The taint of acid was a sulfuric stench, faint but unmistakable, the effects visible in the holes that had been burned in the trailing edge of the elf's robe. "And she has brought her kin-dragons, awakened from the heart of the Khalkists."

The wounded elf arched his back, his jaws clenching soundlessly as he thrashed at an imaginary foe. Aurican leaned forward, touching him gently upon the forehead, and the fellow's struggles immediately ceased. His good eye opened, but the madness was gone. Instead, he stared with a desperate, pleading intensity.

"They came from the skies . . . all of them, red and black and white and the rest. And on the ground, ogres, charging from the woods . . . and warriors like snakes, snakes with arms and legs, bearing cruel swords. Those came from the swamp and butchered all of us who tried to find shelter there. We fought them . . . we killed and we died . . . but there were so *many*. . . ."

"What about Silvanos?" asked Aurican. "Does he live?"

"Aye, at last word before I was carried away. The three brother mages were there . . . the three robes . . . red and black—and the white one, too. Their magic was the only thing that enabled us to survive the first onslaught . . . walls of sorcery around Silvanost. The city stands, for now. They sent me here to find Aurican . . . to beg for help!"

The elf's words burned with shame at the admission, but again the serene figure of the altered gold dragon laid a hand upon the injured messenger's forehead. At the touch, the battered fellow once more drew a deep breath and apparently relaxed.

"You have done your job well, my friend. You must rest here, and grow strong. Know that I shall fly in response to your need."

Abruptly Aurican was a dragon again, rearing high above the younger serpents behind him. He raised his mouth to the skies and, with a trumpeting bray, summoned the other nestmates from their hunts and meditations among the peaks of the High Kharolis.

"Who are these brother mages?" asked Auricus.

"Three elves I knew centuries ago," the elder replied. Clearly he remembered the quest to the realm of gods, and the gifts that had led to spell magic on Krynn—and the three moons that, ever since, had loomed in the night sky. "They are still alive, and still mighty. Indeed, it sounds as though their magic is the best hope of elvenkind—at least, until I can get there."

Soon the brood of his own offspring and his nieces and nephews had joined him, several dozen bright males and females of copper, brass, and bronze, together with Callak and his brother Arjen, and Auricus. One of the females, Dazzall's sister Krayn, took charge of the wounded elf, bearing the messenger into the depths of the undermountain and its sacred grotto.

"I return to Silvanesti," announced Aurican, fixing his stern glare upon the restless wyrmlings. "While I am gone, I expect that all—"

"We're coming with you!" declared Callak, rearing up with a fluttering of silver wings, staring belligerently into the eyes of his ancient tutor.

The other wyrmlings cringed back, expecting an explosive response, but Aurican merely sighed heavily, sending a puff of warm smoke emerging from his nostrils.

"You cannot," declared the elder. "You—all of you—are too young. Bold and brave, I know, but neither will keep you alive against the cruel dragons of the Dark Queen. And though our nest is here, we have no eggs, no clutch to guard. It is too great a risk, for we gamble with the whole future of our kind should I let you come to war."

"What worth is a future if we allow the Dark Queen's dragons to rule the world?" demanded Auricus quickly, raising a question with vexing logic as he came to his brother nestling's aid.

Despite himself, old Aurican allowed himself a measure of pride in his youngster's argument as he replied. "There is no cause to panic. It is not out of the question that I myself, with the aid of the brother mages, may deal with the threat."

"But this is not your task alone!" asserted Callak. "Is not Crematia responsible for my father's death, as well as those of our other patriarchs?"

"And you've told us how, during that war, the red dragon was not captured in the gem of life-trapping with the others!" silver Arjen insisted. "Now is our chance to slay her!"

"There are many wyrms of evil, are there not?" pressed crippled Agon, bobbing his head high to be heard in the midst of his silver siblings. "Surely you could use our help. At the very least, we could guard your back and warn you of ambush!"

"No more argument!" snapped Aurican sternly. "This is an affair of ancients, and my business to complete. Now go, all of you, and guard the grotto!"

"But there are other kin-dragons who don't know about the danger," Callak objected. "Flash and Brunt are gone, and Tharn! And my sister Daria, too . . ."

"Then *that* is your task! Find your nestmates and bring them here!" insisted the ancient gold. "I command you, in the name of the Platinum Father. Gather the kin-dragons to the grotto and await my word."

Then, without a backward glance, he took wing toward Silvanesti . . . and war.

Chapter 21
Pride
<u>Pride</u>

2693 PC

"how do we find Tharn and flash? And who knows where Brunt's lair is?" Callak asked, forlornly watching Aurican's golden shape winging into the sky. Abruptly the gold dragon vanished from sight, and the younger wyrms knew he had teleported to Silvanesti.

Their bronze nestmate laired far away, though none of the other dragons knew exactly where. It was common knowledge that Tharn, on the other hand, had claimed the ancient copper lair of Blayze. The location of that cavern was also secret, but at least they knew it was somewhere in the eastern foothills.

"Well, we'll have to split up. Tharn and Flash will be in the foothills somewhere," said Auricus. "As to Brunt, he always flies west from here, and everybody knows he goes all the way to the coast."

"Daria spends a lot of time hunting on the eastern part of the range," Callak remembered. "I'll see if I can find her. Maybe she can help locate the coppers."

"And I'll teleport to the coast," Auricus added with a nod of agreement. "I'm the only one who can get there fast, and that gives me the best chance of finding Brunt. The rest of you wait in the grotto, as Aurican said."

"Let's go!" Callak cried, leaping into the air and angling for the crest of the High Kharolis. He looked back to see Auricus disappear and the other dragons take wing toward the tunnel leading into the grotto.

The silver male flew with all haste over the snow-swept ridges of the highest part of the range. He relished the icy air against his scales, the pristine frostiness of each deep breath. The exhilaration of flight, as always, brought him a sense of serene contentment, even joy. But he knew that he couldn't complete his task in these lofty reaches, so as soon as the terrain beneath him spilled toward the low-lands, he tucked his wings and tipped into a shallow dive.

How should he find his silver kin-dragon? He tried to think, knowing that Daria was the biggest of the silver females and had demonstrated a streak of independence as powerful as any of her male nestmates. Callak knew she favored hunting in the wooded, venison-rich heights of the foothills, far enough from the plains so that human hunters rarely ventured there. Once, after warning him not to plunder her game, she had shown Callak several of her favorite valleys, and it was to these that he now glided.

He searched diligently, gliding through the hours of daylight, seeking some glimpse of silver scales. Callak flew high enough to see over the serpentine ridges of the foothills, but not so lofty that he would miss details on the ground. He took a deer each night at sunset, generally selecting a yearling with a plentiful layer of fat. Yet despite the good eating and pastoral scenery, he grew increasingly agitated by his failure to locate Daria as the days passed.

After the fourth sunrise of his search, he saw a flash of reflection from a ledge just below the summit of a rounded mountaintop. Stroking upward, he found the silver female coiled regally in a rock-bound aerie, sleeping off the aftereffects of her feasting. Daria was growing plump and shiny, Callak saw, and he was startled by the allure he saw in that glimmering, serpentine form. He wondered why it had been so long since he had sought her, or desired her company.

But this was a time for more pressing business. He brayed a greeting as he swept downward, and the female quickly raised her head, blinking drowsily as he came to rest beside her. Curling his tail onto the ledge, Callak bowed, lowering his neck to parallel hers.

"What is it, Cal? I was sleeping!" she snapped petulantly.

"Trouble," he said, shaking off any further objections with his firm tone and stiff-winged bearing. Briefly he told her of the elf's report and the summons of the ram's horn. "Aurican wants us all to go back to the grotto and wait for him there."

Nodding, Daria uncoiled with supple grace. "Are all the others coming as well?" she asked, stretching her wings, allowing her tail to jut stiffly behind her.

"Brunt, Flash, and Tharn are gone to their lairs. We know that Tharn, at least, comes over here. I wanted to ask you if you have any idea where we might find him."

"Yes!" Daria said, her eyelids lowering shrewdly. "He doesn't know that I found his lair, but I've seen him there several times."

After a short flight, the two silvers landed on the smooth lip of a lofty cliff. Callak was surprised to see a shadowy cave mouth in the mountain wall before him. The cavern was dark, and moist, musty air, tainted with the sulfuric scent of acid, wafted from it. "It's completely screened by the overhang," he remarked. "You can't see it at all from the air."

"Or from the ground, either—not if you're dead!" The voice, speaking in the copper dragon's unmistakable growl, came from the darkness within.

Instinctively Callak whirled toward the opening, wings spread, his own head jutting forward on his stiffened neck. He felt the rumble of frost in his belly and stood alert, waiting for any sign of Tharn's blast of acid, ready to reply with a withering attack of his own ice.

"Wait!" cried Daria. "We're here with news!" Quickly she told the copper about the return of the chromatic dragons. "We've got to gather in the grotto!"

"Aurican has gone to do battle. He has commanded us to wait, to be ready," Callak added.

"I'm safe right here!" snarled the copper dragon. "I have no intention of going back to the nest like some pathetic wyrmling, seeking my sire's protection!"

"But together we're stronger—we have a better chance!" the silver male argued.

"Then *you* go back and be 'together,' " replied Tharn mockingly.

"What about Flash?" Daria asked, her tone surprisingly calm against the heat of the males' emotion. "Can you warn your brother of the danger?"

"Flash?" Now Tharn's voice was filled with unmistakable fury. "If you see him, kill him for me. He stole one of my treasures two winters ago!"

The two silvers tried for the rest of the day to convince their recalcitrant kin-dragon to accompany them, but he adamantly refused. Finally, in disgust, they took off and flew side by side toward the ancient lair of their clan.

Callak felt the hot, angry eyes of the copper burning into his tail as they flew toward the sunset. Strangely, the sensation lasted even after the valley of Tharn's lair was long out of sight.

Chapter 22
Tharn's Quandary

2693 PC

Deathfyre watched the pair of silver shapes until they were long out of view. The two dragons of argent were big, but they flew like neophytes, wyrms who didn't acknowledge the possibility of danger anywhere in the sky. The red felt a tingle of pure hatred, and only with difficulty did he restrain the urge to attack. Still, he knew his purpose here, and he wouldn't risk that mission for a momentary act of violence, however tempting the targets.

When they were gone, he allowed the spell of invisibility to fall from his scales. Deathfyre relished the sight of his serpentine, blood-red body, and only reluctantly had he employed magic to mask his beauty from the world. Still, the concealment had served a useful purpose. He was certain that the silvers hadn't seen him when they winged with such urgency out of the low, tree-shaded valley.

Regretfully, much of his current mission required him to travel in a state of invisibility or other magical disguise, such as the body of the soaring condor that he often employed. Deathfyre was proud of his crimson shape, but he was able to overcome that pride in order to serve the needs of concealment—and to hasten the chances of winning this war.

For a moment, he reflected on the grand, swift invasion that he and Crematia had led against the elves of Silvanesti. The bakali had proved to be loyal and effective troops, and with the skies overhead filled with chromatic dragons, they had accompanied the ogres in an irresistible onslaught. The northern border of Silvanesti had been breached in a series of swift battles, the elven garrisons caught before they could entrench. The magical barriers that had risen along the invasion routes into the forest realm had given the attackers only momentary pause, as the lightning and acid breath of blue and black dragons had quickly breached those arcane barriers.

When Deathfyre had left the battlefields a few seasons earlier, the armies had been surging southward with ruthless violence. They should be nearing the island capital of the elven realm by now, and it was Deathfyre's devout hope that he would complete his mission and be able to return to the south in time for the final destruction. That conquest, so long overdue, would be Crematia's greatest triumph—and the dawn of Deathfyre's mastery.

But his mother was right about one thing, a lesson she had carried with her from the Abyss: They must always strive to find their strongest enemy and destroy him. And, despite the power of the three mages, that most lethal enemy was unquestionably represented by the metal dragons of Paladine, and their golden patriarch in particular.

Two crimson shapes popped into view beside Deathfyre, the pair of female red dragons coiling sinuously beside their leader as they inspected the valley beyond the concealing ridge.

"Did you mark the lair?" asked Cynysi, her tongue flicking along Deathfyre's neck as she whispered the question.

"Yes, my pet, though I cannot know for certain if the two silvers were leaving their grotto or returning to it."

"How shall we tell?" asked Kyri, jealously pressing close at his other side. "Perhaps they are flying back to the great lair, not departing from it. Then we shall have lost them."

"I have a way to find out. Mask yourself, my females, and wait for me here."

Once again Deathfyre regretfully cast his invisibility spell, not daring to be discovered. Taking to the air, diving through the long shadows cast by the setting sun, he investigated the place that the silvers had left behind with such precipitate haste. He had been embarked on this search for a long time, but now he allowed himself to hope, for—thanks to his lucky glimpse of the two silvers— it seemed he might be drawing close to his goal.

Soon he saw the small cave mouth, and he settled to the cliff just above it. After insuring that a stiff wind blew up the face of the mountain, a breeze that would keep his scent from any nostrils within the cave, he sniffed—and was immediately rewarded with the stench of metal dragonkind, which hung thick in the air.

Yet the odor was dominated by the overriding, acidic stench of a copper dragon, and as the wind blew the last of the silvers' spoor away, Deathfyre knew that this was not, in fact, the true object of his search. Instead, it was more likely the lair of a single, solitary dragon.

Deathfyre, with the help of Cynysi and Kyri, had been charged by Crematia with finding the lair of all the good dragons, and he all but growled at the thought that he still hadn't succeeded. Still, this was closer than he had ever come before. When he had seen the two silvers, he had guessed that they had been departing from the great nesting lair of the metal dragons; now it seemed more likely that the mysterious hidden cavern had been their destination.

With an inaudible snarl of frustration, Deathfyre looked back to the west. The pair of silver serpents were long gone by now. He would never be able to catch sight of them.

But he was close; he knew it! There had to be something . . . and then his snarl turned to a rasp of quiet pleasure as he seized upon a plan.

When he leaned over the cliff to sample the air with his great nostrils, the scent of the copper was stronger than ever, strong enough to convince him that one of the good dragons remained within. Once again Deathfyre let the mask of invisibility fall away from himself. He took to the air, flying a roundabout course away from the copper's lair. Finding Cynysi and Kyri, he gave them explicit directions, then left to wing strongly, and in plain sight, up the valley below the hidden cave.

"Here me, my kin-dragons!" he bellowed, his voice powerful enough to rattle rocks loose from the bluffs. Averting his head, he nevertheless eyed the lair from the corner of his eye. Soon a lanky shape moved there, crouching low but unmistakably staring outward.

"Come to me, my red sisters, my kin-dragons of black and white, my blues and greens! I have found the lair of the good dragons!" Now he allowed a hint of exultant triumph to enter into his voice, sensing the stiffening posture of the hidden listener. He bugled his words, filling his chest with air, shouting with forceful volume.

"Their nest lies to the west of this great ridge!" He extended his head toward the crest of the High Kharolis. "Gather with me in our sacred clearing. We will mass there. Tomorrow we attack!"

With perfect timing, the two females came into view, hurrying to join with Deathfyre's steady flight. "This way!" he called, more loudly than was necessary. "Come with me as we gather our numbers!"

Propelled by a final pulse of his wings, Deathfyre lifted himself up and over the ridge flanking the valley, with Cynysi and Kyri flying right behind him. As soon as they were out of sight of the cave, Deathfyre again became invisible, then circled back to watch.

Coming to rest on the crest opposite the cave, he saw the slender copper emerge. The serpent's agitation was clear in the stiff, twitching restlessness of his wings, and in the jerking of his head back and forth. The quandary was obvious to the sinister watcher. The dragon was torn between staying in his cave, or flying to the secret lair to carry the warning to his kin-dragons. Obviously it was not an easy decision.

Finally the copper made up his mind. He took to the air, flying with visible urgency, staying as near to the ground as he could. His course was the same as that taken by the two silvers.

And he was completely unaware of the massive, winged shape that glided silently and quickly and invisibly in his wake.

Chapter 23
Aurican's Revenge

2693 PC

Aurican teleported by memory, bringing himself not directly to Silvanost, but over the northern forests of the elven realm. He wanted to approach the capital with a plan, so now he flew as an eagle over the woodlands, winging steadily southward. His great feathered wings bore him quickly, and if he was spotted, the enemy wouldn't know that a dragon approached.

The evidence of war was everywhere across the landscape below, and it was with grief that the gold dragon thought of the lives lost, the destruction wrought by the Dark Queen's legions. A mighty rage swelled within him, and he desperately wanted to find Crematia and kill her. Yet almost immediately the anger passed, replaced by a wave of melancholy as he thought of his precious charges back at the grotto.

They're too young—all of them! The ancient dragon all but groaned at the prosect of renewed warfare, knowing of the vicious and implacable foe awaiting them. Even the mightiest of his youngsters, Callak and Auricus, were mere neophytes at magic, lacking all but the most insignificant of spells. Too, they didn't possess the size and power needed to face a full-fledged serpent of the Dark Queen in open battle. Any mature black or green would be able to blast one of those wyrmlings from the sky with a single lethal expulsion of breath!

That was why he kept them there, where, at the very least, they would be safe. Deep in his heart, he knew that even if the elven nation fell, if he himself were killed, the race of metal dragonkind would survive.

But how could the elves hope to stand? It broke Aurican's heart to see the wrack of war, the horrors he had thought vanquished more than five hundred winters earlier. But now fires had again ravaged the lush woods, and towns and farms were torched into ruin. In places, the ground was black and utterly dead, marking the killing swath of an evil dragon's breath—be it acid, frost, or any of the other lethal assails of the chromatic wyrms. Trees were splintered, and though fires still smoldered here and there, he could see that, for the most part, the war that had claimed this borderland had moved relentlessly on.

Aurican flew at a very high altitude, for the gold knew he would need surprise and speed to accomplish anything against his deadly foes. He winged steadily onward, seeing that the devastation was sweeping, even worse than it had been in the first war. The dragon soared over the ruin of a crystal-walled town whose stone barrier had been melted into shapeless muck by infernal heat. The buildings had been smashed into splinters, and areas that must have once been serene gardens were now trampled expanses of mud and ruin.

Flying onward, he found more smoke, sensed that war still raged in this region. He saw columns of troops marching through the wrack, great files that must certainly be ogres. Fury flared again, and he forced himself to resist the urge to dive, to incinerate a hundred ogres with an expulsion of his fiery breath. He would be patient, retaining the eagle's body, saving his first appearance for an opportunity to strike at the crucial enemy: Crematia.

As he flew, the gold dragon's eyes swept the ravaged forest, seeking some sign of a target. Finally he saw the crystal towers of Silvanost rising to the south and took some comfort from the fact that the elven city still stood. Magic shimmered in the distant air, and he knew that the three wizards had sustained some kind of defense, a barrier against the city's ultimate collapse and destruction. The tenuous protection seemed to ring the island city but left the rest of the realm vulnerable to the invaders.

And then he saw a flash of crimson scales, a scarlet shape flying low and fast above the river leading toward Silvanost. He followed the serpentine form, saw the huge size of his target, the winged shadow flickering over the murky waters of the river. Aurican expanded into his true form, spread his golden wings, and made ready to dive. The blood-red dragon was Crematia, he knew, and the knowledge brought his hatred surging into a consuming emotion, a boiling fire in his guts.

The majestic gold tucked his wings and leaned forward, forming the deadly missile that was a diving dragon. Neck extended, belly rumbling with the pressure of surging flame, Aurican plunged swiftly downward. He watched the serenely gliding red grow larger in his vision. The wind whistled past his head as he descended, and his forelegs reached with unconscious tension, straining to rip sharp talons through crimson scales, to rend Crematia's hateful flesh with the sudden onslaught of his attack.

The red dragon flew with a curious lack of caution, as if contemptuous of the very notion of danger. She glided without effort, crocodilian head swinging back and forth with arrogant unconcern. Auri thought he knew the reason: Everywhere Crematia looked, she saw only devastation and destruction, proof that her armies held sway over all this vast forestland.

Closer plunged the gold dragon, gases of angry fire now building irresistibly, seething toward inevitable release. A moment before collision, Aurican's eruption of flame sizzled forward in a jet of searing fire, roaring like an inferno around the crimson form. He knew the blast— lethal to almost any creature alive—wouldn't seriously injure this monstrous wyrm, but he hoped the surprising onslaught would give him an initial advantage when the two great bodies met. The gold dragon hurled himself into the dissipating fireball, clawing and striking, slashing talon and fang against—

Air! The massive crimson form had disappeared! There was no target here, only . . .

In that instant's reflection, Aurican recognized the trap and acted with the speed of his thought. He whipped his head upward, arching his back to pull out of the dive as the space below him suddenly erupted with a hellish fireball of hissing, crackling flame. Crematia swept past, her deadly ambush foiled by his instantaneous evasion.

But then another crimson form smashed into Aurican from the other side, powerful jaws rending his wing, claws tearing golden scales from his flank. Flames roared, masking his vision even though the heat could not penetrate his golden scales. He bellowed and twisted, his reaction too slow to clamp his jaws into the supple red dragon that pushed away, Auri's blood trailing from his claws and teeth.

The gold flipped onto his back, pitching desperately through a roll to come out in pursuit of Crematia. His wing was torn, but he could still fly, impelled as much by a monstrous, consuming rage as he was by the strength of his aging limbs. The other red, a creature that was much smaller than Crematia, fell rapidly behind as the gold's plummeting speed carried him away. There were more of them now, a half dozen young red dragons swarming in pursuit.

Aurican muttered a quick spell, teleporting himself in front of the evil matriarch, avoiding another slashing attack by the youngsters. He reared, wings spread, jaws gaping, ready to meet his ancient foe.

Crematia and Aurican crashed together in a tangle of rending fangs and slashing talons. Clenched in a lethal embrace, the two serpents tumbled through the air, rolling and plunging toward the ground. Grimly Aurican seized the red's neck in his foreclaws, ignoring the stabbing jolts of pain as her rear legs ripped into his belly.

Only at the last minute did Crematia break away, throwing herself outward and flailing her wings in a desperate attempt to gain altitude. Sensing his enemy's desperation, Aurican cast another spell, an enchantment that went against the very nature of his enemy's being.

A cone of cold blasted outward, searing the fire-loving red in a shivering onslaught of deadly frost. Crematia shrieked, straining to stay aloft, but by then Aurican flexed his own wings, trying to pull himself out of the headlong dive. Breaking away, Aurican saw the ancient red smash into the treetops, plunging downward to crash into the ground. She lay in a shady grove, twitching spasmodically, then growing still.

And then there were chromatic dragons coming from everywhere, blue and black, green, white and red. Aurican quickly masked himself with invisibility, but he knew that wouldn't long deter the magic-using wyrms. Changing shape quickly into the body of a tiny hummingbird, he dived toward the ground and darted under a frond of leafy fern near the great crimson body.

Soon the clearing was crowded with dragons, a seething nest of bright scales slithering and coiling around Crematia's motionless body. The wyrms were shocked, trembling with fury, growling and hissing as they glared here and there.

"Where's Deathfyre?" asked one, a black.

"I come."

Now there was another red dragon here, a surprisingly huge wyrm that was nevertheless as sleekly muscled as a young adult. He came to rest beside Crematia, and the other chromatic dragons fell back. The hummingbird that was Aurican, still and soundless, watched from beneath his leafy concealment.

"My matriarch!" groaned the red dragon, laying his neck alongside Crematia's bleeding form as that great serpent stirred slightly, moaning in pain. This newcomer was Deathfyre, Aurican knew, and he realized with a shudder that the ancient red had left behind a very powerful heir.

"We shall have our revenge!" the one called Deathfyre declared, his voice a wicked and hateful hiss. "For I have found the grotto of the good dragons. I followed a fool of a copper until he showed me the entrance. Now we go there, and we kill!"

"I am proud of you, my son," gasped the dying red. "Strike your blow swiftly, and then return here. Remember, find your strongest enemy . . . kill him. Mercy is weakness . . ."

". . . and weakness is death!" hissed Deathfyre.

"Good, my son . . . Kill as many of the metal wyrms as you can . . . but then return here. The elves, with their magic, are mighty, and you dare not leave them unguarded for long."

"We shall complete the revenge," Deathfyre promised.

He might have said more, but by then Aurican had already teleported back to the cavern in the High Kharolis.

Chapter 24
Dragonflight

2693 PC

The golden patriarch appeared in the grotto, just above the nest. With a flap of his vast wings, he settled to the ground as the younger wyrms stirred and hissed in shock at his sudden appearance. Wings buzzing, the throng of metal wyrms faced their sire. The agitation quickly settled as the nestmates recognized Aurican.

"Quickly, take wing, my wyrmlings! You have very little time!" declared the venerable gold, the urgency in his voice piercing any vestige of normalcy held by the younger serpents. Looking around, Auri saw that all the nestmates had gathered. Even Brunt was here, smelling of fish and brine.

"But why, sire?" demanded Auricus, trying to speak

calmly. "And where do you command us to go?"

"The dragons of the Dark Queen are coming. Crematia is dead, but she has a scion, called Deathfyre, every bit as wicked as herself. And he's learned of the grotto!" His eyes fell upon Tharn, who hissed and glared about, ready to fight. The gold dragon said nothing about what he had overheard, though he felt certain Deathfyre had somehow discovered Tharn's lair and then followed the hot-tempered copper to the grotto beneath the High Kharolis. Yet there was neither time nor purpose for recriminations. They had to *move*.

"They will be here as soon as they can gather and teleport. As to where, you must divide into your clans. Callak, you take the silvers; Auricus, you lead the golds. Tharn, Dazzall, Brunt—you take charge of leading your siblings to safety."

Agon flapped his wings loudly, rearing onto the withered stumps of his rear legs, the limbs that had been wrinkled and twisted since his birth. "Should we not fight them, Grandfather?" he demanded.

Aurican sighed, wishing he had time to explain. He shook his head, regretful but firm. "There are too many of them. You must take wing. Our only hope lies in the future—and then only if you can escape."

"We go!" cried Callak, sensing the urgency. He pounced to the nest and reached out with a foreclaw to lift the silver chain of the ram's horn, allowing the precious artifact to slide over his neck. Agon, Arjen, Daria, and the other silvers padded after, ready to follow their brother from the grotto.

The wyrms of the brown metals, too, as well as Auricus and his golden nestmates, also buzzed wings, surging in agitation. Only Aurican looked back with a momentary pang of regret, knowing that they departed a place that had been hallowed by the metal dragons for ages. It was an ignominious departure, and his throat tightened with rage and frustration as he considered, only for a moment, how much he wanted to remain here, to fight the chromatic dragons for this place.

But these wyrmlings were still too young. They would be doomed in any fight with the mighty serpents of Takhisis. Such foolish sentimentality was more fitting for a human or elf, creatures with the emotional vulnerability to know love. He wondered for a dazed instant: Could the two-legs, those creatures who spoke so enthusiastically of love, learn to love a place? Was such a thing even possible? With cold reality driving the moment of reflection from his mind, he reared above the brood and glared sternly about.

"I will lead the way. If I must fight, I will, but the rest of you are to flee with all haste. Leave me, if you must, but *escape*. This is my command, and the command of your Platinum Father as well."

The wyrmlings took wing, buzzing through the air behind Aurican as he flew from the door cave into the vast chamber of the underground lake. There was no sign of the enemy here, but this didn't surprise him. From the words he had overheard, he suspected Deathfyre had discovered the cave leading from the Valley of Paladine, but doubted that he had risked coming in this far. It seemed likely that, if he had, one of the nestlings would have noticed the intrusion.

With this thought, he wheeled into a tight spiral, whirling through the darkness above the great subterranean lake. A thousand thoughts tumbled through his mind as he sensed that this was the last lesson he would ever bestow upon the young wyrmlings.

"Make your lairs far from here, in secret places," he told them. "Be true to each other, for you are the strongest allies your nestmates will ever have. When you have eggs, guard them with the last breath of your lives! And know that each of you is strong, strong in his own way. Find those ways, my children, and survive!"

He was about to dive toward the exit cave when Auricus pulled him up with a word. "Sire, can we not prepare for this battle with spells?"

"Yes!" he agreed, chagrined at his own impetuous speed. "But not for battle but for escape." Aurican spiraled tightly, thinking. "Those of you who have learned the haste spell, cast it upon yourselves."

He knew this would allow most of the golds and silvers to fly with great speed. The patriarch cast his own spells of haste on Dazzall and Krayn, giving the two largest brass wyrmlings the advantage of magical swiftness.

"I will cast mine upon Tharn," little Agon said, startling the copper with the abrupt enchantment, then turning to face Aurican's scowl. "Should we not see that two of each color, a male and female, have the best chance to escape?"

"And my spell goes to Horim!" Arjen agreed, enchanting the copper female before she knew what was happening.

"A good thought, my brave wyrmling," Aurican agreed, powerfully moved by the crippled silver's sacrifice. Brunt and Dwyll, the largest male and female bronzes, were also enchanted with the spell of speed. "Now fly to the Valley of Paladine and beyond!"

In moments, Aurican burst out of the entry tunnel in a golden explosion of speed. The sun blazed in a cloudless sky, and the shimmering brightness of daylight seemed an incongruous contrast to the darkness in his heart, the grief and shame that would be the legacy of their flight.

And there was Deathfyre, poised above the entry, already sweeping into a reckless dive. Two crimson females flew close at his sides. Other flecks of color appeared in the sky, widely scattered over the High Kharolis, and Aurican immediately understood the reason: Only the trio of reds had been able to teleport with accuracy, since the other serpents had formed their destination based only on Deathfyre's descriptions. Still, a pair of blues plunged swiftly toward the valley, and more spots of color appeared in the near distance.

Aurican's mouth gaped wide and fire spewed forth. The three reds flew through the flames, breathing infernos of their own. Golden claws reached out, tearing a crimson wing, and one of the females shrilled a cry of pain and fury. Aurican felt talons rending his own flank and knew that Deathfyre had whirled around to attack from behind.

The mighty gold flipped and twisted, slashing down at the other female but unable to reach the tenacious foe clinging to his back.

"Get the rest!" cried Deathfyre, in a shrill tone of command, and Aurican knew that his nestlings had flown into view. "Kill them all!"

"Fly, my wyrmlings, for the Platinum Father. Escape and live to gain vengeance!" Aurican roared.

Then there was a shape of black wings, like a monstrous, snake-limbed bat, poised before him, and a blast of acid seared the golden scales of Aurican's chest. He groaned, an involuntary explosion of pain, and then felt his body pummeled by another smashing blow. Dazed, he wheeled in the sky, vaguely surprised by the sudden silence that seemed to have descended. He felt no pain, merely a gentle serenity. Only when the scent of ozone stung his nostrils did he realize he had been struck by the lightning of a mighty blue.

Frost and fire blossomed around him, and the serpent writhed in renewed efforts to escape, to fight. His fiery breath seared a black, but more lightning hissed into his flanks, ripping away his wings, gouging deep into his ancient flesh. A cloud of noxious gas swirled as a green dragon dived past, and Aurican's desperate thrash tore at an emerald-colored wing, shredding the membrane and sending the wyrm spiraling into a doomed descent. Once more he breathed, the great fireball engulfing several blues and a screaming white.

But then more power, another barrage of deadly dragonbreath came together with lightning and fire and cold. For a moment, Aurican's struggling body was lost in a cloud of murky sky.

And then that murk closed in, darkening his vision, finally seeping through the pain to draw a final curtain across his life.

Chapter 25
A Valley of Corpses

2693 PC

Deathfyre turned into a reckless dive, shocked at the speed with which several of the young wyrmlings were fleeing the deep valley. He had expected the creatures to fight to the death and had not anticipated the desperate flight that drove them toward the high ridges. Clearly the cowardly serpents intended to escape.

Now the powerful red twisted in the air, seeing that many of the metal dragons had in fact remained to do battle. Other wyrms swept above, and he saw a blue dragon shriek and writhe in the clutch of several silvers and a brass. A red pulled through the melee, rearing its head to blast a desperately maneuvering bronze from the sky. Recovering his own equilibrium, stabilizing himself on his powerful wings, Deathfyre curved through the air, still looking for victims.

The memory of Crematia's death was a fire within him, a driving force for vengeance. Her loss was not a cause for grief—there was a clear advantage that came to Deathfyre, heir to the Dark Queen's empire—but it was a wrong that called for revenge.

Deathfyre wheeled to pursue the fleeing dragons, but he saw several silver shapes slashing toward him, and his instincts compelled him to protect himself. Though all of them were small, they flew with deadly purpose.

Twisting like a corkscrew in the air, Deathfyre whipped his neck toward the enemy attackers. Jaws gaping, he belched a cloud of roaring flame, a billowing fireball of death that wrapped two of the silver shapes in its killing embrace.

Pushing down with hard strokes of his wings, Deathfyre fought for altitude, trying to avoid the scorched bodies that would tumble out of the dissipating ball of fire—but there *were* no bodies! The remaining silver serpent curled around, and the red barely pulled his wing out of the way of a vicious blast of frost. He saw that this young silver was a cripple, that its rear legs were weak and shriveled, but that did nothing to tame the deadliness of its breath weapon. Deathfyre tumbled backward, out of control, with a burning pain of ice freezing his tail.

At the same time, he knew how the crippled silver had eluded him. It had been the simple spell of the mirror image, an enchantment Deathfyre himself had known since his first hundred winters. Yet when it was used against him, the simple trick had fooled him completely. There had been only one silver dragon, not three, and his lethal fire had been wasted against a pair of magical impostors!

Infuriated, he swept after the silver as that gleaming serpent flew close to the ground, carving a wide arc back toward the battle raging in the skies. Some of the wyrmlings had escaped, aided by magical speed, but most of the brood had remained to fight. This silver newt was small, little more than half of Deathfyre's awesome length, but he proved to be a surprisingly fast flier. The withering of his body clearly did not extend to his wings. Straining to the limit, Deathfyre found that he could close the distance only gradually. Finally he breathed, spewing a hellish cloud of fire that surrounded the impudent silver for a searing, fatal instant. The red dragon was already wheeling away as the wrinkled, charred carcass tumbled from the sky.

Clouds of dragons whirled through the sky overhead. A young bronze tumbled, horribly slashed, while blues and blacks caught a pair of coppers in a deadly crossfire of acid and lightning. Fire and smoke drifted through the air, and flashes of flame and clouds of green and noxious gas added a surreal beauty to the scene.

And still more chromatic dragons winged toward the fight, with vengeful challenges ringing through the air before them. Several greens dived from the heights, sweeping toward the smoldering patch of sky, and a wedge of whites, laboring hard to gain altitude, winged speedily closer, their pale, serpentine forms standing out clearly against the mountainous landscape to the north.

Another metal dragon, this one a golden female, plunged downward, writhing and shrieking in pain. As the pathetic creature tumbled past, Deathfyre saw that her entire face had been burned away by a blast of black dragon acid. Another gold, this one a larger male, roared in and torched one of the blacks with a breath of fireball, but then the gilded wyrm was forced to flee for his life as the other blacks whirled about in furious pursuit.

Then suddenly the skies were empty of Paladine's dragons. A few of the metal serpents had buzzed over the high ridges, scattering away from the mountain valley. They fled in full panic, knowing their clan had been decimated, and for now the chromatic dragons let them go.

Looking down, Deathfyre saw dragons of every color lying in the ghastly stillness of death. The battle had littered the valley floor with corpses, great shapes scattered like bright scars on the ground itself. Here a blue wing twitched, or there a copper tail lashed back and forth, but for the most part the serpents on the valley floor were utterly and irrevocably slain. Even from this height, the awful wounds inflicted by breath and fang and claw were clearly visible, leaving great rends in the scaly bodies.

And central to this killing ground was the mighty golden serpent, Aurican. It pleased Deathfyre to know that not only had the mighty patriarch perished, but also that fewer than a dozen of the metal dragons had escaped the carnage. The few that had fled were no threat for now. They would be hunted down and killed at his leisure.

His mother's teachings, the words of Takhisis herself, came to Deathfyre in a clear flash: Find your strongest enemy and kill him. . . .

Now, with the dragons of Paladine defeated, he knew where that enemy lay. The power of magic still screened Silvanost, and it was time to reduce that stronghold.

There would be time for the metal wyrmlings later.

Chapter 26
Exiled

2693 PC

The surviving nestmates gathered in a dark, marble-walled gorge in the tangle of the Kharolis foothills. There were but ten of them, young dragons of metal who had departed the grotto in desperate, magically enhanced haste, with memories of violence and death licking at their heels.

Callak and Auricus were the last to land, after insuring that the evil dragons made no pursuit. The pair had circled for a long time over the Kharolis Mountains while the others tucked their wings and dived to the shelter of the secluded gorge. They all understood that there would be no returning to their ancient lair. Once on the ground, the remaining dragons of the Platinum Father could only huddle miserably together for warmth and comfort.

"Aurican is dead," Auric whispered, his voice numb with disbelief. "He died so that we could live."

"He was so wise, so mighty," wailed Blythe, the golden female who now coiled dejectedly beside Auricus. "How will we survive without him?"

"And so many of our nestmates . . ." Dazzall said numbly. "I saw Flash perish after he tore the wings from a blue."

"And Agon," Daria said, her voice catching. "He led that mighty red away from me . . . from all of us."

"Ten dragons of metal . . . we are all that remain." It was Callak who called for the attention of the others. He nodded his silver head sadly, reflecting on the brothers and sisters they all had lost.

"Are we safe here?" asked Daria, the only other silver to remain alive.

"We cannot know for sure," replied Auricus, in tones so deep that he sounded startlingly like his sire. "It may be that Deathfyre or another has tracked our flight, knowing we came here to hide and lick our wounds."

"At least they felt the sting of our claws, the bite of our fangs!" asserted Tharn with a menacing growl. "I saw Arjen kill two blues . . . before he perished."

He sighed, lowering his sharp, angular head to the ground in acknowledgment of the truth they all understood: In a few short minutes over the Valley of Paladine, the good dragons had been dealt a devastating defeat. It had been a tragedy of unprecedented and far-reaching proportions, culling most of their number, slaying their patriarch, reducing these nestlings to a band of pathetic survivors.

True, they had killed some of the Dark Queen's wyrms, perhaps as many as they themselves had lost. But that, in the balance, still left scores of chromatic dragons, many of them fully mature, arrayed against these five pairs of young serpents.

The dragons of Paladine finally slept, abandoning themselves to torpor. A sunrise and sunset passed, but the nestmates didn't stir. Instead, they rested, allowing their wounds to heal . . . but even the passage of time couldn't quell the rising of despair.

Daria awakened them all with a braying cry of alarm. The silver female regarded her nine nestmates seriously.

"I have had a dream," she said, her tone low, awestricken. She looked at Callak, then at the others, shaking her head in wonder. "I saw a great Spear of Paladine. Someday there will come to us a weapon that will allow us to battle the dragons of evil."

"Where do we find this weapon?" growled Callak.

"It will find us, but not for many hundreds of winters. Until then, we must leave this place." Daria looked at each of the wyrmlings, and the finality of her tone was enough to quell most objections.

"Leave the High Kharolis?" Auricus was the one who voiced the disbelief felt by all of the young dragons.

"New people will claim the grotto—not our enemies, but not our neighbors, either. They will mine these mountains and build great cities on the lake. And we must be gone."

Callak thought for a moment about debating this point, but in the end, he deferred to his kin-dragon, knowing that the grotto held nothing for them now. And he understood instinctively that the power of her dream was not a trifling thing.

"We must separate, as Aurican said," the silver male declared. "But we cannot forget each other. Remember, in our differences are we strong."

"I will keep the fires of vengeance burning," growled Tharn. "That we, or our children, shall know the price our nestmates have paid . . . and shall one day exact an accounting."

"And I shall record the history of our grotto, and our leaving, so that none of our wyrmlings may ever forget." Auricus made the statement, and they all knew that it was a solemn oath.

"The humans must learn what has happened," Dazzall announced. "And I shall tell them to insure that they remember us."

"Be strong, my nestmates," Brunt declared, his thick,

wedged head dipped into a bow. "For in strength, we will survive."

"But for now, we must fly," concluded Callak.

The mountain range was abandoned under the clear skies and bright full moon of the spring equinox. As Callak took to the air, with Daria by his side, he saw that the landscape of the High Kharolis was still a blanket of uniform white, sparkling glaciers and pristine snowfields reflecting the dazzling brightness of the midnight sky. Even the lake where his mother was buried had vanished beneath the layer of whiteness.

The wyrms of metal flew for a long time under the full moons, circling the high ridges in their matched pairs. Fate had seen that the ten who survived could still plant the seeds of future generations, for their numbers included five males and five females, a single pair of each precious metal color.

Finally they winged upward and away, soaring over the ridges of mountains that encircled their sacred realm. To an observer, it might have seemed that each pair of dragons chose a different point of the compass for its destination. Yet there was no such calculated plan to the dispersal. The divergent courses were merely the result of the good dragons seeking refuge in far quarters of Ansalon, places where the vengeance of the evil wyrms could never reach them.

Many years remained to pass before these young serpents would breed, produce eggs, and eventually restore the numbers of their kind. They would need to make new lairs, to hide themselves in such wilderness as remained in the world, seeking to live that their descendants might someday have a chance to be born.

Yet in their survival, they knew hope, and in their memories were the tales that would fashion their history and their destiny.

And perhaps, in the unknown future, that destiny might lead them to revenge.

Chapter 27
Wild Magic

2688 PC

Three robed figures gathered in the highest chamber of the Tower of Stars, Silvanost's loftiest promontory. Aside from the colors of their robes, which were black, white, and red, respectively, the trio of figures might have been stamped from a single mold. Each was hunched low, grimly taut in posture, with the cowl of his robe pulled forward to hide face and features.

Although the clear skies allowed the light of a million stars to illuminate the room, the three remained fixed upon the floor, almost as if they were unwilling to regard the heavenly brightness. A pattern of arcane symbols was barely visible on the tiled surface, glowing slowly brighter until a pattern of illumination passed like a web though the room.

"Do we dare?" asked Parys Dayl, he of the white robe. "We have no way of knowing what effect the spell of wild magic will have, beyond that of capturing the wyrms of the Dark Queen."

"What else matters? If the chromatic dragons are allowed to come on unchecked, everything is lost," declared red-robed Fayal Padran.

"Yes." Kayn Wytsnal's voice was a hiss. "And since the dragons of metal have failed, there is no other hope. Our power may wrack the world, but if the serpents of the Dark Queen are defeated, we shall be well rewarded."

Another figure came into view. His golden hair, gone slightly white with age, glowed softly in the starlight that filtered through the tall, crystal windows. The three wizards looked at him expectantly and with obvious respect.

"How fares your council?" asked Silvanos. Though the elven patriarch's voice was as dry as parchment, the three listeners knew this was not because of age, but rather due to the profound nature of the proposal now being considered.

"Bah!" Kayn's voice cracked like a brittle twig, snapping from beneath the black cowl of his robe. "They know what must be done, and yet they are afraid to do it."

"And you are not afraid?" asked Silvanos, gently raising an eyebrow.

"Of course I am, but I am afraid of the results. They fear to take the chance, while I clearly recognize that we *must* cast the spell. We have no other choice."

"And you?" Silvanos asked, turning to Fayal.

"I fear my colleague is right, though he cares little for the effects that may result. Magic could wrack much of Silvanesti, even the whole world."

"And the dragons?" Silvanos inquired patiently.

It was Fayal who replied. "All the portents indicate that, whatever else its effects, the casting will seize the chromatic dragons and draw them into the fundament of Krynn. They will be entombed."

"And that is the only effect that matters!" Kayn declared. "Anything else can be survived! For if we do not cast this spell, our barriers will inevitably collapse—perhaps within the next winter or two. Then Silvanost, and everything else, will be lost."

"And the spell will work?"

"That is a good question," Parys admitted. "We have aligned the poles of wild magic so that they have a powerful attraction for the wyrms of Takhisis. We *think* it will work. But in truth, all we can do is hope the summons will be enough to drag them down, to trap them."

"But the defensive barriers will otherwise fall . . . this is a certainty?" inquired the elven patriarch.

"Aye," said Fayal, with the other two mages nodding in agreement.

"Then it seems that we have no choice," declared Silvanos with a finality that the others could only respect.

* * * * *

Deathfyre had wasted no time in renewing his onslaught against the elven realm, for he knew that the Silvanesti would be able to recover and rearm far more quickly than the dragons of Paladine could possibly hope to restore their depleted numbers.

So it was that the evil army returned its attentions against the south. Relentless hordes of ogres and bakali marched, led by ruthless minotaur raiders. Dragons of blue and black, of crimson, green, and white dotted the skies, answering to the mighty Deathfyre's commands.

Coss, a great, acid-spewing black serpent, and Spuryten, an ancient blue, were Deathfyre's chief lieutenants. The trio of dragons led three great spearheads converging onto the elven capital of Silvanost. And all the wyrms of Takhisis took wing against elvenkind, drawing in an ever-tightening noose about the besieged city on its once-pastoral island. Still, the barriers of the brother mages held them off, foiling every attempt to complete the conquest, to carry the destruction into the crystal city itself.

And the campaign progressed with relentless savagery and irresistible might. Bakali swarmed through the marshes of Silvanesti, driving the elves from the well-watered lands that provided so much of their food. Ogres bashed at the walls of every fortified strong point, often aided by the crushing power of dragonbreath. Gradually the doomed outposts were destroyed one by one, leaving increasingly large stretches of the forested elvenhome a bleak wasteland.

Only the magic of the three brother mages prevented the ultimate triumph of the evil armies. The wizards used their mighty sorcery to maintain the enchanted barriers that held the serpents and their land-bound allies away from the city of the elves. These potent blockades of stone and flame and magic and ice resisted all efforts of the advancing tide, though the rest of the realm was, little by little, overrun.

At last all the outposts had been overrun or destroyed, and only the stubborn island city remained. Three great armies, commanded by Coss, Spuryten, and Deathfyre himself, surrounded Silvanost, ready for the final onslaught. It remained only to plan the culminating attack.

"What news of the siege?" demanded Deathfyre when Coss reported to him on the progress of the campaign. "Has the city's defense been breached yet?"

"It proves stubbornly defiant," the black wyrm replied grimly. "The elves have gathered those three powerful wizards in a high tower. They have used sorcery to hold us at bay, but they must fall when all our power is concentrated against them."

"All the dragons are ready to attack?"

"Aye, lord, though you should know that the numbers of our ogres and bakali have been depleted by the long campaigns."

"I will find us more troops, and soon . . . soon we shall prevail," the great red pledged. His thoughts turned to the past, remembering the golden killer who had brought about his mother's death. Yet he remained aware that the metal dragons who had escaped remained too few, too young, to cause him any worries. Only when the war was won would he turn his attention to vengeance.

"Be ready for the final onslaught. I shall return soon with fresh armies."

Deathfyre flew rapidly to the north, where, in the smoking Khalkists, evil men had built a teeming city in the place where Darklady Mountain had stood. This was a place called Sanction, a city of fire and smoke, a nest of thieves and murderers, where the worship of the Dark Queen was a thing highly regarded. Deathfyre was lord here, and the men had built great monuments to his name. Many of these wicked humans willingly joined the legions of his army, ready to butcher as cruelly as any bakali or ogre when they marched to war.

But before Deathfyre could return to the south, the three brother mages cast their great spell, an enchantment calling upon the fundamental power of wild sorcery, the fundamental power that abided in the very center of the world. The strength of this magic was a thing unknown on Krynn before or since.

With the exception of Deathfyre, all the dragons of the Dark Queen had gathered for the onslaught against the elven city. Before the attack commenced, the brother mages worked their enchantment in the Tower of Stars.

Coss, Spuryten, and all the others watched in awe as light flared from the lofty windows, and electricity—like bolts of deadly lightning—exploded into the sky. The ground shook, and the trees swayed to a fundamental disturbance, a disruption of the natural laws of the world.

Then, with a sharp *crack* like thunder, waves of sorcerous destruction spread outward from Silvanesti, wracking the land as they passed. The power of the spell sucked the chromatic dragons downward, trapping each serpent of Takhisis in a lingering well of darkness.

The ripple of magic reached Deathfyre as a trailing effect, for the center of the convulsion lay hundreds of miles to the south. Even so, Deathfyre hurled himself into the air, sensed the power sucking at him, trying to drag him down.

He made it as far as the smoking Khalkists before the power caught up with him. Then the ground rose up, and a great hole yawned below him. He could not prevent himself from falling in, and then the walls of stone and fire surrounded him, and everything he knew became darkness.

PART III

Chapter 28
Silver Lords

circa 1400 PC

The wild elf maiden was a blur of laughter and speed. Arms and legs pumping, silver-white hair trailing in the breeze, she sprinted like a deer along the forest trail, ducking a mossy limb, casting a merry smile over her shoulder as she put on another dazzling burst of speed. She leapt a mossy fallen trunk, ducked around a tight corner, and without hesitation splashed through a gravel-bedded stream. Silver drops of water sparkled in the sunlight, and her bright cry of delight rang in harmony with the trilling of the water as she sprang onto the far bank to fly onward with a pounding of bare feet against the path.

She was a creature of exquisite beauty, this fleet elf of the forest. Muscles rippled in her limbs, yet her body possessed a lush fullness that made her doelike speed all that much more astounding. Her skin was a pale, almost translucent pearl, now a white blur in the semidark shadows of the forest floor. The small strip of foxskin girding her loins did little to preserve even a semblance of modesty.

Not that modesty had any place in the mind of the one who chased the elusive maid through the forest. Harder footsteps thudded behind her, and a wild elf brave came into view. Head low, he dashed forward with single-minded determination, leaping in a single bound the stream that had slightly slowed his alluring quarry.

The warrior's body was covered with whorls and leaf patterns of black tattoos. A trailing horsetail bound his shock of long black hair, a plume that, suspended by his speed, floated like smoke in the air. He, too, sprinted with an easy grace, a fluid rippling as the trail straightened and he slowly closed on the elfmaid. Like the female, the brave was unarmed, though he bore the horn of a great ram on a silver chain around his shoulder. He lacked even the limited clothing that encircled her waist.

Head down now, drawing deep and measured breaths through his flaring nostrils, the runner seemed unaware of the woods passing in a blur on either side. He was blinded by the beauty, the scents and sounds and sights that combined to draw him after his exquisite quarry. Now he was desperate to catch her, to bring her to ground.

With another teasing refrain of laughter, the female elf darted through a blossomed bower and sprinted into the clear. The brave followed, eyes fixed upon her lush form, mind blinded to all thoughts except this alluring maiden that led him so tantalizingly onward.

"Hargh! Heads up! Looks like we've got some prizes, me lads!"

The bark of alarm, harsh and deep, was the elves' first clue that the clearing was already occupied. Huge shapes stirred to the right and left, rushing from the shady bowers along the meadow's fringes. A pair of brawny, two-legged figures, each bearing a heavy, knotted club, advanced to block the path of the two Kagonesti, while more of their hulking comrades closed in from all sides.

"Ogres!" gasped the maiden in quick recognition, skidding to a halt as a dozen or more brutish cohorts rushed to join the two blocking her path through the clearing. The brave whirled to see more of the monsters charge from the far sides of the sun-swept meadow, blocking any attempt they might have made to return the way they had come.

The elfmaid spun in a swirl of silvery hair, casting looks to either side, placing her back to the brave's. The two Kagonesti stood barehanded, facing at least two dozen of the burly humanoids. Clubs raised, drooling tusks exposed, the brutes closed in for an easy kill.

"I dislike the odds," murmured the lean warrior, with an attitude of mild concern.

"I agree," replied the maiden, nodding as she frowned at the encircling ring. "Do you think we should change them?"

"Immediately."

Silver scales swirled into view, coiling around the place where the two wild elves had stood, as a pair of huge serpentine bodies took their places on the ground. In a flash of reflection, mighty wings flapped and grew, driving gusts of wind, dust, and debris into the faces of the startled ogres. Many of the brutes shrieked in terror, turning to flee from the pair of menacing silver dragons that suddenly loomed before them. Others fell to the ground, wailing and groveling, begging for mercy or trying to claw a place of concealment into the hard soil.

Only one displayed the courage, or foolishness, to continue the attack. This was a brutish chieftain who hurled himself at the male dragon and was met by a savage, darting snap of those great jaws. Lectral bit hard and felt the crunch of sturdy bone. He killed the ogre instantly and, with a contemptuous spit, hurled the burly body into the faces of its companions.

Heart's blast of deadly frost exploded from her silver jaws, a white cloud of death roaring outward in a magical blizzard, expanding with hissing violence through the warm spring air of the clearing. The dragonbreath froze a dozen ogres in the garish postures of instant death even before the brutes realized they were being attacked. Still more of the monsters threw themselves onto the ground, and the wailing of their abject fear echoed through the woods.

Lectral pounced, crushing an ogre with each forepaw, snatching up another in his great jaws. Breaking the muscle-bound body in a crushing bite, he tossed his neck and sent the creature's remains tumbling into a pair of fleeing ogres. His silver tail lashed around, crushing several more of the monsters, sending the great, brutish warriors tumbling like children's toys.

Smashing with his great body, the silver dragon settled heavily downward until the desperate thrashing underneath him was crushed into stillness. Whipping his head toward a band of the brutes huddled beyond his left wing, he belched a cloud of killing frost. The lethal breath expanded through the clearing, freezing flowers and bees in the same swath that slew a dozen fleeing ogres.

In an instant, the rest of the monstrous band had vanished into the forest. Terror wafted in their wake, an acrid stench in the air. Lectral saw that many of the brutes had even cast their weapons aside, shrilling cries of utter panic in their haste to reach the imagined shelter of the forest paths. Abruptly four or five more broke from a nearby clump of brush, lumbering toward the trees, casting terrified glances behind.

Heart's jaws gaped again, and she expelled a cloud of white gas, a forceful explosion of her breath that gusted strongly toward her targets without the roaring destructiveness of her deadly frost. Nevertheless, the monsters saw the mist churning toward them and screamed in panic, sprinting desperately to get away as the vapor swept forward and enveloped them.

When the mist dissipated, the remaining ogres were scattered across the ground, limp and motionless—except for the slow rising and falling of chests stirred by deep, placid breathing. Eyes wide, those ogres lucky—or unlucky—enough to be lying on their backs stared in mute horror at the two serpents looming overhead, masters of this sunswept patch of meadow. Others, facedown, grunted and groaned but were obviously unable to move a muscle.

"Why didn't you kill them?" Lectral asked, with a raised eyebrow. Like all the metal dragons, he and Heart possessed a nonlethal breath weapon as well as their deadly expulsions. Still, he was surprised she had used it on the ogres. He prodded one of the motionless brutes with his foreclaws, rolling it onto its back to inspect the tusked maw, which now gaped slackly, allowing a copious spill of drool to soak the ogre's chest. "They're just paralyzed."

Heart shook her great silver head, though her own expression was also a trifle puzzled. "I didn't have to kill them, so I didn't. It seemed a good time to show mercy."

"Well, as Regia says, we dragons could kill all the ogres, and the humans and bakali, too, if we wanted. But why waste the breath?" Lectral replied.

"Our golden sister is too inclined to think in terms of the abstract. It's more that the threat is gone now . . . and I don't feel like killing any more."

"That sits well with me as well," Lectral agreed. He leaned forward, trailing his head along Heart's neck. "In any event, Regia is not the female who concerns me just now."

The silver male's lids drooped lazily over his eyes as he reared back and regarded the supple curves, the shimmering scales, and gleaming wings of the silver female. He squatted before her, ready to pounce, waiting for the flick of her tail that would recommence the tantalizing game that had just been interrupted.

But Heart shook her head. "No, Lec . . . let's fly, together."

He was about to protest, but he knew she wouldn't be swayed by any argument he could make. Too, with the passing of her teasing manner, his own excitement had rapidly faded. Heart seemed to him once more as she had always been: a silver nestmate who had grown to adulthood at his side, a friend and comrade during the hundreds of winters through which they and their kin-dragons had ruled the skies of Krynn.

Callak had been their sire, and their matriarch, Daria, had raised them in her lair, deep in the mountainous wilderness of western Ergoth. For the first century or two of their lives, they and their silver nestmates had been alone in the world, insofar as they had known nothing of other dragons. They had, of course, engaged in social intercourse with elves and humans, and both had formed strong friendships—particularly among the Kagonesti, in Lectral's case. Heart had enjoyed the company of the wild elves, but also displayed fascination with humankind, most notably the armored and heroic knights who ruled the realm of Solamnia.

After Callak had grown old, he had given Lectral the clan treasure: the horn of the great ram that he now wore on the silver chain around his neck. The silver dragons had grown to maturity with an understanding of the deep bonds between the Kagonesti wild elves and the dragons of argent.

Only after reaching adulthood had Heart and Lectral encountered dragons of other colors—first in the person of the sociable brass dragon Kord, scion of Dazzall, who seemed to know everybody and everything. He had become a good friend to all the silver nestmates, and in turn had introduced them to the less extroverted wyrms of the copper and bronze clans. Lectral had developed a grudging sense of respect for a copper male, Cymbol, who had once demonstrated great speed and quickness in stealing an elk that Lectral regarded as his rightful prey. Eventually the two wyrms had reached an understanding, and Lectral had learned that Cymbol's barely contained fury was a constant thing, a drive for vengeance against the chromatic dragons that had been inculcated in him by his sire, Tharn. Unfortunately—at least, so it seemed—neither of them had ever encountered one of the Dark Queen's dragons. To all appearances, they had ceased to exist during the time of their sire's early life.

The bronze, Bolt, had been less hostile initially than the copper had been, but neither had he been overly friendly. Still, Heart, Lectral, and their nestmates had learned from Daria the tale of the grotto and its abandonment, and it had been good to discover for certain that the others of the metal dragons had also survived to breed.

Lectral had been impressed by the differences even more than the similarities between the five clans. One of the *most* different was the dignified and studious Arumnus, a gold of approximately Lectral's age. Scion of Auricus, he was wise and thoughtful, if a trifle dull as a companion. And his sister, Regia, had been only haughty and aloof.

Lately Lectral had been dazzled by the changes he had sensed in Heart as the two of them approached full maturity, a feeling that matters between them were progressing toward something magical. The thought of her elven form fleeing through the woods caused his silver scales to shiver, and once again he regarded her with a sidelong inspection, wishing that she would flick her tail or arch her neck in that gesture of invitation.

Instead, she spread her wings and crouched, ready to take to the sky. With a sigh, Lectral, too, stretched wide, scooping downward as he leapt after her, dragging himself slowly into the air. The grasses of the meadow swept by, and finally he had enough speed to pull upward at the edge of the trees.

The two silvers steadily climbed, moving into the clear skies of late spring. A perfect day, thought Lectral, for flying, or hunting, or doing any kind of living at all. But still, as they flew side by side through summery skies, he pondered the questions of Heart's strange allure and the mood that had been shattered by the bothersome presence of the ogres.

Of course, the brutes were no real threat to a nearly mature silver such as Lectral or Heart, save the unlikely circumstance of a bunch of ogres coming upon a sleeping dragon. In fact, the world of the two nestmates' lives contained nothing that was a real threat.

"I wonder what it was like when the evil dragons still lived," mused the great male, pensive as the measured strokes of his wings carried him forward. "When there was real danger in Krynn . . . threats even to mighty dragons."

"Perhaps those old stories were just to scare us," Heart replied, teasing. "Have you ever seen a dragon that wasn't gold or silver or one of the brown metals?"

"Regia and Arumnus believe in those old legends!"

Lectral replied, rising to the bait. He shivered, unwilling to admit that he, too, sometimes pictured in his dreams a vague, five-headed image, a being he regarded with considerable unease. "And how else do you explain the small number of our forefathers, the five pairs who escaped the great scourge of Deathfyre? Or the wild magic that wracked the land, that caused the three brother mages to be hunted down and killed by vengeful elves?"

"Good stories, all of those. But I still think those gold dragons spend too much time in libraries!" Heart declared. "They should get out and fly once in a while!"

"There's nothing like flight to clear one's head," Lectral agreed, relishing the sweep of wind across his face, his wings, and his scales.

"Oh look—there's one of the knights!" cried the female, with a sudden dip of her head toward the brown plains. Lectral looked down and saw a great war-horse with a fully armored rider. The knight was trailed by a retinue of a half-dozen squires and pages, each mounted on a lighter, smaller horse. The party was riding across the dragons' path of flight, and apparently none of the humans had yet noticed the serpents.

"Come on, Lectral! Let's go talk to him!"

"Not again," groaned the male, knowing it was useless. Heart had already dipped her wing, sideslipping into a gliding dive that would carry them to ground out of sight of the riders, allowing them to land behind a screening line of tall pines.

By the time Lectral had settled to the grassy turf, Heart had changed to the form she preferred for these increasingly frequent encounters. Cloaked in the body of a tall, beautiful human woman, garbed in a typical noblewoman's silks that were perhaps a trifle more revealing than modesty would require, she strode forward into the roadway. Experience had shown her that an appearance like this would invariably bring the armored rider to a halt, no matter how pressing his business.

Lectral barely had time to assume his own disguise. In the form of a severe warrior, avuncular of appearance yet still strapping and capable in physique, he followed Heart as she waited for the rider to approach. The male dragon reflected that, if Heart's appearance was certain to get the knight to stop, his own stern and glowering visage was calculated to prevent the human from lingering for too long.

"Ho, my lady!" cried the warrior, lifting the visor of his helm with a gauntlet-covered hand. "And your honored grandfather as well!" he added hastily as Lectral advanced protectively at Heart's side.

"Greetings, Sir Knight!" The shapely maiden dipped into a polite curtsy.

"Stand your horses there, men," the rider directed, sending his followers into a nearby meadow as he dismounted.

"It is a pleasure to encounter you," Heart declared breathily. "I see that you bear the mark of the rose."

"Aye, lady. Methinks you know somewhat of the three orders that make up our ranks."

"Indeed I do, brave sir. And I know that, though crown may be mighty and sword strong, it is the rose that is most pleasant upon the senses."

"Indeed!" The knight positively beamed, the tips of his curling mustaches rising with his expression. "Er, is there a matter upon which I may be of assistance? Ogre trouble, perhaps? The brutes are reported to abound in this area."

"We have seen ogres, but they're dead now," Lectral replied grimly.

For the first time, the knight regarded the strapping form of the maiden's escort. Lectral's gray eyes met the human's frankly, and he allowed the sinew to ripple along his arms.

"No mean feat," admitted the armored rider. He hesitated, but Lectral made it clear that he wasn't about to wander away.

"Quite. Well, er, if your matters are in hand, there is business that calls me to Dargaard, else I would be certain to linger," he pledged, with a deep bow to Heart.

"Wait!" she cried as he swung back into his saddle. "Would you carry this . . . for luck?"

She lifted a scarf of shimmering silver, so light that it seemed to float like a spiderweb on the gentle breeze.

"It would be my honor, fair lady!" cried the knight, clearly moved.

Heart kissed the plume of silk, then handed it to the rider, who wasted no time in lashing it to the tip of his lance. By that time, his retainers had mounted, and with a cheery farewell, the band took to the road. Only after they were out of sight did the two dragons change shape and once again wing into the sky.

"Why did you do that?" grumbled Lectral, strangely disturbed by the memory of Heart's flirtations.

"Oh, Lec, it was such fun! And it's harmless!"

"It's not harmless. It's mischief!" retorted the glowering silver male.

"What about you and the wild elves? You're always talking to them, traveling among them. Don't tell me they all know the truth of your identity."

"That's different," Lectral declared. "You know of the special bond we have with the Elderwild, going all the way back to Darlantan and Kagonos."

"Now you sound like an old fuddy gold!" teased Heart. To punctuate her words, she dipped a wing and dived away from Lectral, flicking her tail teasingly across his belly as she began an upside-down loop, then dropped into a straight plummet toward the ground.

He plunged after her and had to work hard in order to catch her. Wingtip to wingtip, they glided toward the dusk, relishing the rosy expanse of sky as the last rays of the setting sun glimmered off their scales.

They came to rest on a high ridge of the Kharolis, knowing that a teeming nation of dwarves dwelt below them. Yet it was still one of Lectral's favorite places, as it had been for years and years, and had been for the generations of metal dragons preceding them. Aloof and removed from such concerns, the mighty serpents watched the growing swath of rosy purple, deeply content as the sunset expanded to encompass the western horizon.

Chapter 29
Heir to a Queen

circa 1300 PC

Deathfyre stirred, awakening in the depths of his fiery chasm. Over an immeasurable time, the spell of suspension that had entrapped him was gradually weakened, allowing the mighty crimson head to rise with glacial deliberation. The Dark Queen's summons was a faint and distant knell, and only slowly did the red dragon become aware of the keening, pervasive call. He puffed a slow exhalation of dry air, unaware of the ashes that wafted from his nostrils or the soot that layered his crimson scales.

Suspended thus, he had slept for a dozen centuries while the metallic wyrms of Paladine had grown complacent in their superiority on the surface of Ansalon. Deathfyre had grown larger and more terrible during his torpor, yet in his awareness, it was as if little or no time had passed.

He knew nothing of his old rivals, Callak and Auricus, nor was he aware of the spreading presence of humankind. Beyond the mountains, more and more lands of ancient wilderness, as well as realms once held by ogres, elves, or dwarves, had been claimed by the relentlessly energetic race of men. Closer by, the Khalkists remained a region of raging fire and eternal smoke, but even here the presence of humankind was penetrating with relentless determination.

Through the murk of his long suspension, Deathfyre was vaguely aware that all of his kin had been slain. The magic of the brother mages had been an irresistible force, and the proud dragons of Crematia's mighty horde had been swallowed by the bedrock of Krynn, where they had withered and perished over the passing centuries.

At the same time, he could not know of the convulsions caused by the violent magic of the three arcane sorcerers. It would have pleased him to learn that the trio of wizards had been relentlessly hunted by the elves, eventually forced into magical banishment or killed outright. So devastating had been the wild magic unleashed by their great casting that elven historians regarded them as villains of the same scope and wickedness as the dragons of Takhisis themselves.

And only Deathfyre had been spared, by fortune, magic, and the blessing of his five-headed mistress. As the epic forces of unnatural magic had wrenched the world, pulling the other chromatic dragons into captivity, he had been dragged to the same cavern in the bowels of the Lords of Doom where Crematia had sheltered more than a millennia before.

Deathfyre's matriarch had emerged from that hibernation to loose a flood of destruction across the face of the world, commencing a nearly triumphant campaign for the mastery of Ansalon. Soon her descendants would be ready to do the same, but the Dark Queen had learned a lesson from Crematia's arrogance and knew that her dragons would not be able to achieve a swift and easy victory.

Instead, Deathfyre's campaign would employ a new tactic, characterized by patience far beyond any Takhisis had displayed in the past. The plan itself filtered into the red dragon's mind over centuries, instilled by long and repetitive dreams. These visions gave to him memories of blood and killing, of plunder and wealth, and they warmed him within as the fundamental fire of the Khalkists radiated against him from without.

Inside his cavernous vault, with its scorching heat and eternal fire, Deathfyre's awareness was gradually restored. The Dark Queen's message was clear, her scheme clever and complicated. Through the timeless centuries, he absorbed her wishes, heard her commands, until, with a shiver of memory, he awakened to the recollection of the sweet taste of fresh blood. Raising his head, feeling the hunger gnaw at his gut, the crimson serpent reflected upon his mistress's desires.

A timeless interval later, after he clearly understood the wishes of Takhisis, Deathfyre took wing within the fiery chamber, circling many times over the lake of fire. He recalled the dreams, knew the path that had been laid out for him, and heard the reminders in the bubbling fury of the lava and the rising tumult of the flaming subterranean storm.

Finally his flight took him soaring from the mighty caldera, crimson wings once again spreading wide, claiming their rightful place in the skies of Krynn. Deathfyre exulted in his freedom and his flight, banking and soaring, slicing through the clouds that roiled and churned around the three volcanic summits. The red dragon longed to fly south, to wreak vengeance on the ancient homes of the elves, but he had heard his queen's commands and he knew that this was not his task.

Instead, he would be patient and—for the first time in his long and destructive life—discreet. He limited his flight to the impenetrable murk surrounding the trio of summits, insuring that he was not observed from the ground. When at last he grew tired, ready to come to rest upon the firmament, he used his magic to change his body to that of a great vulture. The black-winged bird settled through the clouds, soaring unnoticed into a valley that had become home to a teeming populace of humans and ogres.

This place was called Sanction, Deathfyre remembered, for it had been founded before the brother mages had cast the wild magic and entrapped him. It was a city and a valley that figured greatly in his destiny. Rivers of fire scoured the streets, and buildings teetered at the brink of destruction as lava churned past, steadily eroding the landscape of the city. Yet new constructions were rising from the rugged slopes, and Deathfyre observed one swath of blackened ground—clearly a slum that had been swept by ruinous fire—where new shacks were already beginning to appear. Furthermore, temples to a host of gods, real and imagined, had sprouted like weeds amid the tangled alleys and byways. The peripheries of the city had become a chaotic nest of arsenals and smithies, while great stockpiles of coal were gathered in huge piles on the city's eastern, mountain-guarded flank.

The tangled alleys leading through the teeming city's darkened heart were lined with hovels and shacks of incredible wretchedness, many of these sprawling in the very shadows of splendid manor houses and palatial residences of prominent merchants and nobles. Within the slums, the population grew and swelled, expanding within its limited confines, building pressure that must inevitably be released in an explosion of consuming violence.

This was a perfect city for his purposes, Deathfyre saw, a place of murder and mayhem, of worshipers who hailed dark gods and practiced rites of grim decadence. It was a city that had a prominent place in his plans, and he would return here.

Yet for now, the wishes of his immortal mistress required him to journey to higher valleys, mountainous reaches much farther to the east. The condor veered with a shriek of arrogant disdain, a cry to subjects who did not know they had just heard the voice of their future master.

His black wings trailed long feathers, like the fingers of a bony hand, as they cut through the smoke and murk with easy grace. Steadily he flew, up the valley leading into the mountain range, leaving the city of fire until a future time.

Deathfyre marked a course over a trackless tangle of mountains, soaring by memory to the lofty cave, a place Crematia had created in her prime. In her later years, she had shown it to her mighty son, and he had marked the place well. Now he approached the apparently featureless cliff, his keen eyes seeking the subtle shimmer of magic. The ledge was concealed by illusion, but the red dragon's power was sufficient to part that disguise, and then to melt away the wall of stone that blocked the passage beyond.

Within the secret cavern, Deathfyre found the great treasure room that he remembered, a cavernous chamber with a floor carpeted by coins of steel and gold and gemstones of every color and size. He rolled amid the mass of treasure, allowing the metal disks to run through his talons, burying himself in a mound of precious jewels and gleaming coins. He searched for and found one particular item that he had remembered only vaguely, but here again he was guided by the images sent to him in the Dark Queen's dreams. This was a fine leather satchel with a pair of latching handles, an item Crematia had tossed aside with almost contemptuous indifference.

Slowly and patiently the red dragon began to gather the coins and gemstones, scooping them into his massive claws and pouring them into the magical sack. Though it took him a day and a night, he was able to conceal the entire vast hoard in the single satchel, doing as he had been commanded in the dream sent by Takhisis.

Carrying this great wealth, he departed the secret chamber and came to rest on the valley floor. Deathfyre used further magic to take the form of a dwarf, and from there he embarked on foot into the realms of the great miners of the Khalkists. He traveled as a rich merchant, gradually acquiring a small caravan of fine horses, several stout wagons, and a retinue of loyal, well-paid servants.

He was welcomed among these dwarves as one of their

own—more to the point, one of their very wealthy own. In the central cavern of their great underground city, the dwarvenking himself hosted a great feast in his honor. The visiting merchant was introduced to the dwarven lords with high ceremony. Many of these worthies brought blushing daughters of marriageable age to meet the exotic visitor, though each of these overtures was met with polite disinterest. Instead, the dwarven visitor announced plans to embark upon an ambitious business venture.

With great expenditures, he bought the services of many a doughty miner, forming a large expedition of experienced delvers. He led this courageous band over rugged trails into the heart of the Khalkists, realms that a thousand years before had been the domains of chromatic dragons. Paying handsomely, as always, the dwarven entrepreneur divided his hundreds of workers into mining parties and set them to work in a series of lofty valleys, commencing a search for precious gems.

And there was added incentive, for the master dwarf was interested only peripherally in such baubles as diamonds, rubies, and emeralds. These finds were to be kept by the workers themselves, and many a dwarven laborer grew rich in the service of this mysterious stranger. Unfortunately, some of the workers also lost their lives, as is ever the way with mines, but the families of these victims invariably received generous compensation from the dwarven overseer.

As to his purpose, the master delver's instructions were specific: He desired for himself only those rare stones that were perfect spheres, pure and unblemished in color. They were discovered in five varieties: black, red, blue, green, and white, and the rich dwarf paid handsomely for every sample brought to him.

When he had collected many dozens of each variety, the dwarven businessman organized another great expedition and made ready to march down from the Khalkists. He prepared to travel with a great caravan of wagons, announcing his intention to seek and purchase trade goods of all kinds. Of course, the party would also carry a generous selection of the rare, spherical baubles of color.

The dwarves who worked for him were hired for a new task now, informed that the caravan would spend years in making a great circuit about Ansalon, and they were promised that the party would return bearing fabulous profit for all. The master delver had proven to be a beneficent and generous employer, so once again he was greeted by many willing offers of assistance.

Eventually more than a hundred dwarven laborers signed on for the duration of the expedition, with the understanding that they might be gone for a score of years, or even longer. The caravan departed with a creaking of sturdy wagon wheels and lowing of oxen under the skillfully wielded whips of dwarven teamsters, with the fond farewells of a great populace still ringing from the mountain heights.

Trekking through rugged terrain, the dwarves carved a road where they had to, hoisting the wagons over mountain ridges, guiding them along precarious ledges above deep, rock-lined gorges. They progressed eastward for a long time, but—true to the master delver's words—they at last emerged from the mountains into well-populated realms that were exotic, remote, and wealthy.

In each city, town, and village that the expedition reached, the dwarven delver, now proving himself a master merchant as well, traded away his precious spherical gems. Sometimes he exchanged them for great sums of steel coinage or bedazzling jewelry, but at other times he seemed touched by a most undwarflike generosity and consented to give up a stone for a mere night's lodging, or in trade for a beaten old nag of a horse. Always the spheres were received with awe and wonder, for they were unique, and therefore precious, among all the treasures of Krynn.

Over winters and summers, through good weather and bad, the trading caravan marked its long and methodical path across much of Ansalon. Beginning with Balifor, the dwarven delver's route extended to Mithas, then passed through the increasingly prosperous realm of Istar, before finally curling back southward through Neraka, Sanction, and Xak Tsaroth. Eventually he even trekked into the distant reaches of mountainous Thorbardin and the southern seaport of Tarsis.

Thus were the round baubles seeded throughout the world. Some were locked in treasure rooms, or placed upon newly sanctified altars by their proud owners. Others were rolled into playrooms, left as children's toys, or placed in galleries and halls for public or private exhibition. Each was kept, mostly treasured but occasionally forgotten, as the caravan rolled on. As the years passed, the spheres were regarded like any other exotic object of great beauty and indisputable rarity—that is, they were prized treasures.

And then, at last, the dwarven merchant and his weary caravan approached the valleys of the Khalkist foothills. Yet the great merchant was tired by the long trek and didn't want to bother to journey all the way to the dwarven realm. Instead, he ate his horses, burned his laborers to death, and settled down to wait.

Chapter 30
Precious Baubles

1191 PC

Rallak Thartan was a stout, elderly cloth merchant, fortunate enough to have inherited a family stall in one of Xak Tsaroth's most affluent neighborhoods. Business was good, as it had been since his great-grandfather had first sent a caravan to Tarsis in search of silk. Through his practice of starting work early and staying late, Rallak Thartan had grown to dominate the fabric market in the entire quarter of the city surrounding his modest shop.

Normally these work habits entailed the diligent merchant arriving at his home well past sunset, long after his competitors had closed up shop. But today, as he had done with increasing frequency of late, he decided to pull the shutters in midafternoon and hurry home to the welcoming arms of his wife.

For, lately, those arms had been very welcoming indeed.

It had all begun with a gift, a bauble Rallak Thartan had given his young wife a few months earlier. A simple red sphere, of large size and pure crimson color, it was an orb that was unique and fascinating in a strange way. The globe was beautiful of shade and perfect of shape, and there was nothing like it in any other house in this part of Xak Tsaroth.

Yet to the merchant, the stone had at first represented neither beauty nor a means toward his wife's affections. It had been, purely and simply, a matter of revenge.

Rallak was still amazed at the fluke of events that had led him to gain possession of the bauble. After all, the orb had belonged for a long time to the House of Garlot, one of the Thartan clan's major trading rivals for five generations. The venerable patriarch of House Garlot had won the sphere more than a hundred years ago in a clever trade with a dishonest dwarven peddler. The Garlots had displayed the crimson orb in their shop's anteroom, and it had long been the envy of Xak Tsaroth's mercantile circles.

Yet time brought changes, and the House of Garlot had eventually suffered a run of bad luck, most notably the state of raving insanity to which the current heir had succumbed. Finally, upon the recent occasion of his rival's bankruptcy, which would have been cause for Rallak Thartan's celebration in its own right, the merchant had gained possession of the crimson bauble.

Though he had at first been unimpressed by the physical appearance and qualities of the sphere, which was too spongy to be an actual stone, Rallak Thartan's wife had been thrilled. She had installed the crimson orb in a place of honor, an alcove in their sleeping chamber, and had it mounted upon a stand of pure gold. Lately he had even wondered if the thing was glowing, for he had noticed a subtle illumination seeping through the shadows of night, a crimson glow that was somehow very similar to that shed by a fading, but still very hot, bed of coals.

Now he hurried home through the busy streets of the

city, anxious to hear the latest word about his wife's treasure. Lately, each day had brought a new development, or so it had seemed. At least, his young bride had eagerly reported to him the details of a seemingly enchanted series of transformations.

She had been pleased to observe the subtle expansion occurring as the crimson orb literally seemed to swell. She had remarked upon flickers of movement within the orb, ripples that periodically showed upon the smooth surface. And, of course, like Rallak Thartan himself, she was delighted by the aura of embers that seemed to emanate from the globe during the darkest hours of the night.

And when Rallak Thartan's wife was delighted, she had a way of making sure that he was delighted as well. He reflected upon his own good fortune with a bawdy chuckle. The merchant was a man of mature years, ample paunch, and carefully cultivated dignity, but his wife was much younger than he. Her own enthusiasms carried over to him, and lately he had found himself feeling more youthful than he had in years, even decades. And so much of it seemed to have to do with this precious treasure—the stone that clearly wasn't a stone at all.

He strolled through the entryway of his palatial manor, mildly distressed that his maidservant had failed to open the door to greet him. Still, even that irritation was fleeting. How could he be angry when his mind was anxiously wondering about his wife's latest surprise?

Up the stairs he lumbered, thinking that the house was strangely silent around him. Where were the sounds from the kitchen, the cooks and maids going about their chores? Still, he wasn't particularly worried, not even when he caught a faint whiff of char on the air. Somebody had merely been careless with the fireplace ashes; surely that was all.

The blood on the satin quilt of his mattress gave him the first hint that something was terribly amiss. The appalling discovery of his wife's headless corpse, lying in the alcove where the treasure was kept on display, provided the second.

The third and final piece of the puzzle was delivered by

widespread jaws surprisingly powerful for their size, and equipped with rows of needle-sharp teeth. The gaping mouth darted like a striking snake from the tangle of a curtain that had fallen and was now bundled carelessly on the floor. Like a vise the crimson maw closed around Rallak Thartan's head . . . and twisted.

* * * * *

Aku Ben Vyneer hauled back on the reins, and the plodding camel shuffled to a halt. With an irritated spit, the animal chomped placidly while the rider climbed down. With a wave of his hand, Ben Vyneer gestured for the file of camels and horses following in his tracks to stop. The men of the long caravan wasted little time in setting up camp. Tents rose with the ease of long practice, and small cooking fires were started, the aroma of strong tea soon wafting through the encampment.

A sea of dunes rolled to the horizon on all sides, unmarred by any sign of an oasis. Nearby, ancient pillars and crumbling walls marked the scene of a waterless ruin. Normally Ben Vyneer would have spent the last few hours of daylight in a steady push forward, urging his tired mounts and men to keep moving, determined to cross this waste in as a short a time as possible. After all, there was no part of Estwilde—or all Ansalon, for that matter—that was so dry, so barren, as this inhospitable desert.

But, strangely, Aku Ben Vyneer had an interest more profound than even the pursuit of profit that normally governed his existence. It was this interest, perhaps even obsession, that had caused him to order the caravan to such an early halt. Now he stalked about the bustling camp with visible agitation, shouting orders, barking relentless criticism, increasingly distraught as he waited for one particular task.

Thus his men wasted no time in erecting the tent of bright blue silk—the shelter he had recently ordered, specifically made to house his greatest treasure. Once the tent had been pitched, the men left their master to his own pursuits. Ben Vyneer entered the tent and took his place on a soft cushion that had been placed before a large chest, a chest for which he alone held the key.

How long and hard had been the road that led him to this end? He reflected on the question with deep pleasure, allowing himself a moment of tantalizing anticipation before he released the lock. For years he had bargained to gain possession of this chest and its unique contents, even selling his most beautiful daughter to the previous owner, in a clear and well-stated exchange.

But then, when that owner had reneged upon his promise, Aku Ben Vyneer had no choice. Yesterday he had killed the wretched thief, then stolen this most precious of treasures during the dark of the night. Today he had led his caravan far into the desert before daring to stop and inspect his find.

With an unsteady hand, he reached out to take the key in his trembling fingers. He turned the chip of brass in the lock, scarcely daring to breathe as he felt the catch of the latch release. He forced himself to be calm as he reached out with both hands, holding steadily to the sides of the sturdy chest.

Aku Ben Vyneer opened the lid, prepared to gasp in delight at the beauteous treasure within.

But instead he grunted in sudden dismay. Shaking, he pushed the lid back, leaping to his feet to peer into the shadowy container.

The blue orb remained there, but there was a pasty flaking to the perfect surface that had not been there a few days earlier when Ben Vyneer had last inspected his—at that time future—treasure.

"What is happening, my bauble?" he asked, reaching out a hand to touch the blue surface that had once been such a perfectly reflective turquoise. "Has someone harmed you?"

To his surprise, he felt a tiny tingle of a spark as his fingers stroked the smooth sphere. And then the orb moved, pulsing with a very definite, throbbing expansion of its upper surface.

Ben Vyneer fell to his knees, pressing his face to the carpeted floor of the tent, and it was in this posture that the blue dragon found him when it emerged. The wyrmling wasted no time in killing the nomad with a bite to the back of his exposed neck.

Then, well contented, the blue dragon hatchling settled down to its first meal.

* * * * *

The hooded priests gathered in their damp cellar, within a darkened shack at the terminus of a shadow-cloaked alley amid one of the bleakest of Sanction's wretched slums. Each member of the cult entered alone, with a careful look back and forth in the dark lane to make sure he wasn't observed. The surreptitious visitors wore robes of dark gray or brown, each walking silently and alone, casting furtive glances that seemed perfectly at home in this city of evil and greed.

One after another the secret members gathered, passing through the incense-filled stall of the spice shop that ostensibly gave this building a reason for existing. Within, each of the mysterious figures repeated the same process: He went to a trapdoor that was designed to look just like the rotted planks of the floor. After checking again for observers, he silently raised the portal and entered.

Moving down the stairway concealed below, the priest joined his fellows in the secret sanctuary, a room of dank, muddy walls, and worn and ancient benches. But these were mere accessories, unimportant attendants to the thing that had founded this order and was now responsible for drawing the group together.

Pulling the heavy cowls of their hoods forward so that each face was fully lost in thick shadows, they huddled around the sacred orb—the treasure that gave them a focus of faith in the tortured chaos that was Sanction. Though the order of secret priests had been in existence for many decades, an air of expectancy had settled around the members during recent months, and this meeting was one of the results.

The orb was a sphere of perfect blackness resting on a

marble dais, raised above the assembly of faithful priests. These hooded clerics murmured quietly, until gradually the sounds rose to a steady, rhythmic chant.

Abruptly a robe was pulled away from a slight figure, and a young woman was revealed. A gag distorted her face, tightly binding her mouth, muffling her frantic pleas and outcries. Cruel bonds wrapped her arms and legs, preventing any movement beyond the frantic twisting and thrashing that she commenced as soon as she was revealed. The woman struggled with a vengeance, her eyes wide with terror as she was stretched on the floor before the orb of darkness. Her bonds were then slashed, but only so that her wrists and ankles could be outspread and fastened with metal-studded straps.

The chanting built slowly, still soft but possessed of an urgency, or perhaps even a hunger, that had been lacking moments before. The helpless victim saw the knife as it emerged from the cowl of a black sleeve. A single scream pierced the gloom, breaking through the confinement of the gag as the blade slashed forward, and then, mercifully, her sufferings were over.

Then the sphere of blackness started to pulse, a rhythmic thrumming that grew in speed and intensity. The priests chanted with frantic hope, all eyes fixed upon the sacred orb. Within the cellar, the sound rose to a keening wail.

The rip came suddenly as something terrible and shiny, serpentine and black, pushed through the surface of the collapsing sphere. Acid spurted, a spume of searing liquid sweeping through a full circle, hissing into flesh and cloth, leaving the priests blinded, writhing on the floor, uttering shrieks that slowly faded to moans, ragged breathing, or utter silence.

These were not sounds worthy of attention in Sanction, so there was none who came to see what had happened.

The black, slime-covered serpent slithered down from the marble dais and crept to the nearest of the priests. This wretch, though blinded and crippled by the acid, was not yet dead, and his groans rose into piteous wails as the serpent began to feed.

Chapter 31
Fury of Deathfyre

1056 PC

"Fly to me, my kin-dragons, wyrms of Takhisis!"

Deathfyre stood tall atop the smoldering caldron of the volcano, sending out a cry that rang across the breadth of Ansalon. The message was swelled, given strength and volume and range, by the Queen of Darkness herself. Riding the wind, the summons reached far, penetrating every corner of the world.

As the great red dragon bugled forth the call from the heights of the Lords of Doom, the populace of Sanction quailed and cried in the valley below. An hour earlier Deathfyre had first flown over that city in his true form, appearing from the volcanic smog like a vengeful apparition. Crimson wings spread wide, as if to draw the entire city into an embrace of doom, the red dragon swept back and forth over mansion and slum.

He had attracted attention with loud roars, drawing the populace into the streets and onto rooftops and balconies, where they stared upward in a mixture of terror and awe. Then Deathfyre spoke to them in their own language, telling them that their new master had come . . . that he was the one who would lead them to power and glory.

"If you do my bidding," he had bellowed, the sound of his voice echoing from the three great mountains flanking the city of fire, "you shall thrive and grow mighty! But if you resist, know that you shall die!"

Men trembled and women wailed at the coming of the mighty wyrm, but the numerous ogres in the city howled and cheered, hailing the vision of a master that arose from the distant fog of their tribal dreams. These accolades still rang out, and a frenzy had spread through Sanction, bringing throngs into the narrow streets, igniting chaotic revelry and frantic prayer in approximately equal proportions.

But for now all these lesser beings, the two-legged throngs of his legions, were beneath Deathfyre's notice. His cry was meant for other ears, some near and others distant, and—unlike the bellows with which he had terrified Sanction—it was audible to those listeners alone.

In the depths of the city's sewers, a black head emerged from the murk, probing for the source of the piercing summons. The young dragon had dwelt here for a long time, ever since it had emerged from the sacred orb that had been the focus of a short-lived cult. Now it crept through the muck, pushing upward, stalking along a street, scattering merchants and mercenaries alike until it took wing, striving without understanding to reach the lofty summit.

Through the arid waste of the Estwilde desert, the cry wafted like a scorching wind, penetrating the eroded columns of an ancient palace. Gusts carried eddies of sand into swirling funnels, marking the clean-picked skeletons of many camels, horses, and men. The hot wind swept on, pushing through the ruins into a barren, dry chamber where dwelt a serpent of pure turquoise blue. That wyrm raised its wicked head, sensing the cry, and then it, too, took wing, rising over the desert toward the horizon of the rugged Khalkists. The blue dragon flew with a purpose, a sense of mission like nothing it had ever known.

In distant Xak Tsaroth, the cry fell from the sky, pushing through a ring of armed guards that garrisoned a cordon about the once-grand home of a wealthy merchant. It had been a long time since that merchant had been seen, and though numerous brave men had ventured into the house to see what was wrong, none of them had ever emerged. Thus this permanent detachment of warriors had been left as a precaution.

Now the guards recoiled in terror as a crimson monster roared forth, scarlet wings flapping wildly, cruel jaws gaping. The red dragon filled the street with lethal gouts of fire, burning numerous men-at-arms and bystanders before it took wing. Once airborne, the wyrmling marked a course for Sanction, like his kin-dragons answering the piercing, intuitive cry.

And from countless other hatching dens they came as well, these dragons born in treasure rooms and dungeons and manor houses throughout Ansalon. They took wing as soon as they were touched by their immortal queen's message, in the first days out of the egg for some, after many years of surreptitious feeding and growing for others. The chromatic dragons were guided by an instinct older than the trio of mountains that surrounded Sanction, the Lords of Doom that had emerged from the chaos of Darklady Mountain's destructive eruption.

They joined Deathfyre over the course of several days, hundreds of wyrms of all the Dark Queen's colors. Greens flew in wide formations, while blues and reds dived and darted, striving for supremacy. Dragons of black came out of the night, and wyrms of icy white flew from the glacial south, all of them awakened and compelled, drawn by the irresistible summons of the Queen of Darkness.

"I blazed my way from Xak Tsaroth in a fury of fire and claw and fang!" boasted crimson Tombfyre, crowing in exultation, describing the men-at-arms who had fallen dead, lethally charred by his fiery breath.

"And I was master of all the sewers of Sanction. There I dwelt in comfort, eating well, until I hastened to obey your summons!" announced black Corro.

"As for me, I was comfortable in the midst of the northern desert," explained Azurus, he of the turquoise-blue scales. "But finally the last of the camels was gone, and I began to grow hungry. And now that you have brought me here, I begin to see my purpose."

"Fly forth, my kin-dragons!" ordered Deathfyre, selecting the greatest among his flock as his agents. "Go to the realms of mankind and ogre, dwarf and bakali—all you can reach within a day's flight of here. Gather warriors to my banners and bid them march to my city with all haste—and tell them that to disobey is to die."

Corro, Azurus, Tombfyre, and many others flew toward the points of the compass, and within a few days they returned, bringing the promise of many troops following in their wake. A wave of warlike frenzy had swept the surrounding realms, and warriors of all races flocked to Sanction with bloodlust and avarice in their hearts.

At the feet of the Khalkists, the ogres once again answered the martial call, thousands of brutish warriors emerging from their dens and lairs. The descendants of a once-mighty and highly cultured race, they now snarled and growled like animals, smacking their lips at the prospects of fresh blood. The ogres were large and strong, and each carried a heavy, sharp-edged blade. As a force on the ground, they were a mass against whom very few troops would dare to stand.

From the lower valleys and fens of the Khalkists came the bakali, recruited by the black dragons, who relished the muck and mire favored by the reptilian savages. The lizard men remembered Deathfyre in their greatest legends, and they willingly gathered in a throng to once more serve their crimson master. The scaly-skinned warriors came by the hundreds and then the thousands, forming great encampments before the walls of Sanction, watched suspiciously by the humans who manned the city ramparts.

Corrupt humans came, too, drawn from Sanction and other realms by lure of treasure, or propelled by fear of consequences should they decline to serve. Barbarian horsemen rode in great swarms from the plains, and nomads marched southward from the deserts. Crude and brutal pirates trekked overland all the way from Balifor, and mercenaries from Tarsis and Xak Tsaroth arrived in increasing numbers, answering the universal lures of treasure and adventure.

And even some of the dwarves of the Khalkists, the children of those who had labored for Deathfyre in the gathering of the dragon eggs, added their banners to the crimson wyrm's horde. Wicked and evil creatures, these cruel dwarves betrayed the proud and honorable legacy of their people, bribed by the dragons' offers of all the gems they could capture.

The dragons that had answered Deathfyre's summons circled the mountains and finally settled to the ground, landing on the flanks of the soaring volcanoes, so that from a distance the summits seemed to be mottled in patterns of the queen's five colors. All of these deadly serpents had been born in secrecy, and many were already quite huge—a surfeit of food supplies had seen to that.

Now the dragons fluttered and roared, watching the troops stream toward the city below. Breath of fire and acid, ice and gas and lightning, blasted the skies in ritual challenge as the wyrms of the Dark Queen grew more aggressive, more anxious to unleash their power against the world. Inevitably fights erupted among them, leaving wings rent, scales torn from flesh, and lives lost as that pent-up fury built to a fever pitch.

And then their leader let them know that the attack would soon begin.

Deathfyre gathered his two-legged captains on the ground before the city walls. He appointed a mighty ogre, Garic Drakan, as commander of the army, and bade the dwarves, bakali, humans, and other ogres to show the chieftain such fealty as they would to the red dragon himself. When the roars had risen to a deafening crescendo,

Garic put his army to the march, leaving Sanction behind as the horde advanced like a tide of ink onto the plains of Solamnia.

"Do we strike against the elves?" demanded mighty Azurus as the dragons fluttered their stiff wings and craned their necks, ready to attack. All knew the grim history of the Silvanesti wars, and vengeance was a powerful compulsion among the wyrms of Takhisis.

"No. This time it will be the humans who feel the brunt of our onslaught!" declared Deathfyre. He clearly remembered his matriarch's firmest lesson: Find your strongest enemy and kill him! "Solamnia has become the greatest realm, the strongest empire on Krynn, and thus it shall be Solamnia that feels the fury of our queen's wrath!"

"I myself will burn a hundred of the enemy warriors!" boasted Tombfyre, who was already a large serpent, capable of expelling a huge gout of flame. He rose to his haunches and bellowed a great fountain of fire into the sky.

"Ah, my son," declared Deathfyre. "I know that you will earn the praises of our queen!"

And when the dragons of evil took wing, they darkened the sky. Aided by their skyborne allies, Garic Drakan's army swept forward on the ground, quickly subduing the realms around the mountains, squashing the peoples who dwelt in the foothills as if these minor kingdoms and duchies were so many villages and camps. Ultimately the great serpents led the invasions from Sanction onto the plains of Vingaard, a tide swarming westward toward the realm of the proud knights.

On the ground, the armies of the ogre Garic Drakan marched forth. Columns diverged across the prairie, destroying settlements, pillaging strongholds, battling any band of armed men that dared to raise a blade. Legions of mercenary horsemen preceded the brutal foot soldiers, making savage onslaughts against every city and town in their path. Bakali lizard men swarmed behind the riders, killing mercilessly, while the heavy ogres and tens of thousands of human footmen plodded relentlessly forward, a crushing wave of irresistible force that swarmed in a lethal tide.

In the face of this onslaught, the Knights of Solamnia rode forth from their castles to do battle. Companies of the Sword, the Crown, and the Rose all formed courageously. True to honor, duty, and the Measure, they faced attacks by overwhelming armies, until the dragons of the Dark Queen flew from the skies, driving the human warriors back with horrendous casualties.

But during these initial campaigns, mindful of the impetuous advance that had led to destruction in Silvanesti more than a thousand years before, Deathfyre held his legions to a more measured pace. Led by Tombfyre and Azurus, the mighty red dragon's wings of flying serpents rarely flew far ahead of the troops on the ground, and those spearheads were held in check as well. Deathfyre insisted that his horsemen remain within supporting distance of the rest of the army, until ultimately the army of the Dark Queen plodded forward in a well-disciplined wave, relentlessly burying everything across a thousand-mile swath of ruin.

And always Deathfyre remained alert for reports of the dragons of metal. Surely they dwelt in the west and would learn of the attack. But where were they? When would they enter the fight? He couldn't know the answer, and so he made certain that he was ready. In fact, this was one of the major reasons for the measured advance of his force. He didn't want to expose a far-flung spearhead to annihilation at the hands of a sudden dragon counterattack.

Still, much of the pride of Solamnia bled and died on the plains of Ansalon. Dargaard Keep fell, and the mighty Vingaard River was crossed, with the castle of the same name besieged. Everywhere the army of Deathfyre met victory and left grieving, ruin, and destruction once the vanguard had passed.

But where were the dragons of metal? Until they flew, Deathfyre knew that his vengeance would remain incomplete.

Chapter 32
Lectral's Choice

1029 PC

Flanking cliffs of white chalk rose from the mist-shrouded depths of a wilderness gorge, concealing an icy torrent of glacial melt that churned and eroded its way through the slash of deep channel. Most of the vast chasm was shrouded in nearly eternal shadows, a blanket of darkness broken only when the sun stood at high zenith. Moss draped the slick white rocks, and tributary streams flowed from constant springs and seasonal snowmelt, trickling down the steep cliffs in a myriad of splashing waterfalls, adding their contents to the raging flowage far below.

High on the north-facing wall of the deep gorge was a wide ledge, a shelf of white rock that remained exposed to sunlight throughout the day, during all seasons of the year. The chalk surface was smooth, though a number of curved indentations pocked the surface near the cliff wall. Furthermore, a steady stream of clear water trilled down the nearby cliffs, gathering in a wide, deep pool before spilling over the lip of the ledge to shower into the unseen depths of the gorge.

This perch was Lectral's favorite place in all the High Kharolis. The flat surface was long enough for him to stretch to his full length and sufficiently wide that he could carelessly gather himself into a loose coil. The pool made for splendid drinking, and on exceptionally hot days, he could immerse himself all the way to his eyeballs in refreshing coolness.

As to the view, he was content to remain within the cool confinement of the white chalk walls. He enjoyed the sight of blue or gray skies overhead, and from within the gap of his secluded gorge, he observed the phases of the moons or watched the constellations as the stars wheeled by. He had learned to anticipate every nuance of lunar cycles, predicting when and where each of the three moons would appear along the overhead rim.

The familiar Kharolis skyline loomed to the east, and though Lectral couldn't see the mountains from his ledge, he could call up their mental image anytime he chose. For now, he was content to let the memory suffice, to enjoy the smooth comfort and sheltered confines of his lofty ledge. Of course, he often left this place to hunt, and frequently those hunts took him over the crests of the High Kharolis. He always made a point to circle the deep mountain-guarded lake where his proud sire, the legendary Callak, was buried.

Yet it had been long since he had visited any of the two-legged folk who lived beyond those heights. He wasn't really interested in that sort of society anymore—with the exception of the Kagonesti. And even then, his protector-ship of the wild elves had become an aloof and distant thing. Often he had observed the tribes throughout the forests of Ansalon, but he did so invisibly, or in the guise of a bird or perhaps a stag or mountain sheep. He held the ram's horn in its sacred trust, but never had he had to use it or to answer its summons from the Kagonesti.

For long periods of time, Lectral remained on his chalk ledge, concealed within his white gorge by himself. Heart, ever his favorite companion and nestmate, had been absent from his life for many winters. He wondered if she were spending all of her time in the guise of human or elf, for even the griffons that regularly brought word of events in the world had heard nothing of the large silver female. With a flash of jealous memory, his thoughts returned to a sparkling moment: the chase of two wild elves through the forest and its untimely interruption by a band of ogres.

It was odd how, in that elven guise, he had felt a warmth of feeling, a deep affection for his nestmates that was decidedly undragonlike. He had heard about love, of course, but as it would be to any centuries-old serpent, the concept was not a thing he could understand. It seemed a silly and vulnerable weakness, useful only to enliven the existence of short-lived creatures who had no real hope of majesty in their pathetic lives.

Sometimes in the years immediately following the time when he and Heart had wandered apart, Lectral, too, had walked among men. After all, as a silver dragon it was somewhat expected. Yet he had never found the appeal in these short-lived, vibrant folk that had compelled Heart and, more recently, her younger sisters, Saytica and Silvara, to live for long stretches in the guise of a two-legs. The Kagonesti, at least, were serene and dignified and lived lives of a properly long span of years.

Lectral was thinking, with fond reminiscence, of the silver female when a cloak of darkness suddenly blotted out the stars. He jerked his head upward, popping out the top of a sphere of a magical blackness, and when he heard a musical trill of laughter, he knew he had been made the victim of a prank.

"Silvara! Come out where I can see you!"

The laughter rose, chiming in harmony with the waterfall, and a small, slender dragon of shimmering silver crept into view around the shoulder of the cliff wall.

"I'm sorry, Uncle Lectral," she said with utter insincerity. With a blink of her great luminous eyes—eyes that seemed too large for the narrow silver wedge of her head—she stretched her wings and dipped a leisurely foreclaw into the waters of the pool.

Lectral, as always, found it impossible to be angry with the impetuous wyrmling. Still, he made a show of scowling and harrumphing, as if she should think twice about working a new spell on him the next time she paid a visit. "And to what do I owe the honor of this visit?"

"Saytica and I were in Palanthas for the winter, but I think I was starting to get on Astinus's nerves," Silvara admitted, with a slightly embarrassed shrug. "At least, that's what Regia said when she asked me to leave."

"Maybe you were getting on Regia's nerves as well," Lectral proposed with a chuckle.

Their golden kin-dragon was widely known for her fanatical attachment to human ways of society and manners. Regia was easily flustered by a dragon who, whether in human or elven guise, lacked a proper knowledge of decorum. It wasn't hard to imagine that the playful young silver had soon grown irritating in the eyes of the haughty gold.

"That could be. Quallathan and I were playing around the Tower of High Sorcery, and she punished him with an extra lesson and told me I should see what was happening in the High Kharolis."

"That sounds like Regia," Lectral admitted. Quallathan was even younger than Silvara, but he was strong and quick, with a keen intellect and sharp wit that had already drawn a great deal of attention from the elders. It was quite possible that Regia considered Silvara a bad influence on Qual, though Lectral refrained from mentioning his suspicion to the lively youngster. "I don't suppose an extra lesson is too much of a punishment for Quallathan," he suggested.

"No. He went right into his human form and started to read a big stack of scrolls Regia gave him."

"Did you know that's why the gold dragons like to use

their two-legged bodies so much?" the silver male explained. "Because it's easier to read with a human's eyes than with a dragon's. Also, human fingers are better than claws for turning the pages."

"I didn't know that. But it was all right, though," Silvara continued breezily, trotting to the edge of the ledge and looking into the misty depths of the gorge, then turning those over-large eyes back to Lectral. "I was ready for a change of scenery."

"Saytica stayed behind?"

"Yes," Silvara replied. "She has an easier time putting up with all the rules."

"Well, she's quite a bit older and larger than you. I suppose that makes a difference," noted Lectral.

"Everyone is," the young female replied sourly, but then she brightened. "Anyway, it's as Daria taught us: Dragons should be flying, not reading."

Lectral chuckled, remembering his matriarch with fondness. Then his brow furrowed. "Have you seen Heart?" he asked, finally getting to the question that was never far from the surface of his awareness.

"No, and Regia hasn't either. She asked me the same thing just before she sent me away."

An eagle keened, circling the ledge, silhouetted by the rosy glow of the sun sinking toward the western horizon. Then the birdlike form shimmered and grew, and it was a gold dragon gliding through the air, curling regally and settling toward a landing on Lectral's ledge.

The two silvers quickly changed shape, using the bodies of wild elves to conserve space, and moved against the cliff wall to leave more room on the narrow perch.

The gold, whom Lectral had already recognized as mighty Arumnus, settled in a downrush of wind and nodded a greeting of stiff-necked formality. The dragon's rather formal manner wasn't because he was aloof, but because he'd been spending too much time with Regia, Lectral suspected.

Smoothly Arumnus changed shape, shrinking, curling upright to stand smoothly in the body of a burly Knight of

Solamnia. Shiny golden armor protected his strapping form, and a great sword was strapped to his waist.

The two wild elf bodies stepped forward. "Welcome, kin-dragon," Lectral said, feeling a surprising rush of affection toward the mature gold. After all, Arumnus was one of the few male dragons who was as old as Lectral himself. Despite his aloof and studious nature, he had been a friend and comrade since making Lectral's acquaintance some three centuries before.

"Have you heard the news?" Arumnus asked, urgency overcoming his traditional gold dragon reserve.

"What is it?" Silvara asked before Lectral could speak.

"War has come again to the world. It has already been waged for several winters in the east, and now it has come against the men of Solamnia. The wyrms of the Dark Queen are awakened, and they, too, have joined the onslaught against the knights."

"Dragons of red and blue—chromatic serpents?" demanded Lectral, tingling with a sudden sense of discovery—and fear. "But where did they come from?"

"They came from the east," Arumnus replied. "Sanction is their great city, but much of Solamnia has felt the torch of dragonfire."

"That is no concern of ours!" Lectral blurted, surprising himself with the outburst and the sentiment. He was aware of Silvara's look of astonishment and the gold dragon's expression of gentle reproach.

"How can you say that?" argued the young and graceful wild elf who was the female silver dragon. "We all have friends among the humans! Think of Heart. What will she do when she learns about this?"

"No!" Lectral barked in sudden panic, knowing the affinity the silver female felt toward the knights. Indeed, Heart would no doubt take wing against the chromatic dragons by herself if need be. "That is, we have to find her!"

"It is already a dragon matter," Arumnus continued. "Young Cymbol has gathered his copper siblings, and at least a dozen of them have flown against the evil dragons in the north. Word is that Bassal was killed, perhaps others as well."

Lectral felt a glimmer of real menace. These were the names of dragons he knew, at least in passing. And now they were falling, slain? "Cymbol has always been an angry sort. Many times I have heard him boast that he would lead the attack against the Dark Queen's dragons if only he had the chance."

"And now he has that chance," Silvara noted, her own eyes alight.

"Regia is considering the golds' response even as we speak." Arumnus looked toward the sky with unseemly urgency. "Perhaps she will have arrived at a conclusion by the time I return," he added hopefully.

"Don't just consider. *Do* something!" Silvara insisted.

Lectral, too, sensed the rising compulsion of a martial summons. "Yes. We silvers shall fight as well. This is the fight that our ancestors waged . . . that drove our fathers and mothers from the grotto."

His mind flashed to a thought of the Kagonesti forest in the realm south of Sanction, and he tried to picture the horror if the scourge of dragonfire and waste should spread there. Guilt surged as he realized that it had been many winters since he had flown over the wild elf realms.

"What now? Who's this?" Arumnus pointed toward the sky, where a silver-winged shape glided across the faces of the rising moons, then settled toward the ledge.

"Heart!" cried Silvara, frantically waving a slender hand.

The elder female silver dragon settled to the ledge, and then she, too, became an elfmaid, as beautiful as Silvara, though with the fullness of a mature woman. Lectral remembered that shape, and again the memories of a forest chase came back. He felt a dizzying sense of emotion, all but staggering as he stepped toward his silver nestmate. He embraced her, felt her arms tight around him.

"Hello, my Heart," he said thickly, taking her elven hands in his own. "It is good to know that you are safe and well."

"And you, my nestmate," she replied, the pressure of her fingers sending ripples of agony through his heart until she broke free of his touch.

"Hello, Sister," said Silvara, going to Heart and quickly hugging her.

"Greetings, Little Sister. And to you, my friends."

Lectral's heart pounded, and he felt a rush of blood in his ears. A raging storm of memories returned to him, and he recalled every detail of the time he had chased her through the woods, had almost captured her.

And, looking at the distant focus of her eyes, he understood that she had, at last, eluded him forever.

"Do you know of the war?" asked Silvara.

"Indeed. The dragons of the Dark Queen have taken to the skies," Heart declared grimly. "Already some of the brown metal dragons have joined the knights, but we silvers should go as well! The humans are brave and fight valiantly, but they need our help. Saytica has already flown to join them."

"Of course!" Silvara said. "And what of Huma?"

Lectral looked at Heart sharply, jolted by the question. She returned his look with an expression of frankness and a plea for understanding. "There is one man in particular . . . the knight called Huma," she explained. "He has moved me with his courage, his goodness. In part, it is for him that I come to you to beg your help for the knights."

"The knights . . . or this *one* knight?" asked Lectral, his tone a soft growl.

Heart's head whipped back as if she had been slapped. Then she raised her chin and met her nestmate's gaze. "I cherish him very much. And I believe that he may lead the knights to victory."

Lectral suppressed a surge of jealousy. A very strong part of him wanted to find and squash this human who dared to enthrall his nestmate, and he worked very hard to restrain an impulse toward violence.

"What about the wild elves, the Kagonesti in the east?" he asked anxiously. "Who knows whether or not they are suffering under the dragons as well?"

"Who can know?" countered Heart. "But there is more. You all remember the Spear of Paladine, the prophecy as foretold by our honored mother, Daria, at the time the grotto was abandoned."

"Yes!" cried Silvara excitedly. "The weapon of the gods that would give us means to strike at the Dark Queen."

"It is a lance!" the elfmaid dragon explained. "A Dragonlance, formed by the hammer of Kharas and wielded by knights from the backs of dragons."

"And you have these lances?" asked Arumnus.

"We have twenty lances," she said. "Many are the knights who have volunteered to wield them. We need nineteen dragons to fly with me. I have already heard from Saytica and Cymbol and Bolt, and Arkas as well."

"And I shall fly at your side!" pledged Arumnus.

"And I!" Silvara cried.

Heart turned her firm expression to the younger female. "You are too small, Little Sister. The lance-wielder must be an armored knight, and I fear the burden would be more than you could carry."

Silvara slumped, but then turned her expression to Lectral. "You can go, too, can't you?"

The silver dragon took a deep breath, for the first time his elven chest feeling like a constricting vessel. He shook his head, still fighting against an explosion of temper.

"By the time you fly to Palanthas you will have your twenty, and many more," he said, with a penetrating look at Heart. "As for me, I must fly to my Kagonesti."

She came to him and placed an elven hand upon his taut arm. "I understand. But know, Lectral, that this man Huma is a good man. And I love him."

"Love?" The Kagonesti eyes flashed scorn. "Have you forgotten you are a dragon?"

"No, I haven't. But perhaps I've learned that even dragons can know love. Perhaps that's a gift we silvers can teach to our kin-dragons. We *can* love."

"*You* can love, perhaps." Lectral's voice was as tight as a Kagonesti bowstring. "As for me, I choose to fight."

Chapter 33
War in the Sky

1028 PC

Lectral took to the air, propelled by a sense of profound rage, driving relentlessly through the skies, leaving the High Kharolis behind. Borne by his fury, silver wings carried him over the broad Vingaard plains. He tried not to think about Heart and her knight, but his mind was aflame with the memory of her last words to him.

Love—and for a *human?* How could she even imagine such a thing? It was an abomination, a blasphemy of the darkest kind! If there was indeed such as concept as love, it belonged to the two-legs—lesser creatures who lacked the majesty of flight, of thousand-year life spans, of inherent magic and devastating breath-weapons!

Powerful wing strokes devoured the miles as Lectral

passed the forested foothills and moved to the fringe of the dusty plain, flying over realms he hadn't seen in many years. Eventually he perceived the great darkness in the north and knew that this was the present area of contention of the Dark Queen's war.

Drawing closer now, he soared above vast legions, a dark tide overrunning the plain all the way to the Khalkists. Dragons of evil wheeled and spiraled amid the clouds, and Lectral masked himself in invisibility. Even in his nearly blinding rage he retained enough patience to know he should study his enemies, should acquaint himself with their habits instead of making an impetuous attack.

From a distance, he observed dragons of red burning villages, landing to tear at human-built constructs of stone and earth. He wanted to strike at them, but he wouldn't, having convinced himself that his duty was to the wild elves. Watching one mighty red in particular, he determined that this was the leader of the Dark Queen's wyrms, and he spotted another crimson wyrm, almost as big, that led many other serpents in the onslaught toward Palanthas. Once, as Lectral circled on the fringes of the battle, that sinister monster raised its head, and the invisible silver shivered to a sensation that he had been discovered.

But Lectral turned toward the east, seeking the foothills of the Kagonesti forests, and the red wyrm turned back to lead his offensive. Closer now, black clouds roiled in the skies, blanketing the plains with a cloak as heavy as the gloom that shrouded the silver dragon's heart. And still Heart's words echoed through his mind, mocking and taunting. Love! Could she really believe it?

He growled, knowing that she did. Again he remembered that wild elfmaid who had led him on the chase through the woods, and a plume of frost exploded from his jaws in an unconscious expression of his rage and grief. If the knight, Huma, had appeared before him, Lectral felt certain he would have ripped the man into small pieces.

But he had his task before him, and the evidence of war was all around. Curving toward the Khalkists, he swept over the great arsenals of Sanction, invisibly watching legions of blue and white dragons wing forth, flying to the east, while countless troops—reinforcements to the main armies, no doubt—marched in their wake.

Only then did he turn his flight directly to the south, ultimately soaring above the forest homes of the Kagonesti. With relief, he saw that the woodlands remained green and untrammeled. At least from the heights, it appeared that this time the war had spared the ancient elven realms. The trees were vibrant and healthy, the lakes clean, streams spilling crystalline and pure from the mountain heights.

The ram's horn was a feathery weight around his neck as Lectral swept low, skimming just above the level of the trees. Unlike the last wars, it seemed that this time the Dark Queen's fury was in fact directed against the humans, not the elves, and for this Lectral was profoundly grateful.

But did even the humans deserve the help of the mighty serpents of Paladine? Although he knew that twenty of his kin-dragons were flying into battle, bearing human riders with their gleaming Dragonlances, he couldn't bring himself to believe they did. And he refused to acknowledge that this feeling was petty, caused by his own jealousy. Instead, he convinced himself that his motives were noble and he was the only hope the Kagonesti had.

And he flew on, winging over a verdant swath of undisturbed forest, trying to ignore the war raging within his own soul.

* * * * *

With Heart as their leader, the dragons of metal landed on the courtyards and plazas of Palanthas. Saytica was there, and other silvers as well, and also golden Arumnus and several of his male and female nestmates. Cymbol and many of the coppers, who had been battling the chromatic dragons for several seasons, had willingly volunteered to bear lancers into the fray. Too, Bolt and the bronzes, and Kord, with six or eight of his brass brothers, had also hastened to the proud city, landing on the increasingly crowded fields.

Lectral had been right, Heart saw. There were more than enough dragons for the twenty lances and the equal number of knights who had offered to bear them. Still, she missed him. His absence left a hole in her being that she knew would never be filled.

Saddles had been made by master smiths and leatherworkers, simple straps of leather and steel, and these were fastened to the great flying mounts. The Dragonlances themselves, gleaming shafts of enchanted steel tipped with razor-sharp barbs sparkling like diamonds in the sunshine, were affixed to simple but effective swivel mounts.

Finally the mighty serpents dipped their heads and allowed the riders to climb aboard. Winds gusted across the parade ground as twenty pairs of wings pulsed and fluttered, driving into the air, slowly lifting the great dragons and their bold lancers toward the skies. The cheers of a hopeful populace rang behind them as the flight, with Heart and her beloved Huma in the lead, angled toward the east.

Clouds roiled and churned, spuming like black smoke high into the sky, marking the scourge of Garic Drakan's invasion. Cymbol had told the others of the terrible devastation taking place, but even so, the taint of soot and ash and death was an affront to the nostrils of man and dragon alike. Yet the flight of metal dragons sped boldly on, venturing into the murk, seeking the sinister colors that would mark the Dark Queen's serpentine fliers.

Crying challenges, braying toward the vanishing sun, the dragons of Paladine swept through the darkness. Silver Heart was still in the lead, with Saytica and Arumnus to one side, each ridden by an armored knight. On her other flank flew Bolt, with a unique rider, a hulking, dark-skinned minotaur. All the metal dragons spread into a wide **V** formation, a sight not unfamiliar in the skies over Krynn, yet this flight was faster and far more deadly than any wing of migrating geese.

Disappearing into the heavy clouds, the powerful dragons fought against gusting winds, struggled to keep their neighboring fliers in sight as they surged through the roiling skies over the plains. And then there were flashes of brightness in the black, alabaster wings and gaping jaws of the same color as a dozen white dragons surged forward to attack. The gleaming tips of the deadly spears ripped into the pale wyrms, and with screams of pain and resonant blasts of lightning and frost, fire and acid, war in the skies was joined.

* * * * *

Lectral was alerted by the cry of a griffon, a keening shriek of alarm that came from a faraway mountainside. Sensing a menacing presence above, the silver dragon teleported a hundred feet to one side a split second before the attacking red dragon incinerated the air where he had been.

The monstrous serpent was huge, and Lectral knew immediately that this was the one who had sensed his presence, the dragon who was second in size only to the crimson monster in command of all the Dark Queen's horde. A quick glance to the north showed him four more reds, all winging swiftly closer, but this great red serpent was the immediate threat.

All of Lectral's rage came together as, with a shrill cry of fury, he flew toward the attacker. His breath exploded in a thunder of frost, but the red evaded it at the last minute, and the silver was forced to veer aside from another hissing fireball.

"Fool!" brayed the crimson wyrm. "Like the pig Darlantan, your ancestor, you are doomed!"

"Spawn of Crematia! It is *you* who will die!" Lectral roared in response, straining to close with the serpentine crimson tail.

He snapped, barely missing the red dragon, then whirled through a tight spin to fly after his foe. Slashing claws tore at the scarlet membrane of a wing, rending a single gash, and then the two monstrous dragons crashed together. Clenching, they twisted and spiraled, clawing in frantic rage, breaking apart to leave a shower of scales, mixed crimson and argent, fluttering downward.

The two mighty serpents dipped and dodged, diving and climbing, first one, then the other in pursuit. And all the time the other four reds drew closer, winging with desperate speed. The newcomers were all considerably smaller than Lectral's awesome foe, but even so, the silver knew their arrival would sway the battle into an unwinnable contest.

"Now, son of Darlantan, you will die!" cried the red, seeing the direction of Lectral's gaze. "I, Tombfyre, will see your life ended!"

Only one tactic gave him hope. Lectral turned southward, pulling his opponent into pursuit, now carrying the fight away from the foursome of reds with as much speed as possible.

"Coward!" brayed Tombfyre. "Stay and fight! At least do your sire that much honor!"

"I am Lectral, heir to Darlantan and Callak," the silver roared, diving, curling his neck to shout backward, underneath his belly. "I would slay you, but I am no fool, to die against five!"

"Bah!" sneered Tombfyre, abruptly veering out of his pursuit. "Then the wyrmlings can kill you. I have more important affairs!"

With a blink of magic, the red dragon vanished, and Lectral guessed that he had teleported back to the battle that was raging in the north. Trembling with rage, the silver whirled about, more than willing to face the four younger reds in a duel.

Flying toward him, the crimson serpents closed the distance fast, spreading apart only slightly as they and the mighty silver converged. Abruptly Lectral tilted into a stall, then pulled himself upward with a powerful push of his wings. The sky beneath him became a hellish inferno of crackling fire, but the silver dragon escaped with just a few scorches on his tail.

Quickly he pivoted, slashing past the reds, sweeping downward in a plunging dive.

Then, as Lectral blasted the nearest chromatic with an explosion of killing frost, there were three. His wings drove him ever faster, and now he was the attacker, trying to close the distance. Clawing at a red body, veering away from another explosion of fiery breath, the silver dragon ripped scales from the flank of an enemy wyrm.

But the trio of red dragons swerved back, and in a clash of talons and fangs, all four serpents came together. A hissing cloud of frost and flame roared like a thunderstorm, engulfing all the dragons in a horrific cloud of mutually destructive breath.

And then Lectral was falling, twisting lazily, watching the trees rush upward to meet him. He tried to break away, but his wings refused to move.

* * * * *

"There!" Arumnus declared in a harrumph of flame. The knight on his back leaned over, studying the distant ground.

"I see them—four or five greens, eh?"

"And the blacks!" the gold dragon noted, banking slightly to bring the rest of the chromatic dragons into view. The gold looked around anxiously. Where were Heart and her knight?

With bellows of vengeful fury, the dragons and their knightly riders dived toward the enemy wyrms. Lances ripped through emerald scales or shredded wings of midnight black, and the skies were full of smoke and flames and screams. Serpentine fliers weaved, slashed, and breathed, while knightly riders wielded their lances with deadly skill. In a few shocking moments of battle, every one of the chromatic dragons had been driven from the skies.

Heart and her rider pulled ahead, winging beside

Arumnus. The silver flew strongly, but her expression was grim.

"I must go," she declared. "We have a different fight to wage."

"But our destiny lies here!" Arumnus declared, indicating a vast wing of red dragons spreading across the sky, angling toward a renewed attack.

"You will take this destiny," Heart replied. "As to me, I must follow the commands of love."

"Love is not for dragons!" Arumnus asserted, but his silver kin-dragon and her rider were already gone.

And a great, five-headed shadow began to loom out of the clouds. Arumnus knew Heart's goal, and he could only pray that she would succeed.

* * * * *

Lectral's body twisted under an onslaught of unbelievable pain. He flailed as one of the scarlet serpents swerved past, catching the red's leathery wing with his sharp talons. Tearing savagely, the silver dragon rent the stiff surface, pulling the red to him, feeling the brittle membrane, frozen by his blast of silver breath, crumble in his talons.

Two more red dragons, smaller than the heir of Crematia but still dangerous, tried to free their comrade, but Lectral clung tightly to the squirming serpent. With a crushing bite, he snapped the wyrm's neck, but then the rippling agony through his own body drove blackness upward into his brain. He struggled, groping for words, for magic, for *something!*

When he crashed into the trees, he was vaguely aware of the two reds flying away, leaving him for dead. Pain swept through his body, wracking agony that seemed certain to kill him.

But he still lived. In a nightmare of agony, he realized his wings were shredded, several of his legs smashed and broken.

Finally he reached out a claw, felt the curving surface under his talons, and raised the ram's horn to his jaws.

Chapter 34
The Wounded Queen

1028 PC

"Sire!" Tombfyre cried, appearing in the air before Deathfyre's flying form. "There is a silver to the south, over the forests of the wild elves! He was pursued by four wyrms, but I cannot say that his life is ended, for I came as soon as I heard your summons."

"There will be time for him later," Deathfyre growled. "Now I need you here. See these humans? They come to us with lances, cruel weapons that have already rent flights of whites and greens."

Corro, the mighty black, fell into formation beside them. He snorted, flexing his midnight wings, with many of his inky clan trailing behind. As Corro passed, Tombfyre felt a new presence, and with awe he watched a mighty cloud seethe upward, growing into a solid entity.

"Show courage, my kin-dragons!" roared the elder red. "Our queen approaches, and if we can win this fight, she will hold sway over all the world!"

Deathfyre led his red dragons in a wedge of lethal flight, bellowing furiously at the sight of the metallic serpents winging toward them. Tombfyre pressed ahead, savage and eager, fires of fury burning in his belly.

Now he saw that the good dragons had saddled themselves with riders, a single human warrior astride each of the serpents. Sunlight glinted from the silvery metal shafts of their wicked lances, but Tombfyre chortled aloud at the realization that his enemies had handicapped themselves with all of this clumsy, unnecessary weight.

The two formations swept closer, and the red dragon bellowed a cry of battle, ordering his serpents into a dive. Corro spat a drool of acid, snarling loudly, leading the remaining blacks and greens—those that had survived the first clash with the Dragonlances. Many blues and whites pulled alongside, and more than sixty of the Dark Queen's wyrms swept downward in an awful wedge of death.

The metallic dragons closed swiftly, with those curiously shining weapons raised, the wyrms bugling bold challenges of their own. Don't they see the odds? Tombfyre was amazed and a little shaken by the foe's tenacity.

"Lances?" declared blue Azurus, gliding beside Deathfyre with a disdainful snort. "As if they could strike us down with mere pinpricks!"

"Beware," countered Deathfyre, "for those are more than pins."

The blue looked scornful, and Tombfyre himself was amazed to hear his sire speak of caution.

"Spread out!" warned Deathfyre, urging the blues and whites to give them room, knowing that the eruption of red dragon breath would be deadly even to his own allies and that the lethal frost of the whites and the crackling lightning of the blues could prove equally harmful to the serpents of his own wing. It was far better to attack the enemy with a widespread formation, concentrating all the breath attacks against different portions of the sky.

Azurus led the way, bringing his blues through a plunging curve, sweeping toward the head of the metal dragon flight. Some of these silver and gold wyrms rose toward the blues, while the rest winged on, bearing steadily toward the reds or warily eyeing the whites that swerved outward to make an attack from the other flank.

Lightning crackled as Azurus spat a flaming bolt at the lead dragon, a large gold. But that serpent twisted away, leaving a cascade of sparks spilling from the dragon-scale shield protecting the rider. Then the lance of the leading attacker ripped through the blue membrane of a broad wing. Mighty Azurus, greatest of the blues, lurched and flapped pathetically, veering to the side, then toppling onto his back while the shredded membrane trailed behind him. With a shrieking cry of fury that swelled to disbelief, then curdled into sheer terror, he tumbled from the skies.

Other keen lances ripped into the blues, and in a few shocking instants, a half-dozen of the sleek, powerful dragons had fallen. The metal serpents veered and dodged, maneuvering to avoid the effects of the deadly lightning breath. Now the dragons of Paladine attacked aggressively, spewing acid and cold and flame of their own, bearing the riders and those wicked lances into the midst of a swirling aerial melee. Slashing with metallic talon and fang, the good dragons desperately sought to rend the evil serpents who escaped the initial killing onslaught.

The whites swept inward, but they were met by a trio of silvers, immune to the frosty blast of white dragonbreath. The metal serpents emerged from the cloud of icy spumes, three riders crouched behind their shields, lances poised steadily, aimed at the ranks of wounded enemy dragons. With piercing stabs, the serpents of Paladine drove relentlessly through the scattering whites, stabbing and slashing many of the alabaster wyrms out of the sky.

For long, deadly moments, the formations wheeled through the sky, an aerial dance of exquisite beauty and lethal consequence. The evil wyrms struggled for the advantage of height, but even bearing their burdensome riders, the good dragons stayed close, stabbing and burning, knocking down one after another of the Dark Queen's serpents. When the chromatic dragons separated, then swept inward for a concentrated attack, the knights on their dragons managed to hold them at bay. Meeting the onslaught with outstretched lances, they forced the attackers to veer up, down, sideways, as the dragons of metal wheeled through a protective circle, each lancer guarding the flank of the man and dragon before him.

Suddenly a great presence loomed in the sky as clouds congealed into a shape, straining to achieve solidity. Again Tombfyre felt a shiver of awe, of lethal and immortal presence. Was it the queen? Would she come here, to Krynn, riding the victory of her legions? Tombfyre saw the writhing heads, the smoky clouds that formed the great immortal body now taking form, and his heart flared with hope.

But one after another of Deathfyre's wyrms were slain, and though a few of the good dragons and their riders were knocked out of the air, the battle developed catastrophically for the red dragon's wing. The serpents of the Dark Queen surged from high altitude or tried to sweep upward from below. But always they were met with those terrible lances, the weapons relentlessly cutting and piercing and killing.

Finally, with a shrill cry, Deathfyre dived away and led the surviving serpents of the Dark Queen in headlong flight, while the good dragons maintained their defensive spiral, apparently content to let the attackers go—until a mighty silver, mounted by an armored knight, appeared out of nowhere. The tip of his lance ripped through Deathfyre's flank, and with a ground-shaking scream, the villainous red dragon, the ancient harbinger of evil who had lived for two thousand years, flipped onto his back and plunged, lifeless, toward the bloodstained plain.

Tombfyre shrieked in rage as he saw his sire fall. But still more of those deadly lances rushed closer, an encircling ring of death, and he knew that this battle was lost.

"We will marshal our forces and return with a hundred dragons!" he bellowed in fury, though the cry sounded hollow even in his own ears. In truth, they had been soundly defeated, his dragons all but driven from the skies.

"My son, scion of Deathfyre . . . hear the will of your queen."

The words reached Tombfyre, and they were clear and precise, as if Takhisis spoke to him from close proximity. He whipped his head around, gaping at the sight of a massive, cloudy shape crowned by five writhing heads of smoke. The heads wailed and twitched, as if the immortal goddess were suffering grievous pain.

"Speak, my queen, giver and taker of all life!" the red dragon begged.

He saw the Queen of Darkness herself as she shimmered in the air. Again he felt a moment of soaring hope . . .

. . . but then he sensed the whole truth. A terrible lance had pierced the gut of the five-headed monstrosity, and he understood that more than a battle had been lost. He thought of the silvers who had killed his sire, who had evaded him in the skies to the south, and he cried out in anguished frustration as he watched the dark goddess fade into the skies.

He knew he should fly, should seek and kill his enemies.

But he couldn't move.

"My chromatic children, you are banished, exiled. It is the price of my survival. You must come with me!"

The will of the Dark Queen reached him through space, and he saw the awful truth: By oath had Huma freed the Dark Queen, and by that oath was Tombfyre bound as well.

Takhisis would withdraw from Krynn, and as she had pledged to Huma, a vow made in exchange for her life, she would bear her children away with her, ordering them into exile from the world.

But as always the Queen of Darkness sought to work betrayal.

And as the chromatic dragons were pulled toward the Abyss, Tombfyre was given a lair of comfort and safety deep in the bowels of the world.

And he felt a destiny of greatness and majesty laid upon his shoulders.

Chapter 35
Farewell to Ansalon

1027 PC

A wild elf brave, Ashtaway, reached Lectral only a few hours after the grievously wounded dragon had sounded the ram's horn. Marked by the spiral tattoos of black ink that had marked his clan since the time of Kagonos, the warrior found the shallow cave in which the silver serpent had sought shelter. Aided by a Kagonesti maid, Hammana, the brave brought venison to the injured dragon, while the healing skills of the elfmaid helped to stanch the bleeding of his worst injuries.

Slowly, dreamily, he allowed them to tend him, welcomed their ministrations and their company. For a long time, he remained under their care, depending on Ashtaway for food, relying upon Hammana's poultices to heal his many wounds. Though the brave was often absent, the maid stayed at his side for many days, and the large dragon welcomed her presence. At the same time, Lectral was aware of a deep irony: He had come to save the Kagonesti, and instead it was they who had saved him.

And in his darker moments, when the two elves left him alone, he acknowledged a deeper truth. He had not flown southward solely to serve the Kagonesti, to fulfill a sense of his own duty. Rather, he had also done so to avoid the painful reality of Heart's choice, her love for a human. Unaware of the course of the war raging in the north, he remained lost in his own musings, occasionally brightened by the presence of the two wild elves.

As he watched them together, saw the tenderness in their mutual looks and hesitant touches, perceived their concern for each other and the longing in Hammana's eyes when Ashtaway was absent. He realized they were in love with each other. He found the knowledge both heartening and sad. The attraction seemed very natural, their joy together almost palpable—and he could only think of Heart. Could she possibly feel this same kind of affection for her knight?

Over the course of a season or more, his injuries slowly healed, though one rear leg and his wings remained badly damaged, so much so that he still couldn't fly. Then, late on a warm day, after Hammana had gone back to her village, Lectral heard a rustle of silver wings and saw a familiar snout peering at him from the sunlit woods beyond his shallow cave.

"Silvara!" he declared, his heart pounding with a joy he had thought vanished forever.

The silver female padded into the small cave. "I am glad I found you, Honored Elder. I feared for you more than I can say."

"And you, Little Sister—you're a sight more welcome than you can possibly know."

"You're hurt!" she declared, moving forward to inspect the red scars of his wounds.

"I have been well cared for. I will live and probably even

fly again, given time. But now, tell me of the war, the dragons and their lancers in the skies . . .?"

"The war is over. The dragons of Takhisis are gone, sent from the world by the Dark Queen herself, in a vow forced upon her by the knight Huma, in exchange for her own life."

"Heart was right about him, then. . . . He *is* a man of true greatness." Lectral felt a stab of shame, sharpened by the fact that he couldn't completely banish a flush of jealousy.

Silvara lowered her head, and with a growing ache of grief, he suspected the next thing she would have to tell him.

"And what of Heart?" he asked, barely daring to breathe.

"The cost of our victory was high. She was slain, perishing at the same time as her knight," the silver female replied.

Lectral was silent for a long time. His thoughts churned in a stormy mixture of guilt and grief, wanting to blame the human knight for the death of his nestmate. With another rush of shame, he found that he could not. If anyone was to blame, it was he.

"Have you heard of the red dragons . . . of the one called Tombfyre?" Lectral thought of the wicked serpent who had taunted and fought him, and now he trembled in profound rage. If he was unable to save her, at least he could look forward to revenge!

But Silvara looked at him sadly, as if uncertain that he could understand her words. "Banished like all the others. He has departed from Krynn together with all his evil kindragons. But there is more, and that is what brings me to you. I come to tell you that we are departing from Ansalon as well."

"We? The silvers?" Lectral was stunned.

"All of us . . . all the dragons of Paladine."

"But why? Did you not say that the war was won?"

"It is another part of the oath, so that the people of the world can rule themselves without the interference of mighty beings."

She told him of the sacred vow that had taken the Dark Queen and all her dragons from Ansalon, and of the price that the good dragons were to pay as well. They would journey to a place called the Dragon Isles, where they would live out their lives and their generations.

"These islands are said to be idyllic realms, perfect of clime, with space for all the metal clans." As she spoke, her eyes turned outward, fixing upon the forests and mountains beyond, and he sensed that, like him, she wasn't ready to leave all they knew behind.

"But how can I go? I cannot fly," he declared.

"Saytica will bear you, but you must assume the form of a two-legs. She comes tonight." Silvara told him that Saytica had been a heroine of the war, bearing the knight who had struck down mighty Deathfyre, the leader of the Dark Queen's wyrms.

And when the mighty silver female came to him later that night, Lectral was able to shift his body. He chose the shape of the white-bearded sage, the same form that had been favored by Darlantan so many centuries before. Finally Lectral straddled the strong, silver shoulders and rode through the skies on the back of Saytica.

They passed over the lands vacated by the fleeing armies of Garic Drakan. The mighty silver flier remained silent, sensing the distress of her battered, grieving clandragon. All around them were the other silvers, a great airborne armada soaring through the cool air, starlight glimmering from a multitude of reflective wings.

Lectral looked helplessly, saw the horizon of the High Kharolis passing to the left, but already the snowy skyline of the mountain ridges had vanished into the distance.

And already, too, it seemed that his once vivid memories of the place were beginning to fade.

PART IV

Chapter 36
Silver Ceremony

127 AC

The rains that had shrouded the Dragon Isles for more than a hundred winters had finally broken, swept over the ocean like so much debris pushed by a giant broom. Rays of sun sparkled from the limitless expanse of seawater; a brilliant array of iridescent facets surrounded the verdant islands jutting from that dazzling surface like soft mounds of green. Though each isle was crowned by at least one summit of dark rock and bright, snow-swept glacier, much of the coastal fringe remained thick and green with tropical growth.

Lectral flew without haste, stretching his wings and allowing the warmth of the sun to soak into the ancient, leathery spans. He rode serenely on a coastal updraft, trying to put aside his thoughts, to ignore the purpose that would soon force him to turn and climb toward the uplands of Cloudhome, the Misty Isle—largest and most populous of the metallic dragons' homelands-in-exile.

Perhaps because of that purpose, he reminisced almost sleepily as he flew through the warm, tropical currents of air. For a moment, he was confused, which was a not uncommon state for him these days. His mind brightened with memories of a young silver female . . . was it Heart? No, Saytica . . . She had been a good companion during the long, uneventful centuries on the Dragon Isles. His mind drifted to the image of the lofty High Kharolis, and he sighed heavily at the thought that he would never see those mountains again.

How long had it actually been since the dragons of Paladine had come to these isles, in their exile that had become a way of life? The question troubled him, for it was becoming increasingly difficult—almost impossible, in fact—to remember the time when dragons had dwelt upon Ansalon.

Many hundreds of winters had passed, he knew, though perhaps it was more appropriate to count the summers here in this balmy, tropical clime. And for most of those annums, it had seemed that he and his kin-dragons had lived without meaning or purpose, merely passing the time from one period of wakefulness to the next. They dwelt in peace and harmony, true, but also in boredom and indolence.

Once again he remembered the purpose that had drawn him to the Misty Isle, and his sense of melancholy swelled into a surging wave. Of course, a farewell to a dragon was always sad, and there was a real poignancy when the deceased was a sibling, one who had been born after Lectral in that long-ago era. Yet still he dallied for a while longer over the wave-washed coastline, enjoying the perfect, infinite turquoise of the shallows within the coral reefs along the shoreline below.

But in his heart, he knew that it was time to go, and with a sweeping turn, he arced toward land. He made a straight line along a deep valley in the foliage-draped massif rising toward the island's center, bearing toward the well-known gathering place concealed there. Certainly many of the younger silvers would already be present, and no doubt Silvara would have arrived as well. But Lectral was the venerable silver, and his presence was required before the ceremony could begin.

Saytica had died peacefully, as was the natural way of elder dragons. Soon her body would be commended unto the gods from the height of the Silver Stairs, and it was not only Lectral's wish, but his sacred duty, that he be there.

He continued to climb, following the winding valley of one of the mountainous island's rapid, plunging creeks. He worked harder now, powerful strokes of his wings carrying him upward, past the steep, verdant walls of the narrow vale. Thankfully, the wind was off the sea, and he was able to ride the current of air inland, focusing his own efforts merely on staying aloft, gaining altitude only as it became necessary.

He saw the snow-capped peaks, where the silver dragon nests, rich with eggs, were securely cached. He remembered the lifelong lesson, passed along by Callak and Daria—guard the eggs! It had been the goal of dragonkind since the days in the grotto, and at least life on the Dragon Isles insured that he and his kin-dragons had been able to accomplish this.

As he flew, Lectral tried once again to remember the passing of the last dozen winters, but he realized that those memories were blurred. It had stopped raining before then, perhaps two or three dozen years ago. Preceding that, storms had wracked the islands for no less than a full century. That had been a dark time, when the world itself had rumbled underfoot, and ash and cloud had darkened the skies in a nearly eternal shroud. It had been an era when Lectral had yearned poignantly for the stability of his beloved Kharolis.

He knew that more recently he had been sleeping for some time, until he had been awakened by the coming of a griffon. The creature had respectfully informed him of the passing of Saytica and presented the announcement that her commending would occur when the sun first reached its zenith following the spring equinox.

Saytica . . . Unlike Lectral, she had flown to war when the call came, had borne a lancer against the chromatic dragons while mighty Lectral had ignored his nestmates and gone off on his own. His regrets had been strong, at first, but now even those emotions had been dulled by the passage of centuries. Dulled, perhaps, but they were still there.

Trying to focus his hazy memories, Lectral wasn't even certain upon which of the isles he had most recently been sleeping. One of the smaller islets, certainly. Was it Jaentarth, or perhaps Alarl? No matter, really. With the exception of Cloudhome, the isles were quite similar, almost interchangeable in the ancient silver's opinion. True, each was for the most part a paradise of plentiful food, balmy weather, and pastoral wilderness. But they were also boring. And after this ceremony, Lectral would eventually find another lair amid the perfect terrain of the Dragon Isles, curling up and going back to sleep. In fact, it would probably be very soon, for there was little to do here except sleep.

With a twinge of sadness, he wondered: was this to be the destiny of all the young silvers as well, the proud and mighty descendants of him and his mighty sire, and their ancestors back through the dawn of time? Would they merely grow large so that they could move from cave to cave, spending increasing periods of their life asleep, too torpid even to note the arrival of a new summer or winter?

In truth, the summers on the Dragon Isles were things Lectral would just as soon spend in the depths of a cool and sunless cave. When he did emerge during the hot season, he invariably sought the glacial heights of the islands' central massifs, where the altitude was sufficient to hold even the scorching heat at bay. A silver's temperament was not made for the tropics.

Of course, the gold dragons seemed to be content in exile, since they seemed to find contentment in everything. Led by Regia and Arumnus, they dwelt in great airy palaces and manors in the City of Gold, spending most of their time in the human or elven guises they preferred. The ancient matriarch and her stolid, ever predictable mate presided over arguments in philosophy or created artworks and poems during their periods of activity and awareness. Of course, the younger silvers had told Lectral that lately even the golds were spending increasing amounts of time sleeping in their silk-draped chambers. It was as if a plague of tiredness was besetting dragonkind, sapping their might and their imaginations and, eventually, even their very animation and spirit.

The dragons of the brown metals had grown wild and disparate during the millennium of exile. For the most part, they chose solitary lairs on the outer islands, or in the deepest wilderness of Misty Isle. Brass, bronze, and copper invariably regarded each other with jealous distrust, and all had become suspicious and hostile toward the brighter wyrms. The silvers and golds, for their part, tended to leave their lesser cousins alone.

On his current flight, Lectral glided across a deep valley that he recognized. Numerous hot springs spouted from the marshy floor, and he knew the bronze dragons nested and laired here. Strangely, he saw no activity in the great lake centering the swampy lowland, and he wondered if the bronzes, like all the rest, had become listless and torpid.

True, some dragons remained restless. Silvara, for example, much as her elder sister had done a thousand years ago, spent long periods of time traveling unknown reaches. Though no one accused her to her face, it was widely rumored that she was violating the stricture against travels on Ansalon. But certainly she, too, would be present for the ceremony of her elder sister's commending.

Shaking his head, Lectral realized that he had arrived, his flight at last crossing the ridge bordering the bronzes' swamp. Now he glided toward the small, circular vale at the foot of the Silver Summit.

True to Lectral's guess, the valley below was flocked with silver shapes, all of them supple and wiry . . . and young. These were not wyrmlings by any means.

Dargentan and Darlant, who cleared a path for their venerable sire, were mighty serpents in their own right. Each was already larger than Lectral had been at the time of Huma's war, though the ancient one was now half again as huge as either of his proud scions.

The sire came to a rest in the middle of the silver throng, and with measured dignity, he dipped his chin in acknowledgment of the honoring bows, heads dropping all the way to the ground, of the younger wyrms of argent. Folding his wings with precise care, Lectral turned his attention to the nearby mountain and its glimmering path of ascent.

The steep slope leading to the Silver Summit climbed in metallic perfection from the base of the valley to the top of a small, pyramidal mountain. Saytica's body lay atop the flat peak, which was a space just large enough to contain the massive silver corpse. Solemnly the gathered dragons raised their heads, all eyes focused on the edge of the mountaintop.

His height allowed Lectral to see that several gold dragons were present as well, standing to the side of the gathered silvers in a little knot of human and elven bodies. The ancient silver knew the golds would claim this was because space in the small valley was limited, but he believed that his golden kin-dragons actually preferred to spend their lives in their tiny two-legged bodies.

"Greetings, Elder Brother," came a familiar voice, and Lectral's heart soared with an emotion he hadn't felt in too many winters.

"Silvara! It's a joy to see you, Little Sister, even in the sadness of our gathering."

"It is a mixed sadness," declared the graceful silver female, advancing to Lectral's side. Dargent and Darlant bristled, holding the rest of the wyrms back from the pair. "I do not mean to be cold, but Saytica had not been truly living for more than a thousand winters."

"No," agreed Lectral. "Not in the way we once lived upon Ansalon. . . ."

"I must confess," Silvara said softly, "I would have

stayed away from here if I could."

Lectral thought of Heart, and suddenly he felt very old and very sad.

"Did you love her? Saytica?" asked the silver female softly.

Lectral shook his head. "She was special to me, a treasure. But I have learned that love is not—or at least, shouldn't be—a concern of dragons. Let the lesser creatures suffer from that whim."

"It is to be wished," Silvara said, but there was a strange sadness in her eyes that didn't quite match her words. Lectral remembered again the rumors, whispered by young wyrmling and wandering griffon, that she had visited the continent in violation of the exile. He wished that he could warn her of the danger—certainly Regia or Arumnus would have been able to—but his heart broke at the thought of forcing her to an unwilling confinement.

A whisper of attention hissed through the crowd, and all the gathered dragons turned their eyes toward the top of the gleaming slope.

Magic shimmered, and a small figure who had been looking down at the throng of dragons suddenly grew, golden scales and wings coming into view, reflecting the bright rays of the noontime sun as Regia loomed above her kin-dragons. The golden female, wise and patient as ever, looked at Lectral with such disturbing clarity that he shifted awkwardly and cleared his throat with an impatient harrumph.

"She was great and wise and mighty . . . and so terribly unhappy," Regia said in dignified farewell. "It is without gladness, but also without grief, that we witness her ascent to the heavens."

"Farewell, Saytica of the Silver Wing," came the deep chant from the gathered dragons.

"I commend thee to the vault of the skies," Regia declared, her tone sonorous and deep as it echoed throughout the small valley. "And may all the blessings of Paladine rise with you."

At that, Regia dipped her head, allowing her snout to

touch Saytica's motionless nostrils. She murmured a long incantation, the words to the spell inaudible to the wyrms gathered below, and then flames appeared, surrounding the silver shape with a sparkling aura.

Finally the ancient gold spread her wings and took flight, gliding from the mountaintop to settle beside Lectral and Silvara.

The gathered dragons held their attention on the summit and its massive, motionless burden. Saytica's scales gleamed more brightly than ever, reflecting the rays of the sun with an intensity that seemed to actually increase the brilliance of the glow. Shimmering like a surface of vibrating liquid, the scales seemed to flow like quicksilver, but the great body remained whole and dignified in its final repose.

Then, as the magic took hold, Saytica's silver shape glowed so brightly that the dragons were forced to watch through the protective screens of their inner eyelids. Yet none turned away from the blinding illumination. The surrounding peaks stood out in brilliant detail, scorched by a flare like burning magnesium, a fire burning so brightly that even the sun seemed to pale in comparison.

Lectral dared not take a breath, so rapt was he at the sight upon the mountaintop. The brightness rose to a truly blinding level, until his only awareness was that spot of light.

Yet the blazing glow was curiously heatless, radiating no increase in warmth. Instead, it consumed the dragon who lay inert at the core of the brightness. When the fire slowly faded into nothing, there was no sign of Saytica.

With a collective sigh, the watching dragons settled, necks relaxing, wings stretching and ruffling in the still air. Many of the youngsters took off in a series of steep, upward pounces that Lectral could only envy.

"It *is* good," Silvara said, and for the first time Lectral realized that she had remained at his side. "Regia was right; this is not a time for grieving."

"You're right, it's not," Lectral agreed, already feeling a familiar, numbing fatigue. "But is it a time for anything at all?"

Chapter 37
The Price of an Oath

296 AC

It was young Dargentan who awakened first, at least among the silver dragons. The young male rose to his feet with a barely contained sense of energy, a feeling of profound unease. Sniffing the air, he crossed with a clattering of claws to the pool of water at the back of his cave. When he found it frozen, he emerged from his lair to blink into the pearly rose light of dawn.

He saw that the surface of Misty Isle's highland was buried under a blanket of snow, a layer of white that glistened in pristine perfection across the pastoral valleys and rolling summits of the highlands. Graceful cornices curled from lofty ridges, and the wind had marked long drifts, scoring sharp lines from numerous trees, rocks, and other irregularities.

All but the highest pines were fully buried, and Dargentan's breath frosted visibly as he snorted from his great nostrils. It was a startling thought, but true, to realize that just a few miles away the island's coastal lowlands were already balmy with the coming of spring.

But when his eyes rose toward the glacier wall, his unease clattered into full alarm. He saw that something had disturbed the snowfields up near the ice-draped nests of silver. Great furrows of dark ground were visible among the snowfields, where the snow had been churned and clawed away.

With a pounce, he took to the air, driving for altitude, fear choking upward into his throat. He flew closer, blood pulsing as he acknowledged a terrifying truth:

The nests had been raided!

He soared above the ridge where the ice-shrouded bowls of silver rested, and one look at the empty mangers confirmed his worst fears: The metallic eggs had been stolen.

Braying in alarm, Dargentan flew among the mountain summits. He knew that he had to find Lectral.

* * * * *

"You say that the eggs—*all* the eggs—are gone? Stolen from the nests?" demanded the ancient silver, a fundamental sense of urgency driving away the vestiges of his lingering fatigue. He rose and shook himself, twisting and stretching his stiff body, sloughing off old scales in a glittering silver shower. "When did this happen?"

"While I was sleeping—while we *all* were sleeping," Dargentan explained breathlessly. "I found them all dug up, and I came to tell you right away."

"That was wise," Lectral agreed, though his guts were churned into an icy ball by Dargentan's news. He stalked, stiff-legged, to the mouth of his cave and looked into the snow-swept valley beyond. From the position of the sun, near the northern horizon of jagged mountains, he knew that the isles had moved only slightly into spring. "Fly with me to the nests. We will see for ourselves."

Together the two silver dragons took wing, stroking toward the valley of the high glacier. By the time they arrived, they found more of their argent clan gathering.

The nests were high on a cliff, cloaked by ice and shadow year round. Here Lectral and Dargentan landed, finding Darlant probing through an empty icebound nest of silver wire.

"Look!" exclaimed Darl as the pair of big males joined him. He pointed to claw marks along the ledge, where mighty talons had scraped the ice. "These were dragons."

"And here!" Dargent pointed to a flake that at first appeared to be a large plate of ice. It lay on the edge of the narrow shelf, near where the protective layer of frost had been torn away from the nest.

Only when he sniffed, recoiling at the crocodilian scent, did Lectral admit the truth.

"A white dragon scale . . . Our nests were raided by the wyrms of the Dark Queen."

"And every one of them is empty," confirmed another silver, returning from a flight over the far end of the glacier-draped ridge.

"Word from below," reported a wyrmling, buzzing up to the ridge where the silver dragons sat in stiff-winged agitation. "The brass dragon eggs were stolen, too, right out of the hot springs!"

"We must fly to the City of Gold," Lectral declared, his voice stern enough to silence all the younger wyrms. "Perhaps the golden eggs are gone as well. In any event, Regia and Arumnus must be told."

In a cloud of sparkling metal that belied the grim foreboding in each dragon's heart, the silvers took wing. By now a dozen or more of the clan followed their venerable ancient as Lectral flew above the valley of the glacier that trailed downward from the massif.

Soon the river of white became a grayish brown, and then it vanished—or was transformed, more accurately, into a splashing flowage of meltwater that spilled downward, through a series of emerald lakes linked like gemstones on a silvery chain. Finally the city of golden towers and lofty palaces rose from the coastal mists.

"Look—we're not the only ones to fly here," Darlant observed, and Lectral turned to view a great cloud of brown metal dragons emerging from a side valley. They were coppers, he saw as they got closer, and together with the silvers, they filled the skies above the City of Gold. The mighty ancient of that clan was Cymbol, and he drew up to Lectral with an air of grim disquiet.

"Your eggs were stolen?" asked the silver, his deep voice barking through the windstream of flight.

"Aye. Yours as well?" asked the copper, with a snort of acid spattering from his nostrils.

"It was the chromatic dragons. We found the scale of a white on the high glacier."

"And a griffon tells me that blacks were seen poking about the swamp that protected our nests."

"Look below," noted the silver, as they crossed over the city wall, a looming barrier of shiny burnished gold. "It seems that many of our kin-dragons have awakened to the same kind of alarm."

The new arrivals commenced a great spiral over the broad central commons. Many bronze and brass dragons were here as well. In fact, the vast plaza that was the city's heart was a virtual sea of metallic scales and twitching, agitated wings. Dragons squirmed and pushed through the throng, some crowding into the great temples raised to either side of the square.

"Let's stay aloft," suggested the ancient silver to his two scions as Cymbol and his band of copper dragons descended, landing with much shoving and snorting amid the tangled mass below.

"Good idea," Dargentan agreed as he and Darlant took position on either side of Lectral's wings.

"Have either of you seen any sign of Silvara?" the ancient dragon asked.

It was Darlant who replied. "I flew past her most recent lair, but it was empty. I don't think she'd been there for a score of winters, perhaps more."

At that moment, a braying cry of alarm rang out from the rear, and Lectral and his two mighty companions curled through a tight turn. They strained for altitude in a sky sparkling with metallic shapes, gleaming wings and scales bright in the pale midwinter sun.

"Look there!" cried Dargentan, who had often demonstrated his remarkable eyesight. "Coming from the ocean, to the south."

A crimson shape winged from the southern skies, flying arrogantly toward the mass of metallic dragons, and Lectral bellowed in stiff-necked fury, propelled by instinctive antipathy. For a moment, he was a young serpent again, flying to battle in the skies over Ansalon. The red dragon brought a flame of emotion more intense than any feeling he had experienced in a thousand years.

But then he remembered that this was the present time, these were the Dragon Isles, and he realized that this chromatic serpent could not possibly be coming to attack. He fell into flanking position, watchfully poised above and behind the red dragon. From his vantage, he saw that the scarlet serpent was huge, as ancient as Lectral himself.

Many silvers, golds, and dragons of the brown metal clans had also winged into the sky, and now they flew in a great oval formation toward the valley beyond the city walls. In grim silence, the metallic serpents escorted the hated intruder.

The crimson serpent flew toward the city's center, on a course leading to the plaza that had been sanctified by many centuries of dragon ceremony. The massive wings tilted into a sweeping curve, gradually descending. But when it seemed as though the hateful serpent was going to land on the city square, Lectral acted on an instinctive wave of fury.

He dived past the red's nose, breathing a blast of ice into the air before the crimson serpent. The red veered away with a growl, but reluctantly settled to the ground beyond the city walls. The younger good dragons remained circling in the air, while Lectral came to a careful rest before the intruder. Regia and Arumnus were there, too, as well as the venerable copper Cymbol.

"Where are our eggs?" snarled the latter, drooling a spatter of deadly acid from his jaws onto the ground. "Answer me or die!" The copper wings buzzed in a fan of agitation, and Lectral wondered if the still-impetuous ancient would spit his corrosive breath at the red dragon right here and now.

"If I am harmed, you will never see your eggs again," declared the dragon, turning a reptilian smile to Regia, ignoring the fuming copper.

"Why do you come here?" asked the golden female coolly.

"To give a chance to save those eggs for which you seem to display such ardent concern," explained the red.

"Who are you?" Lectral asked abruptly.

"I am called Harkiel, Burner of Copper Scales," the wyrm said, grinning wickedly at Cymbol, "and I speak for Takhisis, the Queen of Darkness herself." The voice rumbled with surprising power, echoing back from the walls of the City of Gold.

"What is your purpose, then? How may we save our eggs?" demanded Regia, with patience that Lectral found almost as infuriating as the red's cruel arrogance. Even so, her golden wings bristled; looking closer, Lectral saw that she was striving hard to control her rage.

"To present you with an oath—a sacred oath, sworn on the name of Paladine and the Dark Queen. If you swear this oath, then your eggs shall remain safe and will be returned to you in due time."

"Never!" cried Cymbol as Lectral shook his mighty head in grim disagreement.

"What is the content of this oath?" Regia pressed, as if unaware of her kin-dragons' agitation.

"You must pledge to remain aloof from affairs in Ansalon, even though you may receive pleas for help from the pathetic wretches who dwell there."

"Help in a strife against your queen's dragons, no doubt," Arumnus intoned, as if discussing an abstract fact of historical insignificance.

"Correct."

Lectral could see the red dragon sneering. He felt a swelling of hatred in his gut, but he forced himself to restrain a violent response. Truly, the golds were displaying the proper attitude. A matter like this could only be treated with aloof disdain. Patience, he told himself. Vengeance could come later.

"And the eggs will remain safe?" asked Regia.

"You have the pledge of my mistress that they shall," replied Harkiel, with a dip of his head.

"Then I do not see that we have a choice," replied the golden matriarch.

With a sad shake of her head, she summoned the younger dragons to her, requesting them to pass among the islands to gather the rest of their kin-dragons . . .

. . . so that all could take the oath to the Dark Queen.

Chapter 38
Betrayal

352 AC

The silver dragon came to rest on the ledge beyond Lectral's lair, the wide cavern near the top of Glacier Peak. During the years since the theft of the eggs, the ancient serpent had taken up permanent residence in this deep cave. He was able to command a view of the oceans south of Misty Isle, and, perhaps even more important, anyone who sought him with news would know where to find him.

Now Dargentan had done just that, folding his wings with an ease that Lectral could only envy. Still, it made him proud to look at his handsome and capable offspring. Dargent was in his prime, a fast and powerful dragon with serene self-confidence and pride. He would one day be a worthy successor to bear the ram's horn.

"Was there a sign . . . any kind of word at all?" asked Lectral, with very undragonlike haste. He looked past Dargentan, as if he would confirm with his own eyes the reports from far beyond the horizon.

"It seems certain that Silvara is not anywhere on the isles," Dargent explained, with a shake of his head. "As to word from the mainland, it is . . . incomplete."

"Of course—because of that accursed oath!" barked the elder, his voice deepening into an unconscious but heartfelt growl.

"Even so, from what I have pieced together from the griffons, there have been no reports of dragons of metal anywhere on Ansalon. The serpents of the Dark Queen, in contrast, seem to be spreading like a plague. The destruction has already blighted more than half the world."

Lectral whirled about, his tail cracking like a whip as he pictured the High Kharolis and smoking Khalkists, Silvanesti and Solamnia, all darkened by the same scourge he had observed more than a dozen centuries before. He thought of the cities of men in which he had dwelt, more than fourteen hundred years earlier, and the pastoral forests of the elves.

Of course, rumors had come to the dragons on their remote isles, tales of a great Cataclysm, a darkness descending over the face of Krynn that had brutally changed the face of the world. Indeed, the gold dragons, and Regia in particular, had held this vast destruction to blame for the hundred winters of rainy weather that had beset the isles before the time of Saytica's death.

"What is the word of other dragons?" Lectral asked.

"Harkiel, who brought us the oath, is in Sanction. Word is that he has become horribly corrupt, sickened. And another great red has appeared . . . one you will know."

"Tombfyre?" growled the ancient silver.

"Aye. He leads the Red Wing and carries their emperor on his back. He seems to be little more than a flying horse," Dargent declared contemptuously. "Albeit, his rider is the greatest warrior in the Dark Queen's legion. That one, the Highlord Ariakas, has fashioned himself Emperor of Ansalon, and the griffons claim that he has hundreds of thousands of troops under his command. Indeed, he is known to have won many battles."

"It's like ancient times—Huma's war, being waged all over again! But this time the queen keeps us out, by virtue of that accursed oath!"

"Regia counsels patience, as always," Dargent said wryly. "She reminds us that the queen is bound by her pledge to return our eggs safely, when at last the course of her destruction is done."

The eggs! For the thousandth time, Lectral pictured the precious spheres of gleaming metal. His guts churned at the thought of the clutch in the hands of the queen's horrible minions. Would they even know to keep the silver eggs cool, or would the wyrmlings wither and suffocate in the midst of oppressive, ultimately lethal heat?

"Does Regia, or any of the golds, even know the meaning of concern, of genuine worry?" Lectral didn't want to scorn his kin-dragon, but his deep exasperation further sharpened the elder's tone.

"There is one bold one—you remember Quallathan. I have heard him counsel his elders that we must at least confirm the Dark Queen's compliance. But they demur, claiming that the oath must stand in its original words, that anything less would be unfitting of us!"

"I remember Quallathan," Lectral noted. "A strong flyer. He's even a little bigger than you, isn't he?"

"Perhaps I'm shorter by a scale or two," the prideful scion replied. "Of course, he was born on Ansalon, before the exile. He flew during Huma's campaign."

"Aye, you're right," recalled the ancient. He reflected, and not for the first time, on the sad fact that his offspring had never seen the wonders of the High Kharolis.

Dargentan continued. "Still, you're right about his strength. And, too, he's one who's not afraid to let his wings show."

Lectral chuckled sharply at Dargentan's phrase, which meant that Quallathan spent much of his life in his actual dragon body, rather than the two-legged forms favored by so many of the golden serpents.

Except for Quallathan, who shared Lectral's and his scions' anguish, the other good dragons seemed to have talked themselves into an air of acceptance and complacency. Regia and Arumnus had retreated to their lofty libraries and serene gardens to discuss matters that Lectral didn't even want to guess about.

Of course, there were other exceptions as well. Cymbol's rage and frustration were well known, and he had whipped a number of the younger coppers into a similar frenzy. Kirsah, a good-sized dragon of brass, was another young firebrand. He had even threatened to fly to Ansalon to seek the eggs himself, until Regia, together with Kirsah's venerable sire, Kord, forbade him forcefully from making the trip. The council of elders, which was a casual board centered around Regia and grim Arumnus, had threatened the young brass with magical confinement if he should dare to disobey.

And so the dragons on their islands had returned to a life of stasis, though it was a life that continued without the eggs that were their promise of a future. Indeed, the earlier lethargy that had possessed the metal clans seemed to have lifted, to be replaced by a nervous energy. It was a place where the dragons didn't do much of anything, but they were taut and nervous in their inactivity.

Until the day that Silvara returned.

Lectral was in his usual post, occupying the mouth of his cave, eyes turned southward. The silver female flew from that direction, waves splashing brine against her belly, so low over the ocean that Lectral didn't see her until she had nearly reached the shore.

And with that first sight, he knew that this was Silvara. He leapt to his feet and bugled a greeting, a long and sonorous trumpet cry that allowed the female to pinpoint his location on the high mountainside. Immediately she swept upward, wings stroking for height.

Then Lectral saw the rider upon her back, and he was struck by a staggering moment of recognition—but how could this be Heart? And certainly that wasn't the human knight, Huma, who rode astride the beautiful silver neck!

He shook his head, once again reminding himself of the present time and place.

No, the dragonrider was an elf, a golden-haired male who rode mighty Silvara with serene grace, though his face was locked in an expression of haunting sorrow.

"Fly with me to the Silver Summit!" cried Silvara as she glided past Lectral's ledge. "I—I have news that must be shared with all!"

Propelling himself into the air, the ancient male strained to catch up to the younger female's swift flight. He felt a deadly chill, terrified by the sounds behind Silvara's words. For, despite the maturity and patience and wisdom that was her due as a dragon of more than a thousand winters of life, she had been unable to keep an edge of raw, hysterical fear out of her voice.

Lectral still trailed behind as Silvara came to rest in the valley below the gleaming massif. Regia and Arumnus were already here, and somehow Lectral wasn't surprised by the fact. He settled to the ground beside Silvara as the lean elf who had ridden her across the ocean slid down from her silver serpentine neck and stood stiffly with a hand on the female dragon's shoulder.

Silvara changed shape before Lectral or any of the others could speak, and the ancient silver found himself looking at a beautiful silver-haired wild elf. He gasped, again moved by the powerful resemblance to Heart. The maid stepped forward and gestured to the sylvan warrior she had carried to the isle.

"This is Gilthanas, an elven prince of Qualinesti," she said, her words spilling out in a tremulous rush, a display of emotion so strong that Lectral felt the disturbing intensity all the way to his core.

"I have traveled with Silvara, and I, too, know of that which she speaks. If it were not for the need, neither of us could bear to relate the tale."

Silvara looked at Lectral, and the elder was struck by the age and weariness in her gaze. She seemed like an ancient herself, wracked by a grief greater than anyone should have to bear.

The elfmaid tried to speak, forced out a stammering word, then buried her face in her hands.

"Take a moment, child," Regia soothed, bobbing her head before the body of the wild elf female. "Let the words come from beyond. Allow yourself to be their filter, but not their creator."

Slowly, tremulously, Silvara began to speak. Her words brought forth a tale of horror and corruption, relating a journey that she and Gilthanas had made into the bowels of the Dark Queen's temples. It had been a long search, which she had conducted always in her elven guise. There, below the festering city of Sanction, she had found the eggs—and at this point in her story, she broke down into tears.

Gilthanas, with grim-faced discipline, told the rest . . . of the precious eggs, corrupted by the Dark Queen's priests . . . of craven draconians, monstrous troops for her evil legions, born from the eggs of metal dragonkind.

The elf's words were brief, his terms concise and mundane as he described the varieties of draconians, the corrupt brutes that were spawned from the hope of metal dragonkind's future. Yet so appalling was the horror revealed by those simple phrases that the entire gathering of metal dragons was struck mute. Wind ruffled, moaning in a sympathetic lament as it coursed down the Silver Stairs. Those steps, when Lectral's eyes shifted to the side, seemed somehow tainted and dark, as if they had been stained by the blood of many dragons.

"Thanks to Paladine that you are alive, both of you," whispered Regia. The shimmer of her scales had darkened, and, in fact it seemed to Lectral that a cloud of mourning had been drawn over all the wyrms, tainting the immaculate perfection of their metal forms. Regia slumped numbly, and the ancient silver was surprised by a pang of real sympathy for the oftentimes aloof gold. But then, he felt sorry for them all, for as he tried to comprehend the catastrophe, he wondered if their entire race, all the clans, were not actually doomed.

Then abruptly Silvara shimmered silver again, rearing

high and roaring a challenge into the sky, a challenge that was followed by an explosive wave of icy frost. Cries of betrayal, shouts for vengeance, rumbled from the gathered dragons. Wings buzzed in the air, and more than one serpent belched forth a cloud of frost or fire or spat a bolt of crackling lightning toward the heavens.

Only then did Lectral note that the elven prince bore a long silver-shafted weapon, a spear that was poised on the ground, its lofty tip of silvery steel a full twenty feet overhead. He sensed the aura of magic within the mighty lance and knew that he beheld a return of ancient might.

"There is more," Silvara declared, her tone sterner, hopeful again. "A weapon of the ages, reforged again, ready to wield against our ancient enemy."

"The Dragonlance . . ." murmured Lectral, suddenly understanding.

"The lances of Huma have been forged!" Silvara cried. "Who will fly at my side?"

Again Lectral saw Heart before him, saw the beautiful silver dragon who had been drawn to the love of a mortal. She, too, had pleaded with him to take up a rider, to bear a lance into battle with the Dark Queen's legions.

And he had refused.

In a vivid instant of shame. he remembered his petty anger, the jealousy that had sent him away—and left him with a legacy of a thousand years of guilt.

"I will fly with you," he said, and he added a silent plea to long-dead Heart, begging her forgiveness—and her understanding.

Amid the accolades of the other dragons, roaring and bellowing in a frenzy of battle-lust, Silvara heard his words, looked at him—and, for the first time since her return, she allowed her eyes to flare with a light of real and genuine hope.

Chapter 39
Allsar Dane

352 AC

The human knight was a young man, powerful and lean and, to all appearances, quick to learn. Like his fellows, he was brave enough to volunteer to fly, was willing to place his life in the hands of a mighty winged serpent, to do battle with the evil dragons of the Dark Queen in the war-torn skies over Ansalon. Now he advanced with a walk of catlike grace, clearly a warrior of self-confidence and maturity.

Yet Lectral took an instant dislike to the first man he had met in something more than thirteen hundred winters. He looked down his great shining snout, glaring between the flexing apertures of his broad nostrils as the man strode boldly up to the great silver dragon. Only with an effort did he avoid a disdainful snort.

The towers of Palanthas rose just past this parade ground, and the lofty ridges of the northern Kharolis range, still limned in the whiteness of spring snow, formed the horizon beyond. Together with a multitude of metal dragons, he had made the flight from the Dragon Isles to this legendary city. Now Lectral had to force himself to lower his gaze, to confront this insignificant human when his eyes longed to fix upon the great mountain range.

The knight knelt, looked frankly at the ancient creature looming over his head, and then bowed his head and spoke in serious, dignified tones.

"Esteemed Ancient One, I beg to request the great honor of mounting your immaculate shoulders and of riding your mighty self into battle. I pledge to strive mightily against the foe of your people and mine. I pray to the Platinum Father that together we can do great injury to the Dark Queen's hopes."

"I don't have 'people,'" Lectral retorted sharply, though he was forced to admit to a certain approval of the knight's bold words and his properly deferential air.

"I beg your forgiveness, Honored One. As you may have deduced, I am inexperienced in the ways of dragons. I can pledge that I will not make the same mistake twice."

Lectral was becoming embarrassed by all the fuss. "It is a minor matter. But tell me, knight, how are you called?"

"My name is Allsar Dane, Knight of the Crown," declared the warrior earnestly.

"You may address me as Lectral." The silver dragon studied the human a little more closely than he had upon his first inspection. The man was tall and strapping, bearing the weight of his heavy plate armor with an easy grace that suggested he was a person of significant strength. He stood with dignity, yet had been able to ask for the dragon's forgiveness without, apparently, feeling that he acknowledged any weakness in his own honor.

That was a lesson that more than one copper dragon might take to heart, Lectral thought with a chuckle. Then he reflected upon his own reaction of sourness at his first meeting of Allsar Dane, and he felt an uncomfortable flush of guilt. Perhaps age is making a bitter old nag out of me, he rebuked himself silently.

Finally he realized that the knight was still standing before him, waiting for a reply.

"Indeed, I agree to bear you in battle." Lectral knew that he could carry the knight, though the thought was still strange. "But I warn you that holding on shall be your own affair, for my habits of flying, like everything else about my ancient self, are rather thoroughly ingrained."

"Of course—if you will allow me the use of one of these rather simple saddles the cobblers of Palanthas have made for us."

"Certainly." Lectral had seen one of the seats, and it caused him to reflect upon the courage of the warriors who would ride them. The saddle was little more than a strap and a set of stirrups attached to a swiveling bracket upon which would be mounted the potent Dragonlance.

"Splendid! I have some skill with the lance, and we can only hope that we'll get the chance to stick a few of the Dark Queen's dragons!"

"Quite," murmured Lectral, taken aback by the young knight's enthusiasm. Still, it was a refreshing change, and he had heard many tales of the deadly lances during his time on the isles. It would be good to see one in action from a closer viewpoint. Again he thought of Heart with a pang and wished she could know what he did here today.

"Of course, most of my fighting experience has been gained with a fishing pole in my hands," Allsar admitted sheepishly. "A rainbow trout is my favorite prey."

"Ah, fishing," Lectral agreed, remembering many pleasant experiences of his own. "Can there be a more perfect food? Myself, I always looked forward to the running of the salmon. Now, *that's* a delicacy."

As hostlers came forward and hesitantly wrapped the saddle around his chest and neck, Lectral raised his head and looked around. The high ridges of the northern Kharolis, and the High Clerist's Pass, guarded Palanthas as they had through all of the ancient dragon's life. When his gaze swept to the south, toward the lands that were lost in the dust of the plains and distant mountains, he reflected on an astounding piece of news he had heard following his arrival in the great city: that there was now a deep ocean slicing through the middle of the Kharolis Range, with open water extending eastward as far as Sanction.

"Can that be true?" he murmured softly, intrigued and amazed by the thought.

"I beg your pardon, Mighty One?" wondered the knight.

"What? Oh . . . I had heard of a great body of water to the south of here, dividing the middle of the Kharolis Range. Do you know of such a thing?"

"Indeed. It's called the Newsea, though many generations of my people have lived since its creation during the Cataclysm. Perhaps you can remember what it was like before then."

"A thousand years before."

The knight was silent, regarding the dragon with a calm and appraising gaze.

"Perhaps we will fly there and see this ocean," Lectral suggested.

"The fishing is said to be quite good," Allsar Dane informed him.

"That's intriguing news, I admit." Lectral felt a little better about this man and was ready to fly. He looked around, saw the fluttering of metallic wings, lances upraised as the knights and dragons filled the plaza before the city.

Palanthas, of course, had seemed pretty much the same as ever to Lectral—that is to say, boring. It was a place keenly conscious of history and fate and magic, and naturally the gold dragons had always felt very much at home there. Yet to Lectral and his silver clan, it had always seemed to be one of the more staid and aloof of the human realms. Generally he had favored livelier places, such as Xak Tsaroth, Tarsis, or even Sanction, to the serene placidity of Palanthas.

Just a few days earlier, that fabled city had been the site of the arrival of the metallic dragons on Ansalon, a homecoming that was accompanied by great celebrations and optimism on the part of the inhabitants. As soon as they had overcome their initial terror, the humans had poured forth and gathered around, until every one of the metallic dragons had been draped with garlands and fed many draughts of fine wine.

In the wake of that spontaneous celebration, Lauralanthalasa, Princess of Qualinesti and sister to the elven prince Gilthanas, had been appointed general of the newly created Army of Whitestone. And for the first time in this bitter strife, the forces resisting the Dark Queen would go to war sheltered by the wings of Paladine's mighty serpents of metal.

"Dragons, make ready to fly!"

The speaker was golden Quallathan, who had been granted the honor of carrying the army's general, Laurana. Lectral had always thought highly of the mature and steadfast gold, and it pleased him that the humans and elves had honored him thus. Looking around, the ancient dragon saw his two scions nearby, each mounted by a lance-bearing knight. Dargentan flapped his wings, ready to fly, while Darlant stretched his neck in visible anticipation. He, too, was ready to hurl himself into the skies.

Mighty Cymbol, the venerable copper, was also prepared to join the flight to battle. He carried a grim-faced elf in his saddle, a silver-armored lancer who looked like a heavier version of Gilthanas. The copper had barely contained his fury, and now the desire for vengeance burned like a fire in his glaring eyes. Clearly he was ready to exact his price in blood. Brass Kirsah sat just beyond, trying to coax an interesting pair of riders into the saddle. One, a dwarf, seemed to be assisted, sort of, by an energetic kender.

Then came the melodious cry from Quallathan, and the dragons of Paladine took flight. Silvers, bronze, and brass formed a great wing to the left, while the golds and coppers arrayed themselves to the right, until the sparkling of metal wings formed a great swath across the sky. The man on his shoulders was a good weight, and Lectral's flight was as strong and steady as ever.

"Never before have my kin-dragons flown in such a great wing as this," Lectral admitted in wonder.

"And never has the Dark Queen had such good cause to fear," added Allsar Dane.

The Vingaard plains were a blur of uniform brown viewed through the puffs of clouds. The flight of dragons flew onward soundlessly, lofty and aloof, over the High Clerist's tower and the pass where the enemy armies had met their first setback.

"It's beautiful!" Allsar Dane declared, his voice a whisper of awe. "You can see all the way to the Vingaard River."

Lectral was silent, remembering the glories of Ansalon as if he had departed here only a season or two ago. He relished the long-forgotten sight of an entire continent sprawling to the horizons below him.

"Look there!" came a cry from the right, and several dragons bellowed cries of alarm.

Immediately all eyes were riveted on the spots of color emerging from the southern sky. The tiny shapes grew, soon becoming tinted with emerald brightness. These were green dragons, and their own riders, with a masked lord in the lead, guided them in a tight wedge of attack. Flying high, they came on in a long double rank, one line flying just above and before the other.

Quallathon brayed his challenge in response, the mighty golden wyrm diving into the fray with tucked wings and arrow-straight neck. Laurana crouched on his back like a veteran lancer, her long-shafted weapon pointed forward and down. Sunlight brightened the tip in a reflective staccato, like sparks trailing away from the razor edge of steel.

Lectral flew swiftly, not at all uncomfortable with the weight of a human rider. Allsar Dane held his lance with the poise of long experience, though this was his first time in the air, and his knees gripped the silver's neck firmly.

Lectral tried to convince himself that the man would actually remain mounted if he were forced to dive, roll, or perform some other aerobatic maneuver. But at best he could only hope. He was surprised to realize that if the man came to harm, the silver dragon would feel profound regret.

Beside him, Dargentan and Darlant flew with strong, steady strokes, each with his rider crouched and ready, Dragonlance pointing boldly toward the foe. The green shapes grew larger, each defining itself into a dragon and a masked, armored rider. Lectral led the contingent of silvers toward an optimal attack position, sideslipping to make an oblique approach against the greens, then tilting forward to commence a savage rushing dive.

The silvery spear jutted proudly past Lectral's shoulder, gleaming in the sun, tilting with lethal purpose toward the nearest of the emerald serpents. That dragon swept closer, the green jaws locked into a grimace of pure hatred. The rider of the Dark Queen's wyrm also bore a lance, though the weapon had a shaft of wood and a smaller, less brilliant tip.

"Now!" Allsar Dane urged, and Lectral sensed his rider's intent. With a violent shift, the silver body curled away, and the tip of the Dragonlance tore through the green scales of the enemy wyrm's belly.

The courageous rider crouched behind his dragon-scale shield as a blast of green gas billowed into the air. Lectral felt the stuff sting his nostrils, but he cleared the cloud away, killing another green in midflight with a powerful exhalation of deadly frost.

"Hold on," growled the ancient silver, lifting his right wing and dipping his left. Allsar Dane's knees tightened, but otherwise Lectral paid his rider scant attention. The man would have to hold on for himself if the pair were to have any chance of making it through the battle.

Lectral veered toward a green that was looping around below, but before the silver jaws could blast their frost, the lance tilted, sending the barbed head tearing through the emerald scales of the enemy dragon's shoulder. Lectral raked his claws through the green wing, but that was a mere aftereffect as, fatally pierced by the deadly lance, the wyrm of Takhisis plunged toward the ground.

Now Lectral pulled out of his dive, curling his neck and tail to help him arc through a level glide, then smoothly soared skyward again. The crushing force of the maneuver pressed the human rider heavily into his saddle, but the man made no complaint as the ground once again fell away below. Lectral reached with broad wings and stroked downward, straining toward higher altitude and the battle that swirled and raged through the skies overhead.

"Over there!" barked the knight in a rudely direct tone. But Lectral bit back his annoyance and followed the tip of the lance, seeing several greens swarming around a mighty gold and its royal elven rider.

"Quallathan!" cried Lectral in alarm, immediately sideslipping and curling toward the savage melee.

Laurana, astride the gold, stabbed with her lance, taking down one of the greens, and then Lectral swept through the melee. Allsar Dane's lance ripped another emerald-colored serpent, and the powerful combination of silver talons and fangs rent a third, leaving it, crippled and shrieking, to plunge helplessly toward the plains far below.

Lectral looked, seeing more of the enemy dragons breaking away, flying toward the eastern horizon. The first battle was over; the evil wyrms had been put to flight. He knew there would be more, and the silver dragon was eager to fight them.

"We've got them on the run now. I'll bet they fly all the way to the Khalkists," Allsar declared.

"Then it is time for us to go there and finish the job our forefathers began," replied the mighty silver dragon.

Chapter 40
Fire in the Sky

352 AC

In a dazzling campaign, Lauralanthalasa, the Golden General, led the army of Whitestone on a rapid counterattack across the Vingaard plains. Under the shelter of metallic wings, the Knights of Solamnia, dwarves of Kayolin and Thorbardin, and free men and elves from throughout the west surged in vengeful attacks against the dragon highlords and their teeming armies. Buoyed by Laurana's success in her initial attack, the forces of Whitestone marched and fought and marched some more, striking quickly, winning one battle after another. Willingly they followed her orders, trusting her natural instincts, constantly keeping the enemy forces off-balance and in desperate retreat.

Laurana led the liberation of Vingaard Keep, and then swiftly ferried her army—on the backs of dragons!—across the river of the same name while that torrent was at the full height of spring flood. Striking quickly, moving with forced marches, and always in the direction the enemy least expected, the Army of Whitestone embarked on a series of blistering, lightning-fast offensives.

The wyrms of Takhisis did not let this advance go unchallenged. After the disaster met by the green dragons, the whites and blacks flew forth but were defeated in quick, sharp battles. Following each of these three engagements, the survivors among the defeated chromatic dragons reeled back to the east, flying into the rugged Khalkists in search of sanctuary.

On the ground, the mounted knights thundered forward in sweeping charges, onslaughts that set the plains themselves to resounding underfoot. Great phalanxes of footmen kept pace, anchoring the line when the enemy forces showed signs of attacking, or hurrying forward in relentless pursuit each time the foe was once again put to flight. Elven bowmen harassed the enemy with deadly missile fire, and doughty dwarves wielded sword and axe, an implacable anvil against which the hammer of the good dragons could strike.

Still the Blue and Red Wings remained intact and under Highlord Ariakas's personal command. That lord's mount, Tombfyre, became as well known as his master, killing many a Whitestone warrior with his fiery breath, cruel jaws, and crushing talons. For the most part, the Emperor of Ansalon patiently held his mighty serpents back from Laurana's army. Yet finally any further patience on the Highlord's part would have resulted in the loss of virtually all the land gained in the previous years' campaigns.

The two wings met in a major battle, hundreds of dragons and their riders wheeling through the skies, breathing death, striving for mastery, and once again the Golden General prevailed. The Army of Whitestone moved on to the liberation of Kalaman, while Ariakas fell back again, withdrawing into the rugged sanctuary of the Khalkists.

But before the campaign could continue to its final triumph, Lauralanthalasa was captured by trickery, her own loyalty used to draw her into the Highlord's snare. She was taken into the heart of the Dark Queen's realms, and all the hopes for victory remained in abeyance. Warriors, dragons, and wizards on both sides felt the world plunging toward a cusp of history, a day—or night—when the Dark Queen's dreams of mastery would either become reality or be shattered into irrevocable defeat.

Yet still the war in the skies continued as the dragons of Paladine fought against the wings under Ariakas's command. Gilthanas of Qualinesti, mounted upon mighty Silvara, took command of the aerial forces, and the good dragons pressed their foes all the way to the fringe of the Khalkists.

For their part in this culminating campaign, Lectral and the silvers were patrolling with the coppers over the great Army of Whitestone, which was gathered at a gap leading into the foothills. The evil forces had fallen back all the way to Neraka, with mountainous barriers screening them against any land attack from the west. Now they watched . . . and waited.

"After the war, let's go fishing," Allsar Dane suggested, lounging in the saddle as Lectral glided lazily above the plains. They had learned to converse easily in the air, Lectral holding his neck arched so that he could hear the man's voice. The posture was too slow and awkward for battle flight, but quite comfortable when, as now, they were gliding on patrol.

"I'd like that," the silver flier agreed, realizing that the notion had a strong appeal. "To the Newsea, perhaps, to see if the salmon are running."

"Ah, but only if we can then go to the mountains, stalking the rainbow trout," replied Allsar.

"I like your plan," Lectral said.

A squawk of alarm drew their attention, and they saw a griffon flying urgently toward them. The hawkish flier bore an elven scout on his back.

"The Blue and Red Wings gather in the high mountains," the scout explained as his laboring steed strained to fly beside Lectral at this lofty altitude. "They're concealed by fog, but they took flight with the dawn. They'll be coming this way soon."

"Thanks for the notice," the silver replied, turning his head to the east. Allsar Dane cinched his belt tight and made sure that the Dragonlance was firmly seated in its swiveling mount.

The coppers, under the leadership of Cymbol, circled nearby. The gold, brass, and bronze dragons were elsewhere, embarked on a desperate search to rescue Laurana. Until the Golden General's return, Gilthanas, astride Silvara, would remain in command.

"Ready?" asked Lectral.

"Let's go," the knight replied.

The skies over the mountains were thick with cloud and mist, a great blanket of white, deceptively soft and pure, billowing upward into the loftiest reaches. After hearing the alarm, the ancient silver stared into that impenetrable murk, waiting for the first appearance of the foe. His rider was alert and poised on his shoulders, and more silvers flew to either side.

The Red Wing emerged from the cloud like a mass of bloodstains seeping through a cotton blanket—dozens, then scores of red shapes growing larger and more distinct, emerging from the foggy nothingness to become bright, vivid spots of color. In the lead came the Highlord Ariakas, Emperor of Ansalon, still mounted upon mighty Tombfyre.

In fact, Lectral recognized the dragon before the rider, for his old enemy was the only wyrm among the opposing force that was the silver's equal in size. Somehow it seemed fitting that the descendant of legendary Crematia should bear the enemy emperor.

The dragons of both wings converged quickly, with no thoughts for the antlike troops crawling on the ground below. A formation of blue dragons flew beside the reds, and the numbers of the enemy serpents seemed to fill the air. Lectral knew beyond any doubt that this battle would be settled in the skies—and, perhaps, finally resolved for all the future of Krynn. His jaws parted instinctively, and he bellowed a thunderous roar, loudly challenging the chromatic dragons, instinctively boasting of his courage and his might.

Answering bellows resounded in the air until the sky shook as though from the force of a thunderstorm. Blues and reds tipped forward and dived, while dragons of copper and silver labored upward, striving for the altitude to meet the foe in level flight. Lance tips sparkled like diamonds, and knightly armor gleamed as bright as the dragons' silver scales.

The two forces converged in sudden silence as the dragons ceased their roaring, concentrating on the grim business now close at hand. Lightning flashed suddenly, a premature blast from an overeager blue dragon. The crackling bolt was met by a spume of acid, scornfully spat by a copper, and the lingering cloud of brackish gas spread a sharp, acrid stink through the air.

Flames roared in Lectral's ears as the first rank of the charging wyrms swept past. Allsar Dane twisted and jabbed with the lethal lance, gutting a blue that tried to fly too close. Lectral's own breath joined the frosty clouds of the others of his clan, mingling as well with the streaming acid of the coppers, until the stench of corrosive gas, exploding lightning, and sooty flame were all mingled into a thick stew of pollution.

Red wings careened past, and Lectral pulled upward, scraping with his talons, tearing away a section of crimson membrane. Lightning from a nearby dragon of blue jarred him, ripping scales from his belly in a painful wound, but the ancient silver was able to tuck and dive, allowing the lancer to pierce the lightning-spitting blue with a fatal stab to the neck.

Another red, this one nearly as big as Tombfyre, dived toward them from above. Lectral cast a spell, the useful incantation of mirror image that created multiple images of his actual self. He twisted away, the magical duplicates diving in opposite directions, and the red's fire billowed harmlessly into the midst of the spell.

The ancient silver turned back then, casting a spell of slowness that seemed to mire his crippled opponent in thick, oily air. The chromatic dragon labored to turn, moaning desperately in the grip of agonizing delay, sensing the doom that swept closer on silver wings. With a barrage of rending talons and crushing jaws, Lectral ripped into his enemy, and seconds later a torn and lifeless red corpse dropped toward the plains far below.

For a long time, the great forces of dragons clashed in the sky, wheeling in a savage circle. Mighty serpents flying alone or in pairs and trios dived away from the fight and then climbed back, a relentless cycle of attack and flight, each side straining to gain the advantage. Ariakas seemed to sense that this was his last chance to win a great battle, for he threw every reserve, every immature wyrmling and naive young lancer that he could find, into the fight. Many perished on both sides, blasted from the air by lethal attacks of dragonbreath or lance or sword or claw.

Often a dragon was not slain outright, but was crippled by a blow against a wing, a wound that would prove as certainly lethal as a thrust through the heart. Lectral watched many serpents and their hapless riders spiral frantically downward, one good wing stroking the air, trying unsuccessfully to restore some grace to the doomed flight. In a moment of calm and clarity, the ancient silver reflected that, if he were stricken, he would prefer the utter lifelessness of an instantly fatal wound to the helpless struggles that gave so many of the falling dragons such pathetic final moments. And the doom awaiting at the end was the same, regardless of how quickly or prolonged the suffering of the dying.

Lectral found himself in a battle with a monstrous blue, a dragon of wily skill with a deadly swordsman mounted on his back. Through a long series of dives and strikes, they dodged back and forth. Finally, attacking with the aid of haste magic, the blue twisted Lectral about in the air, sending the silver tumbling into a frantic dive, forcing a desperate try to pull out of the headlong descent. Allsar Dane hung on without a murmur, his knees pressed tightly against Lectral's flanks as he clung hard to the leather strap of reins.

Finally the silver dragon recovered his balance, pulling out of the dive with a sudden loop that took his pursuer completely by surprise. Allsar Dane stabbed the dragonlance through the back of the blue's rider, then into the wyrm's flesh, driving it deep between the azure dragon's shoulders. With a shriek that rapidly faded into a moan, the serpent died, falling from the sky with its lifeless rider toppling from the saddle to tumble limply at the dragon's side.

But before Lectral could start to gain altitude again a great crimson shadow spread overhead and Tombfyre was there. The silver twisted, trying to dive away, but Ariakas struck, and Lectral felt Allsar Dane's blood warming the scales of his back. The dragonlance hung limply by the silver dragon's side, and the man didn't respond when the mighty serpent repeatedly called out to him.

Tombfyre veered away, bearing the shouting Ariakas toward the eastern skies. With a backward look, Lectral saw that the battling dragons had dwindled away, and now the mighty red seemed bent upon making a complete escape.

Roaring, Lectral plunged after him, driving his silver wings through the air, striving to overtake the hateful red. The aerial battlefield vanished to the rear as the pursued and pursuing dragons flew over the foothills of the Khalkists. The Emperor of Ansalon fled on a course that would take him well north of Sanction, as if he had a purpose, a destination in mind other than mere escape.

The ancient silver came steadily after the red. Now Lectral forgot about the stiffness and the other infirmities of age; his wings, his whole body, felt young again, as if he were a powerful serpent in the prime of his life. For a long time, the two dragons raced through the skies, leaving the battlefield far behind, until at last the eastern horizon before them had darkened and, to the rear, the sun had slipped past the jagged teeth of the foothills.

A great temple loomed in the distance, a place that the maps had marked as "Neraka." It was a dark and dolorous place, and Lectral understood that this was his enemy's destination. The spiraling of great dragons, dozens of them, cut colorful swaths through the air above the Dark Queen's fortress. They roared, swarming forward, ready to protect their stronghold against this impudent silver.

Knowing it was certain death to pursue any farther, Lectral could only wheel downward in frustration, watching the red dragon and his arrogant rider disappear over the next mountain ridge, winging steadily toward the twisted, distorted edifice.

Chapter 41
Tombfyre's Dilemma

352 AC

The ghastly fortress rose from murk and shadow, shrouded by dark fog, a twisted monument to the Queen of Darkness thrusting high into the war-torn skies of Ansalon. Tombfyre, bearing the grimly silent Ariakas, flew onward through turgid air, watching the grotesque shape emerge into clearer view. The red dragon seethed with fury and resentment.

"Find your strongest enemy and kill him!" This ancient dictum, the command of Crematia and Deathfyre through the ages, rang through his mind, demanding that he turn back and fight. And yet his rider, his "master," had ordered him to flee from the battle.

"You will land there, in front of the temple," declared

the Emperor of Ansalon flatly.

Without reply, Tombfyre dived, scrutinizing the awful edifice. At one time—and in another place—this might have been a grand temple, with sweeping balustrades connecting a ring of supporting towers to the vast central monolith. High walls encircled a broad courtyard, and many balconies, bridges, and ramparts marked the interior surfaces. Yet some of the outer towers leaned chaotically beyond the fortress wall, and the central pillar itself rose more like a diseased and warped trunk of cypress than a construct of stone and mortar.

Chromatic dragons of all five colors wheeled and spiraled in the skies over the queen's fortress, and Tombfyre suppressed a bitter urge to rebuke them. Where were they when battle was raging in the skies over Vingaard? Victory had been within their grasp, he deluded himself. Surely another score or two of dragons would have given them the supremacy they deserved!

With the memories of the battle, the red serpent felt the bitterness of his flight and knew that this fortress was not where he chose to go. His place was in the skies, battling the serpents of Paladine—and, especially, defeating the ancient silver dragon, descendant of those who had thwarted his clan for so long.

"Land!" repeated Ariakas. "And then I desire that you wait for me."

Tombfyre growled his resentment, the sound a dull rumble of rage that Ariakas certainly felt through the stiff leather of his saddle.

"You must obey!"

The Highlord's voice was as taut as a bowstring, giddy and terrified at the same time. Anticipation tried unsuccessfully to dominate his fear, and the result was halfway between a plaintive plea and an arrogant command.

"No! I must fight! I must destroy the silver dragon!" roared Tombfyre, snorting a cloud of fiery smoke in frustration. "He is the heir of the wyrm who slew Deathfyre, and it is my destiny to kill him!"

"Your destiny was set out by *me* when I freed you from

your tomb so deep beneath the Khalkists!" snarled the Highlord. "Would you have had me leave you there to rot?"

"If you had left me there, you would still be there as well, for it was my wings that bore us both to the surface of the world!" growled Tombfyre.

"You will obey me," Ariakas declared grimly, and Tombfyre admitted to a grudging respect. Certainly no other creature in the world would dare to speak to him like this.

And what Ariakas said, for the most part, was true. Tombfyre's destiny *had* been laid clearly by the Dark Queen, and he was bidden to bear this Dragon Highlord where he would go. Bitterly Tombfyre followed his rider's instruction, winging toward the monstrous, twisted shape that now seemed to rise higher than ever into the sky. He felt an immortal presence behind that grim structure, knew that Takhisis herself was again drawing near Krynn, seeking the portal through which she could enter and gain mastery over the world.

"Your vengeance can wait," Ariakas snapped, as if reading the red dragon's mind. "Our mistress—your queen and mine, should I need to remind you—will pass through the Foundation Stone gate tonight. Would you not be in attendance?"

Ariakas had regained his composure, and now his voice was as cold and arrogant as it was when he was sentencing some wretched prisoner to torture or execution.

Tombfyre glowered into the gathering darkness, declining to voice an answer, for in truth, this was a time when the will of his mistress was but a faint and secondary compulsion compared to the hatred that drove him to take wing against the ancient silver. He thought of victories won and disasters suffered during millennia of strife between the two forces of dragonkind. Certainly all that history had been meant to lead to this dramatic resolution . . . now, here, tonight!

Of course, he knew of other tales, legends, and predictions. If the prophets were true and the alignment of the

Foundation Stone properly established, than Ariakas was right: Takhisis herself would pass from the Abyss to Krynn on this bleak eve. The pieces of her mighty spell were in place, and though her armies had suffered setbacks on the fields of battle, the opening of her mighty gate would allow the Queen of Darkness herself to rule upon this world that was her destined plaything.

And Tombfyre's greatness would again be eclipsed, as it had been during the reign of Deathfyre, was now by his human lord. His mistress would be here as well, and she would command the troops of the army. Ansalon would be *her* empire, and Tombfyre would have yet another master upon Krynn.

"Do you *hear* me? She *comes!*" The Highlord's voice was increasingly shrill, as if he sensed his mount's growing reluctance.

"If the queen passes her gate, then she will summon me at her pleasure," Tombfyre declared, tucking his wings and slicing a downward course through the air. He glided with serene grace toward the massive clearing before the twisted, deformed edifice that was the Temple of Neraka. In grim silence, he landed and waited for more arguments from the human emperor. But Ariakas made no sound. He merely slid to the ground and turned his back upon the mighty dragon.

After the Highlord had started toward the gates of the Dark Queen's fortress, Tombfyre once again took to the air. His eyes remained fixed upon the Khalkists, where his clan had reigned for thousands of years.

The silver dragons, gloating from their victory in the skies over Vingaard, would be gathering there, he knew. And certainly there he would find the mighty Lectral.

And Tombfyre would find his destiny as well.

Chapter 42
Life and Death

352 AC

Allsar Dane's life seemed to have lasted but an eyeblink of time, a fact that Lectral found curiously saddening. He looked at the pallid, drained features of the knight, saw where Ariakas's mighty sword had pierced the armor and the flesh of Dane's back. The blade had torn through the metal plate, puncturing the body to a relatively shallow depth, at least by the standard of a dragon's wound.

Yet in a man, it had been enough to be lethal.

After landing, the silver dragon changed shape, but only long enough to shrug out of his saddle, to release the slain knight's buckles and armor, and to lay him in state on a low hillside, overlooking a lake of pure, clear water. Eyes closed as if in slumber, the knight's face was gray and pallid. To Lectral, it suddenly seemed to look very old.

Again silver scales gleamed as the mighty dragon assumed his true shape. Sadly Lectral scooped a grave in the rocky ground of the Khalkist shale, remembering his first reluctant acquaintance with this brave man.

"Ah, my friend, you were a worthy foe for Tombfyre, and for the Dark Queen herself, whether they knew it or not."

Gently the silver dragon lifted the limp body and laid it in the grave. With a few scoops of his massive forelegs, Lectral poured dirt and gravel over the motionless shape until the grave was a slightly mounded spot atop the low hill. He patted and smoothed the surface for a long time, wanting to insure that the surface was perfect.

With a shimmering of magic, the mighty silver shape contracted, faded to a mundane gray, and rose to stand upon two feet. The figure of a proud knight stood beside the burial site, head bowed, hands clasped before his armored chest as he remembered the brave warrior's last moments.

"O Platinum Father," murmured Lectral. "Please see that this courageous Knight of the Crown receives the honors due a hero of Paladine . . . and know that he will be missed, by humans and dragons alike. By the Oath and the Measure, he fought well and died as a hero."

Fighting a curious twinge of emotion that thickened his throat and misted his eyes, Lectral looked to the placid lake just below the hill. Many ripples spread across the surface, marking the feeding of numerous trout as they snatched flies and water bugs from the surface.

He wondered idly if they were rainbows. He hoped they were, for that trout had been Allsar Dane's favorite.

"Good fishing, my friend," murmured the silver dragon, once again a gleaming serpent.

With a respectful nod, Lectral spread his wings to catch the mountain breeze, gliding low over the sparkling blue waters, then stroking powerfully upward to soar above the encircling ridge. Gusts of wind swirled, lifting him higher, but he used his strength to hasten his ascent, no longer content to ride the breeze like some carrion-hunting bird.

He thought of Silvara and Heart, of their talk of love. Surely that was not an emotion for dragons . . . but was it true that it could be learned? Is that what he felt now, the emotion that was causing him such grief? Perhaps it was true that a dragon, a *young* dragon at any rate, could in fact learn to love.

Perhaps, in fact, that was the silvers' unique gift to the clans of their kin-dragons. It was the counterpart to the learned reflection and the magical mastery of the golds, the genial sociability of the brass or the stolid strength of the bronzes. Even the vengeful coppers had shown that, through the ages, there was a need for violence and fury, and the clan of Cymbol had borne that torch bravely and well.

And for the silvers, was it their place to show the kin-dragons the value, even the mere *existence*, of love? Perhaps that and, of course, to embody the pure beauty of flight, the thing that the silvers did so much better than any of the other metallic dragons.

Lectral considered the question. His life was his flying—that was the thing that gave him the purest joy. Indeed, if there were such a thing as love, perhaps flight was its purest expression. Finding himself among the heights again, he didn't lapse into a leisurely glide. Instead, he strived like a youngster, pulling great scoops of air with each powerful beat of his wings, lifting himself higher than the surrounding ridges, vying for the altitude that was the province of the high peaks of the range.

He knew the other silvers were dispersed, hunting perhaps, or waiting for word of the night's developments. The evil dragons had fled from the skies over Kalaman and the plains, falling back to the twisted fortress that Lectral had glimpsed during his pursuit of Tombfyre. No doubt they still circled there, anxiously awaiting the arrival of their queen.

A ram bleated, with a clatter of rocks, and Lectral looked up to see the creature skipping with uncanny precision along a lofty cliff. But something else moved above it, and in the instant of that awareness, he threw himself forward, wings extended to catch an immediate lift.

Tombfyre appeared seemingly from nowhere, attacking with a blast of fire that cruelly seared Lectral's tail. The silver dragon careened wildly down the mountainside, avoiding craggy outcrops, barely airborne. A crimson shape swept past, roaring in triumph and glee.

What a fool I was! Lectral rebuked himself furiously. He had been alone and careless, lost in his pathetic musings, making a splendid opportunity for a vicious and implacable enemy. If not for the bleating of the frightened mountain sheep, the battle would have ended at once—a fatal ambush leading to a solitary and anonymous kill.

Struggling for equilibrium, Lectral saw the ground whirling upward and knew he was about to crash into the mountainside. With a quick word of magic, he teleported high into the sky, pulling out of his spin as Tombfyre roared a fiery ball of frustration below.

But then the red dragon disappeared, and the silver whirled in sudden alarm, ready for a magical attack from above or behind. There was no sign of Tombfyre anywhere in the sky, until Lectral cast another spell, one that allowed him to see objects masked by a spell of invisibility. His enemy stood clearly revealed, the mask of magic ripped away as the red dragon strived higher and higher through the air.

Replying in kind, Lectral blinked out of sight behind a spell of his own invisibility. Tilting his wings, he angled toward the infuriated red. From the fixed nature of Tombfyre's glaring eyes, the silver knew that his enemy wasn't fooled by the spell. No doubt Tombfyre, too, possessed the ability to detect objects concealed by invisibility magic.

The silver dragon circled at a lofty height, as high as he had ever flown before. He watched the red laboring through the thin air, striving to reach him, and once more Lectral knew the pure joy of soaring even above the birds. He felt a serene sense of calm, knowing now that this was a proper destiny for him and his clan.

Finally Tombfyre reached that great altitude, and the

two dragons swept together, jaws gaping, widespread wings sweeping forward in a mutual but deadly embrace. Combined roars echoed like thunder from the surrounding heights while the serpents rushed toward a violent merging.

No longer would Lectral try to evade his archenemy; neither would he flee nor give chase. They would meet here, a mile or more above the mountaintops, and they would resolve a fight that had been waged over thousands of years. Here, now, it would be finished.

Lectral filled his lungs, started his blast of frost as he saw the first tongues of flame erupt from Tombfyre's horrible maw. A blast of cold and fire mingled with thunderous force as the two ancient wyrms smashed together. Tombfyre's fireball encircled Lectral, while the blast of frost exploded outward to envelop the hateful crimson wyrm. Locked in a clench of claw and fang and serpentine tails, the pair of monstrous fliers plummeted downward.

Lectral was sorely hurt, and he knew his wings had been seared beyond their ability to carry him in flight. His enemy, too, had been crippled by the deadly expulsion. The silver dragon clenched his jaws tightly over Tombfyre's throat, preventing any sound, any attempt at spellcasting that the red dragon might make. Silver talons punctured scarlet scales, ripping into the red dragon's flesh, clutching him in a merciless embrace.

Tombfyre squirmed frantically, desperate now as he sensed his enemy's intention. Wind whistled past their scales, soothing the burned flaps of Lectral's wings as the ground suddenly seemed to rush upward with blurring, reckless speed.

At the last moment, Tombfyre made a frantic twist, a final, desperate try to escape. But Lectral just pulled him closer, and together they completed their final dive, merging with terrible violence into the world of their ancestors.

Epilogue
Home at Last

352 PC

The clans of Paladine's dragons dispersed with the scattering of
the Dark Queen's armies and the final failure of Takhisis
herself. Ariakas stood at the gate, but he died before he
could witness his queen's frustration—and the freeing of
the Golden General. As the tower of Neraka collapsed, the
dragons of good and evil took wing, once more flying free
in the skies over Krynn, unbound by oath or pledge, by
master or mistress.

Many of the metal dragons who had borne riders
remained in the company of those humans, elves, or
dwarves, aiding them in the strife that still raged across
the face of Ansalon. Battles continued to rage in many
places, but these were mere skirmishes by comparison to

the vast campaigns of the war.

The brass dragons, led by Kirsah, resumed their social interaction with mankind. Many of the golds returned to their studies, and the coppers, vengeful until the end, hunted the evil wyrms throughout Ansalon. Some of the bronzes continued to fight as well, while others went back to their lairs beside the sea.

Two silver shapes flew side by side through the Khalkists, fighting chromatic dragons wherever they could find them, though for the most part the surviving wyrms of the Dark Queen took pains to avoid the massive, vengeful serpents of argent. Always the two flew slowly, one or the other carefully studying the ground.

After a long search, Dargentan and Darlant came around the shoulder of a smoking volcano to spot a mighty shape lying in the valley below. The two adult silvers settled beside the body of their great sire, still entangled as it was with the twisted remains of Tombfyre.

A tattooed figure emerged from concealment, coming forward to bow to the two mighty wyrms.

"I was waiting here, watching" said the wild elf brave, a warrior who bore the ram's horn at his waist. "I knew you would come."

Carefully the two silver dragons pulled their sire free, and with a spell of alteration, they rendered his body into that of a wild elf brave. It was a fitting tribute for now, and even more important than his appearance, it rendered the mighty ancient into a form that one of the dragons would be able to carry aloft.

"We shall bear him home," Dargentan told the wild elf.

But that home would not be in the north, did not exist on the pastoral isles waiting off the coast of the continent. Without discussion, the two silver scions took wing, Dargentan carefully bearing the body of his sire in his mighty foreclaws. Their course took them over the plains, past the victorious armies of the Golden General.

For the first time in their thousand years of life, and the last time in the history of their mighty sire, they were going to their true home—home to the High Kharolis.

Acknowledgments

Every story of Dragonlance draws its heart and soul from the work of Margaret Weis and Tracy Hickman. They told of the War of the Lance in the Chronicles, and laid down much of the history of the world in the Legends trilogy and other works. Their writing has been an inspiration to me for more than a decade, and I am grateful to have a chance to share in the wonderful fantasy world of their creation.

In this novel, I have taken the liberty of peeking into several previously existing tales, including the books of Margaret and Tracy, Richard Knaak, and several of my own earlier Dragonlance novels, presenting new interpretations of some scenes that have already been described. I have always employed a different point of view, and hopefully a fresh perspective, to these episodes—but I could not have done it without the original works for inspiration and detail.

In addition to my gratitude to Margaret and Tracy, I would also like to thank Richard Knaak for the story of legendary Huma. Here, again, I have approached the history of Krynn from a new viewpoint (that of the dragons, of course) but have tried to blend my tale in a manner that is true to the stories already in existence.

Also, thanks to Mary Kirchoff, Dan Parkinson, Harold Johnson, and Sue Weinlein Cook, for their previous work and current input into the ever-changing world of Krynn. And, of course, thanks to my Dragonlance editors: Bill Larson, J. Robert King, Pat McGilligan, and Brian Thomsen, all of whom have helped these stories more than any reader will ever know.